OUT OF LINE

"Good night," she said, "and thank you."

"My pleasure." Neither of them moved an inch.

They came together as if both thought of it at the same moment. Like a magnet meeting a piece of lead. She breathed in the scent of bay rum and smoke and . . . just plain man.

With one hand, he tipped her chin up. "Lady, for a kiss—"

"No!"

"—I'll donate the entire thousand dollars it'll take to build that school."

She came to her senses. "Have you ever gotten anything without buying it?"

A cynical smile split his handsome face. "I don't keep track, but I'll make you a bet—"

"I don't bet."

As she turned to go in he yanked her back and held her fast by her elbows. "Sweet little schoolmarm, I'll have you where I want you before that new schoolhouse of yours is built. Asking me for kisses."

The sound of her hand slapping his face rent the still night air.

❧   ❧

Don't miss HARVEST SONG, a Diamond Homespun Romance by Karen Lockwood:

Diamond Books by Karen Lockwood

HARVEST SONG
WINTER SONG

WINTER SONG

KAREN LOCKWOOD

DIAMOND BOOKS, NEW YORK

This book is a Diamond original edition,
and has never been previously published.

WINTER SONG

A Diamond Book/published by arrangement with
the author

PRINTING HISTORY
Diamond edition/November 1993

ISBN: 1-55773-958-7

Diamond Books are published by The Berkley Publishing Group,
200 Madison Avenue, New York, NY 10016.
DIAMOND and the "D" design
are trademarks belonging to Charter Communications, Inc.

PRINTED IN THE UNITED STATES OF AMERICA

10 9 8 7 6 5 4 3 2 1

To "Tucker Sage," my first writing teacher

aka
Pat Cavanaugh, Ruby Fisher, Patti Sherlock,
Sherry Roseberry, and Lillian Yeoman
with gratitude
for sharing so many Friday nights
of encouragement

and

to all my former students,
for your continuing inspiration.
Someday, I'll explain why. . .

On the blackboard of Castlerock School, August 22, 1893:

PENMANSHIP

Oh give me a home where the buffalo roam.

ARITHMETIC

Once upon a time, there were thirty million, and today there are a hundred. How many times does one hundred go into thirty million? How many times does zero go into thirty million?

CHAPTER

~ 1 ~

Montana, September 1893

Jennie Beasley hadn't thought anything *else* should go wrong that Monday, but trouble, she'd learned, in a small town like Castlerock, could rumble through before you saw it charging. And when trouble came this time—just five minutes after the third-year readers had lined up in a row for recital, she smelled it first, wrinkled her nose at a faint acrid smell, distinctive from chalk and dirt and horses. Acrid and sweet . . .

Something was burning!

She stood so suddenly her chair crashed backward, and the table tipped; her gold watch brooch, which she'd unpinned from her shirtwaist, clattered to the floor. All over the room

1

children started, looked up from their books, wriggled their noses, and grew wide-eyed.

"Smoke!" Susanna Vane squealed, and fifteen wary children turned as one toward the stove that sat at the rear of the room.

Lord Almighty, but black smoke wafted out of the chimney pipe, like a dragon belching.

"The stove's burning!"

"Of course it's burning," Vernon Higgenbottom said with sarcasm. "Why else do you think it's here?" Then he slunk down in his seat, a superior smirk on his face.

Jennie studied the stove, searching for the source of the smoke. "Hush now. It may just be green wood. Remember, it's the first day we've lit the stove." In her heart, she knew different. The smoke wasn't from something burning in the potbelly of the old black stove; it came from up higher, somewhere in the stove's craw, its stovepipe.

"Last year my aunt's stove blew up!"

Susanna Vane stood up in the aisle.

"Now, let's not alarm everyone, Susanna," she chastened.

Jennie, heart pounding, for the children's sake tried to look composed. But it was, after all, a Monday, and that meant anything could be burning in that stovepipe, especially if Vernon had been in here for Sunday services the day before—and stayed after to "sweep up." Vernon never wasted his Sundays in prayer—not with opportunity galore to set up pranks and booby traps inside and out the school building.

"Vernon Higgenbottom?" She looked from the minister's son to the smoking stove and back again.

Vernon folded his knees and slunk down further.

"Did you stick a chicken up that stovepipe?" Every teacher who'd endured a student like Vernon had endured a smoke-filled classroom at least once in her teaching days.

"Did you?"

Vernon only smirked wider. "Maybe. Maybe not." Tall for his sixteen years, bigger than Jennie, Vernon slumped down on the bench. "Maybe the stove's just worn-out and tired of being in school all day." His drawl was surly, just like when she'd caught him outside the schoolhouse smoking illicit cigarettes. And behind him the Armstrong sons, lanky farm boys, smirked too. Vernon was their personal hero.

Jennie hurried to the side of the room, where she pushed up a rusted, dusty window. "For impertinence, Vernon, you will stay after—"

"Miss Beasley!" She turned to see the stovepipe enveloped in smoke, black and putrid. Those sitting closest to the stove jumped up. Children coughed or covered their faces. And Jennie forgot all about what she'd been going to say.

It was past time to leave. Diving into the middle of the little desks to the row nearest the stove, Jennie pulled Ole and Gunnar Slocum away from their bench and shoved them gently toward the door.

"Class," she said in a voice that suddenly trembled, "leave your books and stand by your desks. We're going to have a fire drill."

Fifteen students were spread among four rows of desks. She started with the readers at her desk. "Hold hands," she said in a calmer voice than she felt, and taking hold of a little hand in hers, quickly turned to the rest of the class. "Orderly now. No one needs to run . . . walk out in a row . . . I want everyone to meet me at the hitching post outside!" she called. "Hurry!"

She'd no sooner said the words than the smoke surged out, as if the dragon had belched again, angry with indigestion. All eyes were sideways on that smoking stove, but the children headed straight for the door. A couple of the sixth-grade boys, taller and bigger than Jennie, pushed ahead. "We're getting out of here. C'mon." And out they ran, leaving her alone with the little ones.

A flame burst out of the stovepipe, and tiny Minnie Armstrong screamed. Jennie swept the littlest student up into her arms. "Hush now. Don't panic." Her own heart thumped as if a bear were on their heels. Smoke swirled about her ankles. Blindly she felt for the wall, stumbled along it till she found the door, and burst out. Minnie's big brother, Will Armstrong, in a change of heart, had waited at the door, and Jennie thrust his baby sister at him. She turned back to the door where the school bell hung from a rope pull up over the rafters. It wasn't a fancy belfry or a large bell, but it served to call the students to line up at nine o'clock. Would it be loud enough to sound an alarm to the town?

Caleb brushed past her. "I forgot my marbles."

Jennie, grabbing him by his overall straps, yanked him toward the door. "Aw, Miss Beasley, it ain't bad. No worse than when my ma burns the bread."

"Never mind your marbles. Out!"

Another child doubled back on her and rushed into the smoky room. It was her own niece, Mariah, heading for the squirrel cage up by the blackboard. Jennie grabbed, but Mariah was too quick and vanished inside the smoky interior.

"No! Mariah. No!"

All she could do was grab a sweater off a hook and dunk it in the communal water basin, then covering her mouth and nose, she dived back into the black smoke, feeling her way to Mariah.

"Leave the squirrel! Mariah . . . Mariah . . ." She couldn't shout for coughing.

Blindly she groped for the corner of the room and then the blackboard. Without warning, she crashed into both the girl and the cage, fumbled for Mariah, pressed the wet cloth to her face, and grabbed the ten-year-old's hand. They retreated the same way Jennie had come—by feel and memory.

Outside, the little girl coughed, and reaching the school steps, Jennie herself leaned over and drew in ragged breaths. "Get!" she gasped at last. "To the hitching post! Get!" She doubled over and gagged on the smoke.

Mariah instead dropped to her knees with the squirrel cage. Weak-kneed as she was, Jennie could only stare, speechless, as her niece unfastened the door to the cage. The squirrel darted out and scampered away across the road.

"Run, Mariah!" she choked finally, but Mariah, still disobedient, just hunched there by the cage, cradling the empty cage in both arms and crying.

There was no more time to waste. By now, smoke gushed out the doors and whatever windows were open.

Groping for the bell rope, Jennie yanked down on it, and the bell pealed out loud and fast. Tears streamed down her face, as with every ounce of strength left in her she rang the school bell over and over. Not the slow ring that was the familiar nine o'clock call to classes, but with a staccato swiftness, that clanged without end.

Please, let all the children be out and safe. Please. Please.

Mariah, the only one in sight, still sat at the foot of the steps in the dirt, coughing, and as for the others, Jennie *had* to find them, had to make sure they'd all gotten out.

Ding-dong! Yank and release. *Ding-dong!* Yank and release.

Somewhere glass shattered as a window broke, smoke billowed out in ever higher clouds, and Jennie, holding one arm over her eyes, clutching the rope with her other, clanged the bell over and over until it echoed the cry in her head.

The children . . . the children . . . the children . . .

The sound of the school bell was at first just another familiar sound to Nate Denison. After all, he heard it every morning and noon. That and an occasional barking dog or rowdy poker game were all that seemed to happen in this sleepy little town.

In fact, after half the summer here, he was beginning to wonder why, once the Yellowstone tourists trekked out of Wyoming and rode off on the Northern Pacific, the residents didn't go stark raving mad. There was nothing to do here but look at steaming hot pools and sniff sulfuric air all day. As for himself, he was already certified insane for building this big fancy house out in the pine-speckled bleakness of southern Montana.

It was one of his few miscalculations in life, but he'd rationalized it quickly. As an easterner come to seek profit near America's Wonderland, this home allowed him to look over his prospects in comfort. And he had a second reason for lingering. Back east, in his well-ordered worlds of Newport, Rhode Island, and Fifth Avenue, New York, with their rigid code of behavior and social rules, life was utterly, comfortably predictable. He'd hoped this would be a well-needed change of pace, an antidote for love lost.

Not that he'd found any peace of mind yet. Nothing but four walls and big blue skies day in and day out. Which was as boringly predictable in its way as what he'd left behind. So days dragged, and he resorted to spending his time—like now—at his big rolltop desk, organizing and reorganizing all the cubbyholes or else composing letters or telegrams to his stockbroker and political cronies back east.

As he bent over his writing paper the school bell broke his concentration. It never rang this long. Maybe some boys had finally decided to try some mischief with it.

And then the door from the kitchen burst open, and his housekeeper came scurrying into the library, yanking off her apron as she rushed to the window.

"Oh, no, Mr. Denison. Oh, no, oh, no, it can't be. . . ."

"What is it, Helga?"

"A fire! A fire . . ."

He looked up, mildly curious. It had been a long dry summer, so he wasn't surprised. "Not too near my house, I hope," he said as he wrote.

"It's the school! We've got to go help."

"We?" he said, scraping back his chair. "My own housekeeper is giving me orders?"

"*Ja,* it's an unwritten law of the west. All able-bodied men turn out for a fire—even the rich ones. For the bucket brigade."

"The deuce you say?"

Then Helga was heading for the front door, his own scrub bucket in hand, without so much as a by-your-leave.

Mouth quirking in amusement, he moved to look out the window and stared, fascinated, vaguely disturbed by the dark smoke that billowed out of the little log shack that passed for a schoolhouse. It was across the road and half a field away—not close enough to pose a threat.

Already Helga was halfway to the torrent of smoke, her stocky hips jiggling beneath her long skirt.

He dug his field glasses out of a desk drawer and assessed the fire through the window, undecided on whether to get involved. Back east, there were fire departments for such emergencies. Personally he'd come no closer to flames than his fireplaces and candlelight dinner parties, but this was the school, his conscience reminded him. As the bell continued to ring, the citizens of little Castlerock came from all directions, all with buckets or shovels in hand. Already he could see a bucket brigade forming, as men and women came running and formed a human chain from the river behind the school.

Then he spotted two of the garish ladies from the saloon run up, buckets in hand. Helga had meant what she said if able-bodied women were showing up. Through his field glasses, he saw children mingling in the smoke-filled yard,

and he frowned, guilty. Next thing he knew he was rolling up
his shirt sleeves. After grabbing a shovel from the toolshed,
he headed down to join the townspeople. Maybe if he did his
bit, he'd fit in better.

Up close, Nate stood stock-still, staring at the commotion,
which resembled the floor of the Stock Exchange in a panic.
No one was in charge, not even the teacher, who, now that
he thought of it, had never emerged from the building. He
walked closer, close enough to feel the heat like an open oven
in his face.

At the smoke-filled doorway, a young woman, barely visible
through all the smoke, still yanked on a bell rope. Flames shot
up the roof of the tinder-dry school, licked dangerously close
to the bell. He didn't know the woman's name, but had not a
doubt this was the schoolmarm.

Though he tried to avoid such idealistic creatures at all costs,
he'd crossed paths with her once at the Castlerock Mercantile;
she was a skinny chestnut-haired mouse who had hidden in
the corner by the flour sacks. Then, too, she rang the school
bell every morning at nine o'clock, waking him up to the same
sight. Brown or black slim skirt. High-necked white shirtwaist.
Hair upswept in a demure bun. Oh, yes. He'd dug out his field
glasses to look at her more than once, cursing her for waking
him. He'd wanted to ring her neck a few mornings. Now he
knew her delicate neck was in far more danger than from
his curses. Throwing down the shovel, he pushed through the
crowd toward her.

A moment later he yanked the bell rope from the woman's
hands and, sweeping her up into his arms, hauled her outside.
He ran a dozen yards toward the road, set her down, and
deliberately fell on top of her. Just seconds later the roof
blew off the Castlerock School. A chunk of wood struck him
a nasty blow to the shoulder, and he lay still, absorbing the
pain, eating the dust in which they lay.

"You meddling fool," the schoolmarm said, squirming left, then right, trying to crawl out from under him. She pounded his chest, his back. "The children! Let me go! Someone's got to sound the alarm!"

"The entire town's already here," he said gently. "Unless you want the whole state to donate buckets, I'd calm down . . . calm down, lady."

"Calm down?" she squealed, squirming again. "You fool! Move! Move . . ." His chest took another barrage of blows from her fists.

Karl, the town's carpenter, ran up to them, overall straps flying loose. "Jennie, are you all right?"

"Not till this—this oaf lets go of me."

That's when Nate realized her hair was tangled in his hands and gently he extricated himself, rolled off, and lay, painfully disoriented, squinting up at the smoky sky.

Using Nate's chest as leverage, the schoolmarm struggled to her knees and glared down at him. Nate's first real look at her was of a soot-covered face—elfin and desperate. A cascade of chestnut hair glowed about her face.

"Miss Beasley!" a child shouted from across the confusion. "Minnie's sick. Come quick."

She rolled off and stood.

Jennie Beasley. That was her name.

"Your shoulder's bleeding," she said to Nate. "Get someone to wrap this around it." She threw a dampish cloth in his face and then ran off in the direction of the child's voice.

He stood and gingerly blotted the blood off his shirt.

Glass shattered again. The air was filled with the smell of crackling wood and cinders, hot and stifling, like a bonfire on a summer day. Next to the smell, sounds dominated everything—screams and crackling flames and prayers for an end to it all. Each bucket of water was about as effective as spit into hell. The bigger danger, as Nate saw it, was if it spread

to Karl's carpentry shop, and worse, jumped the dirt street
and did away with his mansion. Already men were digging
between school and carpenter's shop, hoping the fire wouldn't
jump the trench.

Wincing at the wound to his shoulder, Nate elbowed his
way up to follow the schoolmarm, but she was lost in the
confusion and smoke. Someone flung a shovel at him the way
he used to fling his gloves at his valet. "Here, mister . . . dig a
trench. Don't stand there like a bump on a log." Mechanically
he began to dig, while keeping one eye out for Miss Beasley.
Where was she?

Desperate, Jennie ran from the obnoxious easterner.
He'd practically crushed the breath out of her and delayed
her from finding the children. Now she fought her way
through the ugly smoke and cinders toward the hitching
post. Milling townspeople, buckets, shovels, tripped her
up every other step.

"Calm down, Miss Beasley," they said, one after the other.

From one after another, she tugged away. "Please, the children . . . please, the children."

At last she found her students, exactly where she'd told them
to go, clustered at the hitching post, watching terrified as thick
black smoke billowed out of their school. Even, praise God,
the two big Armstrong boys, who for once had risen to the
occasion and were riding herd on the others. They all held
hands, like in ring-around-a-rosie.

Hastily Jennie did a head count, saying names, reciting the
roll by heart as she found each precious head.

Susanna . . . Joshua . . . Mariah . . . Caleb . . . James . . .
Minnie. The littlest student gagged and choked, then while
Jennie held her head, recovered. She began her head count
over again. James . . . Minnie . . . Annabelle . . . Sam . . .
Eddie . . . Thaddeus Jr. . . . Will . . . Ole and Gunnar . . .

Three times she walked around, counting, reciting names.

"Where's Vernon?" she cried.

"Aw, he ran off," Will Armstrong said. "He messed with the stovepipe all right, and now he's gone."

"I'm scared," little Minnie cried, clinging to her brother Will's leg.

"Don't cry," Jennie soothed, clutching two sobbing school-girls to her. "We're safe now." And as the walls of the school collapsed in front of them, she urged everyone to think of something else. Of home. "Don't look. We're safe out here. The river's near. Your parents are coming to get you. Think of home. And aren't we lucky everyone got out safe?"

"I left my marbles," Caleb moaned. "My glass allies."

Susanna put on a brave air and stared in fascination at the fire. "Well, I took off my brown stockings, and I'm glad they're burning up. Now Ma can order me grown-up stockings."

"Shut up, Susanna," Will said.

"Will, Will," Minnie cried. "I left my thimble doll in my lard pail. I left it." She sobbed quietly.

And somber Mariah stood there, quiet as always, dark bangs plastered against her forehead, dark braid coming undone, staring off into the distance, in the direction where her pet squirrel had scurried off.

They stood in silence, finally, except for the occasional cough or tear wiped away, and each lost in his private thoughts, watched the fire engulf their school.

Because it was such a glorious Indian-summer day, Jennie hadn't even been going to light the stove today, but had changed her mind at lunchtime. A smart teacher never waited till it was cold enough to need the stove. She always tried it out, worked out the bugs while the weather was still favorable. Just her bad luck.

Over and over she said the opposite, though. "Aren't we lucky?" As if by saying it, she could block out the cinders in the air, the crack of logs burning—the realization that every desk and book and slate the town possessed was gone. Even her gold brooch with the watch dangling from it—a gift from her sister, Grace—was destroyed. Usually it was pinned to her bodice, but today she'd unfastened it. Two holes in her shirt-waist were all she had left to remind her of it. But material possessions meant nothing compared with life.

Kneeling, she embraced the little ones, two at a time, while their tears dampened her shirtwaist, their clutching hands tore at her hairpins. "It's all right," she said over and over. "Every-one's out. Your parents are going to put the fire out."

The wind shifted constantly, and every few minutes smoke blew against her face. No matter how many times she swal-lowed, she couldn't rid herself of the taste of fire. Rubbing her eyes only made them run with tears.

The parents—the ones who lived in town—ran up and collected their offspring. Jensen. Vane. Zane. Slocum. The Armstrongs rode in from their ranch, and fourteen-year-old Walt drove his little sisters home. Will stayed to work the brigade.

One family at a time, they were claimed, until Jennie was left with only the Gordon children. Four big boys and a girl. Her nephews and only niece. Children of her sister, Grace, who was practically bedridden with a difficult pregnancy. Grace would have heard the bell and wondered. Torn between the fire and the children, Jennie decided on the children.

Once again Jennie counted heads.

One . . . two . . . three . . . four . . . five. Yes, only Gordons remained, and taking the hand of the youngest, she walked them up the street and into their father's mercantile, where a startled seamstress was just clipping off some yard goods for herself.

"Where's Thaddeus?" Jennie asked. Jennie's brother-in-law not only owned the mercantile but was head of the school board.

"He's down at the river," Ingrid Jensen replied. Her face colored. "I—I was just helping myself. We might need to make bandages. . . . Thaddeus can add it to my account."

"My, what quick thinking, Ingrid." Jennie spared a brief thought for the eastern dude whose shoulder was cut. Brief. Then she handed Mariah off to the seamstress. "I need your help with the children right now, not bandages. Keep Grace occupied with chatter. Let her see the children. Reassure her it's not too serious."

"It's not, is it?"

"Haven't you looked?" Jennie was incredulous. Smoke enveloped the town. "Never mind. Your Bertha can stay there too. Please help Grace."

"What about you? You're not going back?" Ingrid, who fancied herself a refined lady, sounded appalled. "Grace will be prostrate with worry. That's men's work."

Jennie had already gathered up a pair of work gloves from the mercantile shelf and now grabbed a brand-new shiny bucket that was for sale. "Of course I'm going back," she said as she pulled on the gloves. "It's my school. I *have* to help."

Times were tough. This school was her last chance, and the job had come through family connections at that.

Jennie ran outside. Cinders were blowing down the street, and even from a distance it was clear the school was a total loss. It'd be a miracle if anything was left. But Karl Schwartz had a carpentry shop right next door that could be protected; the barbershop flanked the school on the other side. Even now the bucket brigade was dousing them with splash after splash of water, to kill cinders that might be smoldering in their roofs. Poor Karl was still frantically digging a trench in the dirt.

She joined the head of the brigade, but it was all disorganized. Will Armstrong, fleet of foot, was running the lead bucket back to the river to be refilled and passed up the line again, but it was the head of the line that was wrong. It begged for someone tall, someone tall enough to toss water high up on the roof of Karl's carpenter shop.

Then Jennie saw the perfect candidate—that big bear of a man—the stranger who'd tackled her into the weeds and covered her in an effort of brazen heroism when the school stove exploded.

She couldn't remember his name, but the town had dubbed his mansion with a ridiculous name.

"Denison's Folly!" she shouted, and when he looked up, she waved him over and handed off a bucket to him. "Douse Karl's roof. I can't throw the water far enough." He stared at her, vague amusement in his eyes. "Well, do it," she yelled. "What are you waiting for? Do it! Now!"

Nate had heard such pleas before, but usually from bored matrons and certainly not ever outside his bedroom door. Intrigued by her passion, he took the bucket and aimed for the roof of the carpenter shop. At once she handed him another. And another.

Water was sloshing over onto his English enamel shoes, and blisters welled on his hands. Still, the schoolmarm outworked him.

"Hurry up. Faster, faster," she urged, sloshing water over his pant legs.

His last tailor's bill, he mused, was probably higher than what it cost to build a new school, and at last, more weary than intrigued, he stopped and surveyed the situation.

By now the school was a smoldering heap of charred wood. No more sparks flew onto adjacent buildings. Karl's carpenter shop dripped with water.

He set down his empty bucket and faced the teacher. In the hubbub he had fleeting impressions, but they were indelible. Long unpinned hair flying in the breeze. Her hair reminded him of copper pennies. And it flew wildly about her face, which had intriguing features: a sensuous mouth; a soot-smudged cheek.

His gaze dropped to her torn shirtwaist. Impatiently she held a bucket of water while behind her an entire line of buckets waited to be handed up.

"Why are we still doing this?" he asked her. "The school's a loss. Nothing else is going to burn down."

She thrust another bucket at him. "What do you know about fires?"

He ignored the question and the buckets. "I know if this shop burns, I could build it ten times over."

"Do you know how little money these people have, you idiot? Karl can't lose his business." She stood there, breast heaving, eyes flashing.

Idiot? Nate had won a fortune from making idiots of other people on Wall Street, but no one had ever called *him* an idiot before. No woman had. Not even the mighty matrons of Fifth Avenue.

"Hell, lady, you haven't got the intelligence to be teacher if you don't know how fires spread. It's going to be up to the wind what burns and what doesn't, and throwing water around all day won't change that."

At least five buckets of water had accumulated near her feet. A backup from the brigade.

She picked up one of the buckets of water and drew it back. "You accusing me of not being qualified?"

"For firefighting or creating hysteria?"

Without warning, he got a bucketful of water right in his face. Water, cold, cold water from the Yellowstone River, sloshed down over his shirt.

"Maybe, Miss Beasley," Nate replied in between spitting out water, "just maybe this town needs a fire department without a temper." He delivered the words in the same cool tone he'd used when Daisy Van Altman had flung a glass of champagne in his face.

Karl stepped between them and disarmed the teacher.

"Time to quit, Jennie," he said, gently disentangling the pail from her hand. "The dude's right. The wind's died down. The fire's out . . . unless you see some more sparks you want to douse on Nate Denison."

"He deserved it." Jennie tossed her mane of chestnut hair. "I hope he drowns."

And on that stinging statement, she stalked away to the smoking rubble of her school. When Nate had finished mopping the water from his eyes and hair, he studied her standing there, shoulders prim, blinking back tears, staring at the heap of charred wood and smoking ash. She looked down at the bodice of her torn shirtwaist, touched it sadly as if something were missing.

It was all over, thankfully, tragically over.

In the midst of the rubble, a glint of brass shone bravely. Silent and steaming amid the charred wood and melted lard pails, only one memento of the Castlerock School was salvageable.

Her school bell.

CHAPTER

❦ 2 ❦

They usually came in pairs, Nate had noticed. Pairs of U.S. Cavalry officers regularly rode up this way from Fort Yellowstone, typically on payday when they had money for the saloon or mercantile.

Usually it was Hirum McAllister and Orvil Rowe, a pair of handsome sergeants, who came to Castlerock, while most of the others chose bawdier towns nearby. Today Hirum and Orvil arrived too late to help put out the fire—which was part of their responsibility on rounds in Yellowstone. With rotten timing, they rode into Castlerock just in time to view the aftermath. Leaving behind the shovels and buckets they routinely carried, they got off their horses and sauntered over to Nate.

"What happened?" They stared up at the easterner, who

towered over them, and clearly it was not the fire they were asking after, but his drenched shirt.

He glowered back, like a contrary grizzly. He'd met these men a week before in the saloon and struck up an acquaintanceship because one of them, Hirum, like Nate, was from New York. "You can draw your own conclusions."

Hirum peered at Nate and smiled slyly. "Heck, after two years in Yellowstone, we've figured out the behavior of every animal except dudes. So a cavalryman could draw a lot of strange conclusions about a dripping wet easterner."

Smart alecks. "Like what?"

"Either you got lost under a geyser, or stranded in the Yellowstone River after a moose gave chase, or fished out of a hot pool—someone's always nudging in too close for a better look. Anyway, anything's possible, Nate."

"Pulled long johns out of another pool too," Orvil added.

Nate's glower deepened. Of the pair, Orvil was given to inane remarks. "Why don't you ask the teacher what happened?"

Hirum and Orvil, both dashing enough in their blue uniforms to turn a woman's head, gave each other knowing looks, and then Hirum threw back his head and guffawed. "Hell, Nate, you didn't have to go close enough to get wet. We could have *told* you what she's like."

As if by unspoken assent, all three of them looked over at the smoking rubble, watched over by the schoolmarm. She was gingerly picking up a charred, wet book. It would be easy to walk over and finish what she'd started. But no . . . Nate didn't do anything impulsively. First he studied a situation, analyzed it from all angles, asked questions. . . . So, to that end, he stared at the schoolmarm's unbound hair. Then his gaze moved to her torn blouse, which afforded more than a little glimpse of her corset lace—Montgomery Ward issue, not Worth's of Paris—Nate knew ladies' corsets and unmentionables almost as well as he knew stockbrokers' favorite cigars.

"A real beaut." Hirum whistled.

"The teacher?" Orvil asked.

"No, you oaf, the fire." Hirum glanced at Nate.

"That it was."

Nate took a closer look at their spit-and-polish blue uniforms. Firefighting, he recalled again, was a part of their job in Yellowstone.

"Has either of you ever, in between tourists and long johns in the hot pools, ever encountered a real fire?"

"We've seen more buffalo than fires, and considering there aren't any buffalo to speak of—"

"You spend most of your time staring at the wide blue skies and pine trees, huh? Soft assignment."

"Soft?" Hirum frowned and cast a weary look at his partner. "You ever imagine spending all day with nothing but Orvil here and the occasional moose for company? Now, do you want us to help or not?"

"What's to help with now?" Nate asked.

"Turning over the ashes and charred wood . . . put out smoldering embers. That sort of thing."

Orvil looked glum. "Just our luck to get leave and have to go to work putting out a campfire."

"Shut up, Orvil." Hirum gave his partner a glare. "This was the schoolhouse. We can help sift through it. Might be worth a free drink," he suggested cagily.

Nate, who was just as interested in their experiences with the schoolmarm, picked up on the idea.

"Why don't you come back to the house after you're done here, have a drink, and elaborate on that?"

He didn't have to ask twice, as he knew. People who lived in shacks or barracks might sneer and call his gingerbread mansion Denison's Folly behind his back, but given an invitation, they jumped at the chance.

And so Orvil and Hirum remained awhile at the scene to volunteer their expertise on salvaging the rubble. Nate, after a last look at Miss Jennie Beasley, walked on back to his mansion, where Helga, like a Viking mother, bandaged his shoulder and scolded him over the wet shirt.

By suppertime, though, the young cavalrymen were in the kitchen of his mansion, washing sooty hands and faces before Helga consented to serve them a supper of meat-and-potato pie and warm bread.

Sergeant McAllister looked through the door into the darkened dining room, appreciative, whistling. "Nice—a real mansion, just like they said." Then he turned. "Last time I was in New York, the society pages had you engaged. Weren't you?"

Sergeant Rowe made himself at home in the kitchen, pulling out a chair, and straddled it with a casualness he couldn't exhibit at the Fort Yellowstone barracks. Orvil appreciated good food, especially free food. Hirum, because he was from Nate's home state of New York, had more to say and more of a twinkle in his eye. Otherwise there wasn't much difference in the two of them. They were both handsome, young, and happy to have drawn such an easy post as Yellowstone.

"Built this house for that high-society woman, didn't you?"

Nate shrugged and kept eating the apple pudding Helga had provided for dessert.

"She changed her mind, huh?"

"Yeah." He scooped a second helping of pudding onto his plate and shoved the dish at Orvil.

Hirum studied Nate, as if he were a puzzle.

"I know—she didn't want to leave the big city, right?"

Nate shook his head. Not even Helga had been able to prod the story out of him, but he was getting tired of holding it in, like a damn prize secret. "She changed her mind about marrying an American."

"Yeah?"

Yeah. Daisy had traded in love for an English title. Duchess, no less. A weaker man would have considered it the ultimate humiliation, but Nate, who prided himself on predicting everything that happened, publicly treated Daisy's change of heart as a mere loss of capital, as if he'd had a bad week on the stock market. Privately it hurt.

Abruptly he changed subjects. "What about you two? What brings you here to town?"

Hirum spoke up. "When summer ends, all hotel help of the female species leaves. Like I told you: it gets lonely in there— even lonelier in fall and winter—with nothing but gushing geysers and us looking for poachers and vandals and fires. And Gardiner gets a mite crowded on payday."

"But Castlerock's schoolmarm won't give us the time of day," Orvil grumbled. "She's no Old Faithful when it comes to menfolks. A she-bear is more like it."

"Unpredictable as a gusher," Hirum added simply.

"She's got a temper too," Orvil offered.

"That's what I *said*, you dummy." Hirum glared at his partner.

"No, you didn't. You said—"

"It's what I meant. Drop it." He turned to Nate. "I'd rather hear how long our friend Nate's gonna hang around here."

Nate shrugged. As a speculator, he couldn't give too much away. "We'll see. I think Yellowstone's going to bring in more and more people, and people mean profits." He pushed a bottle of brandy at Orvil.

"More people. More poachers," Hirum said, holding up his glass, waiting his turn while Nate poured.

Nate opened the pie safe, pulled out yesterday's cherry pie for Orvil. Then he stared out the backdoor to the veranda. Unbidden came the sensuous features of that little lady at the fire. . . .

"You didn't mean it about buying buffalo, did you?"

Nate looked around. "A done deed. I bought a few from an Indian in South Dakota. He had a whole herd of them collected. Now they're mine."

"That's crazy. They'll wander off—if your foreman even gets them to agree to make the trip here." Orvil sniggered.

Nate returned to the table, cherry pie in hand. "My foreman's got a crew here fencing five hundred acres—they'll have plenty of grass growing and a stream running right through it." He handed a plate of pie to Hirum, who stared in disbelief.

"You'll never succeed."

"Why not? It's not a crime to make a profit off buffalo. Heads went for up to a thousand dollars back east. Or I might just raise them, breed them. Whatever pays best." Back east, Yellowstone had a reputation already as a place for the elite to visit, to brag about. He'd come here, with no better prospects back east, to make money off what was left of the west—off the vanishing buffalo, off the silver up north, off Yellowstone Park to the south, off the Northern Pacific Railroad.

"Unless you've got a good foreman to ride herd on them, buffalo will walk right through your fences." Hirum downed his brandy and reached for more. "They're not cattle, you know."

"I know that. I'll put them far away from people. Nothing's going to disturb them. One way or another, they're going to make me lots of money."

Aware the sergeant was silent, he turned to find himself being studied.

"Does everything have a price to you?"

"Yes."

"Even women?"

Especially women.

If there was one thing he prided himself on more than the stock market and eccentric investments, it was women. They were utterly predictable. Even Daisy, in marrying a titled Englishman twice her age, had in a way been predictable. A man was entitled to a loss now and then. But he didn't want any more losses with women. Only successes.

"What else do you know about the pretty little schoolmarm?" he asked as casually as possible.

Hirum, smiling, looked up. "She's new, and she's the sister to Thaddeus Gordon's wife. I already told you she's a hard catch. And believe me, plenty of us cavalrymen have asked her out for rides and picnics. Oh, she'll talk to you and pretend, then run off. Not even a school fire can warm her up . . . and don't try offering her a ride to go view buffalo."

"You've already tried and failed, uh?"

"Unpredictable and contrary and full of sass." The sergeant colored. "Yeah, I tried. So'd Orvil here." His tone was defensive. "Too prim and proper to consort with a pair of cavalrymen."

Both of the good sergeants needed spectacles. No normal man could have missed the sight of Miss Beasley with her shirtwaist half torn off.

"Yessiree, I predict she'll die Miss Beasley. I'm just telling you they'll carve an epitaph on your tombstone someday, and it'll say, 'He died trying.' "

"A man could do worse with his time out here." He maintained a nonchalant tone.

"Hand over that pie," Orvil said, licking his fingers. "I'd rather die eating."

Nate handed the pie to Orvil, whose table manners distinguished him from Hirum as well.

While his guests finished, Nate thought on his prospects with Miss Beasley. He could still see the curve of her neck, the smudge of soot on her cheek, the long flowing copper-penny-colored hair. Nate half smiled. This woman was earthy and sensual, even if she didn't know it yet, and she had just started something, as surely as if she'd slapped him with a glove, and Nate always followed through.

Hirum finished his brandy and a few minutes later pulled his fellow cavalryman away.

"You won't get Miss Beasley, not at any price," Hirum said in a joshing voice as he walked back to his horse and the ride to the fort. "Yessiree, that schoolmarm's unpredictable as a sapling in a windstorm, especially now that she's lost her school."

"Every woman's got a price, especially one who's just lost something."

"Then maybe you ought to bribe her with a new school!" And laughing, they headed back down the road to Yellowstone.

Let them laugh. No woman was that unpredictable. They all wanted pretty clothes, a roof over their heads, and money to spend. He'd never met one who was different. No matter how many buckets of water they threw on a man. Nate would find out this one's price, and knowing women as he did, he suspected it wasn't necessarily a mere school.

Money. Money. Money.

That night at dinner Mariah stirred her food and wished her pa would for once use his mouth to eat and not talk. But if he had to carry on, you'd think Pa would see fit to mention how lucky he was his children got out of the school fire, or at least be too tired from fighting the fire to talk. But no . . . all Pa could talk about was how much it was going to cost the town to build a new school.

Her big brother poked her. "Pass the gravy, runt."

"I'm not a runt," she hissed, and when she handed him the gravy, it sloshed over onto his hand.

"Sloppy," she said as her brother licked his fingers.

Then Pa looked her way. "Mariah, stop fiddling and either listen or eat."

She put down her head and, ignoring the sympathetic look from her aunt Jennie, jabbed her fork into a mushy potato. Aunt Jennie was nice, but it was hard having your aunt be your teacher and live with you. All the other girls accused her of being teacher's pet when they thought she wasn't listening, and at home she was "runt."

"Mariah, pass the pickled beets." Pa tucked his napkin under his chin and, as he ate, proceeded with his daily news report of the town happenings. As owner of the mercantile, he was privy to everything, even more than the women, and how long dinner lasted depended on how much news he'd heard and seen that day.

This, Mariah feared, would be a very long dinner, and she spared a longing thought for the pet squirrel she'd rescued from the fire. Poor Ben Franklin. That was his name, and she hoped he had friends in the hills who'd let him share their food and live with them during the winter.

"Today," Pa rumbled in a tone that made Mariah jump, "is a landmark day in Castlerock."

Thaddeus Jr. glanced around, expression sly. "Can we stay home—since there's no school to go to?"

Aunt Jennie looked up in alarm. "We can't close school."

Pa, who abhorred interruptions, cast a warning look at everyone, and Jennie immediately stared down at her lap. Aunt Jennie needed her teacher money; Mariah knew she saved every penny in a cigar box except the two dollars a week she gave Pa for board. Without school, there'd be no salary for Jennie.

"School *will* go on, won't it?" Jennie asked softly.

"That remains to be decided."

"The weather's still decent. We could hold school outside."

Shaking his head, Thaddeus drew a napkin across his mouth and beard. "Too many wild animals stray in here. We'll discuss the school later, after the rubble's cooled." He chomped down on a beet. "Meanwhile the new man in town, the dude from Denison's Folly, that ostentatious mansion, finally mingled with us common folk today."

The golden-haired Gordon boys all giggled and cast furtive looks at their aunt.

"What's so funny?" Pa snapped.

"Jennie threw a bucket of water on him," Thaddeus Jr. said.

"How do you know?" Aunt Jennie, who was usually quiet at supper, asked, then blushed pink.

"Will Armstrong said so. He heard it from Karl."

"Boys. Eat." Ma, who looked tired, didn't waste time on big words.

Mariah slipped a crust of bread to Paddy. Paddy was a black-and-white sheepdog, and Mariah had hopes she might be growing puppies. You could never tell this early, but she could hope.

"Mariah, sit up straight," Pa said, then when Mariah pulled up ramrod prim, Pa continued. "That man is not one of our kind," he informed his family, adding with a significant look at Jennie, "You've seen that mansion he built. Jennie's looked at it every day on her way to school. She knows."

"Knows what? What's wrong with it?" one of the younger boys asked.

"It's obscene, that's what, when men have money like that to throw around, and do you know what he calls it? His cabin in the west! While our modest little school burns to the ground, and the Lord knows where the town will find a thousand dollars to build a new one. It'll be around the block from that obscene piece of architecture. As head of the school board, I can guarantee that."

"Why?" his oldest son asked.

"Because it's a bad influence on plain children like you, thinking you can grow up to have things like that. The man doesn't even work like a decent man. He's a speculator." And before anyone could ask what that was, Pa told them. "That's not a man who works the land or carves out a modest business for a living."

He paused. "Where's the coffee? Pass me some more of those pickled beets."

Jennie got up to retrieve the coffeepot from the stove.

Pa kept on. "He's an eastern dude, one who'll milk our lives dry if he sees profit. Why, already some Indian over in South Dakota has sold him a dozen buffalo. Needed the money for winter, the Indian says, but what do you think a man like Nate Denison cares about buffalo? Certainly not to put meat on his table for him and a housekeeper. No, profit making, that's what. He's here to prey on us and our way of life."

Mariah squirmed, anxious to be dismissed.

"You name it, but it ain't hard work that dirties his hands."

"Maybe he'll get bored and go back to New York," Jennie ventured timidly. After that dunking, she rather hoped she never had to lay eyes on him again.

"Maybe, but no one within a thousand miles has the money to buy that house from him. Why do you think it's called Denison's Folly? No . . ." Pa wiped his mouth on his napkin, a hopeful sign that he was nearly done talking. "No, it's not normal when a man receives a dozen telegrams a day at the depot. And then plans to collect buffalo as if this humble town needed a zoo. Don't get too friendly with him."

"He's the one been hiding in his house."

"Well, I hope he goes back to it. You boys know the motto I live by, and my father before me. 'Labor, all labor, is noble and holy.' Period."

"He did help with the fire," Ma ventured. At her husband's glare, she lowered her eyes. "Ingrid Jensen told me."

"Well, he's got a decent streak . . . anyone would in an emergency. I'll give him that, but he's not one of us."

At last Pa scraped back his chair, and the instant he got up,

Mariah scrambled to the floor to cuddle by Paddy and rub her ears. "Oh, please, Paddy, please have pups," she whispered. She had good reason to hope. Mariah wasn't dumb about how animals mated, and she'd seen Paddy nuzzling noses with the Slocum mongrel. In heat, and being nuzzled. Oh, she wished there were a way to tell for sure besides staring at Paddy's tummy.

She looked up. Pa was staring down in displeasure. Children, of course, were meant to do chores, not play.

"Get out from under the table, runt, and help your aunt Jennie do the dishes. While your ma's with child, you know you have to do extra."

"Yes, Pa."

Scrambling up, she began to collect plates from the table while Pa went outside for his after-dinner smoke.

"I'll wash," Jennie said tiredly. "You want to dry?"

Mariah nodded. She didn't mind doing work really, especially with Aunt Jennie, who liked to listen when she chattered on about her pet animals. Even about the white mouse. So chores weren't so bad.

It was the runt part.

She was tired of being Pa's runt, and that's why she wished so much Paddy would have pups. Because between Ma having a baby and Paddy maybe having pups, Mariah wouldn't be the littlest anymore and so Pa would quit calling her runt.

After the dishwater was thrown on the vegetable garden, Jennie went straight to the tiny lean-to room at the back of the house. Suddenly exhausted, she sank down onto the bed and began to unbutton the dress she'd borrowed from Grace. Now she'd have to borrow a watch too. Of all the things lost in today's disaster, her pin-on watch had had the most sentimental value. Still, she'd never been more thankful for a roof and a bed, however humble.

Once a woodshed, this room had been converted to a bedroom for her and Mariah. Not much more than a bed—metal-
framed and plain of quilt—and a washstand fit in the place.
Luckily Jennie had few clothes; these hung on pegs from the
wall. More personal items were under the bed in a mercantile
box, her savings in a cigar box. The floor was bare of anything
save dirt and one small rug.

An opening had been cut out of the kitchen wall to connect
them with the house, and their only privacy was a curtain
of red, white, and blue calico. But for all its spartan qual-
ities, it was all theirs, including the most prized possession—
a mattress of straw and wool ticking and real pillows in cases
hand-stitched from flour sacks.

Because it would have cost far too much to cut a real window
out, Jennie had, with a black crayon, drawn a pretend window
beside the washstand and Mariah had pinned pretend curtains
to it. They imagined their view—a different one each night at
bedtime. Not vistas of sight, but of the imagination, of their
futures. Mariah always saw a life with animals—perhaps she'd
be a veterinarian, and she'd grow up to be the tallest girl ever.
Jennie said she'd like to attend a real university when she could
save enough money and after that found a female seminary.

"Aren't you going to marry, Jennie?" Mariah would ask
almost every night.

Always there was a pause. Jennie had spent so long caring
for people, her parents, now her sister, that she'd never considered marriage. Of course, she'd never gone near enough men
to have a beau, but she couldn't picture herself married. What
man would agree to the ideal Jennie had of marriage?

"I doubt it," she'd say, and lying quietly in the dark, wonder
what having a beau meant. She'd never have both a seminary
and a beau; it wasn't done, and so she always made herself
picture the female seminary out that imaginary window.

Now Jennie Beasley looked at the double bed she shared

with Mariah. Mariah sat on the edge pulling off her itchy long johns and throwing them over the metal bed frame to join her long brown stockings. Then she stared at their "window."

Jennie looked at it, too, but could see no further than tomorrow and the nightmare of not even having a school building.

"I know what you're going to say, Jennie. That we hold school in an imaginary building."

Jennie smiled.

"Buildings are replaceable, Mariah," she said quickly. "The greatest blessing of all today is that everyone got out."

"And every animal."

"Blessings on them too. But, Mariah, you must never run into a fire again. Run away from fire, but never into it."

"I had to save Ben Franklin."

"But what if we'd lost you? Every possession in that school can be replaced, but not people, Mariah. That's all that counts. And I want you to think about that."

"I'm sorry." There was a distinct catch in her voice.

Jennie hugged her niece. "I'm tired. Let's go to bed." She poured water from the pitcher and fumbled in the old sardine can for their bar of soap. The cool water washed away the memory of heat and destruction. She pulled a soft nightgown over her head and sat down for the nightly ritual when she and Mariah brushed each other's hair. Slowly, as Mariah worked the brush, she began to relax.

"How can blessings help build a new school? Pa said it'll take a whole thousand dollars."

"Tomorrow we'll figure that out."

"Everyone will help build a new one, a fancy one painted white." Mariah was so hopeful.

"I hope so."

"Will it have a belltower?" Mariah was trying to cheer her, trying to engage her in their game of fancy.

"A grand belltower."

"And a cloakroom?"

"Large enough for the squirrel cage."

"Then I'll help build it too. Everyone in town will."

Teaching was her all. She might never have pretty dresses in abundance or money. But she could be the best teacher ever. Unbidden came an image of the stranger who'd helped with the fire and stayed to help pick up debris. He was Nathaniel Denison, Thaddeus had said. The man responsible for that monstrous mansion, Denison's Folly. Thaddeus had acted derisive because Mr. Denison was rich; he'd certainly dressed rich.

She tried to pull out of her fancy thoughts. Except . . . except she kept thinking about that bear of a man. That rich man. How it had felt when he'd thrown her to the ground and covered her with his body. Fancy.

"Jennie . . . I was thinking of the bell."

Even now it sat outside the livery, cooling, a symbol of hope.

"It's safe," Jennie reassured her.

"Good. It's the spirit of the school. Don't be too sad. You'll see. Pa may keep on calling me runt, but he'll make sure you've got a new school."

Jennie pulled the quilt up over them and doused the kerosene lamp by their bed. The stranger who'd rescued her bell, the owner of Denison's Folly, stalked her still, even when she closed her eyes. Blue-eyed, magnetic, and oh, so tall, broad of shoulder. And she'd dowsed him with a bucket of water. If she wasn't so tired and worried for her job, she'd be thoroughly ashamed of her rash behavior.

After a pause Mariah added, "Since there's no school, Jennie, can we go looking for the squirrel tomorrow?"

Jennie rolled over. "There'll be school again. Didn't you hear your pa? School goes on, even if we have to hold it in the street."

CHAPTER

~3~

Aghast, Jennie stood in the middle of the crowd of town parents who'd gathered in the mercantile. "Don't make jokes, Thaddeus. It's only a month or so till Karl will have the new school raised. We'll hold it right here in the mercantile."

Thaddeus shook his head. He was not a big man, or an outgoing man, but his golden whiskers and steely eyes commanded people's respect, or maybe that was due to the reluctant way he gave out credit at the mercantile. For Grace, it had been love at first sight. Jennie abided him—just.

It took patience to listen to him now as he held out an arm and swept it around the room. "Now, Jennie, where would I put fifteen—fourteen kids and still have room for loyal customers like Ingrid Jensen to come in and browse through the calico and canned goods? That herd of kids would scare my customers away."

For a town man, Thaddeus Gordon was ruthless about children being seen and not heard . . . seen *working* preferably. He worked her nephews and her niece mercilessly, though that was not for Jennie to interfere in.

"I'd sooner put them in the saloon. It's not busy in the daytime."

Jennie exploded. "I can't teach in a place with spittoons and liquor and . . . and—" What other vile influences had she heard about? "Pictures of naked ladies."

The saloon keeper stepped forward, outraged. "Hellfire—I mean—land sakes, Miss Beasley, we ain't got no naked ladies in Castlerock. That's over in the Gardiner Saloon."

"Exactly. Our saloon has antlers on the wall." Mr. Vane was the lawyer, and his remark earned him a poke in the ribs by his starchy wife. "I've interviewed clients in there. It's business."

Laughter rippled through the crowd. Well, it might be good for a lawyer's business and Gordon's Mercantile, but it wasn't good for school.

Slowly Jennie's gaze swept the room, looking for support from among the parents. They stood looking back, apathetic.

"School don't have to be that fancy," Mr. Slocum said. "Just a place for readin' and writin'. I don't care where you have it."

Ingrid Jensen, the widowed seamstress, adjusted her spectacles as she stepped forward. "Well, I for one will withdraw my Bertha from school if it's to be the saloon." She folded her arms over her chest, while her spectacles dropped to the bridge of her nose.

"Come to think of it, Jennie," Thaddeus added, "if we closed for a month or two while we build a new school, the money we save on your salary would pay for the new desks."

Jennie felt the blood drain from her face. She earned thirty-six dollars a month, and two dollars a week went to board at the Gordons' house. Shocked at the suggestion, for the first time in the few months she'd been in Castlerock, Jennie was at a loss for words.

She stared at her brother-in-law. How Thaddeus Gordon had managed to sweet-talk Grace was beyond her, and if all men were like this one, she never intended to enter the bonds of matrimony. Never. But if she didn't do that, she needed to teach.

Thaddeus stuck a toothpick between his lips and gave her a lazy smile, like he knew he had her. Men. He was determined to get her to knuckle under, same way his wife and kids did. Thaddeus Gordon had saddled her sister with a passel of kids without asking Grace's by-your-leave, and now Grace was laid up with another pregnancy. And Mariah . . . little Mariah, his only daughter—well, she was plain afraid of her daddy, hungry for a word of affection.

As Jennie saw it, it was high time someone in Castlerock stood up to Thaddeus. "You can't close it."

"Don't cause a scene now, Jennie. The school board's always been the province of us men. We'll take care of you."

She saw red. "No say in it? Take care of me?" Unlike docile Grace, who took what Thaddeus Gordon dished out, Jennie was having none of it. She advanced on him, and the watching town backed away. "You're forgetting, Thaddeus, aren't you, that this town has the worst reputation in six states for keeping teachers?"

"That isn't true."

Nothing could stop her now. "There aren't enough potential husbands in this nothing town to draw all the sweet young things from New England who might come west to teach. This is last on every teacher's list, and the only reason you've got me is because I'm Grace's sister. This town is supposed to be trying to raise standards, bring some civilization to families, and the best idea you've got is to stick the children in the saloon."

Thaddeus Gordon, looking her up and down with boredom, rolled the toothpick between his teeth, then with a neat crunch broke the toothpick in half.

"Heck, Miss Jennie Beasley, if it's fancy refinement you want to teach the students, you could climb up that ridge above Camas Street and go knock on that dude's door. See if the owner of Denison's Folly will let the school take over his fancy quarters."

"Don't be absurd. It's too far out of town." A long walk . . . almost too long for town youngsters, who were used to running up the block or across the street.

Still . . . She paused as possibilities turned in her mind.

Thaddeus nourished her courage. "Go on," he dared. "One rich man rattling around in a mansion like that ought to have a spare room for a few kids, and I bet he's too refined to have one spittoon or toothpick in the whole place."

"The other night at dinner you said he's not one of us."

Thaddeus shrugged. "Heck, you don't think he'll say yes, do you? I just want to see how desperate you are to keep your teaching salary, Jennie."

"Why don't *you* ask him? You're the school board."

"Because I'm not the one standing around complaining that I'm too good for Castlerock's humble buildings."

Jennie looked down at the counter, pondering her reply.

Actually the idea held merit. After all, how many rooms in that mansion could one man possibly occupy at one time? But how could she sashay up there like Teton Sally—the upstairs lady at the saloon—and boldly ask for a favor? It would be totally audacious of her, especially after dowsing the man with a bucket of water.

On the other hand, Jennie prided herself on having audacious dreams and schemes. The invisible window in her and Mariah's bedroom, for example, was audacious.

As was her dream of attending university.

And dreams never came true if you weren't bold.

Whether she could go toe to toe with that arrogant big bear of a man up in Denison's Folly was another matter.

Ingrid Jensen, pushing her spectacles up with one finger, leaned close and whispered in her ear. "I think you should at least ask. That way you'll get to see inside his house. Helga says he's got a lead-lined bathtub—the kind that drains itself."

Jennie's mouth dropped. Ingrid shrugged. "I'd give anything if Bertha could see the bric-a-brac and parlor furniture; educate her in the ways fine people live and then maybe she won't marry the first hayseed who comes along."

"Ingrid, I don't know—"

"Do."

The parents took up the chant. "Yeah, do, Jennie. And we'll all be waiting right here for the inside story."

"Maybe if he says yes, Thaddeus will loosen the purse strings and build you a fancier schoolhouse."

It was becoming a regular joke. At the youngsters' expense.

Thaddeus raised his eyebrows. "Seems the parents want a friendly bet. Get him to say yes, and I'll let you have complete say in what we put into the new school. Fancy desks and double cloakrooms. White painted siding. The works."

He was exaggerating. "I am not a betting woman."

"Go on, Jennie," Ingrid urged. "For Bertha's sake."

Jennie took another step forward, then catching a glimpse of the fancy house through the window, she stopped. She'd called Mr. Denison an idiot.

Profane words and raucous laughter drowned out the rest of Jennie's thoughts and that did it. The town fathers were acting like the cavalry let out of Fort Yellowstone on payday. Things were going downhill fast, and as schoolmarm, it was her duty to leave no stone unturned in bringing culture to the children. As it was, with winter breaks, learning was slow . . . her salary stopped . . . the dream of university that much further away.

"Do it, Miss Beasley."

"There's nothing to lose."

"Do it . . . do it . . . do it."

She turned for the door, then stopped. She'd always been the brave one. When Grace had played at dolls, Jennie had played wild horses.

No . . . she simply couldn't do it.

Then how in the world would she ever achieve her dream of a female academy if she couldn't look one rich man in the eye and ask for what she needed? She could at least offer an apology for the bucket of water . . . and maybe thank him for helping.

Dreams, if they were to come true, happened one step at a time. She walked outside. Almost at once she was flanked by two of Castlerock's most eligible bachelors, who pushed through the crowd at the same time, each vying for her attention.

Blond Karl was tall and lean as a two-by-four. "You really gonna ask that eastern dude about using his house? It was built by out-of-town carpenters, you know . . . St. Paul men." His voice held a wounded note as if the very words "out-of-state workers" were somehow traitorous. The way his Adam's apple bobbed made Jennie long to take a hammer and nail it down.

"Don't worry, Jennie," he said shyly. "I'm going to volunteer every spare hour I've got to put up the frame. You won't be out of a real school for long."

"Thanks, Karl."

On her other side, Edgar wiped his brow with a gray handkerchief and stuffed it in a pocket of his vest. The buttons

strained against a paunch that was as swollen as the bank
coffers at harvest time. "You certainly don't have to lower
yourself to ask favors of a stranger, Miss Jennie," Edgar said.
"If the town puts up a certain amount, I'm sure the bank will
help finance a new school. The ladies are already talking about
holding a bee of some kind to raise money. The bank would
look kindly on that." Above his celluloid collar, his smile
displayed uneven teeth.

Grateful, she looked from one to the other. "Thank you, both
of you, from the bottom of my heart, but I can't sit idle nor can
the children. Their school year is too short as it is. School will
resume."

With Karl on one side, Edgar on the other, and her
brother-in-law watching from behind, Jennie had never felt
more hemmed in by men, none of whom she much admired.
Not that Karl and Edgar weren't sincere. After all, in this
town's pecking order of bachelors, Karl and Edgar were
next in line to claim the hand of the schoolmarm. But
Jennie didn't intend to be claimed by either of them, and
without a school open season on schoolteachers would start
early.

"Do either of you want the children?" she asked them.

"In the carpenter's shop with all those sharp tools?"

"In the bank with real money lying around?"

Their incredulous questions came on top of each other, like
flapjacks popping onto a plate and sitting there cooling.

"So neither of you wants to provide space either."

"Aw, Miss Jennie, it's not that. . . ."

That settled it. "Excuse me, gentlemen, and don't worry.
Mr. Denison will probably say no, too, but I'm leaving no
stone unturned."

And with that, she marched up the boardwalk, headed for
the turreted gingerbread extravaganza. Denison's Folly was
about to receive another fool for a guest.

* * *

Helga, Nate's Norwegian housekeeper, announced that he had a visitor with the same casualness she announced dinner or complained that his fancy furnace was growling through the floor vents.

Engrossed as he was in reading the batch of Western Union messages he'd received up from the railroad depot that morning, Nate wasn't in the mood to be disturbed. He expected some town matron had come to snoop about all the fancy furnishings and then report back to the other ladies at the mercantile.

"Who is it?" he asked.

It was a damn nuisance the way people ran around out west without calling cards. His elegant calling-card dish sat empty save for a spent bullet left there by a joking Sergeant Orvil Rowe.

"A lady."

He looked up at that. "Someone's certainly wasted no time in coming asking for donations for a new school."

"Or else it's about the bee they're organizing—"

"A bee?" Nate had hated bees ever since he'd been stung as a child.

Helga pinned a patient look on her employer. "For a fancy man, you can be pretty dumb."

"You've told me that." Helga, who delighted in teaching such a sophisticated man about the ways of the west, knew it.

"*Ja*, well, some things bear repeating. You see, out here a bee is a social gathering for the purpose of helping each other. We women have quilting bees, where we all help a woman finish a quilt." In her haste, she pronounced her w's as v's. "Or the men will have a school-raising bee."

"Where everyone works for free, I gather."

"There's more helping hands than money in a place like this, Mr. Denison. Sturdy hands are always needed."

"Why is it called a bee?"

"Because the people who work are busy as—"

"Bees. Of course."

"And when I learn what kind of a bee it is, I'll tell you, but rest assured, it's not a bumblebee. Now about the schoolmarm. Do you want me to show her in or do you want her to stand out there till the snow flies? What do you want?"

"Vant" for "want." It always took Nate a minute for Helga's subtle accent to sink in. His mind backed up. What had she said before "vant"? Schoolmarm?

He sat up straighter, suddenly interested. "You never said it was the schoolteacher come to call."

"Did it matter? She is too prim and nice for the likes of you . . ."

"Nice? She threw water on me, Helga. Tried to drown me."

His housekeeper shrugged. "If you were a rugged Viking, you would not care. Remember now, she will be the wife of Karl or Edgar. They claim the next schoolmarm."

His memory called up a fine figure of a woman, especially with her clothing in disarray. Anything but prim. Too fiery for yokels like Karl and Edgar.

"Is she in the parlor?"

Maybe she was coming to apologize, and if so, he'd make her grovel a bit, see how much stern stuff Miss Beasley was made of. Above all he looked forward to seeing her loose-flying copper hair again, the passionate intensity of her face . . . and her delightfully casual way of dressing. She showed a shirtwaist off to far better advantage than any pen sketch in a mail-order catalog.

He stood and eagerly made his way to the parlor. In the doorway he paused, looking her up and down without her knowledge.

She stood with her back to him, bending over, admiring a most exotic object, a peacock feather in a vase that Daisy had favored. His heart hardened, and a knot formed in his stomach. Were women all alike, right down to their taste in ornaments?

"It's from India," he supplied, and she, turning, caught him off guard. The sensuous woman had vanished, to be replaced by a stereotypical prim and proper schoolmarm. "Imported directly from Calcutta courtesy of a friend of the viceroy's."

She clasped her hands in front of her and looked at him as if she'd never heard of India.

He gaped, hardly able to believe the change in her.

"Sit down, Miss Beasley." His voice sounded faint.

He sank into a chair opposite her and quickly took in this very different schoolmarm.

Her hair—that stunning coppery hair—was pulled back into a severe knot. It was all wrong, made her forehead too high, her mouth too thin, her eyes too brown. All of her too vulnerable. Rigid, she perched on a velvet chair like a nervous robin, back ramrod stiff, tan cape tied demurely up to her neck, the rest of her hidden by a long skirt.

"What can I do for you, Miss Beasley?"

She looked down and then swiftly back up from under her lashes. An innocent but fascinating movement. "I came to apologize for dashing you with the bucket of water. I was dreadfully upset."

He sighed, disappointed. There'd been so much promise in that female who'd poured a bucket of water over him. Today she was as predictable as all the other women he'd ever known. First they all apologized and then made their request for favors. Still, he liked stringing the predictable little game out as long as possible.

"Don't worry about it. Did you rescue the school bell?"

"Some of the fathers did, yes. But of course, until we build a new school, there's nowhere to hang it, so it's being stored in the livery. I wanted it in the mercantile, but Thaddeus Gordon says there's no room what with a load of canned peaches and flour sacks expected in. With him not wanting to use the place for a substitute school, I can't imagine why I thought he'd want the bell there either."

Suddenly he knew what she wanted. As it did when he was predicting the future of a stock, his adrenaline ran faster.

"Brandy?" he asked, looking at her sturdy woolen cape and black button shoes.

"No, thank you." Oh, the words had a righteous ring to them, but sure as he knew money, he sensed this oh-so-prim Miss Beasley was just a facade.

"What is it you want? A donation for this bee?" Ask it. Prove me right. "What is it?" He looked directly at her.

Jennie stared at him, mortified. She felt like a church mouse come to rob the offering plate while he, the robber baron, stood waiting for her to try it.

"Is your shoulder all right?"

"It hurts, but that's not why you came."

She shook her head. He was standing over her, taller than ever, wider of shoulder than she'd realized yesterday in all the commotion. His trousers were nubby wool, his shirt white silk, the two items bound by dark suspenders. She craned her neck back to look up into his face, into forbidding blue eyes and hair the same dark brown as strong coffee, hair that looked as rumpled as a telegram he'd just discarded. "Ask me, Jennie Beasley."

"You'll say no."

"I'm more persuadable than people give me credit for."

Words fell off his lips like gold dust off a lode. She held his gaze and said it all in a rush. "I came to ask you if you would mind lending the school one of the rooms in your house as a temporary place to meet . . . for the school to meet." The words tumbled out so fast she wasn't sure he heard. "Just for a month or so, until Karl can raise up a new school."

And then he stood there, staring at her so long she was even more positive he hadn't heard. "I came to ask if—"

"I heard you the first time." The quick sip of brandy was a toast to himself and his clever guess. He looked sideways at her embarrassed blush. It shouldn't be too hard to discuss this. "You want to rent a room from me? I don't run a boardinghouse."

She paused, moistened her lips, swallowed. Oh, but he wasn't going to make this easy. "Not rent. Borrow."

Intrigued, he decided to spar awhile. "Give me a minute, Miss Beasley, to take in the magnitude, the ramifications of this request. You said borrow?"

"Yes, borrow."

"As in a cup of sugar? My housekeeper informs me borrowing is done all the time out here."

"Being so remote, we run out of things. I'm sure you—coming from a sophisticated and urban city—have noticed a . . . lack of certain items."

"Champagne and chocolate toffee. Canned cherries are rare too. And a man would be hard-pressed to replace cuff links."

She drew herself up straighter. "You're being facetious. In this case it's a lack of buildings suitable for a temporary school."

"Ah, yes, the fire. Pity."

"And the only place in town willing to lend us space is the saloon."

He raised his brows in interest, and debated the wisdom of smiling.

"Which isn't at all proper because the place has not a single book and altogether too many cuspidors and . . . those kinds of things. . . . You plan to say no, don't you?" Quick as a robin, she was gone from the chair and had darted to the doorway. "I know it's all because I threw water at you. I'm very grateful you pulled me out of the burning school, you know, and terribly sorry about the water."

In half a dozen long strides, he caught up to her and shut the door. If he wasn't careful, she'd slip out of his fingers.

With a hand on her arm, he turned her around, and the lily-of-the-valley scent of her drifted up to him.

"Miss Beasley, would you stop running away from me and answer a few questions?"

"Such as?"

"Which room did you have in mind?"

Her expression thawed considerably, and hope filled her eyes. "You've got plenty. You could choose."

"I suggest the dining room—for its table."

"You mean, you'd actually consider letting the school come here?"

Careful not to betray too much enthusiasm, he nodded. "Would you like to see the room?"

Jennie nodded back, unable to believe how agreeable he was.

Following, she kept her gaze on his back, on the width of his shoulders. She'd known he was tall, but never realized how big a man. Suddenly he stopped and found her staring at him. "Here it is. Aren't you going to look?" he asked, and moved aside.

She gasped in wonder. It was the most beautiful room she'd ever seen—all bottle green and Pompeiian red. A room of consequence, like all the rooms in the house, she guessed. The brass light fixture said it all. As did the bank of bay windows hung with lace and red velvet. Awed, she headed straight for the walnut sideboard, the likes of which she'd never seen. Why, it even boasted a carved angel head.

"It's lovely." She stood staring at it till she was aware he'd said not a word. Turning, she saw him staring at her in a queer way, as if she'd grown two heads.

"Did I say something wrong? Don't you like this piece? Or is it from the same friend as gave you the feather?"

He gave a stiff nod.

"Oh—well, it's exquisite."

"You may like it, but I don't. Nevertheless it's worth a fortune, so keep the schoolbooks off of it, Miss Beasley, and the chalk and the slates and whatever else you bring in. That is, if you still want to use the room."

"It's nice and light," she said politely. It was, she was dismayed to find, directly across the hall from his personal library. "You mean it, don't you? I thought you'd be too rich to want a bunch of town kids in your house."

Nate meant it all right, but he didn't have philanthropy on his mind. He yearned to slip his fingers through her hairpins and yank them out, and whenever Nate Denison felt that longing, he predictably followed through—be it with an eastern debutante or a bored Fifth Avenue matron. Oh, but he'd never felt more corrupt: while Jennie Beasley stood here quaking and talking about the morals of children being threatened, he thought about the many ways he could seduce her. "I mean it."

"You're very generous," she said softly. "Especially after my rude behavior."

He shrugged. "I'm not generous. I'm a businessman. How would you repay me for my loan?" Pulling out a carved walnut chair from the table, he indicated for her to sit, and stunned at his unexpected question, she sank down, knees suddenly weak.

She furrowed her brow, then cast a baffled look at him.

"I mean," he explained, sitting down opposite her, "when one neighbor borrows a cup of sugar, she can return a cup when the next train load of goods comes into the mercantile, correct?"

He was logical to the point of absurdity. "But how can I possibly return the lending of a room?"

A mischievous smile flitted across his face. "We'll work out a barter system. My dining room for your full cooperation in keeping the youngsters from running loose. They're to stay confined in one room."

Her outrage had to be showing on her face. "They're children, Mr. Denison, not a herd of wild animals."

For a long moment he was silent, staring at her. At last he spoke again. "Did you have something more practical to offer in exchange?" His gaze slowly moved down to her bodice and just as slowly up again.

Immediately she drew herself up in her chair. "You're toying with me. I have nothing to offer you in return, and you know it."

He sat and leaned back in his chair, hands linked behind his neck. "Ah, then this is really a charitable donation you're asking for."

Their gazes locked. She looked away first, down at the polished walnut surface of his antique dining table. Sighing, she admitted the truth. "Yes, all right. I'm asking for charity . . . but not for long," she added hastily.

"How long?"

When she glanced up, his face was as noncommittal as uncracked eggs, and so she tried to look optimistic and force a casual reply. "Only until Christmas."

"Christmas?" Nate echoed, surprised by his incredible good fortune.

He could have any woman he wanted in one week flat, and she was talking in terms of twelve weeks—a bonanza. Twelve minus one gave him eleven weeks of sensual pleasure. More if Karl and the other volunteer carpenters were uncommonly slow.

"That's a long time," he said, frowning.

"Well, it could go faster, but we'll need to order some of the fixtures from back east. You know the desks—real ones with inkwells this time, and a slate board, and—"

"I get the idea. Those things do take time, and that I know from building this house."

He'd been right about the dusting of freckles on her nose. His gaze swept over her from the frog closings on her tan cape to her black button boots. Nate gave his imagination free rein.

"Even though it's charity," he said slowly, "I think that we need some sort of rental agreement . . . borrowing terms . . ."

"Rules?" she said cheerfully. "I'll come early to light the stove. Wood's always chopped by the students, so you don't need to lift a finger."

"Miss Beasley, this house is heated by a real furnace."

"Oh." That explained the noise coming out of that grate in the floor. "Then I'll do all the janitorial work."

"I have a housekeeper."

"Nevertheless I'll clean up after the children."

"They're not messy, are they?"

"Oh, no," she hastened to assure him. "They're very neat. And quiet. Well behaved."

"And capable of burning down a building."

She blushed. "That was Vernon's doing, and he's run away now. You can trust us."

"That's what the Great Fathers in Washington keep saying to the Indians, isn't it?"

"That's different."

"Not at all . . . I trust your lessons are quiet."

After a brief pause she nodded. "But you have to agree to provide a playground for recess."

"I have a yard. Just so they don't stray off toward the buffalo pen."

"Buffalo?" She looked at him askance. There were hardly any left anywhere. She was surprised he'd found some.

"Don't worry. The pasture begins a couple miles out, and the animals aren't here yet."

"Oh, well, then, that's fine. Just so at recess the youngsters aren't near them."

He stood. "The class is perfectly safe."

Why, though, did a little flutter of danger flit through her stomach? As if *she* should be worrying about herself.

"Is there anything else I should have ready?"

Frowning, she looked about, spotted the glass-covered bookcases.

"May we borrow some books too?"

His gaze raked over her. "Help yourself. You may want to pull a few titles that are less than suitable." Half his collection was European. Daisy had presented many of them to him for shock value. "I think you'll find some classics in there, and I'll donate writing paper."

"Thank you, Mr. Denison. Everyone in town—the parents, I mean—predicted you'd rebuff me."

"The town doesn't really know me then, does it, Miss Beasley?"

His smile was ironic, and she stared up at him. So tall. Such intense blue eyes. He had an air of sadness about him that not all his handsomeness could dispel.

"When shall I expect the arrival of the Castlerock School?"

She came to her senses. "Monday. I'm never late. Without the stove to stoke, I'll come early to prepare lessons. You're a true pillar of the community now." Anxious to leave, she reached out her hand. He covered her gloved hand with his own—rather, engulfed her in a bear paw. She felt . . . all liquid and warm. This had been easier than she'd anticipated.

The Castlerock School was back in business.

It would all work out . . . if only Mr. Denison stayed out of her way. For her part, she certainly planned to stay out of his.

CHAPTER

~4~

The thunder of hooves came closer and closer. Buffalo were running like raw syrup across a flapjack—one great brown puddle engulfing the horizon, their hooves pounding in a steady drone. Running thunder.

By the time they crossed the railroad tracks, the train had stopped and unarmed passengers crouched low. Nate's uncle, a portly man with a giant watch chain, swung his rifle out the window. In his haste, he shot too soon, and the hat of a lady up ahead flew off. Every man on the train had a gun pointed out the window at the buffalo who blocked the tracks. The sport was in counting how many a man could take before the train got going. Like Punch and Judy puppets, they fell. Through the window, ten-year-old Nate stared eye to eye with one mangy brute, its tail flicking, staring danger down, dumbly.

"Get up. Out of the way!" His uncle's commands were sharp; the barrel of his rifle pointed right at Nate, who stood blocking his uncle's shot. "Get away!"

And then, amid shrieks, the beast lumbered down the aisle, and Nate was running, bison at his heels, running, running, and at the coupling he fell off the train, thunder rolling over his head, while he swallowed dust, waiting to be crushed or shot, whichever came first. The thunder climaxed in one crescendo as the herd came closer, closer, and he couldn't get up in time to escape.

"Don't shoot!"

A crash resounded, and Nate, shaking, sat up, rubbed his healing shoulder.

He opened first one eye, then the other. The sky above was green, the clouds made of plaster.

Then he realized he was in his bed.

And the year was 1893. Montana. And this wasn't a boyhood trip out west with his uncle. He lived here now. Now. And the room was empty. The stampeding buffalo had vanished. The rest was all a dream of days long gone, as gone as Daisy. A pale morning light filtered through his curtains.

Beneath him another crash echoed up through the floorboards. And now he knew he hadn't dreamed the thunder.

There were thundering feet beneath him, and boyish shouts.

Buffalo in his house? Where the devil was his foreman?

He lay back, remembering. His foreman was in South Dakota, organizing a crew of men to bring home the dozen buffalo Nate had bought—animals so rare Nate might be able to resell them to the Smithsonian—at a profit. But at the moment the hundreds of acres of land behind his house was empty.

So what was loose in his house? He searched more recent memory.

Ah, yes, he remembered a schoolmarm, copper hair flowing out in the wind, her slim body silhouetted against the flames of a burning schoolhouse. The passionate woman vanished and in her place stood a meek spinster in his parlor asking to "borrow" his dining room. And then he remembered the impulsive bargain he'd made with Miss Jennie Beasley.

The schoolchildren.

He rubbed a hand over his stubbled chin, raked his fingers through his hair.

A look at the clock told the tale; his aching head provided the footnote about his late night entertaining Hirum and Orvil. How long had they traded tales about the poachers who got away? Until 2:00 A.M.? Three?

Their gossip had taken Nate by surprise.

"The wives at the fort are the ones doing all the talking and wondering," they'd said over their whiskey.

"Wondering about what?" Nate had been cautious. Women . . .

"Well, on whether you're sweet on the teacher and whether you're the sort to have designs on her . . . and who you've got chaperoning here."

"Helga's here, and as for the other, neither one is true. She's a respectable teacher who needed a classroom. I'm a good citizen with a too-big house."

"I betcha want to flirt with Miss Beasley."

"Leave her alone."

"Ah, now we're getting protective."

Only in the way that a man is protective of his own prey.

"Haven't you two got some poachers to be looking for?"

"Yeah, well we keep our ears open when we're in town too."

"I'll bet whoever's poaching loves bragging about it with a pair of blue-uniformed cavalrymen eavesdropping." He couldn't keep the ironic tone from his voice.

"You never know what you're going to hear," Hirum said defensively. "In fact, we've got our eye on that Gordon fellow.

Your schoolmarm's brother-in-law."

Nate looked up. "How so?"

"He's got an old hunting shack out in the woods, just a ways out of the park. It looks like it's been used lately. Perfect place for a poacher or two to hole up."

"Got proof?"

Hirum scoffed. "Catching him in the act? All we can do is confiscate gear and throw them out, and every old trapper knows it. We need to find some hard evidence. Until then, we puff up and huff a lot like the big bad wolf who's lost his dentures." To illustrate, Hirum sucked his lips over his gums, then took a deep breath and blew the foam off his beer.

Orvil fell off the chair laughing.

"It isn't funny, Orvil."

True. The law had no teeth in it. But these wet-behind-the-ears cavalrymen had just handed Nate the perfect justification for letting Jennie Beasley and her students into his house.

He leaned forward conspiratorially now and lied. "All right. You win. Do you want to know the true reason I agreed to hold school in my dining room? Because she'll have fourteen—fifteen youngsters under her thumb all day . . . loose at recess and lunchtime running about my house—all bragging about their daddies' hunting trips."

"What do you care for?"

"Remember the little herd of buffalo I told you are coming? I want it on the hoof, not poached."

Orvil stood, disgusted. "Poachers be damned. The upshot is the prettiest teacher to hit Castlerock in three years gets confined in the same house with you, a guy who doesn't know nothing about kids or setting traps for poachers. You'll just get caught yourself."

He'd dueled over debutantes. "I can take care of myself against a homegrown schoolmarm any day."

Another crash echoed up through the floor of his bedroom, and this one broke into his thoughts. Dammit, the fourteen youngsters were supposed to be sitting around his dining-room table, reading and reciting. Furthermore Miss Beasley had said they'd behave.

He burrowed beneath the pillow, wishing they'd all go away. What had possessed him? Had the schoolmarm looked that good?

Yes, she had.

But did they have to make so much noise, and what the deuce was crashing? Fully awake now, he found himself thinking of all manner of bric-a-brac: silverware, a stereoscope and dozens of viewing prints, a mechanical bird in a gilded cage, an entire étagère full of porcelain objets d'art, wax fruit, candles. If he had to list it all for his lawyer, he'd be in bed all day.

Clearly he'd have to get up and investigate.

He pulled on his trousers and hiked the suspenders up over his underwear, grabbed a denim shirt, and headed for the stair-case, where he stood bellowing at the top of his lungs for his housekeeper.

When Helga appeared, he leaned over the banister.

"Where's my shaving water? My coffee?"

"I'm sorry, Mr. Denison," she said breathlessly. "I'm a tad bit late. I have the cocoa to make first."

His stomach roiled. "What cocoa?"

"For the students," she said, beaming as she wiped her hands on her apron. "Oh, but a houseful of little ones is just what this place is lonely for. Now I won't quit when my grandchild arrives."

He gritted his teeth. "Why the devil are you brewing cocoa?"

"Because of course the students expect something hot to drink after playing out in the cold. Like in Norvege, we eat more in the cold. But you haven't got a potbellied stove in your dining room."

"Why should I?"

"Because all good schools—even schools in Norvege, have potbellies."

"Really?" She managed again to make his grand house sound inferior to Viking huts.

"So . . ." she said, beaming. "I volunteered to make cocoa on the kitchen stove, and one of the little girls is my helper. And I get to give a lesson on how to make lefse. Miss Beasley said so."

"The deuce you say." This was not part of his agreement with the teacher. She was taking over before he even had a chance to seduce her.

"I approved their drinking out of the Bavarian china. There's nothing else but—"

"What'd they drink out of at the school?"

"A tin dipper and tin mugs from home—all ruined in the fire. Now, you've more than enough dishes to go around, and they won't break a one."

Below, another crash shook the rafters, not the crash of china, but the heavy thud of something solid hitting the floor.

"I'll fire you if I don't have coffee in five minutes."

"*Ja*, sure you fire me. Where do you think you find another housekeeper who can clean up after fourteen children, eh? You would have to send for my good sister in Norvege, and she's already read my letters about what a cantankerous skinflint you are—"

"Me? A skinflint?"

"*Ja*, I've known poor men who are more giving than you are, Mr. Nate Denison of Fifth Avenue, New York. The Vikings would have tossed you overboard halfway to Greenland." She turned to head back to the kitchen, her domain.

"Helga?" he called, trying to sound like he was in control of his own house.

"*Ja?*"

"What's all that crashing?"

She shrugged. "The teacher is showing the boys and girls the principle of gravity, I think."

"Using what?" The mechanical bird cage crossed his mind.

Helga shrugged. "What does it matter? You've too many gewgaws to dust anyway. I wish my boys had had a teacher like her. Maybe they could write a decent hand."

If Helga's sons could write, maybe they'd get jobs in far-away places and would quit coming by to take her away for visits. But that was beside the point. "The students are not supposed to enjoy school." God knows, he hadn't. "They're supposed to sit and be quiet. What kind of teacher is she?"

"Oh, most inventive. Pretty enough to catch the eye of the bravest Viking—"

"Hang the Vikings! Where's the stereoscope?" he asked with some alarm. "She can't use that." He'd promised her access to his books, but not the bric-a-brac. "She'll pay for every piece they break. And they're not to touch the plate from the exposition. Or smudge the stereoscope prints with their grubby fingers." Nate had accumulated a large collection of prints for his viewer—everything from Paris to the Colombian Exposition.

"Hush," Helga said. "Don't hurt the teacher's feelings. Such a sweet young thing and so clever. I thought you were going to lend the school some equipment?" She didn't say the word, "cheapskate," but it was written all over her face.

"Books and paper. And if they don't like my books, they'll have to borrow from the country school." As long as Thaddeus rode the twenty miles out to get them. "And the children aren't to roam the house. Keep them in the dining room."

Helga placed her hands on her considerable hips and glared up the staircase at him. "Mr. Denison, if you're going to be such a grouchy troll about these children, then kindly hide away in your library."

Hide away. In his own house? What had he gotten into? Completely cowed, Nate retreated to sulk in his room and await his shaving water and his coffee, which Helga delivered without a kind word of good morning.

When he finally came downstairs, the house was quiet—inside. Mercifully quiet. At last Miss Beasley had them under control. Satisfied, he made his way to his library, but slowed when he tripped over a pair of high-button shoes in the hallway. Kicking them aside, he finally made it to his library and locked himself in to await recess.

That's when he heard the rain against the windowpanes, followed a moment later by the clatter of a bell going off next to his eardrums.

My God, the teacher had found another bell.

A hand bell. And she was turning all those little feet loose.

And suddenly his head hurt. There had to be easier ways to come up with a woman in this lonesome land.

Instead God was sitting up in heaven laughing his head off at his practical joke with the weather and the children—big and little—of Castlerock School. All those muddy little feet had to return to his Oriental carpets and imported Hepplewhite chairs with the embroidered seat covers.

On and on rain pattered against the window. This was a freak happening. The rain would blow through. Indian summer would return. The new school would get built. The children would leave for good.

He got no mercy. Instead, a moment later, his windowpane shattered and crashed to the floor of his library with absolutely no advance warning. An agate marble flew in with the debris and rolled to a stop, wet and trailing mud, right near his foot. After scooping it up out of the glass shards, he stalked to the door and glared across the hall at the empty dining room.

When the children finally returned, he was standing in the doorway of the library, staring in horror at his dining-room table as one by one they scraped themselves into chairs about it. One boy sat twirling a gold drapery cord; another twirled the opposite cord, and within a minute they were batting the fringed cords at each other.

His gaze met that of Miss Beasley, who stood uncertainly in the doorway of the dining room, color staining her cheeks a ruddy hue from the cold. She glanced guiltily at the shiny marble balanced on his outstretched palm.

A girl no taller than his knees came down the hall, complaining loudly, "He's got running water in the bath-room. Real running water, but it doesn't shut off. It fills up the sink."

"I'll get it," the teacher said quickly, and hurried to the bathroom down the hall to turn off the water.

As she passed him he remained there in shock, still staring into his dining room. To his horror, ugly lard tins sat on top of the antique walnut-finished table. Lard tins and handfuls of marbles. Marbles all over the place. Now, recalling the initials and crosses he'd carved into the wooden desk in his own days in the schoolroom with a cantankerous governess, he went slightly queasy. How could he have forgotten what bored schoolboys would resort to, to get even with schoolmarms?

But this was no scratchy old desk. This was an antique wal-nut table. A duke and duchess, so his father bragged, had once made love on top of it, an earl had shot his rival across its per-fect surface. The Prince of Wales had once eaten dinner at it.

And now fourteen runny-nosed, ragged western children sat around it and stared back at him, the little ones dubious, the older ones smirking. Like Yellowstone tourists, they all of them gawked at him as if waiting for him to erupt in anger.

As Jennie rushed back by, Nate caught her arm and stepped aside so she could survey the glass on the library floor. "I'm sorry. They're excitable the first day in a new place, but they'll settle down." She turned to go, then paused. "Would you like to come in and learn their names? I'd be pleased to introduce you—"

"Miss Beasley, as far as I'm concerned, they all have the same name—schoolchildren. School kids. Everyone one of them looks the same to me—"

"There's no need to talk as if they're animals."

The comparison was too obvious. "What's the source of all the noise?"

"I'm sorry again. I was using a marble to teach cartography. And then I must have lost track of it because I found a real ball, which is bigger. To explain why when the earth is round and maps are flat, it's impossible to draw—"

He glowered. "Enough. I understand the concept. But that doesn't mean they can bounce marbles off my windows."

She put a finger to her lips. "Quiet, please. You'll upset the children."

"Your philosophy of education is too lenient."

She sighed in resignation. "All right, I'll pay for your window, even if it takes an extra year to save for the university. Does that satisfy you?"

"For now," he said with a crooked grin.

Grabbing the marble, she rushed across the hall, slid the door shut, and disappeared into his dining room, his laughter behind her.

Again, he had the sensation of being a geyser, and deep down inside him steam was pulsing, wanting to erupt into angry words. Words he'd not want delicate young ears to hear.

But erupt he would, as soon as school was dismissed.

He turned on his heel and shut the library door. He'd study his telegrams, which he paid the Western Union operator to have delivered daily. The one on top was from South Dakota, from his foreman, the man in charge of herding twelve buffalo here.

Its message was terse.

BUFFALO CONTRARY. STOP. DO WHAT THEY WANT. STOP. DON'T WANT TO BE CONFINED WITH WHITE MAN ANY MORE THAN INDIANS DID. STOP. EXPECT DELAY.

An ironic smile crossed his lips. Jake's telegram made it sound as if buffalo had invented the notion of contrariness. If Jake could listen in on the noise coming from the dining room right now, he'd not be so surprised by a few contrary buffalo. Hell, the buffalo would probably be docile compared with these kids Nate had let into his life.

From across the hall children's voices rose in exuberance, as if they were all talking at once. Miss Beasley clapped her hands and called for quiet, but the chatter continued . . . and continued . . . and continued.

Mercifully, Nate's hangover died and the hands of the clock moved to four o'clock. Finally the house emptied of children, wet feet, and lard pails.

He stood in the doorway of his library to verify it was so.

When he was certain they were all gone, he walked across to inspect his dining room.

Jennie Beasley was down on her hands and knees picking up paper from underneath the table, and one strand of hair had fallen loose from its pins. Her shirtwaist had come untucked.

At the sound of the door sliding open, she peered out from under the table. "Oh, Mr. Denison." Hastily she scrambled out and stood, brushing back the errant strand of copper hair.

The sight of her brought back the reasons why he'd agreed to this bargain: for a chance to get close to the sensuous woman he'd first seen standing highlighted by the crimson glow of flames. Now, as she smoothed her dark skirt over her hips, that attractiveness was not lost on him.

He cleared his throat. "We need to clarify some of the fine points of this agreement, I believe."

"Yes, we didn't discuss what to do in case of rain and snow, did we? I've warned them about playing with the gold sash cords and about confining their marbles to the ground, not the air. We also discussed company manners."

"Heck, wild animals have got better manners," he shot back. The frustration of the entire day overcame his calm.

"There's no need to denigrate them. Furthermore it's unfair to compare them to animals. Children, while impulsive, are still learning to behave properly. Their natural instincts are not under control yet."

What the schoolmarm knew about instincts he could put in his little finger.

While she stood gaping at him he stalked the perimeters of his dining room, pointing out fingerprints on his imported green wallpaper. "Everyone should arrive here with clean hands."

"Of course. If they don't, I'll have them wash up in your bathroom. That's quite a novelty for them, you know, and I suspect they're going to come with dirty hands just for the thrill of using a real sink with running water."

He gaped at her.

"They wash at home. Only clean hands get admitted here." He was glowering at her sensual little mouth.

"Was there anything else?"

"Yes, there's the matter of lard pails scratching my antique dining table. Can't they come without lard pails and skip recess so they won't track up my house with mud?"

Jennie Beasley smiled at him. "Mr. Denison, obviously you've forgotten all about the realities of being a child."

With parents who roamed the world and left him in the care of hired help, he'd never actually known a childhood. "No, I haven't, but I had either a governess or tutor."

"Ah, yes, the privileged minority. Allow me to explain the realities of school life. Children, to begin with, are people, not buffalo or cattle or whatever you intend to pen away."

"Buffalo," he offered, tugging at the neck of his shirt. It was getting warm in here.

"Yes, well, like animals, Mr. Denison, children need to eat, hence the lard pails. Since you don't like them eating on your precious table, may we adjourn to the kitchen instead? That table looks more practical and it would be much closer to the soup in any case. I appreciate your generosity very much, you know."

He'd nearly forgotten Helga's soup and doubted Helga would give him a choice. "I'll instruct Helga to continue making it daily," he bluffed. As if he had a choice. "But recess has to go."

"You're crazy."

Pert little lady.

"Mr. Denison, children can't learn without breaks to exercise so they can sit still later for long stretches of time. A recess naturally must be held. You may dictate whether or not you want them on your veranda. Naturally no one will stray as far away as your outbuildings or animal enclosures, but they need a part of the yard for games."

"No marbles. Period."

"Jump ropes and hoops."

He nodded. "But no screaming or chanting that rhyme about 'Rich man, Poor man . . . ' "

"Red rover. Thread the needle. So laughter is allowed."

He nodded curtly. "But they play on the other side of the house from my library." Let Helga listen to them.

"Is that all?"

"This business of clothing cluttering my hallway won't do."

"Your hall tree wasn't designed for fourteen coats," she pointed out with maddening logic. "Nor is there a shelf in your hallway for fourteen pairs of boots—fifteen counting mine."

"Can't you leave them outside?"

Her face flushed; her voice rose. "Children are not endowed with natural fur coats and thus have to dress in coats and mittens and boots, which means when they arrive at your house with its fancy furnace, they then become warm and need to leave their outer clothing somewhere warmer."

"You're patronizing me, Miss Beasley."

"If you're so clumsy that you trip over clothing, I suggest you designate a place for storing fourteen coats and fourteen pairs of boots."

"The back porch."

"It's cold."

"Helga hangs laundry there. Take it or leave it."

She nodded. "Is that all?"

Again she nodded. "Quite satisfactory."

He felt as if he'd been trampled and left to pick himself up. Her chest moved in and out, and when it did, the little pleats and rows of lace moved with it. He didn't want to negotiate the petty details of school days anymore. He wanted to cup his hand about a row of lace until he could feel the beating of her heart, the swelling of her breast beneath his hand.

"Was there anything else," she asked brightly, "or have we covered everything?" She was pulling her little cape over her shoulders, the wool one with a moth hole near the hem. And while he watched she pulled a ridiculous stocking knit cap over her beautiful thatch of coppery hair. Seconds later matching mittens covered her hands. Homely mittens of brown yarn. Hand-knit. She scooped up a batch of papers with childish-looking scrawls on them.

"I'll be off then." She headed for the door, then as if on an afterthought turned. "The children from out of town take the school wagon. Mr. Armstrong, their grandfather, is the driver, and he comes promptly at four o'clock, but if he's ever delayed, I trust it's acceptable for the children to wait just inside your door out of the cold? Your house is a bit of a walk from town, you know."

Numb, Nate nodded. Next she'd ask if it was all right to mount the school bell outside his window. "Did you say there was a meeting to plan the new school?" It couldn't happen soon enough.

She stopped in the middle of fastening that silly hat beneath her chin. "Did you want to come?"

Truth be told, he wanted to lay the cornerstone of the new school and get those kids out of here, but he wasn't ready to lose Miss Beasley yet. "I'm too curious to stay away."

"It's a box social."

He'd never been to one, and his dumbfounded expression must have given him away, for she smiled. "It's like a bee. You do know about bees?"

"My housekeeper's explained the basic idea."

"She's a wonderful woman," Jennie Beasley said with a warm smile. "In any case, you're invited to the box social and the bee and everything the town plans to help raise funds for a school."

"I'll be there." Next time, Miss Beasley. Fourteen school kids were not going to alter anything. He'd get her where he wanted her yet.

"What a pleasure for Castlerock to have you grace us with your presence." Her innocent smile belied the barb behind her words. "See you there," she said sweetly, and was gone.

He stuck his head out the door, debated returning her smart remark with one of his own, then decided such sparring was beneath his dignity. Darn right he'd see her there. He'd started this, and he'd finish it.

CHAPTER

∽5∾

Nate had no idea what the etiquette of a box social was compared with, say, a ball at the Astors'. But since it involved the exchange of money, he was confident he'd be a quick learner, quick enough to bid on and win Jennie Beasley's box, and force her to sit with him.

He arrived at the mercantile late and overdressed. Oh, his shirt and tie were the same style as the other men's. It was just that his were custom-tailored and so he stuck out in this room of callused hands like a well-manicured thumb. Not that the matrons of Fifth Avenue—the Vanderbilts and Astors—would have put any stock in this humble affair. But to the women here, it was the biggest event of the fall, and they'd dragged out their best muslin and heirloom brooches and polished their black high-button boots. A big stack of box suppers sat on the mercantile counter right between the licorice-stick can and the cash register, and filled the room with the cinnamon and spice aromas of chicken and apple cobbler.

A busybody in spectacles was running the show—Ingrid Jensen—the town seamstress. She was also, it turned out, a widow and mother to Bertha Jensen, the best-turned-out girl in school. He learned all this in two minutes flat from the Gordon girl—the child with dark pigtails—who took it upon herself to welcome him. He suspected this was due to her intense curiosity about his buffalo. Truth be told, he was grateful to young Mariah for putting out the effort to make him feel at home instead of staring at him like everyone else. Even more gratitude was owed Mariah for alerting him, in her naive way, to the widow's wiles.

That explained why the woman had eyes for Nate the instant he walked in, and since he'd vowed after Daisy jilted him that marriage was synonymous with poison, he promptly faded farther into a corner. All he wanted was to buy Miss Jennie Beasley's box supper and get her alone somewhere to flirt. No busybody widow was going to change his plan.

"The bidding is anonymous," the Widow Jensen announced smugly, pulling off her spectacles and adjusting her ridiculous hat, the only hat in the place save for Stetsons, one of which Nate had yet to purchase.

"Anonymous?" Karl the carpenter groaned.

Smugness was never becoming on a widow, especially on Widow Jensen. "Anonymous," she said.

More men groaned, Nate among them. At once he sought out Helga. "How do I know which belongs to which woman?"

"You don't. I made certain there'd be no decorative signs giving them away. Every box was donated from the mercantile, and you'll have to take your chances on your supper companion."

"You could have warned me how it worked," he complained.

"*Ja,* sure I could. But it's more fun this way."

"I didn't come for fun."

"What? No Viking spirit of adventure? Like Vikings sailing for new land, you take your chance here—"

"I'm not a Viking, Helga."

"You have surely bought something sight unseen?"

As a matter of fact, he had. "Buffalo." And those mangy beasts had better be an easier gamble than this affair.

One by one the Widow Jensen held up the boxes—each tied with identical string from the spool on top of the cash register.

One by one hungry men were poked in the ribs by their wives, made bids, and exchanged dollars for boxes. As various married women went off to eat with various married men, Nate grew hopeful.

Without warning, his hopes were dashed. Jennie's box got bought, and lucky Karl, the carpenter, blushed as he led her to a pair of chairs. No one had bought the Widow Jensen's box yet, and only Orvil, who loved to eat, and Nate, were boxless.

At last only the Widow Jensen was left unclaimed.

But two boxes sat up on the counter. Only one was tied with a double length of string.

Everyone stared at Nate, waiting to see what he'd bid on.

The Widow Jensen held up the two boxes and offered them both at the same time.

Mariah edged up to Nate. "If I were you, I'd bid on the box that's got string wrapped double on it. It broke and I had to redo it."

For a quiet little girl, she was remarkably astute. He'd never have noticed the difference in the string if she hadn't pointed it out.

The Widow Jensen held out the other box and smiled flirtatiously at Nate. Visions of eating supper with the aggressive widow haunted him, but Nate, ever the betting man, put his trust in the little girl.

"Two bucks," Orvil bid.

Nate took in the hopeful looks of the good widow in her plumed hat and glanced down at Mariah, who whispered again behind her hand, "Take the one with double string."

"Five for both," Nate said.

"Hey, that's not legal," Orvil complained.

The widow frowned at him and turned back to Nate with a hopeful smile. "Of course it's legal. This second box doesn't count. I'm the only woman left, so it's probably a practical joke and full of rocks. Five for both. Going—"

"Five-oh-one," Orvil bid, suddenly scared of ending up with nothing but rocks for dinner. "I'm hungry," he said when Hirum hooted at the price.

"Five—fifty," said Nate.

"Do I hear six?"

Silence.

"Going . . . going . . . gone."

They were both Nate's. To divide up as he pleased. He dug out his money and then magnanimously handed one box to Orvil. "Here, I'm not that hungry."

"Hey, thanks."

Nate took the box wrapped with double string. "He won me. Denison's Folly won me!" Mariah Gordon bounced up and down.

The widow had already proudly walked over to Nate, ready to lead him to a chair, when she stopped in her tracks. "But that's not legal," she moaned with a flinty-eyed look at Mariah. "No one said children could enter. My Bertha's eating with the children. I raised her to know her place among adults."

"You said there were no rules," Nate reminded her, and led the little Gordon girl to a pair of vacant crates.

Already Orvil had broken the string and opened the lid to

pull out a brown plume that matched the feather in the widow's head. "Guess Sergeant Orvil Rowe is your dinner partner, ma'am," he said politely to Ingrid Jensen. "He's a big eater, so make sure he gives you some too."

"Well," the widow said, flouncing off, face florid. "The sergeant is getting the better meal, I'm sure."

Nate didn't care what he ate, just so the food didn't come with husband-hunting widows attached. He was, for now and ever after, a confirmed bachelor and world-class rogue. It was enough.

"Jennie made my box too," Mariah said, handing Nate a biscuit and a piece of pie. "You can eat dessert first."

As he ate he tried to ignore all the eligible females glaring at Mariah. Not since the Astors' Valentine's Day ball when a dowager grandmother had drawn his name out of a box had so many females cast dagger eyes at him and his partner.

"What's your buffalo's name?" Mariah asked.

Reluctantly Nate dragged his attention back to the little girl. "I've got twelve, and I've yet to lay eyes on them."

"Well, did they have names before you bought them?"

How should he know if Indians gave their buffalo names? "They have to have names," she insisted.

Their fate was up in the air. Why name animals he might sell for their heads? "If you'd care to suggest some, I'll consider them," he said politely.

Mariah's solemn little face lit up, and she pushed her dark bangs out of her eyes. "Oh, yes. May I?"

There was a spark in her eyes that he'd never seen. How easily she could be made happy. Even if buffalo didn't have names and his foreman called him a greenhorn ten times over, he knew then that the Denison buffalo would be named. "I'd be honored. Especially after sharing dinner with you."

"Do you want presidents or Greek gods?"

He thought a minute. "Presidents."

"All right, I'll have a list Monday."

Nate was content. Not only had the child indeed turned out to be an animal lover and hence a soul mate, but if the subject of animals faltered, they could always discuss Miss Jennie Beasley, with whom, he'd learned, Mariah shared a bed.

While he chatted about the animal kingdom with Mariah he surreptitiously watched Jennie Beasley, who struggled to make conversation with the lanky Karl. If this was Castlerock's most eligible bachelor, then no wonder the schoolmarms didn't linger. Still, he stared. Jennie's coppery bun was anchored by so many hairpins a man could stake a claim on the metal . . . after he was done running his hand through her tresses.

Mariah stood and brushed crumbs off her skirt. "We have to do the hugging bee now," she announced.

Nate stared at her, wondering if he'd heard right. A hugging bee? You mean, this wasn't the end of it?

"Don't worry," little Mariah assured him gravely. "All the men bid on their wives. They do it every time they need money for the school. We need lots of money this time. A whole thousand dollars, so that's why we're having two events in one night." With solemn efficiency, she gathered up the remnants of supper and stuffed them in the box along with the double length of string.

"Who do the bachelors get to hug?" he asked, suspicious.

"Oh, everyone. Even Aunt Jennie, though she'll cost the most."

"Naturally. Does your aunt know about this?"

"I don't think so. She wasn't here last year. She arrived just ahead of you."

"I see." In his heart, his hopes of stealing some kisses from the schoolmarm took a leap. He could tolerate being called greenhorn and his mansion Denison's Folly a lot of times for a chance like this. At last he had Miss Jennie Beasley exactly where he wanted her, and he'd never been more sure that riches could buy happiness.

Moments later Ingrid Jensen clapped her hands for order while another mother, Mrs. Vane, the lawyer's wife, sprinkled cornstarch over the floor of the mercantile in preparation for dancing. "This hugging bee is a ridiculous idea, Ingrid," she complained. "Those haven't been done since you were a girl, and you know it."

"Oh, don't be a goody-goody, Susan," Ingrid said, "we can't raise money dancing. It's an old fun game, and what could be more fun than to show the young ones the ways we had fun in our youth? Certainly times can't have gotten more stodgy, or are you afraid your husband will part with a dollar to hug another man's wife?"

"Certainly not. Have your fun then, but my daughter is not allowed to participate." The women stood nose to nose.

"Good!"

As Mrs. Vane backed off, the widow Jensen once again clapped her hands for attention. "Hugs will cost you now, but it's for a good cause."

The old saloon keeper waved his dollar bills in the air. "I'm all in support of education. Won't see me shirking my duty where the future generation is concerned."

General laughter greeted this, and even Nate found himself smiling.

Widow Jensen barked out instructions as quick as if she were sticking pins in a hat. "Old maids go two for a nickel."

Everyone howled, for of course in this town women were scarce. No one was an old maid.

"What about the schoolmarm?"

Nate managed to sneak a glance at Jennie, who was flattened against the back wall, looking as if she were going to her own lynching. Clearly no one had informed her about this event, nor of the fact that she was the fatted calf, the sacrificial lamb.

"Married women are a dollar, but our schoolteacher is five dollars."

Karl, the lanky carpenter, raised his bill. "I bid on the teacher. Five bucks."

Jennie flinched, and as Nate looked, her soft brown eyes met his, silent, imploring him. Pansy brown. Something tugged at his gut.

One way or another he'd bought every woman he'd ever had, and that's all this amounted to. But it struck him as more cold-blooded than his conquests.

Moving forward, he had his five dollars already in hand and more. "I raise him four dollars."

A murmur of shock ran through the assembled crowd. Ingrid Jensen looked nonplussed at this extravagant bid and stared at Karl, who'd slumped against a wall.

"Karl?" she prompted, tone anxious.

"I'm not a rich man," he said, and shook his head, dejected.

Turning back to Nate, the widow put on a brittle smile.

"You're the lucky man." There might have been a touch too much sugar in her voice. "She's back there, looking white as the cornstarch under your feet."

"C'mon, Jennie," her brother-in-law taunted. "Get away from that wall and let the eastern dude have his hug. This is your cause, you know."

Nate turned back to Ingrid in her big hat. "Is there a limit to how many hugs a lady gives?"

Jennie cringed while Ingrid smirked. "Five per lady per night. No more."

Good. Reaching in his coat pocket he slapped more bills in Ingrid's hand. "I'll buy all Miss Beasley's turns then."

In a minute he was at Jennie's side and grabbed her hand.

"C'mon, a hug, Mr. Dude," Thaddeus Gordon goaded. "It has to be in public or it doesn't count."

"Is that so?" Nate looked right at Jennie Beasley.

Jennie looked up at Nate Denison, scared and beyond mortification. If the floor had swallowed her up, she'd have been grateful.

"Hug her! Hug her!" everyone called. The sergeants crowded close. "If you don't know how, we'll show you," they offered in bawdy tones.

Arms stiff at her sides, she shut her eyes, as if waiting to die. She'd hoped against hope that Nate might help her. How foolish could she get?

As Nate pulled her to him in a quick hug, arms loose about her waist, bodies barely touching, she held her breath.

"Heck, Mr. Denison's a raw dude even when it comes to hugging," Hirum jeered. "He don't know how us ordinary folks do it."

Inwardly Jennie melted. Why, it was the chastest hug in the world, the sort the minister gave when he was consoling a weeping parishioner. The difference was it lasted forever, so long she had to breathe, and when she took a breath, her chest rose and fell against the buttons of his jacket. She inhaled the masculine scent of bay rum, the comforting scent of wool. Then at last he let go and set her apart from him.

Her eyes snapped open, questioning. "Is that it?" Just one? And then a brief flicker of disappointment, quickly replaced by a brave smile. Her blood went all tingly and her face warm.

His jaw was taut, eyes giving nothing away. "It makes up in length for what it lacks in quantity. I'm a firm believer in quality over quantity."

He was smiling down at her in a kind way, as if amused at her for actually asking for more hugs.

Cheeks burning, she busied herself smoothing down her shirtwaist. "That's fair enough by me," she said, and turned away.

And she knew then what he'd bought. He'd bought her out

of the humiliation. He'd bought her freedom from this silly game. Rescued her after all.

"I'd better go," she murmured to no one in particular.

He was right beside her. "I'll walk you."

"No. You already said you received your money's worth."

"Miss Beasley, in New York, no proper young lady goes home without an escort."

Orvil overheard. "Yeah, Jennie. Maybe he'll hug you in private."

Everyone guffawed. There was no arguing, or the crowd would only carry on more. Let him walk her. She only wanted away from all the curious leers as fast as possible.

As they left, strangely, she couldn't shake a vague disappointment. For ever since he'd tumbled her to the ground at the fire, she'd been curious as to what a real embrace from the man might be like. And that thought shocked her. Had she really been wanting a man like Nate Denison to embrace her? What a wild wanton idea. A stray cat jumped across her path and with a meow darted into the sagebrush. Involuntarily she moved closer and their bodies brushed against each other.

It was a short walk from the backdoor of the mercantile to the little Gordon log house down on Camas Street, and in a matter of three minutes they had spanned the distance.

"Good night," she said, "and thank you."

"My pleasure." Neither of them moved an inch.

They came together as if both thought of it at the same moment. Like a magnet meeting a piece of lead. His hands were gliding up her back, and then after lingering on her hair, they slid back down to her lower back and spanned her waist. She breathed in the scent of bay rum and smoke and . . . just plain man.

With one hand to her chin, he tipped her chin up. "Lady, for a kiss—"

"No!"

"—I'll donate the entire thousand dollars it'll take to build that school."

She came to her senses. "Have you ever gotten anything without buying it?"

He had the grace to look abashed, only for a second, then a cynical smile split his handsome face. "I don't keep track, but I'll make you a bet—"

"I don't bet."

As she turned to go in he yanked her back and held her fast by her elbows. "Sweet little schoolmarm, I'll have you where I want you before that new schoolhouse of yours is built. Asking me for kisses."

The sound of her hand slapping his face rent the still night air.

"I wish you'd go back east where you belong."

"What, and leave you alone to let fourteen kids tear up my house? I may be rich, Miss Beasley, but I'm not a fool. You're the one who asked for the temporary schoolroom."

"Well, maybe I'll just take the school out of there."

"Where to? The saloon?"

And then she slammed the door in his face.

Women. East or west. They were all as predictable as snow in January.

Chuckling softly, he walked off through the darkness, his boots clicking on the boardwalk of Camas Street. Somewhere behind him he could hear Ingrid Jensen singing, slightly off-key, but melodious, and people were laughing, hugging, dancing, finishing off the evening. His mood grew serious as a memory tugged at him.

Miss Jennie Beasley. He could still see her trapped expression when he'd looked at her in the mercantile. Just for a second, before he'd reverted to his obnoxious behavior, she'd looked to him for rescue. Trusted him. And he'd rescued her.

No woman had ever been safe around him before, and now

for the first time, just for a few seconds, he'd played the gallant. Fifth Avenue would never believe it. He touched his face right where Jennie Beasley had slapped him. It didn't sting anymore. All he felt was some vague regret.

"He ain't like the rest of us any more than that Theodore Roosevelt is. They play at being rough and tumble, but it's all a game. Mr. Denison is not a man to copy 'cause none of you'll ever have the money he does, and in any case money like that corrupts a man. Look at his highfalutin behavior last night."

"No, Thaddeus, that's not a subject to have the children look at." This from Mariah's mother, who had ventured to a rocking chair to share dinner with her children.

Pa looked temporarily abashed, then scowled at his wife. "I know what I'm doing. You be still now. They're growing up, watching you with child, wife, and it's time they understood a few facts of life."

Ma sighed, like always, and Mariah settled back on the bench.

Mariah's pa was once again using dinner to lecture them all, and once again the subject was the rich Mr. Denison, who for some reason irked her pa no end. It was the night after the box social and hugging bee. Mariah sat quietly, petting Paddy's tummy with her stocking foot. Gently of course. Feeling for the thump of baby puppies. Still hoping. Paddy had to have puppies. She just had to. Mariah had waited so long.

Wait was all she seemed to do. Even for dinner. The entire family sat on either side of the table waiting while Pa dished up first his potatoes, then his gravy, then his beans, the stewed venison, and last his favorite pickled beets.

Only then did the dishes get passed on down to the children.

"Mr. Denison's expecting some buffalo for his rangelands. He's going to raise them." Mariah said this innocently enough, thinking to change the subject.

"Mr. Denison's a fool," Pa thundered, fist banging the table. "And trying to haul buffalo God knows how many miles, then pen them inside a fence and raise them proves it. Ain't natural. Buffalo are wild and were put on earth to feed Indians and white men. Nothing else."

"I believe," Jennie offered softly, "that he considers the buffalo an investment . . . since they're rare." Immediately she ducked her head. She could feel an unwanted blush steal up her cheeks—an embarrassing schoolgirl blush—all because of the hug Nate Denison had given her last night.

"Buying buffalo ranks with buying hugs from the teacher."

To her mortification, everyone turned to stare. Thaddeus, thank goodness, thundered on, and their attention swiveled back to their pa.

"Buffalo have got minds of their own. You can't just throw a lasso around their necks and expect a herd of them to meekly follow along like a cow. He'll lose them all. Trust a dude to come up with a ridiculous idea like making money off buffalo."

He paused to pile more food on his plate. "And on top of all else, we've lowered ourselves to using the dude's dining room for school." And on that note, Thaddeus Gordon began shoveling potatoes into his mouth.

"Thaddeus," his wife admonished with an apologetic squeeze of Jennie's hand, "I'll thank you to remember that my sister is doing this town a favor, continuing to teach in makeshift conditions, and the least you can do is worry about the new school getting built instead of ranting on about things we can't change. Preacher's son burned the school down. Direct some anger to *him*."

"Hmmph. Preacher says his son joined a Wild West show. The whole world is going crazy." Thaddeus Gordon shoved venison into his mouth and chewed. "Pass them pickled beets," he said in between mouthfuls.

Mariah had been studying her pa and then Paddy's belly.

Finally, when Pa shoved in a large forkful of venison and was too occupied chewing to vent his anger on her, she ventured a question. "Pa, what if Paddy has pups?"

Reaching for the gravy, Thaddeus Gordon barely looked at her. Her brothers all looked at their sister as if Mariah were the dumbest girl in the world.

" 'Course we'd sell them, runt." Thaddeus Jr. delighted in mimicking his father.

Mariah poked her brother's ribs. "Don't call me runt."

"Why not? You're the puniest runt in school."

"I'm not." Quick tears stung her eyes, and she dashed them away. Tears egged her brothers on all the more.

"Boys, go do your chores." With that one command from their father, the Gordon boys' faces lost their mischievous looks. One by one Mariah's brothers filed out to the woodpile or the chicken coop or to the mercantile. Then Pa turned to Mariah. "If pups show up, we're selling them."

"We'll keep one for a pet, won't we?" she asked hopefully. "Paddy's getting older."

"Animals aren't for play. They're either food for a family or else they help do the work."

"Then what's different about our pups and Mr. Denison's buffalo?"

Pa shoved back his chair. "The difference, runt, is that puppies would bring money to this family. Mr. Denison's buffalo are a pie-in-the-sky idea. A lot of hot air on his part, and I'll believe he's more than a schemer when I see a few buffalo roaming about his range. Now get all these ideas about having pet puppies out of your head. I've indulged you enough letting you keep a squirrel in a cage."

"That's been instructional to the children at school," Jennie put in.

His gaze swung to Jennie. "Keep your wits about you and your feet on the ground while you're at his place. And count us lucky we've got enough money raised and volunteers to get a new school built. I wouldn't want you to spend too much time in close proximity to such a man."

"He likes animals," Mariah said defensively. Whatever the grown-ups were talking about eluded her. For some reason, Aunt Jennie blushed deeply.

"Start the dishes, runt."

Stung, Mariah stood. She hated the name runt, she hated having straight dark hair while her brothers ran about with toffee-colored curls . . . it wasn't fair. It just wasn't, and someday she'd get Pa to tell her why he wouldn't call her by her proper name. Even the animals had better names than she did. And recalling that she'd promised Mr. Denison a list of names for his buffalo, she calmed down. She had important things to do, and as she gathered the serving dishes from the table and took them to Jennie, she silently reviewed all the names of presidents that he could use for his buffalo. Jefferson. Cleveland. Harrison. Garfield—no, he was assassinated same as Lincoln, Aunt Jennie said. Not lucky names for buffalo. She'd have to look in some books at school for other presidents, but certainly no animal in Mariah's acquaintance was going to be plagued with a name like runt.

CHAPTER
6

The crash echoed up through Nate's bedroom floor, right through the Aubusson carpet . . . and the pillow that was wrapped over his ears.

Nate removed the pillow, spit out a feather, and opened one eye, not very wide, just enough to determine that it was daylight.

With a moan, he rolled over. How long had he lingered at the ball last night? And how much champagne had he drunk before dancing with the bride?

Another crash jarred his head . . . and then reality intruded.

This wasn't New York, and his hangover was caused not by champagne but by cheap whiskey. The ball had been in his dreams. All of it had been in his dreams . . . except for Daisy's wedding, which had really happened. He could still see her—

the beautiful brunette for whom he'd built this house—walking down the aisle to wed another man. The wedding between Miss Daisy Van Altman and the Duke of Windermere had been the event of the 1890 New York season. It all came back in a lonely rush. Daisy's stinging rejection.

Followed by a door in his face.

A door in his face?

No, that hadn't been Daisy. That was the icy rejection by Miss Jennie Beasley after the box supper and hugging bee. Smiling, he opened both eyes wide. How the snooty matrons would have dropped their fans to see him bidding on box suppers at a humble mercantile. Come to think of it, it hadn't been all that bad—much more enjoyable than one of the Van Altman balls. Jennie Beasley, all soft in his arms . . . Jennie Beasley, slapping him with passion that amused him . . .

Groaning, he rolled over and dangled one foot out to test the floor. Cold. He'd never liked to get up to both a cold floor and a hangover. He'd give Miss Beasley five minutes more to rap a few knuckles. Then he'd get her alone at recess time and suggest that this whole school business started too early. This was the second time in a week they'd awakened him. She'd have to change the hours so he could sleep.

The next crash shook the bedstead right through the ceiling. Childish shrieks followed. Where was Miss Beasley?

What if she'd made good on her threat never to come back to his mansion to teach school? But she'd held school yesterday, hadn't she? Put duty over anger?

Yes, she was too dedicated.

She was also too prim and self-righteous to allow him to take liberties. No, she'd put duty over her anger again today. After all, she was a predictable woman.

This time a minor earthquake shook the floor from below. These kids, on the other hand, were disturbingly *unpredictable*.

His feet hit the rug, still cold.

And then it hit him.

If the floor was this cold, that meant the furnace was not on, which in turn led to several conclusions.

The furnace, which Helga usually started in the mornings, was not lit. Either Helga had quit, leaving Jennie Beasley to start the furnace—in which case his mansion was in imminent fire danger—or else Jennie, idealistic Jennie, had made good on her threat to quit using his dining room as a school, leaving Helga to teach . . . or hell . . . he was going to have to get up.

After groping about for pants and a shirt, he managed to stumble downstairs.

"Miss Beasley!" Wavering, head throbbing, he moved closer to the open door of the dining room.

Girls squealed as a pair of boys skidded along the hardwood floor between his rug and the imported wallpaper. His letter opener flew through the air and landed on the sideboard, chipping the nose off the carved angel. Folded telegrams floated down from the ceiling like so many paper kites, and someone stuffed a slingshot in a back pocket.

"Goddammit! You worthless buggers all sit down!" Nate didn't know he could shout that loud, but it worked. No more than ten seconds later the students were all lined up on the chairs, prim and proper, while he stalked up the side of the room, yearning for a cup of coffee.

"Where's Miss Beasley?" he growled.

"She's not here." Will Armstrong provided this illuminating information.

Not here. Bloody hell. Was he going to have to play substitute teacher? Was that his punishment for trying to steal a kiss?

"Helga!" he yelled.

No answer.

He eyed the energetic students, who eyed him back, warily.

"You look like a pirate," Ole Slocum observed, staring at Nate's bare feet, bloodshot eyes, and tousled hair.

Nobody sassed Nate before he'd had his coffee. "No talking. If I hear one more word, you'll be out shoveling buffalo chips."

"You ain't got any buffalo."

"I will. Meanwhile I've got cows and wandering buffalo from the park." He grabbed the scruff of Will Armstrong's neck. "Get out and shovel."

"My pa says I don't have to do no chores for any rich dude."

"Your pa's not volunteering his house for a school, is he?"

Will shook his head.

"Out and find your own way to my barn." Nobody sassed Nate before he'd had his coffee. Nobody.

Helga appeared out of nowhere.

"Where've you been?"

"Trying to start the furnace."

"Where's the schoolmarm?"

"I'd ask the Gordon children. She boards with them."

He looked at the sea of faces—little, big, scared, belligerent. Hooligans all of them.

"How should I know which are which?"

"Have you tried asking their names?" Helga suggested.

He steeled himself, trying for patience.

"If you'll please see to my morning coffee, then as far as I'm concerned, they can all call themselves George Washington."

If he'd been smart, he'd have pushed the prim Miss Beasley out the front door when she came asking for favors.

"Why is the teacher late?" he growled.

"Ma had pains, and Aunt Jennie had to stay with her."

Aunt Jennie. A clue. "You must be one of the Gordon boys."

The boy grinned, but it wasn't a look to be trusted.

A dozen or so pair of eyes stared back at him. He scanned the room, looking for someone familiar, slid by a solemn-faced little girl of about ten with long dark braids, then slid back to her again. It was the little girl whose box supper had rescued him from the Widow Jensen.

Mariah sat squeezed between two golden-haired boys. Since they each resembled the boy who'd called the teacher Aunt Jennie, he assumed he was closing in on all the Gordons. That would be enough names for starters.

"Don't you have schoolwork to do, Mariah?" he asked cautiously.

Mariah shook her head. "The oldest girl is supposed to take over when the teacher's delayed or called away."

"Where is she?"

"Absent."

Bloody hell.

"Then you're all dismissed."

Before anyone could make a move, Will Armstrong stood up. "You can't go anywhere," he said with a smirk. "Us ranch kids can't get home without the school wagon, and it won't come till four o'clock. If we have to stay, then everyone does. That's the rule. Miss Beasley said so."

And Nate just bet a silver dollar that Will Armstrong didn't obey a thing when Miss Jennie Beasley was here. But if Will Armstrong wanted to battle it out over buffalo chips and schoolwork, Nate would take him on.

But what the devil was he supposed to do with fourteen— no, thirteen kids in his dining room for the next six hours or so? It was probably too early for recess. He eyed them through narrowed lids and sipped gratefully at the coffee Helga finally brought.

"What do you usually do first?"

"Reading."

"Shush your mouth, runt," said one of the golden-haired brothers.

Nate panicked. "What about arithmetic?" He was an expert in stock-market numbers.

"We never have arithmetic until just before lunch."

"Why not?"

"That's the way it is."

"Did anyone visit the Chicago fair this summer?" he asked conversationally, grasping at straws. They could, he supposed, discuss current affairs.

But the only reaction was widened eyes or furrowed brows. Not a hand went up. "Where's Chicago?" little Minnie asked, followed quickly by, "Does the chain pulley in your indoor privy really empty the bathtub?"

No, come to think of it, these humble families probably hadn't traveled east of their little town. He settled down in the chair at the head of the table and, for want of anything better to do, began to tell them how he'd built this house and why he'd bought some buffalo. Dude talk. It was, unfortunately, about all he knew, and a stopgap measure at best.

At ten o'clock, out of desperation for something to keep the class busy until it was late enough for arithmetic, Nate set to the one other task he knew besides talking: writing letters to Congress.

He dictated the first sentence, tongue in cheek.

"Dear Congress: Please give Orvil Rowe some teeth."

"What for?" Thaddeus Jr. asked.

"So he can eat."

"Eat what?"

"So he can eat greedy poachers. Now write, all of you."

Exactly three minutes later two students set down their pencils and looked up at him, smug smiles on their faces.

"I'm done," Susanna Vane said, echoed by Joshua Zane. Or was it Susanna Zane and Joshua Vane?

"Elaborate."

"What's elaborate mean?" little Minnie asked, squirming. "Will," she asked her big brother who'd returned too quickly from shoveling. "Help me, I forgot how to make a big 'D.' "

"Elaborate means to make up some more words." He pulled little Minnie's paper over and scratched out a big "D" with the pencil, then shoved the paper back.

"What letter is next in 'dear'? 'D'—"

" 'E.' " Damn. Damn. Damn.

At last, for a blessed few minutes, they bent with their heads over the papers and pencils scratching. Nate, more exhausted than when he'd awakened, presided at the teacher's chair, head practically on his arms, another mug of coffee in front of him.

Gunnar Slocum raised his hand and Nate eyed him suspiciously.

"You got a question or a complaint?"

The hand slid back down.

At 10:15 the front door blew open. Nate looked up and there at last came Miss Jennie Beasley, complete with that funny-looking knit hat.

Her cheeks, pink from the nippy morning air, made her look uncommonly pretty. Wisps of hair fell about her face and down her neck. Nate, who still hadn't buttoned his shirt or put on shoes, rose, pulled up his suspenders, and strode through the dining room to greet her.

"I don't feel good," Gunnar whined, dropping his pencil in frustration. "My head hurts."

"Hell, so does mine." Nate kept his eyes on the teacher.

"Mr. Denison," Jennie gasped, clearly out of breath from running. "I do not appreciate you swearing at the children."

Stopping a scant two inches from her nose, he stared.

"And I don't appreciate your students scuffing up my floors and using my letter opener to play darts with the sideboard. You're late for school, Miss Beasley."

In truth, he'd never been more glad to see her in his life, from her copper-penny hair to her scuffed little boots, and he had to exercise supreme self-restraint not to pull her into his arms and hug her for joy.

"Where have you been?"

Jennie gulped and stared at his bare feet, then let her glance slide all the way up. She'd expected the class to be running wild or at best for Helga to have them in the kitchen feeding them cookies.

He stood practically on top of her, so close she could count the whiskers on his unshaven chin. His beard, if it grew in, would be dark, darker than his ruffled brown hair, much, much darker than his stormy blue eyes.

"I'm . . . sorry I'm late." She was breathless from running here. Grace had needed her; she really had, and there'd been no choice about coming late.

"Let them out for recess." His words were terse.

"I just arrived."

"But I've been here for over an hour, and I want very much to talk to you. Alone." His voice vibrated huskily. "If you don't recess this class, then I will."

Stepping around him, she unbuttoned her coat, moved to the head of the table, and pulled off the funny knit hat and pushed odd strands of hair back into place.

When she looked up, he was staring at her in a way that made her bones go limp, the way she'd felt when he'd walked her home. It was time to restore order.

"This might be your house, but it's my class, and it's not time for recess. If you'd like to talk, it'll have to be after school hours."

Quickly she collected the students' papers and, without looking at any of them, thrust the pile at him.

She was unfastening her cape and sliding it off. He lingered, staring.

"What do you want?"

Nate merely smiled and raised his eyebrows with great mystery and his laughter rumbled low.

What did he want? Hadn't he made that clear?

All he wanted was what he wanted with every other woman he laid eyes on favorably and that was to get her alone, to see how quickly she'd squirm beneath his kisses. Given the innocence of this schoolmarm, she was almost too easy. But if there was one thing he'd learned in his wanderings through the salons of the wealthy, it was this: Women were predictable. They might act like they hated you, but at the first touch of his lips on theirs, they all responded in either of two ways. They'd either melt against him or resist. The only fun was wondering which of the two reactions he'd receive from Miss Beasley.

Without another word he left the dining room, then he stopped.

He could hear her humming a melody Daisy had used to play on the piano. A Mozart melody. Daisy, in summertime, before she'd met and become enamored of her English duke, had been fond of picking the flowers after which she was named and plucking the petals in front of him.

He loves me. He loves me not.

It was an old ploy to keep a man off his guard, but always Daisy would manage to pluck the last petal in time to, "He loves me," and then melt against him.

He wanted to know what it would feel like when prim Jennie melted against him. When all that starch melted into the passion he'd seen at the fire. There wasn't any question he could call up that passion . . . eventually.

All afternoon he bided his time.

At four o'clock he watched the students troop out to the school wagon, waited till old man Armstrong flicked the reins and nudged the swaybacked horses into motion, then he went to find Jennie.

At last.

This was the chance he'd been waiting for.

"Good afternoon, Miss Beasley," he said briskly, walking into his dining room. Like a driven man, he stalked her at once, needing to hold her, needing her to help him forget Daisy.

But he'd no sooner backed her up against the lace draperies than she scooted under his arms and escaped, the scent of her perfume left taunting him. The faintest aroma of lily of the valley came from her hair when she moved. He wanted to pull the pins out.

He whirled, ready to give chase, but just as quickly pulled up short, taken aback at the sight of a boy in the doorway. He hadn't expected her to have a chaperon. "Who's this?" He frowned in consternation.

"This," Jennie Beasley announced, "is Gunnar Slocum." She stood stiff as a board, prim as starched sheets in her dark skirt and white shirtwaist. "He's staying after school for extra help with penmanship."

A man couldn't steal a kiss with a child looking on.

She smiled prettily. "Now, what did you have to discuss with me?" Her eyes were wide, soft brown, and oh so innocent.

He stared at her till she blinked and turned away.

She couldn't fool him. "You held that troublemaking child after school on purpose." He advanced on her.

Shaking her head, she backed away around the table.

"Mr. Denison, are you chasing me?"

"What makes you think that?" Even as he spoke they kept moving until finally she backed into the sideboard.

He swallowed.

"What did you want?" she asked softly.

His glance swung to Gunnar Slocum and back. The boy was staring at him and the teacher. Nate turned back. "I thought since you and I share the same house . . . by day . . . that we could talk."

"Yes? About what?"

Darn that kid. With him here eavesdropping, Nate had to make the conversation innocuous.

"How fast are they going to have the new school built?"

On a still morning you could hear the sound of nails pounding as Karl the carpenter boarded in the framework.

"It's going well. I'll ask Karl."

Something about that notion disturbed him as much as the soft brown of her eyes. Again she was a robin ready to fly.

"If it's not ready, you needn't worry that we'll stay here too long. School is always dismissed in winter. We'll be gone by then."

Their eyes locked and held.

He looked over his shoulder to see what the bothersome child was writing.

Thank you, Mr. Denison . . . Thank you, Mr. Denison . . . Thank you, Mr. Denison.

He looked up to find her watching him, eyes warm with amusement. "That will do, Gunnar." And as the obviously grateful child laid down his pencil, she took the paper and handed it to Nate.

"Thank you, Mr. Denison, for arranging to meet me after school on the very day Gunnar was detained. You'll give him a ride, won't you?"

"Can't he walk?" Like a chess game, they were moving slowly and deliberately.

"He lives at the farthest end of town. I'm sure his mother is worrying." Checkmate.

He nodded. "I'll take him on horseback."

"And I'll walk." Before he could make his move, she'd grabbed her coat and hat and was gone.

Later, when the house was empty of both students and Miss Jennie Beasley, he sat alone, his only company the day's mail.

A letter had arrived from South Dakota from his foreman.

Regret the delay. Two of the buffalo acted up, just
put their heads down and refused to move. We had to
lariat both their horns, then they both broke loose and
jumped the fence. They're unpredictable critters and
hate to be confined. A man'd have more luck trying
to corral a school full of contrary kids, and that's the
God's honest truth. Bringing in more experienced help
to try and round them up. Yours sincerely, Jake.

A week ago Nate would have rushed back a letter firing the
man for incompetence. Now, to his own surprise, he crum-
pled the letter in frustration. They could have a contest to
decide which were more contrary—kids or buffalo. It was
probably a tie.

But it was neither kids nor buffalo that occupied his mind
right now. It was his frustration over the contrary schoolteacher.

Homespun Jennie Beasley wasn't any different at heart from
Daisy. Daisy's price had been a title; Jennie Beasley had her
price too. She simply didn't know it yet.

Nor did he know why she kept managing to keep the upper
hand.

She'd managed to dowse him with a bucket of water.

And she'd had the nerve to invite her school into his house.

And she'd slapped him after he'd graciously rescued her
from an embarrassing game.

And she'd blithely come late to school and thanked him for
playing substitute teacher.

But he'd get her. He'd been humiliated by Daisy, but he'd
be darned if he was going to be outsmarted now by fourteen
kids, twelve buffalo, and a prim unsophisticated schoolmarm
with wild coppery hair, freckles, a funny hat . . . yes, he smiled,
it was a funny hat, but somehow charming. And the scent of
lily of the valley lingered on the papers she'd handed him. He
began to thumb through what the students had written. Not bad.

Relax, Nate, he told himself, all women are the same. Totally predictable. All he had to do was figure out a way to separate Miss Jennie Beasley from those kids, and he'd win their little power struggle as well as a kiss.

CHAPTER

❧ 7 ❧

Mariah, beside herself with happiness, patted Paddy's head and gave a longing look at the dog's belly. The sheepdog was stretched out as near the mercantile fire as possible, eyes shut, stomach bulging. It was just as Mariah had hoped. In the past day Pa had confirmed it. Paddy's milk had dropped, which meant Paddy wasn't just getting fat. Puppies were on the way! For *sure*.

Mariah pressed her hand against Paddy's tummy. It ought to be possible, so her brothers said, to feel the puppies kicking. But she was frustrated by all the stomping about in the mercantile. Boots clumping. Doors banging. And deep male voices.

All the men did was talk and talk about poachers in Yellowstone and why they shouldn't be put in jail. It was the same old arguing and grousing. If caught, they were stripped of their gear and walked out of the park. High-handed cavalry! Sometimes an old trapper wandered into Castlerock, wanting to borrow a horse so he could ride back down into Yellowstone and find his outfit before another trapper stole it. And Pa, whose father before him had been a trapper and miner, sputtered on about the waste of effort it was having a cavalry coddle animals and take liberties with expensive gear. Mariah could hear it in her sleep.

"Animals weren't put on earth to coddle," Pa said. "They were put on earth to do their part. Same as children." He looked at his daughter. "Have you done your chores, runt? Helped your aunt Jennie?"

"Aunt Jennie's helping Ma wash her hair, and they don't need me." Gently she stroked Paddy's stomach.

"Well, then get some kindling for the stove here. Watching that dog won't make the pups come sooner."

"Hey, Thaddeus, think I can poach a pup from you?" Mr. Zane asked, tongue in cheek.

"Poach my pups?" Thaddeus Gordon glared at his taxidermist friend. "Pups go for real money, especially to you. You can have pick of the litter, though."

Mariah, ears pricking up at that statement, scooted up to her knees. "Pa, couldn't *I* have pick of the litter?"

"Get the kindling, runt, and never count your chickens— or mongrel pups—before they're hatched." The men laughed, and Mariah, staring back instead of forward, tripped over a flour sack.

Reluctantly she stood. Carrying kindling was usually the boys' job, but because of the men talk around the stove, the boys got to listen in.

But she could be as patient as the next person. Just so Pa gave her one puppy. All hers. A real pet. Not a white mouse or a squirrel or a toad. It would be the kind of pet all the little girls she'd known back in St. Louis—their former home—had owned. A real fluffy dog of her own to follow her about and for her to give a fancy dog name to.

"Mariah," Pa snapped now, leaning forward in his chair and frowning at her. "Now, before the fire dies."

With a last lingering look at Paddy, she headed outside to the woodshed, kicking at a rock in her way. It didn't matter if she brought back the biggest armful of kindling in the world. Pa would never treat her the same as the others, as the boys. Never. She had no idea why, except that they were boys with golden curls and she was a girl with straight dark braids. Whatever the reason, she just knew she wasn't the favored child, knew it like a body knew that summer was over when they felt an autumn snap in the air.

Snap! Somewhere, sagebrush had just been trampled on.

Standing in the door of the woodshed, she stopped dead in her tracks. Just at the edge of their lot, where some pines and scrub brush marked the property line, stood a pair of animals—a female buffalo with a russet-colored calf dogging her heels. Why, with just a pair of knobs where horns would grow and just the hint of a hump on his back, the calf wasn't even half-grown.

There were just a handful of buffalo left in Yellowstone; Pa said if they ended up extinct, it'd be God's will. But Mariah's heart pounded, half in fear and half at the secret thrill of seeing them up close. At this time of year, the animals would be migrating down to lower ground for winter feeding. These two had moved a lot farther from the other buffalo than normal. She stood still, scarcely daring to breathe.

Anyone who lived a week in Castlerock was used to the occasional wild animal straying out of Yellowstone Park. From the day they'd moved here from the big city, Mariah herself had been instructed not to go near wild animals. When she persisted in chasing the smaller creatures like pikas and marmots, the order was amended: on no condition was she to go near any

animal larger than herself. If she glimpsed a bear or moose or
buffalo, she was to run home. The warning was by now as
familiar as the one against venturing too close to the geysers. If
she disobeyed, Pa would dunk her squirrel cage into a bubbling
hot pool. And if he didn't punish her, the cavalry was there to
remind her.

Now, staring that calf in the eye, Mariah did not forget what
she'd been taught. It was one thing to rescue a squirrel from a
burning school. But this was a stray buffalo and calf! Of course
they didn't know they were strays, but in the minds of those
men in the mercantile, they would be. And who knew if one
of them might not be a poacher on the sly.

Buffalo, with those big humps and horns and shaggy bulk,
weren't the sort of creatures you wanted to throw rocks at to
scare off; neither did they deserve to get shot. "Dumb lummox,"
she whispered. "Get going." In their own good time, they'd
wander back to join the small herd—wherever it was.

All Mariah could think of was to grab some kindling, run
back inside, and keep the men inside talking until the buffalo
had time to wander away out of sight. Deliberately, she dropped
the wood, and Pa bawled her out with a "Gawd Almighty . . .
can't you forget them pups and do something right?"

The townsmen good-naturedly told Pa to lay off and helped
her pick the wood up. She dropped her stack again—on purpose. And again.

And when the kindling was finally stacked and Mr. Zane
made a move to leave, she tugged his sleeve. "Joshua says at
school you can't beat him at dominoes. Is that so?"

And when he laughed, she dragged the dominoes over to
the stove. "Who wants to play? A tournament for pennies?"
Games bored her; she'd much rather be with her animals, but
this was different.

Everyone reached into their pockets and threw pennies in
a tin mug where Pa usually kept jawbreakers. For the next

hour they took turns beating each other at dominoes, while outside, Mariah prayed, the buffalo would move back closer to the pathetic little herd. The last of the buffalo.

While Mr. Slocum and Mr. Zane were sweating over the last three domino pieces in the fourth game, Mariah snuck out back and peeked out the door.

The buffalo and her calf were gone.

All clear.

"Zane wins," Pa shouted at Mariah. "Now sweep this mess of dominoes off my floor so I can do some business."

This time when Pa gave his order, Mariah obeyed with a smile, and when Jennie came in to snitch an egg, she was still smiling.

Jennie stood at the dining-room table, watching the class practice penmanship. If wishes were smiles, she'd take two— one for herself and one for Mariah. That smile a few days ago in the mercantile was a rare one for solemn little Mariah. And as for Jennie, the days dragged without reason. For several days after Jennie's late arrival at school, she'd scarcely seen Nate Denison. School, except for its elaborate setting, was just business as usual.

An hour later, with absolutely no warning at all, Nate Denison burst into the dining room during penmanship.

The oak door slid open so suddenly that papers blew to the floor, and the heavy draperies swayed. Nate had ordered Helga to tack sheets over his fancy green wallpaper as a protection from fingerprints, so she wouldn't be surprised if next he had the drapes taken down for safekeeping. Fussy man, worrying so over material possessions when the education of poor children was at stake.

"Miss Beasley!"

At Nate's arrival the students pivoted on their chairs and gawked.

Unexpectedly her heart leaped, and she smiled—for the first time in days. It was a smile rooted deep inside her.

But it wasn't returned. Nate glowered.

Her own smile faded, as if a cloud had passed over. "Is something wrong?"

By way of answer, he strode over to the three biggest boys—the rich Zane boy and two of the Armstrong ranch kids.

"Which one of you did it?"

"Did what?" Jennie laid down her book.

Nate ignored her and spoke to the big boys. "Which one snuck into my kitchen when my housekeeper wasn't looking and put a toad into the coffee tin?"

"A real toad locked up in a tin?" Mariah's eyes grew wide with concern.

"Real. It nearly scared Helga to death. I still don't have my morning coffee."

As teacher, Jennie should appear more concerned about mischief. Instead her concentration was taken by the way Nate Denison's shirt was unbuttoned, by the way he advanced on her with predatory grace, closer and closer.

It was hard to think straight, or even breathe. Such wanton reactions from her body were unbecoming to her station. She straightened her shoulders and cleared her throat, prepared to do verbal battle with him once again.

"Where's the toad?" Jennie asked innocently.

"Where?" He laughed mirthlessly, and it was a good sound. He ought, she mused, to laugh more often.

"How should I know?" he snapped. "For all I know it's jumped into the flour sack or sugar bin, and Helga's threatening to quit again. Someone in this room planned it, and I want to know who."

Jennie had never seen so much passion . . . well, anger, in a man. While the students squirmed and hid their faces in their books, she stood rooted to the spot, staring with brazen longing at the master of Denison's Folly. His hair was all disheveled, and his eyes, which normally gazed at her with a half smile in them, snapped still in anger.

"Answer me, anybody." He scanned the table full of students.

Jennie couldn't help thinking like Mariah. "I wonder where in the world someone would find a toad? We could have used it for a science lesson."

"Miss Beasley!" Nate Denison's fist came down on his precious antique table so hard it shook.

"Well, that's the sort of prank Vernon Higgenbottom would have pulled, but his father claims he's joined a Wild West show."

He glared, fury in his gaze. "I want the culprit."

She tried to stare him down, but those cool blue eyes were formidable. "Mr. Denison. You can't accuse without any proof, and you cannot burst into the classroom like this. All over a toad!"

He'd been heading for the wide-eyed Armstrong boys, but now he turned on her, blue eyes blazing. "Miss Beasley, this is my house. I'll come into this dining room whenever I feel like it and most certainly when I find my housekeeper sprawled up to her armpits in mud because she tripped in her haste to run from the kitchen. And now instead of cooking my dinner, she's at the scrub board washing out her stockings and—"

"Mr. Denison!"

The class snickered. Jennie advanced on him. "Your choice of words is not appropriate for these tender listening ears."

Boldly his gaze raked her up and down. "Then perhaps you'll step outside into the hallway with me."

Something in his tone didn't brook arguing, especially with fourteen wide-eyed children memorizing every word for the entertainment of their table dinner tonight.

"Very well." She turned to Susanna Vane, her oldest female

student, and instructed her to read aloud to the class.

Everyone listened to Susanna read. Not only did she have pleasing diction, but since she had acquired a corset over the summer, she was able to hold the older boys' attention.

On her way out Mariah stuck up her arm and waved. "Miss Beasley! May I leave the room?"

Jennie sighed and nodded. The indoor fixtures—a rarity in this little town—held an endless fascination for the children and probably aroused curiosity about engineering principles. Jennie couldn't see a reason to refuse reasonable requests to leave the room.

But Thaddeus Jr. jumped to his feet. "It's the toad she's after, Miss Beasley. Can I leave the room?"

"No."

"Can I leave the room?" Will Armstrong mimicked, and the class snickered.

"No more leaving the room until I resolve the mystery of the missing toad."

In the hallway Nate waited, arms folded, glaring.

She spoke first, voice low, outraged. "How dare you walk in like that and undermine my authority in front of the students?"

"What authority?" He unfolded his arms and grabbed her by the arms, and while she tried to pull away he kept up a barrage of angry words. "Are you defending them for scaring my housekeeper?"

She drew herself up, tilted her chin up in defiance. "I never intended to be a conventional boring teacher."

"Believe me, Jennie, you're not."

"Well, you may own this house, but I'm the one in charge. It's like the code of the range. You may own things, but the foreman is in charge. That's how our school operates while I'm borrowing your dining room. I'm the foreman, and we'll do things my way."

"Is that so?" His gaze moved down to linger on the in-and-out motion of her lace-trimmed bodice. The more he stared, the faster her heart beat.

A quick glance down confirmed her shirtwaist was all buttoned. She looked up and caught him smiling into her eyes.

"You make a lousy foreman."

"Thaddeus hired me." She withered under his blue eyes. "You can't understand what it's like to teach boys the same size as me. Boys who only come to school because they were wanting out of chores at home. Boys who only come out of curiosity at being in a rich man's house. For your information, some boys only come twenty days out of the year and then to ogle the girls they're sweet on."

Suddenly the gleam returned to his eyes, and she realized he was still ogling *her.* "Please don't laugh. I know you don't understand, but—"

"Oh, but I do, Miss Beasley. I stuck a few tacks on chairs in my school days—mostly out of boredom."

Flustered, she patted her hair into place, reassuring herself she looked prim and proper. She felt horribly wanton and warm. "I'm sorry about the toad. Will you forgive the class?"

Jennie was silent under his scrutiny, then turned vulnerable brown eyes up at him. Something turned over in him, especially when she got that helpless, trusting expression on her face.

"I have to succeed here, Mr. Denison. Already Thaddeus is blaming me for the school fire, and if things go wrong here, I'll have no job."

Tears glittered in her eyes. She wasn't going to tell him how she'd failed at the last school. She couldn't bear his ridicule. "The only reason I'm here is because Grace needed me at the same time the school needed a teacher. I know I can control those boys, Mr. Denison. I want to still have a position when the new school gets built. I want to save my teaching salary.

I want to help my sister if need be—"

"You want a lot for a teacher with a toad loose in my house."

"Are you quite done?"

Nate leaned back on the newel post and studied her briefly. Too little. Too prim. Too much the scared robin. Why, she couldn't organize a tea party to save her life.

Looking mortified, she blushed and then pinned him again with that look of helplessness he'd seen the night he'd upped the bidding and bought her out of the hugging bee. He had her, had her alone out here in the hallway, and he couldn't take advantage of those quivering lips, that fragile figure that begged to be embraced. Why did he feel this way? She was no different from all the women he'd known. They wanted no more than money, jewels, and gowns. This one: a new school.

She tugged at something in him, the way an animal caught in a trap did. He'd been raised to go ruthlessly for the kill. But this time he couldn't. Hell, the west was supposed to toughen a man, not weaken him.

"Have you ever considered going to a bigger town, where you could teach young ones and leave the big boys to someone tougher?"

"I am tough."

Out of the corner of her eye Jennie saw a pair of students sneak out of the dining room and head down the hallway after Mariah. And then another pair. Sweet mercy, she couldn't concentrate.

In a slow trickle the youngsters were sneaking out of the dining room. She positioned herself so she was facing the dining room, which forced Nate's back to it. Three more students snuck out and tiptoed down the hall. She gulped.

"Are you quite done?" she asked again.

He smiled and, despite his good intentions, reached out and

chucked her chin. Suddenly a screech rent the air, and Nate whipped around to the dining room.

"It's empty!"

"I'm afraid they followed Mariah."

At once he spun around. "You saw them go?"

"A couple, but—"

"Hell." Already he was stalking down the hall toward the kitchen, where to his consternation he found the entire class surrounding Mariah, who was doing the squealing as she leaped after the toad and finally captured it under a coffee mug. Clutching it to her chest, she backed away from the big boys, who crowded her. Someone knocked over a kitchen chair.

"It's mine now," she declared, "and I'm going to let it go."

Will Armstrong reached with one hand for the collar of her dress, with the other for one of her braids. "That toad belongs to my brother and me, and you can't have it, runt."

"Don't call me runt."

"Then don't steal toads what don't belong to you, runt. Runt. Runt."

Still berating her with the hated nickname, the Armstrong boy lunged for the mug containing his toad.

Nate Denison in turn lunged for the Armstrong boy and captured him by his overall straps. "Ah-ha," he said, "now that the villains have given themselves away, we can punish them after all."

Mariah, all wide-eyed, sat on the floor, her precious toad still clutched tight. "It's mine. It's mine!"

Helga returned to the doorway and peered in cautiously. "Is it gone?"

Nate turned to give a reassuring smile to his housekeeper. "Almost. Mariah, take it out and turn it loose in my barn."

Mariah was off and running while Helga, breathing a sigh of relief, pushed through the group of youngsters to retrieve the coffee tin. Gingerly she lifted the lid and peered in.

"Class, it's time to return to the dining room," Jennie said, with as much authority as she could muster.

"All but these two." Nate, standing head and shoulders above anyone in the class, held each of the Armstrong brothers by the scruff of the neck.

"What are you going to do?"

"That's between me and them." Turning to the older one, he ordered, "Head for the woodshed, now."

The woodshed! Leaving Jennie Beasley to her charges, he followed the renegades of Castlerock School outside, pausing in the doorway only long enough to shout one parting remark to Jennie. "Meet me in the library, Miss Beasley. We have more rules to discuss."

"I'd sooner meet a grizzly." Did he think her a fool? "You're a hypocritical rogue, acting all high and mighty about buffalo, but stalking defenseless teachers and children—"

"Tsk, tsk, Miss Beasley, the children's tender ears."

Giggling, the youngsters ran back to the dining room. Jennie followed and slid its fancy oak door shut with a slam.

Helga stood at the stove, warily eyeing the coffee tin, then looked from the hall to the backdoor. "Something's gonna give in this house, and it won't be the Tiffany lights. Not on my Viking ancestors' watery graves."

That night when the youngsters left, Jennie went with them in the wagon, all her papers stuffed into her satchel to grade at the Gordons. She had a fleeting glimpse of Nate Denison, brandy glass in hand, watching her from his window, and she felt quite pleased at herself for outwitting him.

But in the end he outwitted her, for the next day both Armstrong boys were absent.

When informed of this fact, she didn't care what Nate Denison might do to her. *Her* fears were irrelevant compared with the education of two youngsters.

The instant Helga appeared with the tray of morning cocoa,

Jennie excused herself. Helga and the cocoa would keep the class busy, and she flew across the hall and barged in on Nate the same way he'd barged in on her class the day before.

Without turning around or even looking up from his desk, he said calmly, "I'm glad you decided to come, Miss Beasley."

"The Armstrong boys are absent. Did you spank them with your hand or with a stick?"

Now he turned and stood up, grim-faced.

"Woodsheds have other purposes besides spanking renegades and stealing kisses. I set them to chopping wood. If they're not here today, they probably decided they can do chores at home as easily as here."

"But I had them almost up to the fifth reader!"

"They were disrupting the others, and my house."

"Did you lend us your house thinking children were going to behave like stuffed specimens in a museum?"

Nate laid his hand over hers, which was warm and soft. He could feel the pulse jump in her wrist. "I did it so I could steal a kiss." Blunt and to the point. "The youngsters are making it hard for me."

She stared at him, brown eyes startled. "Good."

"You know what you need?" He couldn't resist touching her any longer and put out a hand to her chin and gently tipped her face so she was looking up at him.

"What?" Her heart beat faster.

"Wallpaper paste—the kind that sticks to the seat of their pants."

Outrageous man.

She looked into his eyes and caught the gleam of amusement.

"I realize now my request to borrow your house was impulsive and overly hasty."

"Too late now, Jennie. You're stuck here until Karl builds you a new school."

He ran his fingers up her face, then leaned down and kissed her ever so gently. Just a whisper against her lips, just long enough for her to melt, to smell the bay-rum scent of him and melt against him. He deepened the kiss, backed her into the door, tangled his fingers in that coppery hair. The sound of children's voices brought him back to reality. That and her voice, soft against his neck. He couldn't move.

"Let me go."

His words whispered against her lips. "That was a lesson to you, Jennie. Control those kids or they'll all end up in the woodshed, and then I'll have you to myself."

Suddenly she broke away.

For a long minute he stood there, until at last he heard the click of the door and knew she was gone. Only when that door clicked did he inhale, trust himself to move.

Here he'd stolen a kiss, and she'd ended up taking his self-control. Once again the pert, prim miss had proved unpredictable. But he had more time. The new school wasn't ready yet.

Helga was suddenly at his elbow. "Jennie has a scent of bay rum to her."

Nate looked up, eyes all innocence.

"And you," Helga accused, "you smell like lily of the valley, Mr. Denison."

He hid his expression by shuffling through his mail. "You keep your nose on the coffeepot, Helga," he growled. She set down his coffee and more mail.

"Yes, sir," she muttered, "something's gonna give."

"Out!"

He turned his attention to his mail and another letter from Jake in South Dakota.

Nate, I'm gonna put it to you plain. I hope you've got that six-foot fence ready, and I recommend doubling

the fence posts. Not much keeps these buffalo critters
in when they want to make trouble. Trust me, these
critters are a handful. Worse than me with a greenhorn
schoolmarm. Yours, Jake.

A bigger, higher, stronger fence.

Nate hated fences, but for the buffalo he'd made one.

He wished he knew how to fence in Jennie Beasley—not
forever, just long enough to have his way with her.

Damnation, but she was proving difficult.

The day after the toad scare, Mariah walked out of the
mercantile to gather kindling and once again stopped dead in
her tracks.

The buffalo was back—this time only one. The calf. All
alone, big brown eyes staring at her from twenty yards away.

Backing up, she retraced her steps and ran for the mercantile,
where, because it was Saturday, plenty of men were gathered
around the stove.

This time her brothers took one look at her scared face and
said, "What's wrong? Something out there?"

"No, nothing." Who could help her? Hirum? Where was
he?

"You're fibbing, runt."

Thaddeus Jr., who'd been unloading tinned peaches, strode
out and from the back door let out a low whistle. "Well, lookee
here, Pa."

Ten minutes later the men who'd circled the stove chewing
the fat now circled the orphaned calf, guns aimed, a pair of
lassos swinging in the air, making ready to collar the baby.

Mariah, watching from the mercantile's back steps, was horrified. She heard Pa say, "Ain't no mother. She's dead."

"Pa, can I keep him?" Buffalo had to have lots of pasture,
but she couldn't resist asking.

"Mariah, go inside." The guns clicked as they were cocked in readiness.

"Think a calf will charge?" someone asked. Even before the question was out, the buffalo calf skittered away a few more yards. There was a lost look to him.

"If I could get him to my pasture, I could put him to a cow's teat," Mr. Armstrong said.

"Yeah, but what're you gonna do when it grows up? Eat it?"

"Pa, no."

Jennie rushed out. "Mariah, come inside."

"No . . . Pa, don't!"

CHAPTER

❧ 8 ❧

Nate Denison was riding into town on this sunny autumn day against his better judgment. Hirum and Orvil had just come off duty and had dragged him off to hear the latest news from Fort Yellowstone. He'd already heard more than enough. Most of it consisted of everyday gossip. The sort of thing the cavalrymen recorded in their journals. Poachers' tracks. Geysers they'd timed. Bubbling hot pools they'd dipped their feet into. Pine trees they'd found vandalized. The merits of Norwegian snowshoes. A wager on the first snowfall. And poachers. And more poachers.

Nate ought to have cared, but he was thinking instead of the herd of youngsters that wreaked havoc inside his house, and of the schoolmarm—her trusting eyes, her copper-penny hair that fell out of that funny knit hat like corkscrews. She had a passion like a geyser—it erupted unexpectedly.

He shouldn't have kissed her. The instant his lips touched hers, he'd felt off balance. Ever since, his blood had boiled as good as any hot pool's. Served him right flirting with prim schoolmarms. Now he'd have to avoid her till that new school got built.

Hirum and Orvil put an end to that plan. Instead of riding down to the saloon, they stopped at the mercantile. Jennie Beasley, who was unpacking a box of apples, polishing each one, looked up. So prim. So idealistic. Most women her age were saving up for wedding gowns. Either that, or squandering a man's money on beautifying themselves.

"Don't you ever get a day off, Miss Beasley?"

Jennie bristled. "I've fended for myself ever since Grace's and my folks died."

Nate had fended, too, but in ways she'd never understand, and he didn't want to pick a fight. Why did this town have to be so small? No matter where he went, there she was. He headed straight for the glass cabinet, the only place in the mercantile that sold anything that could be called a luxury. Idly he looked down at a lady's pocket watch with a rose engraved into the brass. And then he eyed both a silk-lined vanity case and a scent bottle. Lilies of the valley were in the air. Jennie had come to stand across from him.

"May I help you?" she asked at last.

He looked up.

The copper hair was primly bound up with pins, but he was getting used to that and liked looking at it, anticipating pulling out those pins and feeling the hair tumble into his hands. To steady his hands, he gripped the edge of the showcase.

Again she took him off guard. She wasn't powdered and primped like the women he was used to, yet it was her very plainness that aroused: the pure complexion, the dash of freckles, the trusting brown eyes, and that copper-penny hair that belied her prim demeanor.

He whisked off his new hat—his first Stetson. Despite it, he still felt like an outsider. "I thought I'd browse."

Ashamed of his roguish thoughts, he stared down at the vanity set. But he could see her reflected slightly in the glass.

For a change, she wasn't dressed in those prim white shirtwaists and dark skirts, her schoolmarm outfits. Today it was something with flounces on the skirt and in a soft color—like new leaves in spring—a pale green with little flowers on it. Calico, he guessed they called it. No woman back east would be caught dead in calico, but on Jennie it looked just right.

Then he pointed to the glass case. "I came to ask the price on some goods. Those there? How much?"

Jennie stared down at the beautiful cut-glass scent bottle and the vanity set—silver brush and comb, and a mirror with a cupid design on its back—all lined up on purple satin. She'd never had anything so beautiful and never imagined she would. And she didn't much care either. All she wondered was what lucky lady in Nate Denison's life would receive these gifts.

"Do you know what they cost?"

She looked down and then up at him quickly. "I—I don't know. Only Thaddeus opens this case, but the items have been here forever. Business on luxuries is a little slow in Castlerock, I guess. Most of the ladies come in for flour and molasses and the like."

His hands were close, resting on the edge of the cabinet. They weren't work-roughened, but they were strong. One finger had a tiny white scar.

"I imagine Thaddeus would take any price I offered?"

She looked up into his eyes. "I—I don't know."

From somewhere outside there was a lot of shouting, and their words were drowned out when little Mariah burst in the back door.

"Jennie . . ."

The child pulled up short. "Mr. Denison!" She headed for him, and seconds later was tugging at his hand. "You gotta come! You gotta! There's a buffalo outside."

"Heck," Orvil said lazily, "we just come in and we didn't see any buffalo stalking the street."

"It's not on the street," Mariah said quickly, in a defensive tone. "It's out back. It just now wandered behind the mercantile from the river, and it's not a big buffalo. It's a baby, and Pa's gonna shoot it!"

Hirum and Orvil shot up from their fireside chairs and headed out back to see.

Nate dragged his attention from Jennie and stared out the back door. Thaddeus Jr., who'd followed Mariah in, tweaked his little sister's ear.

"Ow!"

"You meddlesome little twerp. Didn't you see what the dude was thinkin' of buying? Now you've gone and lost Pa his best sale in two years, and we could have used the money for Christmas. I swear, Mariah, if someone has to do without hard candy come Christmas, it's gonna be you—"

"I don't care," she said, on the verge of tears.

"That's all right," Nate said. "She's right. It's a long time till Christmas. Come and show me this buffalo calf."

Thaddeus Jr. shrugged. "All right. But you better hurry. Five more minutes and it's liable to take off running."

Outside the townsmen swung lariats at the calf while Hirum and Orvil stood nearby arguing with Zane the taxidermist over whether to shoot.

"You cavalrymen want to handle this?" Nate asked.

The calf skittered a few more yards away.

Hirum shook his head, all the while watching the calf. "Can't do a blamed thing. Not outside the confines of park boundaries. Maybe if we'd seen the critter first . . . it's up for grabs now."

Nate marched toward the group, aware of their amused snickers. There was going to be a showdown between the mercantile owner and the dude from Denison's Folly. A fight to the finish over a scrawny bleating buffalo calf.

Nate didn't waste time or words. "Let me take him back to my pasture and raise him."

The other men, obviously impressed with the dude's solution, lowered their ropes and guns. But not Thaddeus Gordon.

"You accusing me of something?"

"Only asking for the orphan before it runs off."

"Why should I give him away?"

The calf wandered off about a hundred feet, down toward the river. Mariah ran down from the back porch. "He's shopping, Pa. Not looking for a handout. Why, just before you found that orphan, he was in the store looking to buy your most expensive gewgaws—the ones in the glass cabinet. The gilt-edged scent bottle, and the silver brush set. Both. And you know you'll never get another chance to sell those."

Thaddeus Gordon eyed Nate. Obviously the thrifty Scotsman didn't want to waste an opportunity, nor did he want to appear the fool.

"That so? You looking to buy some fancy items?"

Nate looked Thaddeus in the eye and then glanced off in the direction the calf had wandered. "Only if the buffalo is thrown in. And it's getting ready to run, so hurry up and decide. I can't buy what isn't here."

Thaddeus gave this about five seconds consideration.

Then he nodded. "Let's go in and wrap the merchandise."

"What about the calf?"

"Zane and Slocum," Thaddeus barked, as if he owned the

town, "you two've got buffalo-colored horses. Get 'em and use 'em to fake that little critter down to Mr. Denison's property, and I'll write off part of your accounts."

"Can I name him?" Mariah whispered.

"I'd be honored, Mariah."

"Brownie. His name is Brownie."

Nate went upstairs a few minutes later to finalize the exchange of money. Brownie was docilely following a horse down the street, urged along by a fake buffalo blat every so often from the town taxidermist.

Nate momentarily paused, his eyes immediately going to Miss Jennie Beasley, who stood quietly watching him.

Their eyes held a moment, and then she vanished into the dim corner of the store, and shortly Nate Denison possessed his first buffalo, as well as a silk vanity case and a scent bottle—impulsive purchases both.

Nate Denison never acted impulsively. Nate Denison was a man of utter control. He'd best be careful and spend less time following Miss Jennie Beasley about the dining room.

Nate, who rode back to town the next day simply because the house had become too quiet to bear, came up behind the children, sight unseen. They were clustered around Mariah behind the mercantile. Every one of her brothers and a few town children for good measure were discussing yesterday's episode with the buffalo calf.

James Gordon, who Nate figured was closest in age to Mariah, was holding forth about Nate. "He ain't gonna bring no buffalo here. He's lying. There aren't any left."

"There are too," Mariah said in a heated voice, always the animal defender. Even now, she clutched a baking powder box to her chest, a tiny box that Nate suspected contained some helpless creature. "He's bought some," she said.

"Yeah, where are they? I don't see a single buffalo in his

pasture—just fences with empty grassland."

"They're coming soon."

"Hah! They're gone. All gone, and he's a dumb dude who doesn't even know it."

"He's not! Shut up, James!"

"Aw, Mariah, you're the dumb one, playing with nothing but mice." He took a swipe at her box, as if to knock it away, but she whirled away just in time. "Pa ain't gonna give you a pup either," her brother jeered.

"When Paddy's pups come, I'll get one."

Her brothers all doubled over with laughter. "Pa's selling them. All you'll ever have to play with is mice like that dumb one you're holding, runt."

"Don't call me that." She turned in place, surrounded.

That only egged them on. "Runt . . . runt . . . runt!"

"I'm not a runt! I'm not!"

"Are so. Look in the mirror. All of us Gordons are tall and blond. You're the only plain Gordon. Maybe you're not even a real Gordon."

"That's not so."

"Oh, yeah?"

She slipped her hand into the baking-powder box, and with a squeal Susanna Vane slapped it away. "Don't bring that mouse out! Take it away!"

As the box hit the dirt Mariah lunged for it and pushed its lid back on.

"Mariah is a ru-unt. Mariah is a ru-unt." The singsong chant began as a tease, and Mariah, crying, stumbled to her feet and ran. They chased her until she ran smack into Nate.

In one fell swoop he reached for both Mariah and the baking-powder mouse bed. He looked around at her taunting followers, whose voices one by one died away.

"Why don't you kids run along?"

He barely got the one sentence out before Mariah's tormentors ran off, vanishing inside the buildings and around the corners of Castlerock.

Mariah looked adoringly up at Nate, who knelt to help her stuff the straw back into the box. The white mouse looked nervous, but unharmed.

"I know this doesn't make it hurt less, but it's nice to know I'm not the only one in town who's teased for collecting animals."

Smiling, Mariah sniffled back a tear and accepted her box.

"Sometimes they tell me I'm a stray that Pa and Ma took in."

"I doubt that."

"But Pa ignores me; he likes the boys better."

"I expect he needs them to do the work. What's your mouse called?"

"George Washington."

"Distinguished. Have you got any buffalo names?"

She nodded. "They're important names, too. Not dumb like Mariah."

"What makes you think 'Mariah' is dumb?"

"It just is. Everyone's got a real name like Susanna and Minnie and Bertha, and I've got this dumb name."

Nate suspected that's why the little girl enjoyed naming animals so. Collecting them too. They were littler than she. Just a guess.

He also guessed she'd accept an invitation to go see how the buffalo calf fared. He was right.

It was the first time he'd invited anyone from Castlerock to visit his rangelands without being asked or paying them for work.

For an hour he and Mariah rode toward the pasture and talked of animals. For another quarter hour they watched Brownie and the milk cow that was its wet nurse roam about.

The child seemed to have forgotten all about the cruel

incident. Nate stood while Mariah sat up on his horse, which
he'd left in a draw, behind a ridge, and positioned so they
could see the buffalo calf but the calf could not see them or
detect their scent. It was doubtful a calf could break down
the wire fence Nate had had built around the pastureland,
but he wanted to teach Mariah right from the start not to
walk up this close to where the buffalo herd would soon
roam.

"It's gone," she said. "It walked over the hill, and now
there's nothing." She held up the military field glasses Nate
had bought from his cavalry friends, and peered off into the
distance. "Nothing's there."

Nate walked up higher on the ridge and looked over. With
the orphan out of sight, the entire rangelands were deserted.
Beneath a wide blue sky with scudding white clouds, tall grass
waved back and forth, empty of life except for the occasional
black bird winging up into the sky.

The milk cow and buffalo calf had wandered over the ridge
out of sight. "There will be . . . soon there'll be buffalo grazing
all over this grassland."

"My pa says it's crazy to pen up buffalo like in a zoo. Some
things can't be fenced in and buffalo's one of them. He thinks
they'll all break down the fence."

Nate smiled. "Not the fence I'll build." Then he turned to
the solemn little child beside him, dark hair blowing in the
breeze, looking out to the horizon, the empty grassland. She
wore, he realized, the same funny knit cap that Miss Beasley
sometimes wore.

"What do you think?"

"I can't wait till they come. I've got all their names ready."

A warning signal went off in Nate. "Don't come up here
alone. You can't get too carried away over animals, you know."
He didn't have the heart to tell her he planned to make a profit
off the buffalo, that at heart he was a speculator. Rare buffalo

would be worth more. If he bred them, supply would outpace demand.

"Of course," the little girl said airily. "I'd never do that. I know buffalo can charge. I'd never go up to one. We don't see many anymore, but I still get plenty of warnings from Ma." She handed the field glasses down to Nate, who took a turn looking through them.

He looked up at her, sitting on his horse, her slim shoulders drooping forlornly. And in his mind he imagined Jennie as a child. He'd bet his bank account that she'd resembled her little niece, and the thought tugged at him.

Alone out here with little Mariah wearing that homely knit cap, he found his thoughts drifting back to Miss Beasley, and Mariah seemed to read his mind.

"Don't worry, Mr. Denison. The new school's coming along, and we'll be out of your house soon. We'll all vanish and never come back."

Suddenly the wind was a bit colder, and pulling up the collar of his sheepskin coat, Nate shivered. He tried to imagine his house without Miss Jennie Beasley's noisy charges in it.

"You'll be glad to be rid of Miss Beasley and us kids, won't you?"

He didn't answer.

"What's the matter?" Mariah asked. "You don't look glad about the new school. You should, you know, because by then you'll be too busy with your buffalo."

He tried to rid himself of the image of a funny little knit hat and trusting brown eyes staring at him. "Yes," he said quietly.

Jennie sat conspicuously silent at the mercantile stove, wondering how in the name of mercy she could slip out of there unnoticed and return home. It was too early for either supper or for Grace's baby, and so Jennie sat politely with the women of

town, who had commandeered the stove, telling their husbands
they were going to exchange recipes and sewing patterns for
a spell. The subject had quickly veered from rice pudding
to the latest Paris paper-doll fashions in the newspapers
back east. It was the mention of back east that led them
inevitably to that eccentric eastern swell, Nate Denison,
and his audacious purchase just the day before of a wild
buffalo calf. At that point Jennie had gotten up and tried
to slip away past the pickle barrel to the backdoor.

She'd taken no more than two steps when Ingrid Jensen
called out. "Jennie, don't go now."

She stopped in her tracks.

At this point there wasn't much choice. The Widow Jensen
was, after all, the mother of Bertha, one of her best students.
And Bertha was a big-boned tomboy, always dressed in the
latest fashion by her seamstress mother. Bertha was sometimes
overdone, so to speak, and next to Mariah was the child Jennie
worried over the most. If Jennie had the courage, she'd tactfully tell Ingrid that Bertha's clothes were out of place in
the classroom, but Ingrid was a formidable woman, from her
spectacles to her new-fashioned slip-on shoes.

"Did you want to discuss how Bertha's doing at school?"

Ingrid waved a dismissive hand. "Bertha's doing fine, I
know. She's finally learning something of cultural value. Tales
about Chicago. And how real draperies are tied back. And
how it feels to drink out of genuine porcelain cups. It's worth
having that nasty little log shack burn down for Bertha to get
inside that house."

"Why do you need me to stay, then?"

"Why, to talk, of course, with us ladies. After all, you're
teaching right in his house every day . . . and both Bertha and
Susanna bring home the most delightful tales from school.
Don't they, Mrs. Vane?" she asked, raising her eyebrows
to urge a nod from the lawyer's wife. Susanna Vane was

uncommonly pretty and usually cast Bertha Jensen in the shade, so as a result the two mothers were not the closest of friends, but today Ingrid had gone out of her way to join forces.

"There's nothing to talk about. The children are . . . coping well with their temporary school."

Ingrid Jensen, who'd been polishing her spectacles on a hanky, gave Jennie a sly smile. "I daresay. Why then are you tiptoeing out on us?" she asked slyly. "Because of all the stories our daughters have told us about the temporary quarters?"

Jennie leaned against the door, thankful she was in the shadows in case her blush showed. "I wouldn't believe everything the youngsters say. . . ."

"My daughter has been taught to always speak the truth and not exaggerate, so *naturally,* when she tried to convince me Mr. Denison told fairy tales, I reprimanded her. She said Mr. Denison has actually substituted for you, and he spent the entire hour telling them first about the Colombian Exposition and then about buffalo. Can you imagine? You know, of course, Mr. Denison spanked two of the big boys." The ladies giggled.

The Widow Jensen was a fountain of anecdotes. "And *then* Susanna says your niece caused an uproar over some animal again—a frog in the fine silver—and as a result, Mr. Denison's had his housekeeper tack sheets all over that marvelous wallpaper—tell us, is it imported from France, truly?"

What a tangle of misinformation. Shoulders slumping, Jennie returned and sank down into a chair by the potbellied stove.

"It was a toad, actually, not a frog, and it was out in the kitchen. The bric-a-brac's been hidden—put away for safekeeping—except for Nate's—I mean, Mr. Denison's stereoscope, which the children are allowed to look at as a reward for good behavior. He substituted for an hour, but they wrote letters and behaved very maturely. No one got spanked, but the older boys helped chop wood."

There. Let that satisfy them. She was not going to reveal any more.

But it didn't satisfy. She could tell from the gleam in their eyes and the way they leaned forward.

"Well, *tell* us more. Anything about the house."

Jennie didn't care about any of the fancy furnishings in that house. The only thing in the place that bothered her was Mr. Nate Denison himself, but she was no fool. "Actually," she said, "it is a great nuisance having to teach in his house. The bric-a-brac, the furniture, the wallpaper, all of it is a great bother when children need sensible surroundings. If anything, it's giving them a taste of things they'll never have."

"Or it might instill ambition in some."

That was true, but Jennie was not to be dragged into a theoretical discussion when these ladies were looking to see if she was enamored of the dude of Denison's Folly. "Rest assured, I can't wait until the town fathers—and Karl—get the new school built, so I can put the youngsters back in a *normal* environment. Other than that, I don't know much about Mr. Denison. All he does is write letters and answer telegrams."

And pursue her . . .

"Well, we've tried to pump Helga, but that stubborn Norwegian woman won't open her mouth except to bore us with talk about grandchildren." Ingrid Jensen sounded as if Helga were deliberately sweeping dirt under the rugs to annoy her.

Jennie sent prayers to heaven that the dear woman would be blessed with a hundred grandchildren.

"I think someone's coming to visit him," Ingrid said, her expression reminiscent of a bear who'd just discovered a honey jar. "You know of course he built the house for a woman."

"How do you know? Does he come in and chat while you

tailor coats for him?" Jennie couldn't resist asking.

After the laughter died down, Ingrid drew herself up righteously. "I know, I tell you. No man builds a house like that for himself." She leaned forward conspiratorially. "Somebody's jilted him, and he kept it secret and finished the house. You've noticed he never spends much time here. Just checks on it once a summer and leaves again—until this fall." She looked at Jennie.

"You didn't know, did you, that this is the longest he's stayed put since he built Denison's Folly?"

Jennie stared at the toes of her shoes. "I believe he's waiting for some buffalo."

Ingrid Jensen laughed softly. "Dear Jennie, he's got a foreman to handle all that pie-in-the-sky animal collecting."

"He's very eastern, you know, Jennie." It was Mrs. Vane who pulled her back out of her brief reverie. "A man used to fancy ladies. As soon as the school's built and he's satisfied his male vanity with this notion of collecting buffalo, he'll leave the place to his housekeeper and foreman again and be gone. You know that, don't you?" Just then the cavalrymen walked into the mercantile.

"Well," Ingrid said, slanting a sly look at Mrs. Vane and then back at Jennie, "it might be tempting . . . or disturbing . . . for an innocent young teacher like you to teach all day so close to such a worldly man."

Jennie stood, insulted—no, humiliated at their presumption that she wasn't good enough for the likes of Nate Denison, who in her opinion was no more than a beast stalking her in his house.

"Excuse me, I need to go check on Grace. I worry now that the baby's getting closer."

"Well, don't run off in a dither. We just wanted to make sure you knew your place where a man like that is concerned. All our previous teachers have married solid, sensible men.

Ranchers or cowboys or shopkeepers. We don't mind if you find a sweetheart before the school year is up, but you'd be wasting your time to think on Mr. Denison, don't you agree, Hirum?"

Before he could answer, Jennie said, "I don't waste my time on such . . . such vulgar thoughts." Her voice trembled. If these ladies knew exactly what she thought of Nate, they'd laugh and snicker till the nails curled in the boardwalk. "I've got my reasons for wanting to succeed and that occupies all my attention."

Worse, if these ladies found out that Nate Denison had stalked her around the schoolroom and the library and kissed her, they'd likely turn on her with jealousy. Especially the married ones who were bored with their lot. She'd found that out in her last post. The married women had been the first to turn on her when the superintendent's son had waylaid her in the cloakroom, alone. Her oldest and densest student— she'd underestimated what the boy knew about women and kissing . . . and the extent of his infatuation with her. Well, that was past. But she didn't need any more scandals to mar her teaching career.

She needed to succeed here, and she needed these women to be on her side—as friends.

"Nate Denison invited me to use his house as a good deed to the town," she said in all innocence.

Now Orvil plucked a dill pickle out of the barrel and, crunching off the end, stepped forward. "Aw, leave the teacher alone. She ain't got no fancy notions, and Nate ain't got any notions either. To him she's just the schoolmarm. Nate says he invited her and those kids into his house so he could help us maybe find the poacher. You know, listen in on the kids talking and all. It's the kids he wanted, not the teacher— ow!" He dropped his pickle as Hirum gave him a swift kick in the shin.

Rubbing his leg, Orvil grimaced. "What was that for?" He reached for his pickle and brushed it off. "I was trying to stick up for the schoolmarm."

Hirum poked him in the ribs for good measure. "It's vulgar to give away a man's motives where a lady is involved, especially if he's got no designs on her. You've hurt her feelings. Don't you have any sense?"

Jennie felt her heart plummet to her toes, and her face must have turned as white as bleached flour. Ingrid was watching every nuance of expression on her face with smug interest.

"Well, Nate never said it was some big secret," Orvil whined. "I thought he'd enlist the schoolmarm's help."

"You're dumb, Orvil. Really dumb! Don't you know the teacher's related to one of the chief suspects—Thaddeus Gordon? Now it don't matter how pretty she is, but Nate Denison isn't dumb enough to tell her he's helping us throw her own family in the brig, huh?"

Jennie stared in disbelief. She wanted to sink into a chair; her head went light. "I don't believe you," she said at last, and in a swirl of skirts, ran out. It wasn't true about Nate. Orvil was a teasing busybody, just the same as Ingrid Jensen.

CHAPTER

❧ 9 ❧

"Oh, Paddy, they're beautiful," Mariah said when the last puppy had been born. Pa supervised and for once didn't shoo her away; neither did he waste time making chitchat.

"Their eyes will be open by Thanksgiving, huh, Pa?"

No answer.

"Why isn't Paddy licking the last one?"

"It's the runt."

The runt? Like her. Something inside Mariah's heart reached out. That last pup born, still slick and wet, was, unlike its siblings who all bore the markings of their sheepdog mother, coal black. Mariah decided to help out Paddy, who, after all, had enough pups to look after. So she ran a warm damp cloth over the tiny black pup and set it down by its mother. Paddy pushed it away, and with eyes shut, it lay on the floor behind the stove crying.

"What's wrong, Pa?"

"I told you. It's the runt."

"But it'll be all right?"

"Dunno, but you leave him to Paddy." Pa shooed her off to bed.

All right, if Paddy didn't have time to cuddle it, Mariah did. If that buffalo calf could make do with a substitute cow teat, then this pup could be fooled too. Just so he survived. When everyone was asleep, she tiptoed into the kitchen, only the cold moonlight spilling in to light her way to the stove. With a rag soaked in milk, she squeezed drops into the pup's mouth. She'd do the same by day, when Pa wasn't looking, if need be.

"You'll be all right, little runt," she cooed. "A week from now you'll be big and chubby."

But a week later the coal-black pup was still struggling, and when school and chores didn't take her out of the house, Mariah stayed close and slept little.

Pa looked glum. "I'll be glad when those pups are weaned. We can use the money."

"Not yet, Pa."

"Six weeks with their ma, but I'll pass the word in town they're for sale."

"Except for the black one."

"Mmm." Pa nodded. "He looks sickly. Leave him be."

Ignoring her father, Mariah knelt and stroked the pup's ears.

"Go help your aunt, runt. You're dawdling too much over that dog."

"Pa—"

Her ma stayed in her rocker, looking half-asleep.

And Pa turned from her and headed to the bedroom.

Why did he never pay attention to her? Why was she always "runt"? Tears filled her eyes, and she rattled dishes off the table and dumped them into a tin pan. Water boiled on the kitchen stove. Dishwater. All Pa thought girls were good for was to do housework. Chores . . . chores . . . chores. The boys got to do all the fun things.

She leaned over the tin dishpan, pouring in hot water, chasing a bar of soap, making it float at full speed. A few bubbles appeared in the water and one by one burst. She set down the kettle, grabbed the soap, and rubbed it against the dishrag. She'd just reached for a greasy plate when someone clumped onto the porch and a moment later knocked so loud the walls rattled.

Jennie, dish towel in hand, went to the door, Mariah at her heels, and opened it a crack. At the familiar sight of Hirum and Orvil, she smiled and had a friendly greeting.

Mariah knew these two—by face. It was the same two cavalrymen she'd seen many times sitting around the mercantile stove smoking pipes and snitching dill pickles from the barrel. They were loud and always had a fancy compliment or a wink for Aunt Jennie.

But late this afternoon they weren't laughing. They looked as serious as they had the time they'd marched into the mercantile and throttled Vernon Higgenbottom for carving his name in one of the Yellowstone hot pools.

Yes, that's how the cavalrymen looked now—serious . . . like they were on official business, because sure as crows were black they couldn't be looking for dill pickles and flirtation here at the house.

"Where's Thaddeus Gordon? We got some questions for him."

Whirling, Mariah dropped the dishrag. Something was wrong. Seriously wrong.

Just then her pa reappeared in the door from the bedroom,

pulling overall straps on over the sleeves of his long johns.

"Pa?" What had he done? "Did you carve your name in a hot pool?"

"Quiet, runt. Stay out of this."

"Send the girl out," the cavalrymen said.

"No . . ." Mariah, stubborn, knelt by the pups.

Pa stood, expression wary.

"Remember that orphaned calf?"

"Nate Denison's got it. It ain't my concern anymore."

"We know that. We also found its mama. Dead. How much did the skin bring? Or was it the head? A few hundred? Enough to tide you over the winter? Business ain't so good this year, I hear."

Pa's face grew stony, and he looked from one man to the other. "You've got the wrong man. I'm no poacher."

"The goods are in your hunting shack."

"No, it wasn't Pa." Mariah couldn't believe it.

"Loyal little girl. Maybe we should question her."

"Leave her out of this. A man's got to feed his family, and I've taken animals that stray outside of the park, but only for food. I've done no poaching in the park. You've got nothing to come after me for."

"Sorry, Thaddeus," Orvil said softly. "But we found hides in an old shack of yours near the boundaries, and so we had to investigate, give you a warning about coming inside the park boundaries. That's our job."

Pa glowered. "Poor folks like us are struggling. If you fellows are done asking your questions, why don't you pay up the account you owe me at the mercantile?"

"Aw, Thaddeus, don't get personal. We'll pay up—next paycheck. You renting that hunting shack to anyone we know?"

Her pa looked up, mouth thin with anger. "No. Any hunting I do is legal. If you want to catch your man, you ought to take your own advice and stay home in Yellowstone. Spend less time up here in Castlerock bothering hardworking citizens."

Heart pounding, Mariah looked across at Aunt Jennie. She had at first looked shocked; now she slumped against the wall, white-faced. Mariah didn't know who to worry about more, Pa or Aunt Jennie, who looked as if she'd been dusted with chalk.

"Your eastern friend—the one who's starting a zoo—he's been making friends with some of my customers. They'd tell him anything. Did he tell you to come after me?"

"That's our business, and as for Nate Denison . . . he's got a right to buy buffalo. That's more honorable than poaching them."

Her pa looked from one to the other. "Yeah, well, I never did trust any man who orders silk shirts from New York. And I don't like cavalrymen in brass buttons walking into my house embarrassing me in front of my wife. Get out."

"Don't say we didn't warn you." Then Hirum and Orvil banged out.

"The dude is in on this." Pa glared at Aunt Jennie. "It was your idea to put my kids with Nate Denison." His voice held accusation. "This is your doing, me being humiliated. I bring you here. Do my wife's sister a favor so you can save money for university." He put a sarcastic spin on the last word. "You and that dude are a real pair, you know that . . . both with fancy ideas. Fancy ideas don't have no place out here. They don't fit in with us hardworking plain folks."

"No, Pa." Mariah ran to her aunt's side. "She's a nice teacher. Don't be mad."

And Pa just got madder.

"Do you want me to be blunt about it? I don't have the money for school. Not to pay my share and your salary. I wanted to shut down school and figured you would if I offered the saloon as an alternative. But no, you had big ideas."

Ma got up and waddled as far as the rocker by the stove. The baby was due anytime, and Ma shouldn't get upset.

"Thaddeus, leave my sister alone and answer me the truth. Are you poaching?"

"If there're pelts in my shack, I don't know anything about them. It's those cavalry fellows that are desperate—desperate enough to blame anyone for lost animals."

"Still, if things aren't doing well, you should be minding the store better."

"You criticizing me, wife? Me? My father came here with nothing and made this store out of nothing."

"Thaddeus, I'm being helpful," Grace said gently. "You're the one who did the accounts—why just the other day you wrote off some of two customers' accounts, all for moving that buffalo calf. And you've ordered way too many luxuries like canned peaches and not enough practical goods. Thaddeus, the children look to you for example. If we're near to broke, the last thing we need is a fine from the cavalry."

Mariah couldn't stand to listen anymore. She ran back to the little room she shared with Aunt Jennie and stared out their pretend window.

Jennie looked from Grace to Thaddeus, each one scared, white. They were her family.

"Please," Jennie pleaded. "If Nate Denison's got any designs on helping the cavalry and hurting you, I didn't know about it. I've got money saved in—in a cigar box . . . or I could tutor youngsters over the winter break."

"We *can't* be fined. They can't prove a thing, and I didn't do anything wrong. Someone's using my shack, that's all. I'm not a poacher, despite what that dude and the cavalry think." Thaddeus Gordon grabbed his coat, slammed out of the house and vanished up Camas Street, walking in the opposite direction from the mercantile.

"We'll make it through the winter," Grace said. "I know we will." Her hands came round her swelling belly. "We have to."

For a minute Jennie felt flattened against the wall, as if a cold weight were pushing against her lungs, preventing her from breathing right. She couldn't take it all in. Thaddeus, accused of poaching. She knew her brother-in-law. Even if he wasn't guilty, he'd think first of his pride, of honor.

As the numbness wore off, the truth of Orvil's words sunk in. The words about Nate. At first, she'd refused to believe him, had passed what he'd said off to silliness, but now— how could she not give it credence? Maybe Nate *had* been consorting with the cavalry, helping them keep an eye on the townsfolk.

Is that really why he'd agreed to allow the schoolchildren to use his dining room? Hoping, like children, they'd brag about their daddy the poacher, whoever he was?

Tears stung. Nate Denison bought everything he wanted— from buffalo to information . . . to . . . kisses.

And that was the worst. For as much as she might have worried about such a sophisticated man sullying her reputation, deep down she'd liked the attention, deep deep down, he'd ignited something inside her. Nate Denison had tempted her with what she thought was soul-thrilling ardor. Hah! False ardor.

And it hurt. It hurt to be toyed with.

Worse than hurt. Cut deep at her heart and soul . . . and trust.

For a minute the only sound was the hiss and crackle of wood settling in the stove, then Paddy whined softly to be let out. The puppies slept in a box of straw and, except for the crying runt, didn't even notice their mother leave.

Hadn't he warned her, though, that everything had a price,

even her schoolchildren? *Her* school was nothing more than a means to an end.

It was time to move into the new school, finished or not.

Moments later Jennie was buttoning her cape and pulling on her knit hat and matching mittens.

"Where are you going, little sister? I don't want everyone leaving me." Her sister was curled up in her chair, expression drooping.

"I'm going to check on the new school. Will you be all right for a half hour?"

At her sister's nod Jennie added, "Grace . . ."

Grace stared down at her chapped hands, which were clasped tightly on her swollen belly. "Don't say anything, Jennie, and I'll be all right." She looked up with a forced smile. "Tell me what you're going to do at the new school."

She shrugged. "I'll find out if the children and I can move in."

"You're no carpenter. What do you know about checking a new building? You can't stick a toothpick in it like you do a cake or look at it for lumps like you do gravy."

Jennie slowed and pulled her hat lower over her ears. She'd not be talked out of this, even if she had to endure some of Karl's stammering and cow-eyed looks.

"I'll know."

"You can't grade it like a spelling paper with a pencil either or listen to it to see if there's a mispronunciation when the floorboards creak. All creaks sound alike." Grace's voice quavered.

"I know that too." There were tears swimming in her sister's eyes. Oh, Grace, stop trying to be so brave. Just give in and cry. Cry. . . .

Because if Grace, her big, pregnant sister, with five, almost six kids and no money . . . if she didn't cry, then how could Jennie?

"I'm going to look for signs of windows and blackboards and desks. Like the stuffing in a turkey. If it's got its insides, then it's almost ready. Luckily it's almost Thanksgiving, and maybe Karl can finish it then."

Jennie studied her sister, saw dark rings beneath her eyes that hadn't been there before, a sad turn to her mouth.

"Thaddeus doesn't mean it," Grace said. "He'll be back soon. Don't let him worry you. You can stay in the mansion dining room. The school shouldn't be at all affected by this. Thaddeus could have put his foot down when you took the school up to that mansion, but he thought it was a regular lark. Now he'll have to live with it."

Jennie paused with her hand on the doorknob, searching for the right words.

"All I ever dreamed of was teaching little ones. Being a teacher, esteemed and pure. But as long as Thaddeus and Nate hate each other, it won't do for me to stay there. It's not fair to my family—to you." Nate Denison was not going to destroy her family. That was even more important than her dreams.

Jennie crossed the sitting room in a few steps and knelt at her sister's knee, pulling an afghan over Grace's belly. "I'm sorry I caused such a ruckus."

"It wasn't your fault. Thaddeus is just a stubborn Scotsman."

Jennie planted a swift kiss on her big sister's forehead. "Now, take care of the baby till I come back. You, too, Paddy," she said as she opened the door and the dog ran in. Then she slipped out into the cold of early evening.

The school was being built on a new site, up north on Moose Street, near the bank. A nicer part of town, and the school would be fancier too. From across the street Jennie paused to admire its framework. This was no log cabin. For the thousand dollars the town had scraped together, they were building a

genuine schoolhouse, one that would double as a church. Not
of logs, but of real lumber and nails. Already there was a
belltower, and on either side of the front door were two open
rectangles where the cloakroom windows would go. She'd
helped Thaddeus Gordon select blackboards and desks—the
real kind of desks with inkwells and pencil grooves and fold-up
seats—from a mail-order catalog, and when those came, Jennie
and the class could move in. If all went according to schedule,
they could at least hold the Christmas pageant here, and then
be ready for reopening in the spring.

Outside, the pines were dark outlines, and the only thing
to blow about in the late-autumn wind were vagrant tumble-
weeds. Crossing the street, she made a track of footprints
in the new snow—not a lot had fallen, just a late-autumn
tease, but the little bit had stuck, and like a child she looked
behind at her tracks. She realized she'd actually forgotten about
Nate Denison for a few minutes, and walked into the school,
excited to look about. A kerosene lantern sat on a stepladder,
throwing out a pool of light. The sound of hammering was
encouraging, and the scent of wood shavings and new tim-
ber wove around her, as homey in their way as new
baked bread.

"Karl," she called.

The hammering stopped, and she called again.

"In here," he called right back. "That you, Jennie?"

"Y-yes, I've come to inspect the place. Are you busy?
You're working late."

A moment later Karl appeared, hammer in hand. Lanky
Karl, pushing straight blond hair out of his eyes. Karl was
the plain, solid man that Ingrid Jensen had hinted was Jennie's
"type."

"This is an honor," he stammered proudly. "Especially to
have two people come to tour at once."

"Two?" An awful dread filled her. Only one other person

might be more anxious than she to get this school built . . . but no, Nate Denison would never bother to come tour a half-built school.

"Mr. Denison's here too. Isn't this a fine coincidence now?" Her spirits sank.

"How nice."

Karl whispered close to her ear. "I wish you'd come alone."

"So do I." Her heart hammered in time to the sound of someone's footsteps coming from the back of the room. *Please leave, Nate.* She tried to concentrate on Karl's words.

"I've got a new potbellied stove to show you. It's still in its crate, but it's advertised as more fire safe than the last one."

"How reassuring." As Nate's footsteps echoed over the new pegged floor, she tried to smile, but couldn't.

Then he was there, sheepskin coat turned up to his chin, his brown hair blowing across his forehead. He was, she realized, amused.

Then he reached across and without a by-your-leave yanked her knit hat off.

"Don't—"

"I like to see the way your hair shines by the lamp, Miss Beasley."

Her heart fell down to her stomach and almost forgot to keep beating.

"It's eggs that make it shine." Her voice held ice.

"Is that so?"

"I wash it in eggs—when Thaddeus has extra." For Karl's sake she tried to remain cordial, polite.

Karl cleared his throat. "It's lucky the school's all framed in before any more snow falls."

"Yes."

"Yes."

Their identical responses fell on top of each other's. Briefly

Jennie's glance slid up to Nate's. His eyes still held a glimmer of amusement.

"Would you like a tour?" Karl said nervously.

She dragged her gaze away from Nate's deep blue eyes to Karl's pale brown ones. He appeared so anxious to please. "All right," she answered.

"Well, you're standing in the girls' cloakroom door. The coat hooks are on order. I'll screw them in about four feet high? Is that right for the children?"

She had to drag her gaze away from tall Nate. "Ah . . . yes, that'll be perfect, Karl."

The rest of the tour didn't take long. They inspected the wall where the blackboard would be mounted, the wall where the stovepipe would be inserted, and admired the floor on which rows of desks would be placed. Without windows or a stove, the place was chilly, and Jennie hugged her arms about herself.

"Karl, do you think I can move the class here Monday?"

Nate cut in and spun her around to face him. "Jennie, let me explain about Orvil."

So he knew already about his turncoat friend. "It's too late." She ducked away from his touch. "Karl, can we come?"

Nate turned to Karl. "Don't rush things. Do it right. The school's staying at my house."

"Karl," Jennie countered, "the school needs to move out of Mr. Denison's house. I need you to hurry."

Baffled, poor Karl looked from one to the other, mouth open, unable to side with either of them.

"Karl, don't listen to her. Jennie's class is well provided for in my dining room."

"Well provided for?" Jennie said, rounding on him. "You call chasing me around the table well provided for? Sending two of my boys out to chop wood well provided for? Forbidding the youngsters to touch any of your precious bric-a-brac?

Why, Mr. Denison? Why'd you invite us up there?"

Karl kept looking from one to the other, and then swallowed so hard his Adam's apple bounced in his throat.

"Maybe you'd like to finish looking around yourselves."

"Are you quitting?" Jennie asked, dismayed. She didn't want to be left alone with Nate.

"Well . . ." Karl shuffled his big boots back and forth. "Actually I'm behind on my coffin making. I try to keep at least two spare ones in the store, and what with the school, I'm falling behind."

"Of course. I'm sorry. I know this is volunteer work."

Quick as a wink, Nate turned to Karl. "I might have a job for you. Not volunteer work, but one that pays."

"You can't slow down the school," Jennie snapped.

"Oh, yes I can. Karl needs paying jobs, too, don't you, Karl?"

Again Karl's Adam's apple bobbed. "What kind of job?"

"A Tiffany window that needs boarding up to . . . protect it."

"Oh, interior work in your place. Yes, sir," the carpenter said eagerly. "I'd be honored."

"The school's more important than your precious window," Jennie cried. "Why, ten families could eat for a winter on what that silly window cost!"

"Then perhaps I'll sell it and donate the proceeds to the town."

Jennie stared at him in fury. Buy. Sell. That's the only way he could deal with people—as commodities.

As soon as Karl left, Nate grabbed her by the arms and stared down into her eyes. The harder she pulled away, the tighter he held her. "Hirum talked to me, told me what Orvil said. It wasn't true. I lied to Orvil about you."

She squirmed away. "Give me back my hat."

"I don't like your hat."

"Why?"

"Because I like your hair without it." He reached out to touch a coppery tendril.

She backed away. "My hair is none of your business. Why did you lie? Why?"

His shoulders slumped.

Nate's face was highlighted by the lantern. "Think about it. A single schoolmarm alone all day in my house with me. They were making some crude assumptions. I lied to protect your reputation."

"But we weren't alone."

And fourteen kids hadn't stopped him from finding a way to kiss her. Nor would her outrage now. They were alone, she was filled with fiery passion, and Nate burned with the need to kiss her.

She pulled away. "You've been toying with my affections."

"Yes, but not for the reason Hirum and Orvil said, and," he said, advancing on her, "you liked it."

"I didn't. That would be improper for a schoolmarm."

"Not necessarily." His eyes dropped to her lips.

She did like it. But that was beside the point.

Her gaze locked with his, and she fought her longing. "Nate, let go . . . please."

His face was close to hers, his touch warm, his lips grazing her cheek. "I knew it would come to this," he said angrily. "And I didn't want Orvil and Hirum talking. I should have said nothing. How can you believe those two idiots?"

While he watched her take in his words, he moved closer, pulled her against the wall between the two western windows, and there where moonlight spilled into her new school, he kissed her cheek, her ear, her throat, her eyelids, and finally, when her arms came up around him, her mouth. Her body melded with his, warm and feverish, a fever she never wanted to end.

Her arms tightened around his neck, and she kissed him back, brazenly allowed his tongue to touch hers, his body to press hers against the wall, even as she melted into him, wanting to get closer.

At last he let her go, and she went limp. By the time the kiss was done, the lamp was low, and a few snowflakes blew in the open windows.

"I want to be a virtuous schoolmarm."

"You are failing in that goal, Miss Beasley. Virtue is not your true calling."

"Don't do this again, Nate."

Even as she said the words she turned to look him in the eye, but he was too close, and their lips met again, came together with elemental force. A long time later she broke away and stood leaning against his shoulder, trying to control her breathing.

"Nate, go away. Leave me in my school."

"Not until you tell me you believe me."

She slid along the wall away from him, wary, longing. "I'm not like the women you're used to."

She was right about that, and that was the trouble. Her hair spilled about her shoulders, glowing coppery in the dim light. His gut clenched. "How so?"

"They may like toying, but I feel wicked, like gravy poured over apple pie."

There was a short pause. "Is that the ultimate compliment from a small-town schoolmarm—to be told my kisses compare to fine gravy?"

"If that will make you stop, then yes."

"Now who do you believe? Thaddeus or Orvil or me?"

She wanted to believe Nate Denison, but didn't dare. "I don't know." And she meant it. She wanted to believe Nate, but needed to believe her family—out of loyalty. Besides, why should she disbelieve Orvil? A harmless puppy dog of a man. In utter contrast to big Nate, with his sensuality, his confidence in having his way with women. Nate got his own way no matter what. But Orvil, like Karl, was an innocent. He'd have no reason to lie.

She hadn't realized Nate had come up so close beside her again until she felt his breath, warm and tempting, on her neck. Her insides melted. Slipping away sideways, she looked at him, so big, so handsome. If he were a trap, she'd almost walk into his arms. The sort of man women died for.

"Who do you believe?" Nate leaned close, demanding a choice.

She was shivering. "I believe Orvil spoke the truth."

"Damn, Jennie Beasley. You don't get it. Orvil did speak the truth. I did say those words. I regret now they've come back to haunt me, but don't you see . . . some words—even false words—are meant to protect."

"Lies never work, Nate."

"Jennie . . ." His voice was husky with frustration.

"I feel wicked, and I don't want to. I'd better go back to Grace and her brood."

And he'd better go back east, where the women took kissing more casually. "Jennie," he said in a voice that sounded almost betrayed. When she turned, he merely handed her the ugly little knit hat he'd pulled off. "Don't forget this."

It was warm from being in his pocket. He reached out and touched her hair, which fell loose about her shoulders. "Here. Put it on. Unless it was your intention to announce to everyone at your sister's house that you've been out here letting someone tangle his hands in your hair. Me, the man Thaddeus Gordon hates so? Or they might think it was Karl, and make you marry him," he teased.

She jammed the hat over her hair. Suddenly he was leaving, any warmth that had been in the room going with him. The scent of cold sawdust drifted up to her.

"Good night, Nate," she whispered, hugging herself against the cold.

She stood at the door watching him disappear in the dark toward that elegant mansion. Built for a woman, Ingrid said.

The rogue. Rushing here to find her the instant Hirum and Orvil told him they'd spilled the beans. Trying to charm her into forgiving his duplicity. And as her heart thudded away she realized there was another matter at stake. Even if she believed Nate, she could never trust his kisses to be true. Another woman haunted his heart . . . the woman he'd built that mansion for.

CHAPTER
~ 10 ~

After a sleepless night, Jennie came to one conclusion. Nate's presence in the schoolhouse was indeed too coincidental. His manner too full of easy words and kisses. The verdict: guilty. Nate was a ruthless man who'd sell her own family to the cavalry for profit. The solution: never let him close enough to touch her again.

First thing the next morning, earlier even than when Helga came, Jennie marched up the cold boardwalk, beneath a gray, cloudy sky, and barged into Nate's mansion with no pretense of stealth. Noisily, she began corralling school supplies—the chalk, the pencils, three books of nursery rhymes, the McGuffey readers borrowed from the county school. All of it got rounded up into a big pile and thrown into straw baskets that an hour ago had held brown eggs on the mercantile counter.

She had no idea Nate Denison had been standing there until she looked up and saw him in the doorway, eyes puzzled, hair so tousled she'd have sworn he'd never heard of macassar oil. But that wasn't at all shocking compared with his clothing. Or rather, lack of it. She blinked and allowed her gaze to rove downward. He was dressed in nothing but a wrapper, not even long johns. Not even long-john material. The garment was wine-colored and resembled the garb those women in the saloons wore. Stifling a grin, she looked away and then back. Yes, the cord at his waist looked as if he'd borrowed it from his draperies.

"Is that an eastern-style nightshirt, or is it left over from one of your seductions of married women, Mr. Denison?" She made no effort to keep the sarcasm out of her voice.

"My reputation seems to have caught up with me."

"Your reputation preceded you. Ingrid Jensen subscribes to the New York papers and reads us all the gossip."

"For Ingrid's information, this is a dressing gown for men, and I never seduce schoolmarms."

"Such vulgar words are unattractive and, after your performance last night, hardly believable."

"You are, Miss Beasley, in over your head on this subject."

"And will always remain so. You may frankly pursue looser women for their physical charms but not me."

"Nothing intrigues a man more than moral superiority."

Such conceit.

A slight smile curved his lips. "I thought we straightened out our differences last night."

"You thought wrong."

"Where are you going in such a hurry, Jennie?"

"What makes you think I'm in a hurry?" She threw a few more items in the basket she was holding.

"Packing a basket like you're late to the Big Bad Wolf's."

"I'm already at the Big Bad Wolf's house, and I'm moving out."

"I thought you were a more trusting lady than that. . . ." He came closer. "You *still* think I'm in league with the cavalry and to blame for your brother-in-law's problems?"

"I don't trust anyone who hasn't sense enough to dress in long underwear in this climate, and that's all there is to say."

"Well, considering how early you've arrived—before I could even dress for the occasion, I consider that a bit unfair." He leaned against the sideboard, watching her. "Jennie, I admitted the truth last night, as well as a few of my faults. I'm a speculator, a financial wheeler-dealer. But I swear I'm not one of those cavalrymen. They're just fellows I pass the time with. I don't care what your brother-in-law does. And maybe my words were hasty, but it was your reputation I was looking out for, nothing else."

"If you hadn't been kissing me while explaining all of that, you might have had more credibility." Oh, he was fancy with words. Tossed out regular crystal chandeliers when it came to explanations.

"Stay."

"Why?"

"Without my dining room, you'll have nowhere to teach school. Stay, and I'll let the youngsters play out front. They can bring balls and sleds to school."

She glared, unimpressed.

"All right," he conceded. "Marbles too."

She tightened her grip on a slateboard as she debated throwing it. At him. After all Thaddeus Gordon had done to get her this teaching position, she couldn't in good conscience remain in this house; worse, she couldn't remain here teaching and vulnerable to the man. That kiss last night had sealed the decision. Spinster schoolmarms had no time to deal with broken hearts. For that's all he'd give her.

"I'd sooner teach in the saloon."

"Not if I buy it."

A silver creamer from his sideboard flew through the air and, as he ducked, crashed into the wall behind him.

Jennie began tearing down the sheet that covered one of his fancy-papered walls. As he started over she held up the yards of white muslin as a sort of barricade to hold him and his satin robe at bay. "Don't come near me."

Nate must have looked as baffled as he felt.

She kept scooping papers into her basket and satchel. "You wouldn't understand what it's like for a woman with dreams like mine. You've bought everything you want. I've had to work and save for mine, you double-crossing, betraying lout."

Nate had to admit her language was more colorful than anything the society matrons had used on him. But she still made no sense. "Dreams?"

She looked up into those intense blue eyes. It was none of his business; he'd laugh at her brave little dream. Well, let him. "Maybe you didn't believe me last night either, but I'm saving so I can go to a university."

After a few seconds of silence he whistled. "University?"

He made it sound as if it were the darkest jungle . . . the edge of the ocean before Columbus declared the earth round. Jennie might just as well have said she wanted to travel by wagon train to the moon.

"What's the matter? I'm supposed to believe *your* story, but you don't believe me?"

Nate stared at Jennie with renewed admiration. The women in his acquaintance considered finishing school a bore, never mind a university. But then Miss Jennie Beasley never had struck him as conventional.

"Why aren't you like the other schoolmarms, who teach until they find a husband?" He looked her in the eye, and she did not blink. The lady meant it.

"That's why I didn't want school closed down when the old one burned. I need the monthly paycheck. Only now Thaddeus Gordon will need my savings if the cavalry confiscates his hunting gear. All my savings! And he's innocent."

"How much have you got?"

"Nearly a hundred dollars," she said proudly, tears glistening in her eyes.

Hell, his chandelier had cost that much, and he said so out loud.

"That's hard-earned money, something you wouldn't know about."

"Especially riding herd, as they say, on those big boys."

The matching sugar bowl flew by, and again he ducked.

In three strides he reached her, his hand staying hers from flinging the next object on the sideboard, his mother's antique silver candlestick. She struggled to get away, but he held her hand firmly down and with his other hand spanned her waist and pulled her hips tight against him.

Doubtless the creamer or sugar bowl had left a hole in his wallpaper, which the organized part of Nate wanted to go investigate, but another part of him was far more intrigued by the passion he'd unleashed. Jennie's hair, which appeared to have been hastily pinned, was falling down about the shoulders of her prim shirtwaist most becomingly.

"Heck, Jennie," he said as she squirmed against him, "I don't care if you want to go to finishing school, but you're not leaving my house yet. The windows for the new school all came in broken."

"Did you do it?"

He laughed. "I've outgrown schoolboy pranks."

She wrenched free, and her shirtwaist came untucked at the same time. At last. A glimpse again of the sensual Miss Beasley who'd caught his eye the day of the school fire.

"I may be a dense student, Miss Beasley, but I'm afraid I

need the teacher to clarify how I've ruined this dream of yours to go to a university. When you're calmed down, would you mind explaining?"

She broke free and moved around the room so the table separated them.

"Grace and I never had a place of our own. We didn't even attend the same school two years in a row. The only thing we had that was constant was Grace's pretty looks and my brains, and so we made a pact. She would marry and have babies, and I'd be the one to accomplish something in this world. I'd make the Beasley name stand for something, and I intend to, starting with a university education. Now, why are you staring at me? Haven't you ever met a woman with an education? Are all the women in your social set brainless nitwits?"

Actually, no. The few women he'd met from places like Radcliffe and Vassar were scholarly, but from wealthy families. A few also smoked and read scandalous literature. He'd assumed they were indulging themselves till they found husbands, except of course for the ones who ran off to Paris to become Bohemians. Definitely not his type. But that wasn't the reason for his temporary loss of speech. Once again she'd taken him off guard with her unpredictability.

"I think a university education is an admirable goal," he said carefully.

"And now it'll never happen," she snapped. "All my savings are going to help my sister and her children." She looked up at Nate. "After the cavalry was done with their warnings, Thaddeus admitted to financial difficulties. He can't afford to lose anything."

Nate frowned.

"Do you think Thaddeus Gordon's a poacher?" she asked.

"Do you?"

"Of course not."

"Well, if he's not guilty, there's nothing to worry about, and you can stay here. Next time I see Hirum and Orvil I'm going to personally hold their heads under the livery pump and scrub their loose-talking tongues with lye soap."

"And then what? Pack up and leave people's reputations in a tangle? Don't you understand? Just accusing Thaddeus tarnishes his reputation, puts doubts in everyone's mind."

"No one seems to care about the poachers' reputations," he pointed out.

"That's different. They're strangers."

"Double standard?"

"Maybe . . . That's what it's like out here. People demand honor of their neighbors, and once that honor is tarnished, it's never the same." She snatched up her satchel as if to go. "Why I'm explaining all this is beyond me. You think you're better than all of us."

At the foot of the table he waylaid her and grabbed her by the shoulders. "I'm not better, Jennie, just richer. There's a difference."

"Hah! You've bought and sold everything." She wrenched away, but he was quicker and blocked the doorway.

Jennie stared up at him, soft brown eyes full of pain. "I'll be as good as you someday, Mr. Denison. It may take me ten years, but I'll do it, and when I've gone to a university, it won't matter that you've got money and I don't. We'll be equals then, and you can put on airs and build a zoo out here and wear all the satin robes you want, but it won't make you better than me. You or your fine ladies back on Fifth Avenue. Now let me pass."

He took one step toward her. "I want you to stay in the house."

"I don't. Move away." She raised her foot, ready to stomp her high-button boot down on his bare instep.

The front door opened, and they both turned to see who'd arrived. Mariah.

"Your students are arriving, Jennie."

She rushed to the dining-room window and looked out. The sky was leaden, and through that cold autumn day lumbered the school wagon, overflowing with children in mittens and hats, lard pails balanced on their laps.

Turning, she planted her hands on her hips.

"Look at the sky, feel the cold," Nate said gently. "You're not going to move fourteen youngsters, half of whom have runny noses, into a frozen windowless school, and you know it. Either stay here one more day or cancel school."

Her shoulders sagged. She'd spent more time being angry at Nate than sleeping last night, and suddenly she was very, very tired. The thought of hauling all the books and paraphernalia to a new school that didn't even have desks yet overwhelmed her. She just wanted to collapse in the dining-room chair and set the children to reading.

"Miss Beasley, it's my turn today to look at the stereoscope." Mariah stood in the doorway.

It was true. Mariah hadn't had her turn yet. Was it fair to punish the students because of her own feelings for Nate?

"All right," Jennie said in a small weary voice. "We'll have lessons here one more day, but then we move."

"You'll leave my silverware, I trust. It's an heirloom, dating back to ancestors who lived during the Revolutionary War, and you promised to keep my dining room orderly."

Already her mind spun with all of his rules, rules she intended to break. "If you like things orderly, then why, Mr. Denison, are you parading about unshaven and in your bare feet?"

The windows rattled against their sashes when he slammed the door to his library. In retaliation, as a start in rebelling against his dumb rules, Jennie grabbed his velvet drapes and pulled them shut. Dressing gowns, indeed! The pompous dude.

Perhaps if he'd been dressed in more civilized garb—no, it didn't matter. Even dressed in western denims and flannel shirts, he'd have the same devastating effect on her.

Well, there it was, and it was up to her to maintain a facade of calm until the end of the school day.

Four o'clock. That's when she'd break the news to the youngsters that they'd spent their last day in the dining room of Denison's Folly.

At 1:30 Nate returned from town and stamped into his kitchen, head still down from the swirling snow. He had a bad feeling about the storm that was blowing in; so did the men who'd been working in the pasture to double the height of his wire fence.

Helga had left a stew on top of the stove and gone to town for a ladies' circle meeting. Nate guessed she'd not be back.

From down the hall he could hear the youngsters noisily discussing why women and not just men should get the vote. If Wyoming could do it, then so could every state. A debate. A noisy debate. Didn't the woman ever stop to look out the window?

When he slid open the door, he discovered why. The draperies were pulled shut, and since the storm had started blowing shortly after lunch, it was just possible no one had had occasion to look out a window. Still-wet clumps of papier-mâché perched all over his sideboard. Soggy birds. At least judging from the pair of pine-cone chips glued to their bottoms, that was his best guess.

Oh, the teacher had gotten even. A washtub full of watery flour paste sat on the floor by his antique chairs and spots of paste dotted his imported carpet. It looked worse in here than it did outside. Spattered white. As if a blizzard had been at work. While one of the Armstrong boys argued with the taxidermist's son—the Zane boy—about whether men or women were better suited to the kitchen, Nate eyed the birds with suspicion. They'd have to go before she got ideas about painting them—

as well as his walls. Helga could move them—no, Helga, with rotten timing, had picked today to go to town.

He moved from window to window, opening draperies, and gradually the room grew quiet. Only then did the howling wind become audible. Before he dealt with the soggy birds, the youngsters had to get home, because from the way the wind was blowing, if they waited till four o'clock, old man Armstrong's wagon would have trouble navigating the narrow lane to his hilltop mansion. It was less the snow, which still wasn't deep, than the swirling wind that was the problem. At least for now.

He turned to look at Jennie Beasley, perched behind an array of lard pails. Mariah was feeding the scraps to yet another squirrel, whose cage sat on his dining table, the same table at which the Prince of Wales had once sat.

There was defiance on her face; the lady was spoiling for a fight.

"School is closed," he said simply, upstaging all her messy efforts with three neat simple words. At least the noisy cheers from the class would seem to indicate so.

"Sit down," she commanded, and for the first time he heard real authority in her schoolmarm voice. She turned on Nate. "Since when do you dismiss my class?" she asked, her voice as frosty as the windowpanes.

"When's the last time you looked out the window?"

"It's snowing," she noted idly without even looking. "But hardly a blizzard."

"Helga's gone to town and there's no sign of her coming back."

She laughed, a quick, short sound that mocked him, and refused to come look. "I've lived out west longer than you."

"By two weeks," he shot back.

"Nevertheless *I* know what blizzards are. The natives don't panic over a few snowflakes. Next I suppose you're going to claim the Vanderbilts and Astors have diamonds the size of snowballs."

"I was going to try to drive the students home myself because I don't think you should keep them here until four o'clock."

He might as well have taken on Jesse James. "You begged us to stay here one more day, Nate Denison, and we're staying, making noise, painting birds, carving up your fancy table, and spilling crumbs, and we're going to do it till four o'clock."

"Have it your way. You brought your nightwear, I hope?" He walked out, the class moaning in disappointment. Contrary woman. She was going to end up being snowed in here, and he didn't care one iota. Let's see how tough she sounded when she had to spend the entire night with him!

Her nightwear? Jennie glared at Nate as he retreated. All he ever did was toy with her. She'd made the right decision. Walking out of here today at four o'clock would be the best revenge. By then, his fancy house would be in total shambles.

As the door slid shut in her face she turned back to the class. The table was empty. Now that Nate had pulled the draperies open, Jennie was forced to look outside. Fourteen students stood with her, noses against the glass, watching nothing but whirling white patterns. Ice crusted the corners of the windows.

She guessed there was a time for pride and a time to eat crow. When fourteen children were at stake, she'd gladly dine on crow. She ran after him. "Nate, I changed my mind. I was wrong. You're right. Hurry and get your wagon."

"I thought I'd try the sleigh."

"Whatever. Just get us out of here."

Turning back to her students, she put on a professional voice. "All right," she said, clapping her hands. "Mr. Denison's kindly come to give you a ride home. Everyone into their coats and gloves." And she swished past Nate to help the little ones.

By the time they were all bundled up and she had opened

the front door, Nate and the Armstrong boys were coming in from attempting to shovel the walkway to the barn.

Snow clung to their eyelashes and eyebrows. Quickly they headed for the kitchen stove to warm up with cocoa. Too soon, it seemed, they went out to shovel again, for in the brief time they'd been indoors, enough snow had fallen to undo all their work. For over an hour the rest of the class watched and waited. And all that time the wind increased in ferocity.

At last Nate led the boys back in, stamped the snow off his feet, right there on his good hardwood floor, and then he looked at Jennie. "Sorry. We can't seem to make headway."

"What does that mean? It can't be that hard." But a sinking feeling told her exactly what it meant. Stay calm, she admonished herself. Teachers had to be calm for the students. There was still plenty of time for the wind to blow the snow on through the valley and let them go home for supper. "When do we get to leave?"

Nate pulled off his gloves and blew on his hands. His breath came ragged. "Simple. Everyone will have to wait in here for the storm to blow through. Don't worry. The worst will probably be over by dark, then we'll shovel them out and walk them home by lantern light. We'll probably meet the parents from town coming the other way."

He sounded more optimistic than he looked.

"Where's Helga?" she asked cautiously. "You're sure she didn't make it back?" This couldn't be happening.

He was shrugging out of his sheepskin coat. "Nope. Only a fool would go walking outside now. You can't see your hand in front of your face—"

"I don't believe you." It was nothing but a lie to get her alone here overnight. And to prove she knew he was up to another trick, she marched to the door, yanked it open as if she were going out to church, and walked out into the swirling white stuff.

She found her way down the steps to the ground, but then six steps later stopped, swaying dizzily. She no longer knew up from down. One more step brought her to her knees.

"Nate!" she screamed, just as strong masculine arms closed about her. As soon as he gathered her to him, she clung, arms about his neck, for dear life. He carried her back to the house, slamming the front door with his foot.

"You little fool," he said in front of all the students as he dumped her without ceremony on her rear end on the hard floor.

Rubbing snow off her face, she blinked up at all the staring students and finally at Nate, who stood, shaking off snow and glaring. "That was a stupid thing to do, Miss Beasley. You just failed basic survival."

"But town's not that far," she argued.

"If you can't go half a dozen steps without losing your way, walking to town could mean death."

She gulped.

"Do you believe me now?"

Nodding, she brushed the snow off her shoulders and sleeves then stood. All right. She could handle this. Her dignity might be bruised, but it wasn't broken.

"You mean it's just you and me?" she asked matter-of-factly.

Looking up, he raised his eyebrows meaningfully. "And fourteen youngsters, Miss Beasley. Now that you're back with us, do you have some more sedate ideas for keeping them busy?"

She looked from him to her students, who stood clustered in the hallway, faces uncertain. The littlest ones clung to the hands of older ones. Jennie might have more differences to air with Mr. Nate Denison, but this wasn't the time. She ran to the window and swiped at it, as if she could rub away the storm with the sheer force of her fist. It was freezing; the skin on her hand nearly stuck to the glass. She turned back to Nate Denison, all her earlier bravado vanished.

"It can't do this. Besides, the school wagon will come for us, and Grace's baby might come. . . ."

Nate came over and spoke softly. "Jennie Beasley, babies come when they come. You can't do anything about that, and no school wagon is coming through this—not till Mr. Armstrong muscles it through."

She looked up into compassionate blue eyes. "But some of these children have never been away from home before, and while you may think your house is a treat, they'd rather see their mothers." As a backdrop to her words, the wind howled like a ghost, shaking the glass and blowing down the chimneys and stovepipes of Denison's Folly. Outside, a pine branch slammed against the house.

Minnie began to cry, and Mariah took one of her hands, Jennie the other. "I want to go home," the six-year-old wailed.

"See, they'd rather be with their mothers," Jennie argued. "Can't you do something?"

"Money only buys so many things," Nate noted quietly, "so you and I are going to serve as substitute parents for a while."

She stared at him, grateful for his strong words, for his surprising support. The Nate Denison she thought she knew would have been laying out rules by now on which rooms the children could and couldn't enter. . . .

"Did you have anything special planned?" she asked.

"Pressing social engagements? No. I was going to read *Forest and Stream*. That can wait." He paused, and they stood listening while the howling wind moaned and the woodshed door banged shut.

"Well, what did you have planned to teach next?" he asked.

"Teach? Nate Denison, they're tired and hungry. I was hoping you'd planned to invite us to dinner."

He smiled. "I think the weather's already taken care of that. But bear with me. I've never had a dinner party for sixteen before."

She looked at him, put her trust in him. If they kept their sense of humor, this could be . . . well, if not fun, at least interesting.

Three hours later, after Nate and Jennie had fed the children Helga's stew, the kettle sat scraped bare, rose-patterned dishes stacked up in the sink. Jennie was exhausted but had a new appreciation for Nate Denison. He might be rich and a tease, but in an emergency he could actually rustle up food.

Now they all huddled in Nate's library, where he'd started a roaring fire and lit half a dozen kerosene lamps. Jennie had rounded up blankets and quilts from every bed and chair and handed them out for the little ones to lie on. She pulled aside a lace curtain to peer out, hoping to see something besides swirling snow. Would the wind never die down?

"Hey," Will Armstrong said, "maybe we'll have to spend the night!"

"Yeah!" put in Thaddeus Gordon, Jr.

"I don't want to spend the night," Susanna Vane said.

From where she'd been trying to distract Minnie Armstrong, Jennie glanced up and found Nate looking at her. A flutter of fear went through her. The night? That would never happen.

"The buffalo baby's outside," Mariah interjected, worried.

"I want to go home," Minnie said on a sniffle.

"The calf's in the barn," Nate said. "And some people consider this the finest home in town."

"It's a fancy house, Mr. Denison," Jennie explained patiently, "but that's not the same as home." She feared the little ones were getting homesick, and the gravity of the situation sank in. They might have to spend the night . . . well, she'd cross that bridge when they came to it.

An elegant black-and-gold mantel clock ticked away the

minutes and every quarter hour chimed. It was the most watched object in the room. Though they'd tried games, even vigorous games like charades drew no volunteers. Again the clock chimed.

Jennie waited while it bonged eight o'clock, then shutting the copy of *A Thousand and One Nights* she was reading, she looked at Nate. "Will *you* read them a story now?"

"Yeah," Thaddeus Jr. said with undaunted spirit. "The Headless Horseman story."

"Naw, that's old," Will Armstrong countered. "Tell us about the buffalo that are coming and who you're gonna sell their heads to." His little sister lay half-asleep across his lap and now sat up.

"No," she said.

Nate shrugged. "Another story. Something for the girls. The little ones."

"Well, I don't want 'Little Bo Peep,'" Will said in a sassy tone, as if confident there'd be no woodshed detail tonight.

Jennie looked at Nate, who shrugged again. "The only nursery rhyme I know is 'Sing a Song of Sixpence.'"

"About money. What else?" she said wryly, then quickly turned her attention to the youngsters who huddled between them.

"Then 'Hiawatha,'" she suggested quickly and passed the book full of verses over to Nate. "Everyone likes that." And as the fire burned low the older students recited the verses by memory, Jennie chiming in, trying to soothe the little ones.

> "By the shores of Gitche Gumee,
>   By the shining big sea water,
>   Stood the wigwam of Nokomis,
>   Daughter of the Moon, Nokomis."

One by one the children's voices died away as everyone forgot the words, but Nate, with the book in his lap, kept on reading. Everyone listened, rapt. Jennie kept staring across at him, at the glow of lamplight on his dark hair, the shadow of beard, the children looking up at him, trusting.

Nate finished, shut the book, and stared back at her for a long moment until she grew warm. "I had to memorize that poem for my least favorite tutor."

"No wonder you read it so nicely." She cast about for another topic of conversation, but he stood up.

"I think," he said quietly, "that it's time for bed."

CHAPTER

❧ 11 ❧

"No!"

The entire class jumped as if Nate had yelled, "Fire!"

They looked to see their teacher standing, clutching a quilt to her bosom. "It can't be bedtime. Not yet."

The idea of Jennie Beasley going to bed under the same roof as Nate Denison was as inconceivable as thinking buffalo would return to roam by the millions.

Pure fantasy on his part.

"We're not going to bed yet." The words were out before she realized.

His smile was a mere indulgence as he stood and pointed to the ornate clock. "It's nearly nine. You put your charges through a hard day constructing papier-mâché birds, Miss Beasley."

158

She glared. "Yes, but we don't want to disturb your house any further. We'll bundle up right here." Even thinking of the bedrooms upstairs was out of the question. She simply wouldn't sleep tonight. "I'd just as soon listen to stories all night," she said as brightly as possible.

"The children can't sit up all night, Jennie. They'll fall asleep in their tracks."

"All you're worried about is whether they might knock over one of your precious antiques." She stared pointedly at the étagère filled with bric-a-brac. If sold, the profit would probably feed these youngsters for a month.

"And all you're worried about is spending the night here— with me."

"Children are listening, Mr. Denison."

"I know, and I wish you would too. The situation's changed, Jennie, obviously, and while I prefer order, I can be flexible in a pinch."

This was more than a pinch they were caught in. It was a trap with teeth the size of a giant grizzly's. And this house— why, it was like being swallowed by a whale.

"Their parents might arrive anytime to take them home," she reasoned with hope. Anything to kill this notion of bed.

Nate gave her another indulgent smile and simply shook his head. "The wind's still blowing."

"How do you know so much about storms out here in Montana?"

"I may be new in town, but I'm not as green as everyone thinks. I came here as a boy."

"You did?" Will, who'd been staring at the mechanical bird cage in boredom, turned with renewed interest.

"My uncle, the only member of my family who showed an iota of interest in me, brought me out on the train."

"When?"

"Oh, twenty years ago. When there were so many buffalo,

the trains would stop for them. That's all I remember. That and the wonderland of Yellowstone. It was no accident I came back here to build my house. I was here long before any of you came, you see, and the place holds older memories for me than for your teacher even."

"Do you think there were ever dinosaurs out here?" Will asked.

"Silly," Mariah scolded. "There weren't trains then, so who cares?"

"I care," Jennie said.

"Why?" Nate looked bemused.

"I'm curious. Is there anything wrong with intellectual curiosity?"

"No. It's just that most women, I've found, prefer the stimulus of money. That's why you baffle me. Don't you have any feminine guile?"

"Pardon me for growing up in a more humble place than you. St. Louis made me practical."

During this exchange the children's heads swiveled back and forth, as if they found the debate vastly amusing.

Noticing this, Jennie used it to her advantage. With a sweep of her hand, she gestured to them, their sleepy faces shadowed by the light of kerosene lanterns and one overhead gas fixture. "The storm's got the youngsters far too wound up. They don't look a bit tired to me."

"They do to me and you do too."

"That's your imagination." Hastily she tucked back a strand of hair and, determined to stay awake, stifled a yawn. "We need one more story. It's Mr. Denison's turn."

Fourteen pairs of sleepy eyes turned on Nate Denison, who stood staring with intense interest at their teacher. Jennie, for the first time in her life, was suddenly ashamed of her rumpled skirt, her demure bun of copper-penny hair. And never had she been more aware of Nate Denison's rugged good looks, his own rumpled shirt sleeves, his tousled brown hair, and knowing blue eyes, which gleamed as he looked around at the children. "Class, your teacher's requested a bedtime story. Can you stay awake while we tell her one?"

"Yeah!" went up a chorus of voices.

Suddenly Nate pinned his gorgeous blue eyes on Jennie. "More importantly can the teacher stay awake?"

"For a man with fussy rules, you certainly have turned into a wonderfully maternal substitute."

"My own parents were often touring the world as I was growing up, so I know how it feels to miss your parents."

"You were going to tell us a story?" she reminded him.

"Ah, yes, the teacher's bedtime story. As soon as I'm done, I've an idea about sleeping arrangements."

"Take your time," she muttered, collapsing into an overstuffed red velvet creation that looked as if it belonged in some Fifth Avenue matron's house. Beside her on a walnut table a mechanical bird sat in a gilded cage and beside it sat a velvet album. Such a fussy house. Such a fussy man. And now he was playing nanny to fourteen kids while she dropped from exhaustion.

How dare he cope with this disaster better than she did? How dare he?

Nevertheless it felt good to sit, and she leaned against a pleated satin cushion and tried not to imagine the feel of Nate Denison's arms about her. So tired. Little Minnie Armstrong sniffled and climbed up to nestle next to Jennie.

"So why did you buy those buffalo? To shoot them and sell their heads?" Will Armstrong possessed the hope of adolescents who thrive on horror stories.

"At first that's what I thought," Nate acknowledged easily, settling into a chair by the mantel clock. "Now I'm not so sure. I'm thinking it over. Do you have any advice?"

Will puffed up. "I know all about animals."

"What about storms? Your teacher needs reassurance."

"That's easy. As storms go, this is a dude. A pipsqueak."

"Indeed?"

"Yeah, you weren't here five years ago when the cattle all died out in the blizzards. I spent the night at the schoolhouse that year too," Will said with feigned nonchalance, as if this experience were commonplace. "And the class all slept on the hard floor with nothing to eat but scraps from the lard pails or else chalk, and no one could leave, especially when the train robber tried to break in our window. His beard was all crusted with ice and—"

"Will," Nate interrupted, "you have a brilliant imagination, but let's not scare the little ones."

Will, grimacing, stretched out on the floor and sighed. "I could have stayed home today," he muttered. "I should have."

"You wanted to know about the buffalo," Nate said. "The buffalo out in Yellowstone—and mine, wherever they are— will do fine. They have natural herding instincts and bunch close together in storms. The calves and mothers bunch in the center and the bulls face out, taking the brunt of the storm."

"What's in-stink?" asked Gunnar Slocum, who defied his exhaustion by sitting up Indian style, attention fixed on Nate.

"Instinct," Jennie said, rousing herself. "I-N . . . we'll discuss it tomorrow, but it means something done naturally, because it's a built-in reaction. Mother Nature's way of ensuring they keep warm."

"Like we're doing," put in Nate, watching as Jennie drew a crazy quilt over Minnie.

She looked up sharply. "What are we doing?"

"Keeping warm," he said calmly, smiling.

"Yes, of course." Nate was a big man, his shadow on the wall even larger, and there was comfort in that. As the clock bonged the half hour his gaze never left Jennie.

"Your story for the teacher, Mr. Denison," she said tiredly. Like a child on Christmas Eve, she was determined not to give in to sleep.

He stared over the heads of the youngsters directly at Jennie. "Once upon a time there was a beautiful but spoiled young lady from New York," he began.

Jennie blinked. Had she heard right?

"And she was very, very rich and turned the heads of all the gentlemen in New York, especially one young man, who had led a lonely life. . . ."

The youngsters were drooped around the furniture, half-asleep, but Jennie was now wide-awake, caught in the spell of Nate's intense blue gaze. This was his own story he was telling her. For whatever reasons, he wanted very much to explain away the woman in his past, the woman for whom he'd built this elegant mansion. Oh, she was wide-awake now.

"There were several beautiful sisters and an ambitious mama, anxious for her daughters to make successful matches. Not for love—"

"Were they princesses?" Bertha Jensen, entranced, asked.

"They had everything except for a title. A tiny kingdom in a faraway place called New York that had a magic password to its doors—money. Only the people with the most money could enter, and the older the money, the better."

"Is that why some money is wrinkled?" Mariah asked.

"Yeah," Will said, impatient. "Let's go to sleep."

"What about the beautiful ladies?" Bertha asked.

"Well, they got bored with money, or rather their mamas did, and so they sought out men who could make them princesses or duchesses or countesses."

"Did they find them?" Bertha leaned forward, thrilled that a man could tell a real fairy story.

"One young lady I knew did. She married a man in need of money, and he traded her the title of duchess and she moved to a new kingdom in England and they lived happily ever after."

"Why did the man want her money?"

"To pay for all his servants and for his fancy house."

"Like this one?"

"Much, much fancier. This would be the servants' quarters for a duchess like Daisy."

Daisy. Of course. Jennie drew a finger along a broken thread of the quilt, then abruptly looked up to find him looking at her, eyes pain-filled, voice more vulnerable sounding than she'd ever heard it.

"But why?" Bertha asked.

"Did they have horses and dogs in her new house?" Mariah asked sleepily.

"Undoubtedly."

"Then it's all right."

He gave a half smile. "Now it *is* time for bed," he said, and stood. "And I need you youngsters to reassure the teacher that she'll be safe in Denison's Folly."

Denison's Folly. Lots of men lived through rejection, but few were left with a monstrous house as a humiliating reminder. Now she saw how cruel the town was in dubbing this place his folly. His folly had been in building this for a fickle woman. Sleepy as she was, Jennie yearned to touch Nate, to reassure him he could trust her as a friend, no matter what her family thought. But trust of women was probably a coin in which he'd rarely dealt.

Now, ironically, she'd be trusting him with sleeping arrangements. "What did you have in mind?" she asked softly.

He looked around the drooping children, as if counting. "Eight boys and six girls," he said matter-of-factly. "Almost even. The boys and I will sleep downstairs. You take the girls upstairs to my room. It's the only one made up. . . . Take some lamps with you, and go first. When you're settled, the boys and I will take what blankets are left."

"Organized and precise, even in a bedtime crisis?"

"It's what I've handled best in my life—one crisis after another—at all hours of the day."

To Jennie, no crisis, not even the school fire, matched this moment of walking up the stairs of Mr. Nate Denison's house. Kerosene lamp in hand and little Minnie clutching her skirt, she headed up the curved staircase of Denison's Folly for her first look at the bedroom of Nate Denison.

At the first room she pushed open the door and held up the kerosene lamp to light the interior. Dark masculine decor verified that this was Nate's private room. She ventured inside, the lamp lighting her way. The room smelled of the same soap mingled with bay rum that she'd come to associate with Nate. It was going to be impossible to sleep here. She'd give it to the girls.

Meanwhile, as she waited for them to straggle up, she skirted the room, looking at the rich furnishings, touching the armoire, the marble-topped washstand, a vintage Civil War trunk. She paused before a settee near the windows. The dark green draperies were closed, but outside the wailing wind still rattled the panes.

At last she turned and warily faced the inevitable—Nate Denison's bed. Even from where she stood, it looked like a great beast, oversized like the man. The high carved headboard of dark wood filled the wall, and the plain quilt was piled with pillows, all snowy white. The whole thing resembled nothing so much as a hulking buffalo standing ankle-deep in snow.

The lamp flickered and her heart with it. She tried to imagine Nate Denison asleep beneath that gargantuan headboard.

Inching closer, the scent of his tonic became stronger, and at last she was close enough to touch a pillow. Just a tentative touch.

"Miss Beasley?"

Jumping, she pulled back her hand and turned. "This way, girls." She'd never been so glad to see Susanna and Bertha and Mariah. Especially Mariah. "You're here. I—I was just turning down the bed. Can three of you share this?" She flitted about the room. "And here's a nice settee that ought to fit Minnie just right. We'll make a bed on the rug for Annabelle and Hannah. There're extra quilts in the armoire, I think."

"Where are you going to sleep, Miss Beasley?" Bertha asked from the fancy marble washstand whose compartments she was opening and shutting, as if taking inventory for her mother.

"Me?" Think, Jennie. Bertha's mother and Susanna's as well would prod their daughters for every last detail about the sleeping arrangements, and of particular interest would be Mr. Nate Denison's bedroom. There had to be no hint of impropriety. No one would call this a compromising situation; blizzards hardly ranked in that category, but Jennie would have to be careful. The children were her only chaperons.

"Let me think," she said, circling in place as the children got settled. "Well, I'll just lie down here near Annabelle at the foot of the bed and use my coat for an extra blanket. I'll be fine. I'm so tired nothing could keep me awake."

"Do you want a pillow?" Mariah asked. "Mr. Denison's got lots of pillows—all with crocheted borders. Wanna see?"

She gulped. "Yes, thanks."

Mariah tossed one to her just as she leaned over to blow out the lamp she'd set beside the child. It was one of Nate Denison's own white muslin-clad pillows, and the scent of bay rum assaulted her senses. Outside, the wind wailed.

"It's fancier than home, isn't it, Aunt Jennie?" Mariah whispered with a trace of awe in her voice. "Wait till I tell Ma about the pillowcases. Store-bought, not homemade, right? Everything."

"It smells like Paris, France," Bertha said.

"How do you know what Paris smells like?" Susanna asked.

"Because of its gowns. Ma says all the fancy gowns come from Paris. She says expensive gowns have a different smell."

"Yes, Bertha, everything smells very fancy." Jennie was tired, cold, cranky. And yet her pulse, like a traitor, was thumping at a blissful pace.

"Mr. Denison's bed is very large," Mariah said. "Are you absolutely sure you want to sleep on the floor? If we curled up our legs, we could squeeze you in at the bottom."

"I'll sleep better here." She settled down on the floor near Annabelle Armstrong.

"You're sure?"

"Positive." Her back was against the hard wood of the bedstead and already the floor hurt. "I'm dead to the world."

An hour later, imagination and memories of Nate Denison's kiss very much alive, Jennie lay there, listening to the girls' sigh in their sleep. During the past hour the wind had finally died down, so that she could hear the girls' gentle breathing. Rolling over, she punched the pillow. She could no longer blame her sleeplessness on the storm. Where in this house, she wondered, was Nate Denison sleeping?

Visions of him standing outside the dining room in nothing but a silk dressing gown counteracted her exhaustion. Of course, tonight it was far too cold for any of them to undress; they'd bundled together in their clothes. Was that the case with Mr. Denison? Was he sleeping in his denim pants and woolen shirt? Well, it didn't matter, because first thing in the morning she was going to round up the students and leave here forever, even if she had to shovel herself out. She sat up. Come to think of it, now that the wind had died down, there was no reason she couldn't start getting ready now.

In the parlor Nate, sheepskin coat thrown over himself for a blanket, stretched out on the velvet settee. He stared at the darkened ceiling, the only pristine object left in his once precisely ordered house. Will Armstrong rolled onto his back and began to snore. The quieting of the wind had not helped Nate fall asleep. His bones ached because he'd given his bed to the females. . . . His house by daylight would look like the blizzard had gone in one door and out the other, thanks to Miss Jennie Beasley and her students. . . . His clothes were rumpled, but he couldn't change because his bedroom was occupied by Jennie. . . . Helga was going to catch hell for going off to a prayer meeting two hours before a storm struck. . . . His own housekeeper was probably bunking with the widow Jensen and laughing at the thought of her dude boss caught up here with all these school kids and with . . . Jennie.

Somewhere upstairs the prim and sassy schoolmarm slept. Try as he might to think other thoughts, his mind stalked back to that one stark fact. He could almost see that copper-penny hair flowing out over a pillow and longed to touch it, to touch her, to pull her once again into his arms so he could look down into those trusting eyes. He envied her that trust, wanted to touch her in the foolish hope that some of her trust might rub off on him. He certainly couldn't buy it. Or sleep.

Five minutes later he lit the lamp and was soaping his face. Shaving was as good a way as any to pass the time. He'd just lifted the razor when he heard the stairs creak. He listened a minute, but heard nothing more, so again he lifted the razor. . . .

Jennie was certain Helga kept a shovel in the kitchen of this house, if only she could navigate in the dark. She tiptoed down the stairs, until she heard a sound from downstairs. Then she stood stock-still, listening.

At last she identified the noise. It was a snore. One of the boys was snoring, perhaps even Nate Denison. Dead to the world. By the time Nate woke up, she'd probably have all the youngsters out of here.

Stealthily she continued down the darkened staircase and at the bottom of the stairs turned left and headed down the hall, past the bathroom, on her way to the kitchen, where she fumbled in the dark, found the shovel exactly where she'd remembered, and headed back up the hall.

The next thing she knew she'd run smack into Nate Denison's arms. She backed against the wall.

"What are you doing down here?" he whispered.

"What are you doing out here?"

"You answer first."

"I—I came for this." His arms were warm about her, and he didn't show the least inclination to let her go, but he did feel his way down her arm till he could ascertain what she was holding.

"A shovel? To protect yourself—or were you going to dig your way home at this hour?"

"I—I couldn't sleep, so I thought I'd round up the shovel."

"What do I have to do to persuade you to wait till dawn, when the shovel will have a fighting chance against the snow?"

"Nothing decent comes to mind, Mr. Denison."

"Funny you should mention it first, but I've been awake, having the most indecent thoughts." He wrenched the shovel from her hands and tossed it aside with a clatter.

She was enveloped in bay rum and the smell of soap. More pungent even than the scent that had been torturing her on the pillow. This, of course, was the real man, and by the sliver of light from the open bathroom door, she could barely see him.

"Your beard is white."

"I was shaving."

"In the middle of the night?"

"It was the only decent thing I could think of to pass the time."

"It seems we're both having trouble sleeping." She paused, then rushed on. "The wind was noisy."

"That's not why, Jennie."

"Oh? Were you uncomfortable, then?"

"Yes." The word was shaded with some primitive longing. "I was damn uncomfortable lying there with instinctive needs I can't do anything about."

"Oh? I'm not sure I understand."

"Instinct, Jennie . . . the reason a man's pulse beats out of control. I believe you said something about teaching the youngsters the meaning of instinct. . . . I-N-S-T-I-N-C-T. Are you sure you can give the lesson?"

She yearned to touch him. "Stop!" She clamped her hands over her ears.

He pulled them down, held her wrists. "The dictionary gives genteel definitions suitable for schoolmarms with tender wards, but the word has another meaning."

Gulping, she wrestled away from him. "You can't run away from it, Jennie."

"From what?"

It was dark, but he found her, touched her hand, then her arm, then moved his hand up her body until he framed her face. "This kind of yearning. Do you need it illustrated any further? Man and woman are in the grip of their instinctive nature when they feel this way." He was tracing the contours of her face in the dark.

Her entire body ached to wrap itself around his. "Please, Nate," she whispered, hoarse.

But then she was in his arms anyway, almost as if her body had acted of its own volition. Instinctive.

She could feel the buttons of his shirt against her cheek, he held her so tight.

"Your hair is pretty hanging down your back," he murmured, stroking it.

"You can't see it."

"My imagination works fine in the dark." He bent to kiss her. Her lips parted, and she got a mouthful of soap. One second later she wrenched free and fled into the fanciest bathroom in Castlerock and stood there at the sink, pouring cold water into her shaking hand and drinking it. Beside her, the claw-foot tub looked inviting. If need be, she could spend the rest of the night here.

"Aunt Jennie," came a childish voice from somewhere outside the door. "Aunt Jennie, I heard a crash."

Drat it all. Pushing back her hair, she cautiously leaned out.

"Mariah?" she called softly. "Don't worry. I dropped something."

Nate Denison was lounging against the hallway wall, waiting, and now he pulled Jennie back into his arms. She melted into his warmth as his hands came up to frame her face while he kissed her in strategic places, all calculated, it seemed, to make her moan.

"Are you all right, Aunt Jennie?" Mariah's voice came at length. "You're not having a bad dream?"

"Tell her to go back to bed," he whispered.

"Go back to bed, Mariah," she said in a stage whisper. "I'll be right up." Where was her anger from this morning, her resolve? Then Nate was kissing her again, and her arms came up around his back while his hands slid up her shirtwaist, tangled in her hair.

"This is indecent, Nate. There are fourteen children in this house."

"I told you not to hold school today, but no, you had to stay."

Backing away from him, she fumbled in the dark for her

shovel. Grabbing it by the handle, she stuck it out like a shield. "Nate, no more. Please . . . I'm the teacher. I have an image to maintain. Don't you understand?"

Nate stood looking at her back away from him, her hair loose about her shoulders, her mouth swollen from the past few moments of passion stolen outside a darkened bathroom in a cold house. Oh, it didn't matter if it was a fire or a blizzard; the schoolmarm, if angered properly, was a woman of great passion. And Nate wanted more. So far he'd earned low marks for his efforts: a bucket of water over his head, angry words, and now a shovel in his stomach.

"Dammit, Jennie, then go back upstairs and stay there!"

She ran through the dark, stumbled her way to the first stairstep. He stalked her as far as the newel post.

"Instinct," he said, and laughed softly. "Instinct about men and women, Jennie. Rich or poor, east or west . . . instincts are the same, and it doesn't take a university degree to figure them out."

"Please, the children are listening." She felt wanton, full of strange yearnings.

All she could do was aim the shovel at him, to hold him at bay.

Mostly because she wasn't sure of what she'd do herself. She'd never given in to instinct before, and it frightened her. Her body wanted different things from her mind. Craved Nate's touch. For the first time she knew what it was to lack trust in her own self-control and that scared her.

"Stay away from me, then." Now it was his words that caressed the darkness . . . and almost pulled her back into his arms. She clutched the shovel tighter and ran upstairs to tuck Mariah into Nate Denison's very own bed.

"Aunt Jennie?" Mariah whispered sleepily.

"Yes?" Jennie's voice was still husky with desire.

"Aunt Jennie, you've got soapsuds on your face." A childish

finger came out to touch her cheek.

Hastily Jennie wiped away the telltale traces of Nate Denison's kiss. "So I do. Good night, dear."

It was not a good night. For she could wipe away soap all she wanted, but there was nothing she could do to wipe away the memory of that kiss in the darkness.

The teacher in her yearned to continue the lessons, and wouldn't Nate Denison laugh to know that!

CHAPTER

❦12❧

A grating sound awoke Nate. The sound of wine delivery on a New York morning? No. The sound of maids cleaning out the grates? No. The sound of some bored matron shredding her Paris gown because Nate had ended the affair? No.

Where the heck was he now?

Vaguely he remembered a blinding November snowstorm, and then in a flash it all came back. Montana. Buffalo. Box suppers. School . . . ah, yes, schoolchildren. Fourteen of them, ranging in age from thumb sucker to wise mouth. And a sassy copper-haired schoolmarm marooned in his house in a snowstorm. What had possessed him to move out here on his birthday last August? Daisy walking down the aisle with another man, a chinless duke? A sense of mortality? A man could die with a lot less trouble than what he'd endured in the past twenty-four hours. Or the past few weeks. He hadn't had a decent night's sleep since Jennie had come here.

He stretched out, groaning. Velvet settees were not ideal camping equipment. Eight boys still snored amid the doilies and bric-a-brac of his walnut tables. He dangled his legs over the edge of the sofa and got up. Fumbling over the sleeping boys, he held the lamp up to the clock. A little past seven in the morning.

On the mantel the clock ticked away. Soft and steady. So what was making the grating noise? His fuzzy brain slowly focused on the rasp of metal against wood. It sounded like a railroad crew digging—like a shovel. Sleepy still, he listened, suspicious, then picked his way across the sleeping boys and headed for the front door.

Jennie Beasley had walked upstairs with a shovel last night. Had probably slept with the darn thing.

And he had absolutely no doubt that the noise was coming from his porch. It was not a deliveryman, a maid, or a paramour.

He staggered to the door, pulling on his favorite sheepskin jacket on the way. When he flung the door open, snow blew onto his elegant hallway floor. Dawn was just breaking over the white landscape. But there, just as he'd guessed, was the source of the noise: Jennie Beasley pushing snow off the porch, like a one-woman rescue crew. She turned guiltily and paused, leaning against the shovel as if out of breath.

"Did I wake you?"

He swallowed back the yawn that threatened while picking and choosing among the responses to her question. If his words were cryptic, that's how he felt this morning. "Wake me? Hardly . . . I was just returning from a society ball."

Slowly she stood up and placed both hands on the shovel handle. "I do not find it appropriate to joke at a time like this."

"You know, before I met you, you used to wake me up with that ding-dong school bell every morning."

"In bed at nine o'clock in the morning? How shocking of you. A life of late nights and late mornings is a sure sign of indolence, Mr. Denison." Bending to her task, she scooped another shovelful of snow off his veranda. The shovel grated against wood and ice. "Why don't you close the door and keep the cold outside," she said while shoveling. "Coal isn't cheap these days."

The furnace wasn't lit yet, but he had more pressing worries than his freezing toes.

"I'm less worried about the cost of coal and more worried about the town matrons."

"They won't take a shotgun to us. We've had fourteen chaperons."

"What makes you so sure they'll count children?" Ingrid Jensen could be formidable in her censure, he suspected.

With a sigh, she stood up and looked at him.

He stared at her, at the ridiculous picture she made in that homely stocking hat. She was all red-cheeked and sniffling from the cold, and every time she brought down the shovel, she hit ice.

"I'll tell you why you don't have to worry about a shotgun, Nate. Ingrid Jensen and her likes would be entirely too worried about how far apart we are in social standing. Out west, it's not supposed to matter, but people like Ingrid still keep track of such things."

"Who have they got in mind for you—Karl, the loyal carpenter who's slaving over your new school?"

"I already made it perfectly clear that I'm not going to marry at all. I'm going to a university to gain a degree. But first I have to get out of your mansion, so either help me shovel, Nate, or go away. I want my class out of here and back to their families, and I'm not wasting time."

With an easy gesture, he pulled the shovel from her and watched it clatter down the stairs and land silently in a snow-drift. "What do I have to do to persuade you to wait till the sun rises higher?"

She strained against the cold wool of his coat.

"Nothing decent comes to mind, Nate Denison." Only instinct.

He dragged her inside to the hallway and with one good kick shoved the door shut. Then he reached for her silly little knit hat. She made a grab for it, but he was too quick for her and watched in satisfaction as copper waves spilled down about her shoulders. She ran a mittened hand across her nose and sniffled.

"I want to go home," she said. "My sister is having—"

"—a baby . . . and the dog has just had pups." He'd heard it all the night before. "You don't think we've been forgotten, do you? Heck, Miss Jennie Beasley, there's probably an army of parents shoveling Moose and Camas streets by now. Why, give them an hour, and they'll have a wagon and team hitched and have cleaned away snow clear to my entrance to rescue you. At least I hope so."

"And if they don't?"

"You hold school."

"It's Saturday."

"Hold school anyway. I'm not having fourteen kids running around my house."

"Why not just have them help shovel out?"

"Because I don't own sixteen shovels, that's why not."

"Could we finish this discussion in the kitchen, where there's a stove and coffee? Maybe after everyone's up and eaten, we can figure out how to dig them out and protect our reputations both." She grinned over her shoulder as she untied her cape. "I do believe you're afraid of being left alone in the house with all those children. They might wake up and want food.

Then what are you going to do?"

Shrugging, he knew she'd called his bluff. "Nothing, Miss Beasley. Helga's stew is gone, and I can't cook."

"We're not expecting caviar and salmon. Just something to fill their bellies till they get home. Oatmeal will do," she said as she hung up her cape to thaw.

"Oatmeal?" Not even Helga had been able to coerce him into trying a spoonful of the mushy stuff, but he knew from the boxes and boxes of it lining the mercantile shelves that it was held in high esteem by the people of Castlerock.

"Don't tell me you haven't got any. How can any house with Tiffany light fixtures lack oatmeal?" She marched down the hall to the kitchen just the way Helga did.

Sassy female. He'd met his share, but they could all be bought off with gifts of jewelry or flowers or bonbons. This one wanted . . . a university degree . . . and oatmeal.

He headed for the basement. The first order of business was to start every source of heat in the house and then . . . since Helga had been stranded in town, he'd have to brew his own coffee. He frowned, wondering where the woman kept the coffeepot, or if he dare ask Jennie to . . . No.

Running a hand over the stubble on his chin, he recalled the feel of Miss Jennie Beasley, soft and pliable in his arms in the dark. Because of her, he'd never finished shaving. But that would have to wait. He ran a comb through his hair, winced at the sight of his rumpled shirt, and after pulling on socks as protection from the icy floor, he headed to the basement. Soon, soon . . . his house would empty of all these youngsters, and he'd have the place to himself again. But that meant Jennie would be gone too.

Reluctantly he sought out Jennie in the kitchen, and when he found her, she was holding aloft a box of oatmeal, triumph in her face. "You have some."

He looked askance at the cardboard container of oatmeal.

Her smile widened. "You not only can't fix wagon wheels, but you don't know how to make oatmeal either, do you?"

"Helga does the cooking," he muttered defensively. He almost apologized then stopped himself. Nate Denison never apologized to women. He hadn't apologized to Daisy and . . . she'd run off and married a duke.

By now, sleepy-headed children were shuffling down the stairs, rubbing their eyes, lining up at the bathroom, worst of all, pressing their runny noses against his windows, staring out at the winter wonderland.

He surveyed the parlor and came back to the kitchen, where Jennie Beasley was stirring an enormous kettle of oatmeal. "They're awake." There was an edge of panic to his voice.

"If you're in such an all-fired hurry to get rid of us, perhaps you'll help shovel while I feed them."

He did. The sky helped by shining blue and blessedly clear, and less than an hour later the veranda was shoveled, and the schoolchildren of Castlerock were seated around Nate's antique walnut table—the same table at which the Prince of Wales had once eaten—devouring oatmeal with brown sugar and pats of butter. Their teacher, who managed to look prim and pretty, sat at one end, and Nate sat at the other, presiding. They looked like one very big, happy, albeit rumpled family . . . and Nate felt at peace for the first time in ages. Not even the gluey papier-mâché birds staring down from his oaken sideboard could destroy his relief that everyone was seated. Order temporarily reigned.

And Will Armstrong and his brother actually asked if he wanted help at the woodshed. "You know, earn some credit for being good," Will said in a sassy tone.

Jennie smiled at Nate and leaned her chin on her palm. "Is this why the Armstrongs have behaved lately? You've been bribing them behind my back."

He shrugged. "Threatening them is the more accurate word.

Behave for the teacher or they chop wood. But since you're moving out, you wouldn't care about that now. Would you?"

She looked down at her lap. "I may have spoken in haste."

"You mean, you'll be back Monday?"

With a sigh, she looked up at him and then got up to help Mariah and Susanna collect bowls. "I think we'll decide after we see how the new school's coming."

An hour later a dozen strong men—all fathers of the children—dug their way up to the Denison mansion, swept in like looters, and took their children and teacher home.

Nate watched them go.

Alone at last.

His mansion was silent. Peaceful. Too peaceful. Too alone. He'd been too alone for a long time now, he realized, not that he'd go around admitting that to anyone.

In the back of the house, Helga, who'd returned with the parents, was rattling pans, making breakfast.

Helga handed him a steaming mug of coffee. "Well," she said brightly. "This will be good for catching poachers. With snow there's footprints."

Inwardly he moaned. That's why Miss Jennie Beasley was so angry at him . . . because the cavalry had had the audacity to question her brother-in-law. And because the bigmouthed cavalrymen had misled her about his motives in letting her use his dining room for school.

She just vanished down that snowy road to town, and all of a sudden the house, for the first time in twenty-four hours, seemed too quiet.

Helga noticed too. "You're quiet, Mr. Denison. Don't you agree snow is good for catching poachers?"

"You're right," he agreed, "with this kind of snowfall, the cavalry's got a better chance of finding a culprit," and headed to the outbuilding where his buffalo calf was quartered with the milk cow. He didn't care who the latest poacher was. He'd only offered to help Hirum and Orvil because it amused him to do so. A speculator had no business with moral principles . . . and after Daisy, he didn't care. But now that he thought on it, he hoped whoever was poaching was not Jennie's brother-in-law. Let it be anyone but a member of her family.

But it wasn't the poacher that consumed his thoughts all the rest of that day. Or his long-delayed herd of buffalo.

It was the schoolmarm with the copper-penny hair.

Would she come back here to teach? Or vanish from his life forever?

Home again, Mariah was jubilant, and kneeling to the floor in back of the stove, she flicked back her dark hair from her eyes and reached for the littlest pup, the coal-black one. The runt.

"Oh, Paddy," she gently chastised the mother, "why haven't you been feeding your runt?" Cradling the pup, Mariah nuzzled it. Between the pups and the baby sister born the night of the storm, the house felt like it was overflowing.

She'd given a cursory look at the baby. Her mother cradled her, fed her at her breast, and said, "Mariah, she's got a dimple in her chin and dark hair. I think she's going to look like you."

"Me?"

"Isn't that nice? You've always complained because the boys all had golden hair. Now you'll have a dark-haired sister. It's fitting," her mother teased tiredly.

Ma must still be feeling poorly from the birth. That bald, squalling infant named Pearl commanded entirely too much attention from everyone, including Aunt Jennie, to ever be a candidate for the title of runt.

Which left the runt pup to take over the role from Mariah. Oh, but Mariah would love to take the runt of this litter and love it to death, make up for all the slights she'd ever felt. Already she loved it. It licked her hand and squealed, and she rubbed her cheek against its fur. As her baby sister's cries drifted out from the bedroom and everyone—absolutely everyone in the house—rushed to see her, Mariah stayed with the black pup.

"You want to eat, pup?" She dipped a rag into a saucer of milk and squeezed nourishment into the animal.

Pa came into the kitchen and stoked down the fire for the night.

"Hey, runt," he said, as he always did, now adding, "Put that pup down."

"She's cold."

"I know. Put her down anyway."

Why did Pa have to spoil everything? Her spirits sank.

Somewhere above her, the iron lid on the stove clattered into place. Pa's voice was stern. "A girl like you ought to be here helping your mother." Nothing had changed. That's all Pa thought children were good for—work, work, work. When she grew up, she was going to be like Aunt Jennie and never marry. She was going to have a whole farm full of dogs and horses and cows and pigs . . . and every animal that no one wanted.

"You've spent more time with that dude than with your own family."

"Pa! We were snowed in."

"I don't mean that. That was a blessing, once I convinced your ma Jennie would have things under control up at that mansion. Made it easier when the baby came—just Ma and me here and Mrs. Vane midwifing. Still, now that you've got a baby sister, you've got to put aside all this animal nonsense. No more riding around to see Mr. Denison's buffalo calf. Soon enough it'll be grown and contrary. It's not a pet."

Quickly she stood. This time she was going to answer her Pa back. "I never helped him . . . well, except to give him a list of names for the buffalo. But they're not even here yet, and when

I mentioned names, he laughed at first and said buffalo didn't need names."

"That's the first bit of sense I've heard coming from that dude."

"He's not a dude. The night of the storm he told us stories. He's been here before . . . when he was a boy."

Thaddeus Gordon looked down at his daughter and frowned, the way he so often did. He smiled at the others, but her he frowned at. What was wrong with her? But of course she knew without asking. She was the runt. The odd one. Maybe she didn't even belong—really.

"That man needs a wife to sweet-talk, instead of meat on the hoof."

"He likes animals." What was wrong with that? Mariah liked animals. If Pa didn't like people who liked animals, then how could he love her?

"He likes selling them. He wouldn't care if they went to a zoo or ended up as a head mounted on someone's wall. Just so he takes a profit. I don't see eye to eye with the man. It's got to do with his money and his excessive way of living. Rich people think different, runt."

Call me Mariah, she wanted to scream. Stop calling me runt.

Pa was making no more sense than Ma. He must be tired from the new baby crying so much last night, because as far as Mariah could tell, she and Mr. Nate Denison had lots in common—especially their fondness for animals, and money never got in the way of that.

There'd be no explaining that to Pa, though. "No child of mine makes pets of buffalo . . . or . . ." His gaze fell on the black puppy she cradled. "Or runt puppies, for that matter. Give him back to his mother."

"Thaddeus," Mariah's mother called from the bedroom. "Come along and don't carry on so." Then the baby whimpered.

"I'm coming, Grace," he called. Turning back to his daughter, he added, "Here I am, runt, with another mouth to feed, and less money than ever. You get busy and help now."

A while later, when her tears had turned to sniffles, Mariah climbed into bed beside Aunt Jennie. "Pa's a grouch. I wish those cavalrymen had never come here."

"Times are hard for lots of people. Your pa's tired. Baby Pearl's had him up late. It'll be all right."

"You know what else I wish?"

Aunt Jennie didn't ask. Mariah told her anyway.

"I wish we were spending the night again at Nate Denison's house. It was nice there, and he didn't yell like Pa."

When Aunt Jennie didn't reply, Mariah said, "Well, haven't you ever wished that you could stay in that nice fancy house instead of here with all us Gordons?"

"No, Mariah, my place is here."

Mariah didn't think she sounded sure.

By Monday afternoon, Jennie was ready to scream from frustration. How had she gotten assigned the job of tracking the eggs brought in for trade? Staring down at the baskets of brown eggs, she decided the storm certainly had done nothing to slow down the chickens.

Or the town gossips, who trekked to the Gordon house to offer congratulations on Grace's newborn girl, and then crossed the lot to sit at the stove a spell trading recipes for both roasting duck and squash bread. School, of course, was canceled because of the roads, and outside, the children continued to shovel the boardwalks. Too soon, talk of everything but recipes petered out. Mrs. Vane and Ingrid Jensen, spectacles perched on her nose, sat there like prunes stewing over the lack of news when a town was snowed in.

Once again, Jennie, who was helping in the mercantile while Thaddeus Gordon met with the banker on mysterious business, hoped she'd go unnoticed. Better yet, she wished her brother-in-law hadn't picked today to vanish. Jennie would much rather be at the house, helping Grace hold the baby.

Sweet thing. Jennie never expected to have any of her own, but the few times she'd held Grace's babe, a twinge of something maternal had swept over her.

On the ladies talked about corn bread and onions and sage, but Jennie knew Mrs. Vane and Ingrid Jensen would not be satisfied till they had their measure of gossip as well.

"Susanna says she got to sleep in a real bed at Denison's mansion the night of the storm. A bed with a headboard."

Looking up, Jennie saw them both watching her.

She shrugged. "I slept on the floor." She hated snow, hated gossips, and most of all hated Nate Denison. But for the first time she allowed as how when he'd tried to kiss her in the dark, she might have liked it. But if he was only kissing her to tease . . . or to keep her from moving the students so he could get information out of them, like Orvil implied . . . well, that hurt. She swallowed a lump in her throat and put on a smile for the sake of the Castlerock ladies.

Ingrid Jensen had been hemming a pillowcase, but now looked up. "You mustn't worry, you know, about what your other suitors will think."

"What other suitors?" Jennie must have looked as baffled as she felt.

"Karl and Edgar—the young banker. They're next in line to marry the schoolmarm, of course. Naturally, sharing a house overnight with Nate Denison was slightly out of order. . . ."

"But of course the storm made it unavoidable," Jennie said.

"Naturally," Mrs. Vane hastened to say. "Everyone knows a man like Nate Denison would never make improper advances to a woman like you."

Jennie stared at the mound of brown eggs, yearning to test their shells against the wall. "A woman like me?"

"You know. A mere schoolteacher. Mr. Denison probably worried about it too. How it could affect his reputation within *his* social class. That's why we *know* he'd go out of his way to avoid impropriety."

To keep them from lingering forever, Jennie put their curiosity out of its misery. "Mr. Denison slept in the parlor with the boys, who were highly entertained by his storytelling."

Mrs. Vane nodded approvingly. "Susanna says his bed has storebought pillow slips—the kind with crocheted borders."

No matter how many times Jennie transferred the eggs from one basket to another, Ingrid would wait for the details. "I believe it might," she said casually. "It was rather dark when I tucked the girls in."

"Oh, but my late dear husband would have scoffed." Ingrid Jensen affected a gossipy tone. "Can you imagine a hardy western woman thinking seriously about a man with frilly pillows on his bed?"

Jennie could still remember the warmth of his embrace, the way she'd felt pressed close against him, the scent of bay rum.

Ingrid Jensen looked up and frowned. "Jennie, you've cracked an egg."

Mopping up the mess took time, but not enough to scare off the ladies.

"Are you going to keep school going in his dining room?" Mrs. Vane asked innocently.

With a sigh, Jennie came out from behind the counter. It was the very question she'd been pondering ever since Nate Denison had pulled her into his arms.

"Are you?" Ingrid asked, adjusting her spectacles. "I don't mean to be a busybody, dear, but I think as long as you hold school there, it will slow Karl or Edgar making a proposal."

"Actually I'm saving my teaching money to study at a university, so there's no rush . . . if they're busy."

Mrs. Vane laughed. "Jennie, don't josh about this, and don't tell anyone else you've got designs about a university education. Why, Karl and Edgar both would turn tail and run away and never propose for sure then."

"Why?" Jennie began to unpack a carton of baking powder.

"You know how men are. They'll never want you if you acquire too much education. You know why, don't you?"

No, she didn't. But she didn't want Karl or Edgar making a marriage proposal if the price was her staying home counting eggs and never thinking about anything except the price of muslin. Grace might be content with that, but it wasn't for her.

"I don't care. I'm going." And walking out, she left them sitting there like a pair of hens who'd forgotten how to lay eggs.

Tuesday morning Jennie awoke to wind, a chinook wind that was melting their early snow and blowing away the last of the aspen leaves. She sent Mariah to pass the word to the town kids that school was open. She wasn't excited about it herself, but if Karl and Edgar considered the schoolteacher theirs, then she had all the more reason to want to go off to a university.

First, though, she and Nate Denison had to get some things straight.

And so at eight o'clock she marched alone through the slush and mud to Denison's Folly, where the boardwalk and steps up to the front door were newly shoveled . . . almost as if Nate were expecting her. But that couldn't be. . . .

Yet she'd no sooner lifted her hand to knock than the door opened. Nate was waiting for her and didn't even blink when she stepped onto his hardwood floors in her wet, mud-caked shoes. Instead he took from her the dry pair of high-button shoes she'd carried.

"Good morning, Miss Beasley," he said with all the formality of a butler.

She nodded stiffly.

They gazed at each other, remembering.

She fastened her gaze on his shirt, on the exact spot where his heart had beat against her face.

He stared at her head, at the ridiculous knit hat she'd worn as protection from the wind. Only a couple of stray locks of coppery hair peeked out.

"I'm glad you decided to come back," he said softly.

She forced herself to stand stiff, her hands at her sides. "You can say 'I told you so,' if you want," she said, adding, "I'm not saying I believe you over Thaddeus or Orvil. I'm only doing what I have to do, not what I necessarily want."

His eyebrows rose as if he were hurt. "I wasn't going to say a word." His gaze lowered to her feet. "Except, of course, that it might be a good idea if you changed your wet shoes."

In a way it was good to be back. Sitting on the steps that led up to Nate Denison's bedroom, she pulled off her lace-up shoes and exchanged them for the dry button tops. Then, with Nate still standing there watching, she headed for the dining room, her school. She'd taken all of two steps before she stopped, staring. The dining room, which had been littered with papier-mâché birds and oatmeal spills when she'd last seen it, was now immaculate. The draperies were open and tied back with bows of rope. The birds were packed away in a crate. Moreover the table, covered in a damask cloth, was set with fifteen mugs, waiting for fifteen people in need of cocoa.

Swiveling, she looked at him. "How'd you know I'd be here?"

"I hoped you'd come."

"Oh." She looked away. "Well, there won't be fourteen. Just the town children, but thank Helga for straightening the room."

"Jennie . . ."

She moved away quickly to stand at the head of the dining table, her place. The first-year readers were piled up there, waiting. "We have only one rule, Nate Denison."

Their eyes met, a question in his.

"Never mention the night of the storm . . . or I'll be late and let you substitute again."

"You drive a hard bargain, Jennie." He took a step toward her, then thought better of it and walked out.

CHAPTER

~13~

By Wednesday, Jennie was short with the children, tired from not sleeping, and jittery, jumping every time the hint of a footstep sounded out in the hall or every time the wind came up outside. Thursday was Thanksgiving, and she'd never been more glad for four days with no school. Maybe, she mused, Karl would have the new school ready after the holiday, though somehow that thought didn't ease her agony. How could Nate Denison reduce her to this quivering female? She hated him. Didn't she?

Or could it be . . . could it really be she was falling in love? Was this physical craving for his touch the natural result of romantic feelings? Oh, it was wanton of her. His eastern morals—or lack of them—were corrupting her, that's what. She stared out the window, past the Pompeiian-red velvet drapes, past the veranda that wrapped his house, to the wide blue sky.

Oh, Jennie, Jennie, she cried inside. How could you be so vulnerable to such a sophisticated man? He was a trap waiting to spring, and like a gullible rabbit, she walked right in and got caught. Well, whatever happens now, she told herself, she must not let him know how deeply he had affected her.

"Miss Beasley . . . Miss Beasley . . ."

"Yes, Mariah." Goodness, how long had the class been trying to capture her attention? She was sitting with a trio of students by the windows, all of them, even Jennie, glum. Usually school let out for the entire Thanksgiving week, so the teachers from two counties could attend edifying lectures at the Teachers' Institute in Bozeman. Jennie, with no school building, could not justify the expense this year. But how she longed to mingle on a real college campus . . .

"Miss Beasley?"

She looked up. "What is it?"

"You've got your reader upside down."

She looked and blushed, but laughed for the class's sake. "So I do. I must have been woolgathering. We're all ready for Thanksgiving break, it seems, even me, the teacher. Well, go on, let me hear you recite the Gettysburg Address."

"Fourscore and seven years ago . . ."

Mariah said it perfectly, and Jennie had to fight to concentrate.

She stood and looked at the elegant clock on the sideboard. "Class," she said. "Because it's the day before the holiday, I thought we'd do something different."

At the dining-room table, fourteen faces beamed back at her, happier than she'd seen them since the day they'd made papier-mâché birds. "To get in the holiday spirit you should each think of one thing you're thankful for."

The beaming expressions on fourteen faces faded to dismay. "Aw, Miss Beasley . . ."

"Yes." It was important that she count her blessings, not think of things she couldn't have. Like a trip to Montana State College. Like Nate . . .

Will Armstrong leaned back in a Hepplewhite chair. "I'm thankful we don't have to come to this prissy house tomorrow. Last year," he complained, "we got the *whole* week off, not just a long weekend."

"No bellyaching now," Jennie said, irritated. "Be thankful you get Thursday and Friday."

He sighed. "Okay," and then intoned in a singsong voice, "I'm thankful I've got a mom and dad who take care of me and my brothers and sisters."

"Say it like you mean it, Will." Little Minnie bawled her big brother out.

"Well, what are you thankful for?"

"I'm thankful we got rescued from the snowstorm."

"That's dumb. You're just saying what the teacher wants to hear."

"It's not dumb. If you want to hear something dumb, ask Mariah."

Mariah brushed her dark bangs from her solemn face and opened her mouth.

Her big brother Thaddeus Jr. piped up. "I know what the runt'll say. 'I'm thankful Paddy's got pups, and the world is full of animals.'"

"Shut up, Thaddeus." Tears of mortification welled in her eyes, and Mariah bent her head to stare at her lap. Dark braids fell over her shoulders.

Jennie could remember the feeling from her own school days. Always, Grace with her blond curls was giggling while Jennie, in her shadow with her strange-colored hair and serious demeanor, had been staring at her lap, trying to ignore the teasing from older children. Where Mariah's solace was animals, Jennie's had been school itself, and that despite strict unsympathetic teachers. She'd vowed then that someday, if she were a teacher, she'd do things different. Now here she was a teacher with the power to do exactly that. To change things.

Jennie rang her little hand bell for attention. "Will's right," she said, and everyone looked up, as she'd expected. "I don't want you to tell me the things you think I want to hear.

"I want you to tell me the things you're *really,* secretly thankful for. The fun blessings."

"The haystack," Will Armstrong said impulsively.

"Our porch swing," Bertha Jensen said.

"Hard candy on Christmas." One of the Slocum boys was grinning widely.

The others one by one chimed in.

"Molasses cookies."

"My rag doll." Minnie giggled and ducked her head.

"My new agate marbles," Ole said.

And on it went until at last it was Mariah's turn. "I'm thankful the squirrel got out of the fire, and I'm thankful we have a new school getting built for Aunt Jennie, one with a real belfry and two cloakrooms."

"That's Miss Beasley's thankful speech," her big brother said.

"What are you thankful for, Miss Beasley?" Will asked. "Aren't you thankful you got such a class of superior students?"

Everyone laughed, for they knew Will Armstrong was not a student many teachers were thankful for.

Jennie was going to be as lighthearted as the students. "I'm thankful for"—she thought of her favorite foods, things she hadn't eaten in months—"the good memories of mince pie and oranges. Real oranges, from the peel to the juice running down my chin."

The class laughed. "What else?" Minnie said.

She grew serious. "I'm genuinely thankful that my bell survived the fire." She thought of the note from the stationmaster telling her a box of school supplies would be arriving on the afternoon train. Progress. "Maybe, if our school desks come over Thanksgiving, we'll have our new school soon. I'm thankful for that."

The class moaned.

"And we're thankful to Mr. Denison for lending us his dining room, aren't we?" She gathered up her books, busied herself.

"I'd have been more thankful if Pa had closed school," came Thaddeus Jr.'s sassy reply.

"I'm not," Bertha said. "Someday I'm gonna have a house like this. I'm going to marry a rich man and have pillow slips from back east."

Jennie didn't want to pursue this subject one thought further. "I think we've gotten in the spirit of Thanksgiving. Class dismissed."

They flew out of Nate Denison's house. They were gone, free for four days, flying through the mud and patchy snow toward town.

Jennie was deeply thankful that the day was over, and as quickly as possible she bundled up and headed for the train depot to pick up the boxes. It was, she admitted, good to have a few minutes to herself before going home to her sister, wailing baby, crawling puppies, and all the housework. Thankful as she was for family, she needed a respite and this detour was it.

If she was lucky, maybe her desks would come, and her new windows. Then she could actually move the students into the new school. On that hopeful thought she arrived outside the crowded depot, and a second later drew up short.

There, standing heads and shoulders above the others in the milling crowd, was tall Nate Denison, broad shoulders encased in his sheepskin coat and looking more and more like he blended in. He was at a makeshift message board on the outer wall, right under the eaves, and he was tacking up a piece of paper.

She was seeing things. She looked out across the tracks and back. He was gone.

A moment later, unable to resist temptation, she turned ever so slightly to see if he was still gone. He was. Immediately Jennie trotted over to the bulletin board to read what he'd pinned up.

Wanted: Top-notch crew of wranglers to accompany one dozen bison via railroad freight from Livingston down to Castlerock. Apply at Denison's house on Camas Street. Prior experience with ornery animals preferred.

She smiled to herself. So the elusive buffalo were still on their way. A train whistle wailed in the distance, and she hurried out to the platform.

There he was, just a few feet beside her.

Their eyes met, his amused, and she whipped her head back and made a great show of studying the railroad tracks, as if there were something very interesting about parallel iron rails.

She snuck another look at him. He was watching her.

"You're following me?" he accused.

"It seems I should be asking that," she retorted.

"I was out here first," he said.

She straightened her shoulders primly and clutched the moth-eaten muff Grace had thrust on her.

"What are you doing? Looking for advertisements for buildings to rent?"

An immediate blush stole up her cheeks. He'd seen her reading his ad. "No need. The new school is almost finished."

Nate stared at her, envying that class of fourteen homely little kids who a while ago had been laughing with her. He'd heard them through the walls and was envious. Their laughter underscored his loneliness. And more. He wished he'd been the one laughing with Miss Jennie Beasley.

"Before you move in, I advise you check out the stove. I'm not offering my house a second time."

She bristled, and fumbled inside her coat for the pocket watch she carried now. When Grace had realized her pin-watch had been lost in the fire, she'd loaned her sister their father's antique pocket model. It ran slow, as apparently did the train. She was growing uncomfortable. Where *was* the blasted train?

"The train's late," he noted.

"Are your buffalo coming?" she asked hopefully.

He turned to her, and she looked back. Only ten paces separated them. Her eyes blazed; his held amusement. "Not yet, but if they were, you can be sure the stationmaster would be stopping the train before it arrived here in the middle of town."

He had a knack for getting her to step in her own naïveté like a gopher hole she didn't see. The subject of buffalo triggered other images—her students running about his house tracking mud and fingerprints. She took a wild guess. "A new velvet settee?"

"Not as long as the Castlerock school occupies my premises." He looked at her so hard tingles went through her. "Some friends from back east are coming out on a holiday jaunt."

"Oh?" Her heart beat faster.

"And you?" he asked, looking across the tracks at the sage-covered butte. "Family coming for Thanksgiving?"

Biting her lip, she stared straight ahead out across the tracks. "I told you. Grace is my only family. Grace and her children . . . I'm here to meet a shipment of school supplies. A surprise package. Windowpanes, I hope."

She stared down at the toes of her sensible black buttoned shoes. Why should he look at a plain prim woman like her? You're a mere trifle in his life, Jennie Beasley, she reminded herself . . . no more than a trifle.

Before your time is up in my house, I'll find out your price, Miss Beasley. Mere sport to a man like him. That's all she was.

As the train came round the last bend and the engine loomed closer, steam rising in the cold air, the stationmaster, walrus-whiskered Chester, joined them on the platform. "Took its time, didn't it?" he said, looking with disgust at his watch. "Damn rich swells delayed everything."

"I beg your pardon?" Jennie said, confused.

The stationmaster tipped his hat. "Pardon my language, miss. Train's late and I've got to make up that time on the unloading." He went on to explain. "Some rich swells wanted their private car added back in Minneapolis and it's thrown every connection off since. We ain't equipped to deal with private rail cars."

Rich swells.

Then, as the train came to a screeching halt, all was commotion, and she lost sight of Nate Denison as Jennie moved to claim her freight.

No windows yet, just a single box of slates and chalk and brand new McGuffey Readers. Sighing, she tucked the box under her chin. Which, of course, is when she spotted the man again, and with her heart in her throat, she stopped in midstep. The box slipped down to her stomach.

Nate wasn't alone anymore, and as he'd indicated, it wasn't a humpbacked beady-eyed buffalo he was greeting.

It was a woman.

Another woman and a man. And yet another couple. Two couples and a spare woman. A beautiful raven-haired woman.

All of them beautiful. Dressed in clothes the likes of which Castlerock had never seen. Jennie couldn't help herself. She stood there, box in hands, and stared.

Nate's wealthy friends, of course, and her gaze flew to the lone woman. Could she be the one for whom Nate had built his house? Come out here to reconsider? To beg forgiveness?

No, impossible; she'd wed an English duke . . . or earl . . . or some title. Jennie never could sort them out. After queen and princess, she was lost, as out of her element as if she'd been invited to read tea leaves and prepare watercress sandwiches.

This beauty, however, seemed not the least bit fazed by anything, including a strange little Montana town or Nate's words.

"Cornelia," Jennie heard him say, "this station doesn't have a covered station for your private car. One siding with a view of sagebrush and pine trees. That's it." Gently he untangled her arms from about his neck.

"Nonsense. Build one for this poor little town, then. Papa will pay for it. We *have* to keep our car protected from the snow. It's Papa's, and you can't expect us to sleep in some western bordello and rub elbows with all the common horse thieves, can you? Mama warned me about lice and bedbugs and is positively livid that I'm missing out on all my dress fittings—"

"It's all you deserve for coming with no more notice than a telegram. Now let the stationmaster handle the rail car his way. He's behind schedule."

The beautiful Cornelia lowered her lashes and smiled flirtatiously. "Oh, Nate, why are you fussing so about the time schedule of some low-paid train employee in the middle of . . . of, well, where exactly are we? Montana? All these western territories look dreadfully alike. Endless sagebrush and rocks."

Jennie, suddenly self-conscious about staring, turned to leave.

"Jennie." A man's voice stopped her. A man's voice, low and close by. Nate.

Slowly she turned and hiked the box up higher as he approached, the lovely Cornelia in tow.

"I was going to drop that box off at the school, wasn't I?"

Not that she knew of, but he was taking it from her.

She stood silent as he introduced her to Cornelia.

"Friends from New York. Cornelia Van Altman. Miss Jennie Beasley, the schoolteacher."

Cornelia paused and her lips turned up in a half smile, especially as she stared at Jennie's hat, then she gave a regal nod. "How do you do? Jennie? Is that short for Jennifer or Genevieve?"

"Neither. Just plain Jennie."

"How charmingly provincial." Cornelia barely favored Jennie with a condescending smile, gave another brief look at her knit hat, then, giggling, swept past as if Jennie were no more than a servant. Nate followed. "She's got lovely skin. But you ought to get her to teach you to spell. Your letters were beyond the pale."

"Your answers were wicked."

Cornelia's laughter floated back from Nate's elegant sleigh as Jennie watched Nate dump the box onto the floor and then help Cornelia in. "But there was a reason," the lovely socialite said. "Everyone knows you need something to help you get over Daisy. Even your maiden aunt is annoyed at your continued absence. We shall have to come up with some sparkling and witty conversation for dinner, something to entice you back to Fifth Avenue. May Deardon's wedding is at Christmas, you know, and . . ." Their voices were swallowed up in the cold afternoon air. Then with a flick of the reins, they were gone down the slushy road to Denison's Folly. Behind them a hired sleigh with the two other couples and an array of packages followed.

Laughter floated out in their wake. A mongrel barked and gave chase to Nate's sleigh, then gave up, and the only sound was the clank of the train as it huffed back and forth while the elegant private car was uncoupled.

Jennie stood perfectly still, hand touching her knit hat, as snowflakes fluttered down, dusting the ground the way sugar would. And still she watched until Nate's sleigh was just a speck, and until her fingers and toes were almost numb.

How do you do? How do you do? How do you do? Over and over Cornelia's silly little words echoed. What should she have said? Something witty or clever. Well, one didn't learn to be witty when one spent all day with fourteen homespun youngsters. And if Nate Denison preferred wit to . . . to McGuffey's readers and papier-mâché birds, that was his choice. *How do I do? I do quite nicely for myself, thank you, Miss Cornelia Uppity Fifth Avenue.*

"Miss Beasley?"

She whirled, guilty at her wicked thoughts, glad no one could read her mind.

Nearby stood the stationmaster, Chester, eyes twinkling. Not much went past Chester. "Not at all our sort," he commented kindly. "You got your box, didn't you? The box from Minneapolis. School supplies?" His walrus whiskers waggled.

"Yes . . . yes, more things for the new school. Mr. Denison took it."

Then picking up her skirts, she ran home to the Gordon house. For once, Jennie was desperate for her brother-in-law to tear into someone, to pontificate on and on about these highfalutin strangers.

Nate couldn't wait for dinner to end. The Van Altman brothers and their wives were polite guests, albeit condescending about what little towns like Castlerock had to offer—including Helga's dinner of turkey and mashed potatoes. Such common cooking, Cornelia sniffed. God knows no one in Castlerock had exactly welcomed Nate with open arms, but the people who called this place home were decent good people who worked hard—even the ones who referred to his house as Denison's

Folly behind his back. Idly he listened to Cornelia gush on about the latest Vanderbilt ball and imagined how she'd fare if all her gowns and jewelry and doting servants were taken from her . . . and she were handed a room full of raggedy youngsters to teach. He smiled to himself as the picture of Jennie Beasley came to him, here in this very dining room, presiding over cocoa and spelling papers.

"Nate, you're not listening," Cornelia complained. "Mother is making me go abroad when I've absolutely no interest in perfecting my French, and I can't make her see reason."

"I'm listening," he said, and he really tried. But by now he'd come to an unexpected realization: while he might not completely fit in with the good people of Castlerock, he wasn't sure he fit in with the Van Altmans anymore either.

He listened to them compliment him on his house. "Not up to New York standards, of course, but it's an adorable little chalet, if you will. Adorable dining room. Adorable housekeeper . . . vulgar town . . . vulgar stationmaster . . ."

If Nate heard the words "adorable" or "vulgar" one more time, he'd smash his champagne glass against the sideboard.

Cornelia, who was indulging a little too freely in the champagne, suddenly peeked under the tablecloth.

"Cornelia!" said her shocked brother.

She reached down to the floor and came back up with a wad of paper. "Look," she exclaimed. "The schoolmarm's been here." She giggled.

Clenching his teeth helped Nate restrain himself from snapping at Cornelia. Actually Jennie had wrought all sorts of damage in here, but now that he thought on it, it was more enjoyable watching her wreak havoc than listen to Cornelia's inane chatter.

The women excused themselves from the table and George Van Altman lit a cigar. "You'll take us into Yellowstone, won't you?"

"It's closed," Nate informed them. "You're too late for the season."

"Closed? You mean, the gate's locked?"

"So to speak. The cavalry's in there."

"Well, bribe them. We can buy our way in."

"No."

George Van Altman's smile was patient. "Oh, come now, Nate. Not turning morally righteous on us, are you? I want one of those buffalo heads for my den. It's the rage."

"You can't go in the park."

His wife, another beautiful and bored society matron, peered around the door. "It's all right, darling. I told you we should have come in the summer, but you're not missing anything. The geysers look the same, gush on the same monotonous timetable as in summer. I'll buy you some prints for your stereoscope."

"Dammit," said George's portly brother, Albert, "I just want to move on out of the cold. Let's push on to San Francisco and sample the restaurants. We can be there by the Saturday after Thanksgiving."

But George was adamant. "What about your buffalo? That's all we read about is your buffalo. Just let us shoot one of them. I'll give you a thousand. Name your price."

"I have no price." Which, he realized, might be the truth. It was the first time in his life he'd ever uttered the words, so he'd surprised even himself.

Gradually the laughter died down, and, curious, the ladies returned. "Nate, don't lie," George said. "You've always had a price. I want a trophy head."

"Then hire a mule and ride on in and bag one yourself, but I'll warn you, the cavalry's out for heads of their own— poachers—and they've got a brig down at Fort Yellowstone."

"Ooh, the Wild, Wild West." Cornelia giggled, sitting down and sipping champagne. She reached over to toy with Nate's hand, seductively running her index finger along his pinky. "We could pour the rest of the champagne in the bath-tub," she whispered.

"You're too wild for this place, Cornelia. They hang men out here for trifling with the wrong women."

Cornelia looked at Nate from under her lashes. "Ah, yes, the quaint Miss Beasley. I don't suppose you ever think of her in a tub full of champagne bubbles, do you?"

He scraped back his chair. "George, take your sister back to the car and put her to bed."

"Throwing us out?" someone said on a laugh.

"You seem to think your rail car's got more comforts than my house."

"Nate's becoming awfully stuffy out here all alone," Cornelia said. "We've got to loosen him up before we leave."

As the others put on their coats, Cornelia lingered, defying all convention by taking Nate by the hand and leading him into the parlor.

"Get my cloak, George, and stop dithering on about chap-erons. At least let me say good-bye to Nate."

She pushed the parlor door halfway shut, enough so it con-cealed her and Nate. Then she reached inside his jacket, spread her hands flat on his chest, and ran them up his silk shirt, the way only Cornelia could. Her perfume was rich, her gown rustled seductively, and as her arms linked behind Nate's neck her breasts pressed against his chest.

"Fifth Avenue isn't the same without you, Nate. When are you coming back?"

"I don't know."

"What do you want? I've got a gold cigarette case of Papa's. Bronze trim and silk lining."

Leaning over, he kissed her cheek. "Cornelia, go on to San Francisco and find Edmund Taylor. I heard he was free now, too, and I know he adores you. Always has. I bet he'll follow you back to New York. And you won't even have to give him the cigarette case. At the very least, by Newport next summer you could have him. And he's richer than me."

Her smile was rueful. "It'll serve you right if you end up having to settle for a homely schoolteacher."

"You're tipsy, Cornelia."

"With buffalo overrunning your house." She giggled.

"I've handled worse."

Hours later, gaslights turned off, a single kerosene lantern illuminated his red plush album. Finally he shut it. The pictures of New York did nothing to him. Which was progress.

The interlude with the Van Altmans puzzled him. Five years ago he'd have taken Cornelia's gold cigarette case and everything she offered. But all evening he'd felt as out of place with them as a kerosene lamp set in the middle of Mrs. Vanderbilt's ballroom.

He wasn't a part of Castlerock and didn't plan to stay, yet he was no longer a part of the Fifth Avenue set.

He'd thought this feeling of displacement was caused by waiting for a dozen buffalo to arrive. Any wealthy man used to having his way would feel frustrated at having to wait for a bunch of shaggy animals intent on making life difficult.

The buffalo had no rules.

New York had too many.

Cornelia's perfume was too rich, not lily of the valley.

The memory of a funny little knit hat kept getting in the way . . . making him smile. Copper-penny hair and prim shirt-waists that smelled vaguely of glue and cornstarch.

Two such different women. Each representing a different way of life.

Nate didn't know where he fit.

At the Gordon house, supper had been strangely quiet, and Jennie grew sadder by the moment. She didn't fit into Nate

Denison's house or life. Yet what did it matter when she hated his money-can-buy-anything attitude?

At last she cleared her throat. "I was at the depot and saw one of those private rail cars come in . . . you know, the kind the very wealthy travel in."

Silence.

"Pass the pickled beets," Thaddeus Gordon said in a toneless voice.

"We're out of pickled beets," Grace reminded him.

His fist came down on the table. "Why did you waste the last ones?"

"They were brought by Ingrid Jensen after the baby was born, and you know whenever Ingrid tries to can anything it's not fit to eat. Try the potatoes."

Thaddeus scowled at the table. "That's all we've got? Potatoes and plain turkey? No trimmings?"

"The boarding house has pumpkin pie," Thaddeus Jr. said. "I heard Edgar talk about it in church."

"We can't afford trimmings," his mother said softly.

"Why not?" Thaddeus demanded.

"Thaddeus," his wife said, "the townspeople aren't buying. We're lucky you sold those turkeys you ordered. The people are traveling to Livingston to the bigger mercantile for things like trimmings."

"Damn Livingston. Does everyone have to be like that Denison dude and have bigger and better things?"

For a minute Jennie had hoped Thaddeus would be distracted and start one of his lectures about Nate Denison and his rich company. But no one seemed to care today. All they talked about in strained tones was the scarcity of food. And then the baby began to wail.

The children sat eating, eyes downcast, forks scraping back and forth.

"I'm not a poacher, you know." Thaddeus had been defensive ever since the humiliating visit by the cavalry. "I can support my family without resorting to poaching."

"Thaddeus, it's all right. Jennie contributed her board money for apple pies. You ought to be thankful."

All of a sudden Thaddeus Gordon scraped back his chair and grabbed his coat off the peg by the kitchen door.

"Where are you going?" his wife asked. "It's Thanksgiving."

"I'm going to the store. To mark down the prices so I can compete with Livingston stores. Damned if I'll depend on my wife's sister to feed my kids. Thaddeus Jr., you get a notice up in the depot to sell those puppies. Today."

The door slammed, the baby wailed, and Mariah, face solemn, leaned down to stroke the little black runt that was nestling beneath her bare feet.

CHAPTER
❧14❧

The idea, Jennie had learned when winter set in, was to dress as quickly as possible and hurry into the warmer kitchen.

Today, though, despite the temptation of the kitchen, Jennie lingered at the tiny mirror above her washstand.

It was the Monday after Thanksgiving, and she was feeling more uneasy than she had in weeks, which was selfish. After all, so many homely joys had come her way over the holiday, joys not measured in any way except by the heart. She'd played with the new baby, with the puppies, with Mariah. If there had been anyplace the cup seemed less than full, it was the holiday feast. Oh, the table had been laden, but a mood of depression hung over the Gordon house like a black cloud waiting to burst. And everyone, it seemed, noticed, but like picnickers wanting to postpone a storm by ignoring it, no one dared say anything.

Now that she thought of it, the cloud had arrived the day the cavalry had come prying into the Gordon affairs, and it seemed Thaddeus had never shaken the humiliation. Not even a new baby or puppies could lift his spirits. And he delighted in making fun of Nate Denison, whom he blamed for everything that went wrong, from sour milk to green kindling. Nate Denison could do no right, it seemed, and his biggest sin was in being rich.

Thaddeus Gordon's attitude made Jennie all the more guilty for her own feelings. More than guilty. She reached for the cigar box with her life's savings—not a lot, but the growing stack of dollar bills and coins gave her hope. She'd lost all she had when her bank in St. Louis went under during the panic, and so she wasn't trusting this money anywhere but under her bed. Was she selfish not to insist that Grace take this money in addition to her weekly board? Was it selfish to have dreams? She felt traitorous to her own family . . . all the more so because of her feelings for Nate Denison. Everyone was right. She wasn't Nate's sort. If there was one lesson from childhood, she ought to be remembering right now, it was the wisdom of her father—a humble livery-stable owner in St. Louis—who'd taught both her and Grace not to be tempted by useless glitter. Be frugal, hardworking, and honest. All else was folly.

Denison's Folly. It was all folly. Yet she couldn't wait to get back to the antique walnut table in the dining room of his house.

No, she corrected herself with the quickness of a teacher putting a red check by a spelling error. It was her class she couldn't wait to see, and ignoring the flutter in her heart, she fastened the top button of her high-necked prim white shirtwaist. She jammed the cigar box under her mattress and rushed out to the kitchen stove to warm herself. The rest of the family was already eating, and she lingered at the stove, pretending to watch the iron kettle.

"Thaddeus has already left?" she asked.

Grace nodded.

"Thaddeus said that fancy railroad car left on last night's train. San Francisco bound." Grace sounded, if not content, at least resigned.

Suddenly Jennie's worry burned as hot in her heart as if it were a drop of water spilled on the stovetop.

It was the sight of Nate with that beautiful woman, Cornelia Van Altman, that worried her. Like a splinter working its way to the surface, suddenly she saw the worry for what it was. Worry that Nate Denison, having had visitors from back east, might suddenly be lured off with them. At the thought her heart ached. What if Nate were gone, off with the beautiful heiress? After all, the lovely Cornelia Van Altman was a part of his world in ways Jennie, with her ordinary upbringing, never could be.

"Jennie, you're daydreaming. Aren't you going to eat?" Grace was in the rocker nursing the baby. "Excited to get back to teaching, I bet?"

"Wishing the new school were ready." Jennie met her sister's careworn look. She began nibbling a biscuit and helped clear the table of oatmeal bowls.

The children were doing various before-school chores. Mariah's lot was dishes, but the black runt of the litter lay at her feet, looking poorly. Jennie finally glanced at the time and moved to the row of pegs by the door.

"Grace, I need to get to school early today. There's a lot to do after the long holiday." The children might hitch a ride with old man Armstrong if they timed it right. As for her, she needed to walk, shake out the cobwebs.

No one objected, so Jennie grabbed her cape, pulled the knit hat over her hair, and donned mittens.

"You're sure you don't mind?" she asked.

Grace smiled. "Run along. I don't expect you to do everything for us, little sister. Dishes. Scrubbing clothes. Cooking. Puppy puddles to mop up. It'll still be going on at four o'clock." She looked into Jennie's face. "Go on. I enjoy imagining it's me going off to school to teach. Go off and do the things I'll never get to."

Taking a step toward her sister, Jennie touched the baby's head. "Grace, I worry so about you."

"Go on." Grace's eyes were bright with unshed tears.

Darn Thaddeus Gordon, the stubborn Scotsman!

Grabbing her satchel of school papers, she was out the door into the cold brilliant morning. Sometimes she wished Thaddeus's father had never left Scotland. Then Grace would have married someone else . . . and Jennie would never have come here and met Nate Denison. . . . She dreaded arriving at Denison's Folly and finding him gone. Dreaded finding out if Cornelia Van Snoot had taken him away in her papa's private car. Oh, blast it all!

At the corner of Camas and Moose streets, the main intersection of Castlerock, she hesitated. The Denison mansion was straight up Camas; the new school was in the other direction, three buildings up on Moose Street.

After a five-second debate, she headed for the new school. She had time to check the progress Karl had made and put herself in a proper schoolteacher mood.

At the new school, the main door was hung in place but unlocked. It squeaked as she opened it.

"Jennie?"

Faithful Karl was inside, piling boxes.

Carefully she entered the maze of crates and boxes that had all apparently come in on a weekend train.

"My goodness, Karl, did we order this many books?"

He turned, obviously pleased, then ran a self-conscious hand through his straight yellow hair. "Jennie?" he said. "You haven't come for so long. I guess you thought I'd never get the new school done."

"You did say one month."

He looped his thumbs in the bib of his overalls. "Well, I know," he drawled, "but I didn't reckon on that train wreck east of here slowing up your desks. It might take a while to salvage the wreck and we may have to reorder the school desks."

"We could just use makeshift benches and tables again." Even to her own ears, her voice lacked conviction.

"You could, depending how fast you want to move out of that fancy house."

She turned away, running a finger along a window frame. "Oh, we're surviving. But I'd like to get settled. You got the new school up so fast."

"Well, yeah," he said, coming to stand on the other side of the same window frame. "That's the easy part. It's this finish work that's slow, and the desks, and then the time of year. . . . Fall's always the hardest time of year to round up volunteers, especially this one, what with the hard times and all. A lot of men are out working in the mines, earning extra for winter. And me, I had to stop to make another coffin. I'm working on the wainscoting in here now, though, and the window panes finally came."

She looked at homely, loyal Karl. "You're a very generous man, Karl."

He blushed, which is the only way Karl seemed able to respond to compliments.

"You've been devoted to this school." She walked around, touching a box here, another one there. Her new school was almost ready. Another few days wouldn't matter. Suddenly she realized Karl had come up behind her, and she turned to see him staring at her in adoration.

"It's you I'm devoted to, Miss Beasley." The words were blurted out, as if he'd been storing them up for weeks. He'd been looking at his boots. Now he hazarded a quick look at her.

For a minute Jennie just stared, not knowing how to discourage him gracefully. Next in line, according to town custom, to marry the latest schoolteacher and so shy. Dear Karl. All hammers and overalls and dependability and loyalty and shyness and Adam's apple. She hadn't the heart to hurt him, but he didn't seem to understand. She was going to remain a spinster.

"You deserve much more of a homebody than me, Karl. The way teachers come and go, it'll happen."

A frown worried its way all over Karl's face and settled at his Adam's apple, which bobbed. "I guess I don't understand."

The smile came unbidden. He was so gentle, so old-fashioned, actually courting her with sweet words instead of trying to . . . buy her. "It's always been the way Grace and I planned it. She'd have the children, but I'd go to school to provide for us, in case anything ever happened to her husband. . . . I'm going to be one of the first women to graduate from college out here in the west. You wait and see."

He shuffled his feet then looked up, awe in his expression. "I think that's mighty admirable."

So much for Ingrid Jensen's wisdom about men not wanting a too-educated woman. A change of subject was called for. The pile of boxes leaning against the back wall provided it. All of this had come in on the weekend train. It looked like enough for an army, she thought, casting a baleful eye on the boxes.

"They must have made a mistake, Karl. I'll bet some of this belongs to the mercantile." That had to be it. She'd pry open the boxes and find sacks of flour and tinned milk that had gotten mixed in with her McGuffey readers, and then she'd send Thaddeus Jr. down to sort it all out.

"You'd better look in those boxes for yourself. Ain't nothing coming for the mercantile. Edgar says the bank can't extend any more credit to Thaddeus."

She stood perfectly still, absorbing that news. "No wonder Thaddeus has been such a polecat."

"What?"

"Nothing." She had no right to speculate about her family in front of Karl. "Let's have a look at this," she said, peering into a box. "Maybe it's for someone else in town—Ingrid's sewing supplies or some such."

Karl smiled. "If it was joiner's tools, I could set up shop in New York and work for the swells."

Already she was flitting from box to box, lifting open wooden lids, gasping at the contents. "Harmonicas! Two dozen of them!"

Below that was a box of piccolos and music books. Again two dozen.

She reached for another. "Watercolors. An extravagance. How stupendous. Or else stupid. Did someone mistake my order for that of a fancy girls' school?"

Karl shook his head. "No mistake. The invoice is from Minneapolis and it gives Castlerock School as the destination."

Jennie exclaimed at each discovery. "A typewriter machine . . . a barometer . . . a box camera . . . three stereoscopes . . . a dictionary stand just like the one in Nate Denison's library . . . Oh, no . . ." The truth dawned suddenly, like moonrise in big-sky country. One minute dark. The next—light.

"Nate Denison bought all this, didn't he?"

Karl, gentle soul that he was, nodded. "There's a big word on the invoice. It's a philan—"

"Philanthropic donation!"

Jennie was not amused. Shocked. Grateful, yes. This was the stuff with which the most advanced eastern schools were equipped.

"There's even one box with a dozen or so tin lunch pails in it. Real ones. Not lard pails."

"Oh, is there?" She had to force herself not to lose her temper. Really, this was too presumptuous of Nate Denison.

"Guess the town owes Mr. Denison for contributing so much," Karl said softly. "I haven't got the means to turn your head with fancy donations."

"Your work is your gift, Karl, and never forget it." Inside, she wanted to scream, throw all her hairpins at the conceited, ostentatious easterner. Fumbling in her satchel, she pulled out the brown knit hat and jammed it over her hair. "What Nate Denison did wasn't generous. It was an outright bribe. A vulgar bribe." She was silent, glaring out the window at the muddy streets, powdered with snow.

"Don't you like it?" Karl asked, looking at her as if he was wondering how to shield himself from a torrent of wrath.

She turned. "I'd love it—if I were a Fifth Avenue governess. I mean it. Your work is worth far more than his bought-and-paid-for gift."

Karl smiled proudly. "I'll have the wainscoting painted next week, and the bell hung, and blackboard nailed up, so if you want to arrange all this other stuff and show it off at the Christmas party, the building will be ready. All you've got to do is name the date."

Without giving dear Karl an answer, she rushed out into the cold morning air and headed up the muddy boardwalk of Camas Street.

All of a sudden she hoped Mr. Nathaniel Denison of New York and Newport, Rhode Island, had gone off on a lark with his society friends, because if he was there in that mansion, she was going to peel a strip off his hide.

*   *   *

Nate Denison had just written *Dear Mr. President* then dipped his pen into the ink bottle when the front door slammed. Before he could turn around in his chair, Miss Jennie Beasley, righteousness brimming from her silly knit cap to her sensible high-button shoes, appeared at the door of his library. Her clothes were as prim and unpretentious as a country schoolgirl's. What would Miss Jennie Beasley, he wondered, look like decked out properly in a big feathered leghorn hat? In a gown from Worth's of Paris? Or better yet, in a silk sheet?

He stood trying to hold back the smile teasing at his mouth as she stormed right into his library. Everything about her held the promise of passion, and something inside warmed at the thought. He didn't even care if ink from his pen was spotting his trousers.

"What are you trying to do?" she yelled, eyes stormy. "Buy your way into the town's affections? It doesn't work that way out here. Even a few mangy buffalo know better than to let you fence them in . . . you—you speculator. And I'm smarter than the buffalo, Nate Denison."

"Oh? Enlighten me and then I can let my foreman and his expert crew in on the secret."

"You can't bribe me."

He looked from her to the nub of his pen, and then hastily set it down on the blotter. "You've been to the new schoolhouse," he guessed.

"Yes, and you can send it all back to whatever fancy store you ordered it from."

"It's staying."

"Why?"

"Because I want to see you get mad every time you have to use it."

"I don't intend to use it at all." Her hands clenched and

unclenched at her sides. "After the way you and your cavalry friends humiliated my sister's husband, when things are already hard—not that that's something you'd know about—I want no bribes from you. Why didn't you leave town with your fancy friends?"

"Is that what you're in such a lather about?" Her blush gave her away. No answer was necessary.

Nate knew women too well, had lived through too many maudlin little scenes in darkened library corners with jealous women not to know what provoked them. None of the regal women of Fifth Avenue and Newport—not even the poised Van Altman sisters, Daisy and Cornelia—ever revealed such raw passion as naive Miss Jennie Beasley.

Nate stared at her, at the hint of passion in her face, and something in him warmed toward her, something he hadn't felt since he was a boy infatuated with a governess.

"Miss Beasley, it's good to have you and the youngsters back. It was a rather quiet house these past four days."

"You're changing the subject." She removed her hat and unbuttoned her cape, aware that he watched her fingers work the fastenings.

She tossed the hat onto his desk, right on top of his letter to President Cleveland. "I can see you're determined not to listen to a word I have to say."

"On the contrary. You have a positive gift for expressing yourself."

Again she balled her fists in frustration. "We shall confine our words to an intellectual level," she said.

Her prim words contradicted her angry eyes and heaving breast. "You can try for an intellectual discussion, Jennie, but I think it's already a lost cause." He looked again at the way her shirtwaist moved in and out with each breath. He advanced toward her.

"Jennie, Jennie, tell me what's wrong with my gifts. I'm truly baffled." In his world the object was to own more than anyone else.

Nervously she tucked her hair back behind her ears, then cleared her throat. "It has to do with intention, Mr. Denison. To be valued, a gift must be freely given, with no strings attached."

"No strings? That's not how I was brought up. Everyone I ever knew or was remotely close to was bought and paid for— from nanny to governess to tutor . . . and then when I grew up, I found out even women came with a price. So now I have to disagree. Every person I've ever known in my life has been bought and paid for."

She gaped at him, as if he were talking Greek, for heaven's sake.

"Are you saying you've never had a friend, a real friend?"

"What do you mean by real friend?"

"One who's always there, without cost? A friend comes with no strings attached."

"That's idealistic poppycock."

"Well, then, you don't know much about anything, Nate. It's no wonder people laugh at your extravagance. You can't buy people. And you can't buy my friendship. When I become a friend, it's for free."

He'd never known such friendship, but wasn't about to admit it. Instead, he walked back to his desk, pulled the rolltop down, and turned to study her from top to toe. Just when he thought he'd figured her out, she did something unexpected.

"Jennie," he said with a smile, "in my vast experience with people, they occasionally laugh at naïveté, but never do they laugh at money."

"If it's used in silly ostentatious ways, they do. You've never tried to do anything for its own sake . . . like . . . like

Karl, over there building the school out of the goodness of his heart."

"Are you saying you like Karl better than me? What does Karl give you? Nails and wood shavings?"

"Don't twist my words. You can't buy a schoolmarm, a woman."

"Wrong. You don't think I built this extravagant place for me alone, do you? I built it for a woman who said she'd come west with me, but who changed her mind."

The charming little frown between her eyes deepened a bit.

He smiled. "Don't worry about making your condolences. She's alive and well in merry old England."

"Your bedtime story." Her anger evaporated.

"I left out a few details for the sake of the children." A lot of details. Mainly his reactions. Anger. Pain. He used to be able to conjure up more. Time was dulling the memory.

But Jennie was standing there, staring at him with soft brown eyes. Eyes that trusted. He'd never known how thirsty he was for trust.

"She sold out to a higher bidder," he said matter-of-factly. "She married a duke, Jennie. He offered a better price, I'm afraid, than marriage to an aspiring buffalo speculator."

Her face softened. "I'm sorry."

"I don't want pity either. In my world women drive hard bargains. Daisy chose to pay for a title. All her friends were doing it. I should have seen it coming, and I didn't. There are very few things I've failed to predict in my life, Jennie. Very few. I predicted you'd like the things I donated to your school."

"I do like them. I just don't want you to give them with strings attached."

"Do they make you happy?"

"That depends."

He was walking toward her, and she backed up. Her sweet little mouth beckoned, her creamy skin, skin that smelled vaguely of lily of the valley. "It makes you happy. Isn't that reason enough?"

She shook her head. "You have a corrupt heart." He was too close for her to think.

"And I suppose you don't want any corrupt friends? Only the pure of heart? Utter perfection? Like Karl?"

"That's not true. But there are other gifts in life I value more than those you can buy."

"The teacher's going to play at riddles. Leave me to figure out what other kinds of gifts can possibly turn her head?"

Jennie stared into those deep blue eyes. Behind her was the door, and inches away, freedom.

"I think you could talk all day and never know what I mean."

"I wasn't going to waste time talking anymore at all," he said, and pulled her into his arms, full length against him, his face buried in her hair. At once, despite her best intentions to remain stiff, she melted against him and her arms stole up about his neck.

His hand was there, forcing her chin up. "Now your eyes remind me of a rainy day. Jennie . . . Jennie . . . a man could own the world and not understand a woman."

She strained against him, but he held her fast, despite her protests. "Don't you understand, Nate, there are some things money can't buy. Respect . . . a good name . . ."

"Sentimental rubbish." He held her, then he pressed his lips to her hair . . . and she clung tighter and then in a hungry frenzy their lips met. And clung some more.

He had no idea of how they'd come to this point, only he suddenly felt like a terribly lonely man, and holding her made him feel less alone.

"Jennie," he murmured in between kisses. "Jennie . . . Jennie," he said softly as he reached up to tuck a strand of hair behind her ear. His voice was husky.

She shut her eyes tight and felt his hands come up to frame her face. Their lips met again, clung hungrily. Surprisingly so.

"Jennie, I can't get this close to you and keep my hands off you. I'm not an unspoiled country boy, and I never will be. You're right when you say I'm a speculator and worse. I'm greedy too. Greedy for you."

Slowly she raised her gaze. Big Nate Denison stood there, vulnerable as a pup, and she was helpless against his loneliness. When he gathered her close, she kissed him back until she was almost faint from giving and giving.

Gradually the sound of children's laughter drifted in through the windows. Suddenly she was tugging away.

"Jennie," he said hoarsely, pulling her back. "This can't go on. Kissing you, then having you back off and preach to me about how teachers are the incarnation of purity. God Almighty, Jennie. Tell me what you want."

The door squeaked, and they sprang apart guiltily. Mariah stood there watching them, looking from one to the other.

"Aunt Jennie . . . Mr. Denison . . ." Mariah bit her lip.

Recovering quickly, Jennie smoothed her hair and excused herself to pin it up. "I'm coming, Mariah. Mr. Denison and I were discussing the new school, of which he's a generous benefactor."

"What's that?"

"He's donated some materials . . . run along, dear. I'll explain later." She turned to Nate, voice trembling. "I'd better go."

"Jennie . . ." He said her name with longing.

"Nate, I need to leave—"

"I'm glad the school's nearly ready," he said coldly. "Move in. Don't ever come back unless you're desperate. I'll send your papier-mâché birds down and whatever else you've left."

She swallowed hard. "I see. Thank you, then, for your hospitality. Without your generosity, we—"

"It was no gift. I did it to get you in my arms, so don't make me sound like some patron saint of education."

He was staring into her eyes, as if looking for something. He set her away from him and, after inspecting her, pushed another strand of hair back behind her ear. "Now you don't look as if you've been in here spooning."

By now, the dining room echoed with noisy children.

"I want you to take back all those extravagant gifts."

"Only if the head of the school board says so."

"That's my brother-in-law, and he'd sooner starve than take your help."

Nate nodded. "So be it. But never doubt this, Jennie. Moral principles won't pay the bills."

The click of the library door was too gentle. He preferred it when she slammed out, when she rattled the bric-a-brac on his étagère and knocked over his stereoscope. Shook the ink in its bottle. He stood there staring at the library door, the faint scent of soap and lily of the valley in the air.

Miss Jennie Beasley, he wagered, would never sell out for a mere title like Daisy had. And though he argued the point just to see her face and voice flame with passion, privately, secretly, he admired her principles. She was the first woman he'd ever known who claimed she'd starve rather than take his money.

It was enough of a game to keep a man amused. And he didn't know now which he anticipated more—the arrival of his buffalo or the arrival of the naive little teacher's piano. . . .

CHAPTER
❧ 15 ❧

When Jennie bumped into the town's banker, Edgar Baskin, face glum, coat buttoned over his paunch, she knew at once something was amiss. He was just coming out of the Gordons' front door.

"Edgar?" she asked, curious.

He plopped his fur fedora onto his head and gave her a guilty look. "Miss Beasley, despite this, I still hold you in mind as the incarnation of purity."

Despite what? If Edgar had seen her in Nate's arms a few days earlier, he'd doubtless characterize her as anything but pure. Nothing Edgar ever did would seem as soul thrilling as Nate's kisses, his embraces. . . .

Edgar cleared his throat the way he did before he made important speeches. "I want you to know that my actions are no reflection of the high esteem in which I hold you. I'm bound by a higher authority—the president of my bank."

A shaft of fear ran up her spine. "What's wrong?"

Instead of looking her in the eye, Edgar looked up Moose Street, packed white after another snowfall earlier in the week. "I'm bound to follow the rules, and I regret if what I've done causes pain. If it's any consolation, it's been a difficult, a most trying year for everyone . . . except maybe that rich man up in Denison's Folly." Doffing his hat, he strode away.

Curious, Jennie pushed open the door and stopped in her tracks. Whatever cloud had hung over the house in the week since Thanksgiving had, at last, burst. Irrevocably.

The once lovely Grace sat, looking years older, face lined, hair straggling from its pins, clutching the baby in her arms, rocking back and forth, saying nothing; she didn't have to speak, her white face said it all. The children were all gathered in the kitchen, equally white-faced, the older ones consoling their mother.

"Pa said for me to look out for you," Thaddeus Jr. said in a bracing tone.

"He told you he was leaving and not me." Grace lowered her face against the baby blanket. "He should have told me. Trusted me . . ."

"Where's Thaddeus?" Jennie asked at once.

No one answered immediately.

"We don't know," Grace said in a shamed voice.

Noticing Grace's red-rimmed eyes, Jennie knelt beside her sister. "What did Edgar say?"

"Thaddeus no sooner left than Edgar arrived. The bank's foreclosing on our house."

"You don't mean it? And Thaddeus has no idea?"

If Grace had to move, Jennie would not abandon her. "I'll help you, Grace. You know that. We'll find a new house."

Grace, who held baby Pearl close against her breast, shut her eyes. "There are no other houses in Castlerock. I threatened to move all the children to the new school," she said with a little laugh that verged on hysterical. "Edgar informed me Thaddeus's not paid our share of taxes. We've always had the most in school, you know, and so paid the most . . . but the school's the last thing on our minds now," Grace said with a tired sigh. She leaned back in the rocking chair and stared up at the water-stained ceiling.

"Thaddeus . . . Thaddeus, I always let him handle it all. He let me think we had enough."

Jennie was rummaging through cupboards. There was food here last time she'd looked. "Where's the food?" They had always been low, but she'd just run to the mercantile.

"Edgar says it belongs to the mercantile and thus the bank. Unless Thaddeus returns with some, I'd guess we've about forty-eight hours' worth. I could stretch it if we have porridge for supper."

"Grace! No." Jennie marched out the door, Thaddeus Jr. at her heels, and headed straight over to the mercantile. At the backdoor, staring her in the face, mocking her, was a shiny new padlock, barring her entrance.

The Castlerock Mercantile was out of business.

Thaddeus Gordon, how could you let it come to this? Her emotions swung from despair and heartache to anger.

This couldn't happen, not to her own sister, her own nieces and nephews. No bank could be that heartless. No town that cruel. No man that improvident, that stupid.

Oh, wait till Thaddeus Gordon tried to show his face around Grace again. How dare he take off right before everything fell apart, and leave his poor wife to pick up the pieces? "Thaddeus Jr.," she called. "Get your brothers. Go hunt for your pa. Look in the saloon, the bank. You know the logical places."

Within a half hour they were straggling back. The message from each was the same: there was no sign of Thaddeus Gordon anywhere in town.

"Maybe he's hunting," Thaddeus Jr. offered hopefully.

"He left his rifle here," their mother pointed out.

And then the youngest Gordon son said, "Chester says Pa bought a train ticket out of here."

"Which way? Eastbound? West?"

No one could quite recall.

Jennie reached for her sister's hand and squeezed it in reassurance, but inside she seethed. The man really had walked out on his family with nary a word.

"Grace, we can take the children and go—"

Grace shook her head. "No, I'm sick, Jennie. I can't go anywhere, so don't talk of starting over. The farthest I'll move is to the boardinghouse. Maybe when I feel less poorly, I can sweep the shop for Ingrid or some such. Thaddeus Jr. ought to be able to get ranch work—after the winter snows thaw."

"That's months from now!"

"I know."

Her brave, foolish sister.

"Do you have any better ideas? You were always the smart one," Grace said.

No. For once in her life, Jennie was at a loss, and she slumped, defeated, angry, down into a kitchen chair.

"I don't," she whispered, "except to feed everyone some oatmeal, and see what comes to mind."

"And don't go selling any of those schoolhouse goods. That's the property of Nate Denison, and I'll not take charity."

"Oh, Grace, this is no time to be proud. Be proud after I help you get on your feet. But now we have to survive."

She hurried to her little bedroom and dug out the cigar box from under the bed. With the salary she'd saved for college she could support her sister's family for a while, certainly buy food. The lid flipped open, and Jennie looked in horror. Empty. Every last nickel of her savings was gone.

Sinking back on her heels, she stared at the meager quilt. Even dressed Jennie shivered, but it was as much from anger as the temperature. Thaddeus Gordon had really done it. Left them destitute with not a banker to turn to.

Well, he'd never break them. No man would. Because even if she had to sell the clothes off her back, her own kin were not going to sit here and starve and get evicted.

And who would buy the clothes off her back? Pay to see her stripped of her last stitch of pride?

Slowly the possibility formed . . . grew as her courage did with it. There was only one man in this town rich enough to help, but he drove a hard bargain.

Before that schoolhouse is built, I'll know your price. . . .

Her price. Standing, she dropped the cigar box onto the quilt and went to the washstand to splash water on her face, dab lily of the valley behind her ears, at the pulse points of her wrists. It was wanton behavior, and she ought to be shocked that she was even considering it.

What did she have to lose? Well, her reputation and her teaching position for starters.

But Nate Denison had awakened something in her during their long hours together, and she wanted to know if he was bluffing, playing a game or not. It was the biggest risk of her life, worse than the risks the men in the Castlerock Saloon took at poker.

Second thoughts pursued her. Don't. . . .

Common sense battered at her heart. Don't. . . .

Pride sat up straight and went, "Tsk, tsk."

And then the baby wailed, and Grace began to weep.

Well, who cared about pride . . . or reputation at a time like this? Why should men have it all their way? This wasn't fair.

They made it through a somber meal of oatmeal. Plain and hot. Grace, turning feverish and beginning to cough, declined food and took to her bed. Jennie cradled baby Pearl in one arm and supervised Mariah in the heating of dishwater. Then she brought Pearl to her cradle next to Grace.

"I'm going out, Grace," she announced.

"Don't beg. I couldn't bear Ingrid Jensen's pity."

"I'm not begging. I'm going to arrange a loan. And don't ask any more questions. Just promise you'll stay here and not do anything rash. I'm going to be rash enough for the two of us."

A minute later she'd pulled on her cape and was still fastening it as she headed out into the wind.

Poor Grace deserved better.

But she'd chosen Thaddeus Gordon for better or worse, and Thaddeus, it appeared, when times got rough, turned tail and ran.

Well, Jennie didn't! And though what she was going to do went against all her principles, there were times—desperate times—when a body was allowed to bend principle for the practical matter of survival.

But so help her, when this was over, she'd find a way to go to college, and whatever she studied, she was going to make sure she was never ever at the mercy of men.

As the icy air hit her in the face, all her resolve froze, like mittens left out in a blizzard. She detoured toward the Castlerock Bank. Maybe, if she talked with Edgar . . . She rattled the doorknob. Locked. And so she trudged along the street to the boardinghouse, where she found Edgar at supper. She waited in the dim hallway till he'd had his fill, till the snow melted into her shoes. Waiting, she prayed that Edgar would be able to help, for if he didn't, she had only one other hope . . . one other chance . . . and the daring of it scared her.

Hurry, Edgar. Bring help to my family.

Edgar, seeing her, pulled up short and fumbled with his waistcoat buttons. "Now, Jennie," he said, before she even got a word out. "It was business, pure and simple. I already explained that."

"Despicable business," she shot back. "You could have foreclosed when Thaddeus was there instead of picking on my defenseless sister."

Edgar's face grew florid. "A bank's a business, Jennie. Ask the rich dude. He'd have done no different."

That was the last straw. "Edgar Baskin, I hope every teacher who comes here turns you down." And as the other boarders stuck their heads out the door, shamelessly eavesdropping, she added, "I for one intend to warn them all that as husband material, you are risky!"

"Jennie—"

She ran out, leaving Edgar sputtering. Let him digest *that* along with his supper and see which gave him indigestion quicker. Picking her way along the snowy boardwalk, she headed down Camas Street toward Denison's Folly, the same as she always did on days she made the long walk to school. . . .

Only this time her errand differed. She was down to her last choice. Nate. Briefly she stopped in her tracks, stared over at the snow-covered ashes where her old school had stood. Courage came and went. Grace's life was in ashes, though. Jennie looked from the ashes of the old school up to Nate Denison's mansion. Her idea, while brazen, was really no more outrageous than what mail-order brides did. She shivered; wind stung her face.

Well, she thought at last, giving in, if nothing else, Nate's mansion offered the nearest place to warm up . . . and he might say yes to her offer. It seemed, after all, to be what he'd wanted all along.

*   *   *

For a long time after Jennie stormed out, Mariah clutched the little black runt to her, trying to absorb its shaking. It was so cold, so skinny, and still Paddy wouldn't nurse it.

"What's wrong with you, Paddy?" she asked. "You're forgetting your baby."

Then her brother was there, pulling one of the pups away. "Quit babying the pups, runt."

"Why do you care?"

"Because I'm gonna make sure these pups all sell and get us some money to take care of Ma."

"Except for the little one, the runt of the litter. He's mine."

There was a pause. Above her, her brother held one squirming pup under his arm while he grabbed his coat from a peg. "The little one, Mariah, is a runt. Paddy's never touched him. He'll die soon."

"I'm feeding him." Mariah already had a rag dipped in milk, teasing at the puppy's mouth. His eyes were wide open now, blue and helpless. Like his siblings, he toddled, though he wasn't strong enough to go far.

"Didn't you hear what Ma said? Don't you know Aunt Jennie's out in the cold right now trying to find our pa? And all you can think to do is feed a runt pup when we don't have food to feed *you*. You're selfish, Mariah. A selfish little runt!"

"I'm not. I'm not using any food, just leftover milk."

"Well, Pa's not raising you to be sentimental. Put the runt down and let it die. And you can turn loose all your toads and mice and spiders and whatever other dumb animals you're coddling."

That showed how dumb Thaddeus Jr. was, for Mariah always let the animals go. The only animal she had to love over winter—besides the white mouse—was that runt pup. Why, that's the reason she'd longed so for the pups, to have one of her own to love over the bitter winter. "It can't die."

"That's a fact of life about animals. If they're meant to die like the buffalo, they die. It's nature's way, and if nature doesn't do it, I'll do it."

"No!"

Thaddeus Jr. reached for the squealing runt, but Mariah backed into a corner, ready to fight for her precious pup. "Leave me be, Thaddeus. You can't make me give it up."

"It's a runt, and it's gonna die."

"No!" She dodged her big brother, but Thaddeus Jr. grabbed the puppy and tossed it in a heap by Paddy. "It's got till morning to start nursing. Then if it doesn't, that runt and I are gonna take a visit to the river."

Stricken, Mariah picked up her skirts and ran to the lean-to room, where she knocked Jennie's empty cigar box off the bed and, pressing her face into the threadbare quilt, wept.

Let him die? A helpless little pup, the pup Mariah had waited and waited for. Mariah's braids tangled against her wet cheeks and she had to brush them away while the tears flowed unchecked.

It was one thing to shoot buffalo, but another to let her runt die. The word stung more than ever. Runts were meant to be abandoned and left to die?

But she was a runt too.

And Pa had abandoned her.

Did that mean her pa planned to abandon her and Ma and them all for good? Oh, it was so terrifying it didn't bear thinking on, and she wished she could hibernate with all her animal friends.

But she couldn't. Aunt Jennie had gone out to find help for the household. That meant Mariah could follow her example and find help of her own.

First, though, she had to figure out what to do. The poachers wouldn't help her—even if she knew who they were. Her brothers wouldn't help. Nate Denison might help, but no, he'd just tell Aunt Jennie. As she lay there, still dressed, even to her long stockings, she pictured the various people who'd come and gone in Pa's mercantile, and finally it came to her, the logical people to help save all the runts of the world. Aunt Jennie still hadn't returned, Ma had finally stopped crying, and as the sounds in the house died down, Mariah lay waiting for her chance. Finally she sat up, pulled on extra socks and a frayed wool sweater.

She'd made up her mind. Out in the now cold, empty kitchen, moonlight slid through the window, illuminating a wintry sky more mauve than black. A good night for seeing where she was going. Kneeling, she felt for Paddy . . . then fumbled for the runt. Her heart soared. It was still there. Still alive. Her pup. Her runt. Hers. Hungry, it chewed at a bread crust, lapped milk from her cupped hands. On tiptoe, she retrieved her coat from its peg and thrust it on, then dug mittens out of her pocket. Stealthily, ever so stealthily, she picked up her runt pup, tucked it inside the unfastened top of her coat, and after looking back to make sure none of her brothers had heard her, carefully lifted the latch on the backdoor.

Dear Mr. Denison,

I send this telegram to advise you of the foolhardiness of your plan regarding American bison. My daredevil crew corralled all twelve shaggy beasts last night, and when we woke up, ten of them behaved more like muleheaded women and jumped the fence and ran clean to the next valley. I'll round them up, though I must warn you I'm getting too old and times are too changed for me to play wrangler. I also caution you to build your fence higher yet—and add barbed wire to the top. That's all I can advise about the contrary creatures—except to add this: now you know why I remain to this day a bachelor and relieved about it.

Are you certain you still want them? A buyer from Canada is interested; if you're reconsidering, I'd snap him up. I await your reply.

Your foreman, Jake Rawlinson

P.S. Don't show this letter to Preacher Higgenbottom, but between you and me, I think maybe God meant them to be extinct—buffalo, that is, not women.

Nate stood under the eaves of the railroad depot and reread the telegram. He supposed he should be worried about what to do next, but given the independence of the buffalo, he'd concluded that there was nothing he could do but put them inside his fence and see if the temperamental creatures would stay.

Maybe, he mused, there were some things a man ought not to try to buy. Comparing them to willful women was stretching a point, he supposed, but there were similarities.

Riding home, Nate allowed himself to admit to frustration. It seemed that acquiring his buffalo was one big delay, and Nate wasn't used to being put off. If it wasn't for that lone calf he'd bought from Thaddeus Gordon, Nate's grazing land would be nothing but an empty stretch of snow.

Helga met him at the foot of his elegant staircase.

"I'm leaving." She was untying her apron.

"Quitting or going out?" he asked dryly. Servants didn't tell their employers what they were doing back east, but Nate, remaining calm, decided he must be mellowing, acquiring some western tolerance. "Or both?"

"*Ja,* and wouldn't you be in a fine kettle of fish if I left you here all helpless."

Damned if he did and damned if he didn't. "What makes you think I'd be helpless?"

"When I came back from the snowstorm. Such a state my kitchen was in." She clucked like a hen taking its chick to task. "It's good I leave for a while, Mr. Denison. Sooner or later you're going to have to learn how to take care of yourself like any other independent immigrant."

"I'm not an immigrant."

"You might as well be, Mr. Denison. You're foreign to these parts."

He glowered. No one had ever questioned his credentials before, his worthiness to belong to any group. "How long do I have the pleasure of dining here alone on water and bread?"

"Until my newest grandson wears me out. *Ja*, not a week sooner."

"Which means you'll be back when you're ready." At her sassy nod, he asked, "What makes you think this job will still be here?"

"Because there is not anyone, not even a troll's mother, fool enough to come work for you. That's how I know it'll still be here. I left you two beef pastries in the safe, and there're apple cobbler and boiled potatoes you can fry up. And if that's all too hard for you, open up the tinned sardines."

Audacious woman, thinking he was going to cook for himself. His expression must have shown his displeasure, for Helga turned from pinning on a little black hat with feathers and shiny ribbon. It looked incongruous over her salt-and-pepper hair and calico dress.

"If you can't live on your own cooking, it doesn't matter how grand your house is. That's the way I was raised in the old country and that's what I taught my own boys when they were growing up. Raised them to be independent, I did. A shame someone didn't do the same with all the men of the world."

Contrary woman, he cursed to himself, deciding a shouting match with his own housekeeper would be beneath his dignity. At the sound of her son's wagon, she blew out into the wind and was on her way to Livingston.

He stood at the library window watching her ride off with her strapping son, a rawboned rancher who lived way out beyond the Armstrong place. Were all the women out here, he mused, so strong-willed? He guessed that's why he let Helga get away with so much, with the kind of talk that had left Cornelia Van Altman gaping. In fact, though he pretended to be gruff with Helga, secretly he'd delighted in the way she'd shocked Cornelia.

"Nate," Cornelia had said, "that immigrant is positively insubordinate. Aren't you going to fire her?"

And Nate had told Cornelia that out here, as long as a woman could cook, she could say what she liked. "Besides, she helps keep the schoolchildren in cocoa."

"You're changing, Nate," Cornelia had cautioned, eyes narrowing, voice turning predictably snobbish. "Who'd ever have thought you'd turn your house over to a prim schoolmarm? What's her name? Miss Beasley? That plain scared rabbit from the railroad depot. You must be desperate for women of culture out here. How, darling, can you stand it? She's no one of consequence. She's really going to damage your reputation with the people who count, you know."

He had clenched his hand a little tighter around the champagne glass and given her a casual smile. "Out here, Cornelia, the people who count are the ones you can count on to help you."

"Oh, you're hopeless," she'd said, much to his relief, and made him admire the new gold bauble on her wrist, a birthday gift from her stepfather. "It's a bribe, of course. He'll give me anything I want if I stay away from home and leave him to Mother, but since we're at daggers drawn over my refusal to accept a proposal from that baron, I could care."

"As long as you get more and more baubles, right?" He guessed he'd sounded more cynical than a gentleman ought. For the first time in his life, a dull flush, rather than paint, had colored Cornelia's cheeks.

"Well, why should I want a baron?" she'd asked. "Daisy's not as happy as she makes you think, you know. Her duke's estate is drafty and shabby. It'll take all of her dowry to put it to rights, and"—she lowered her voice—"rumor has it the good duke's only waiting for an heir before he himself takes a—"

"Cornelia, spare me the details of Daisy's marital life. She made her choice."

Cornelia, who was, if anything, more mercenary than Daisy, laid a consoling hand over his. "And I've yet to make mine," she purred. "New York isn't the same, Nate, not without you there. You're the last of a breed, which may be a blessing to all the brokenhearted matrons you left behind."

Last of a breed. The notion struck his fancy. "Then perhaps my stubborn buffalo and I deserve each other."

"If you say so. But I think it's a waste."

"Don't waste time worrying about me, Cornelia." And that was his last flirtatious exchange with the brunette beauty.

If Cornelia reflected what Nate had been, then he hoped he was changing in some way.

Home now, alone, he paced his mansion in the dark, finally retiring upstairs, feeling like a caged beast.

More and more, evenings were becoming something he dreaded. After the noise and bustle of the schoolchildren, he ought to have welcomed the peace and quiet, but all he did each night was pace the place, stand at his window at the early dusk, watching the lamps begin to glow, one by one, in the windows of the town folk. And then he'd retire upstairs to stare out the back bedroom windows at the vast pastureland that stood, snowy white and empty of all life, save for one lone buffalo calf and a milk cow . . . and here and there the steam from shallow hot pools.

Without warning, someone rapped on the front door. Three sharp raps, as if his surprise visitor were in a hurry. Expecting the cavalry, glad of any company on this blustery night, he hurried down, lamp in hand, and pulled the latch.

There, bedraggled as a stray cat, hair blowing in the wind, stood a haunted-looking version of Jennie Beasley. His blood ran a little faster, and instinctively he pulled her inside out of the wind. How the so-haughty Cornelia would condemn this unexpected visit. How very glad Nate was to see the prim little schoolmarm.

So glad that he had to make an effort to restrain himself.

"No calling card preceded you, Jennie," he said with unnecessary formality. "You've taken me by surprise."

"Calling cards?"

He was teasing and didn't like himself for it.

Instead he leaned against the door, staring in disbelief. The schoolmarm had a decided look of passion, especially when she shook out her hair.

"I've had a change of heart," she said, her tone prim and crisp.

But she looked all wind-ruffled and red-cheeked from the wind. He wanted to take up with her where the outdoor elements had left off. The words and the appearance were at odds, and intrigued, he asked, "A change of heart? In what—what way?" Husky, his voice came out sounding like a schoolboy's. It was all there for him in her eyes; he knew women that well. But he still didn't believe it. "What do you want, Jennie?"

After peeling off her mittens—those homespun homely mittens—she cleared her throat and ran a nervous finger across her lips, then through her hair. All too aware of his stare, primitive, predatory, she choked the words out nonetheless.

"I've come to tell you I was wrong. I do have a price after all."

CHAPTER

∾16∾

Jennie had never thought herself capable of barter, except for the box social and hugging bee, and was uncertain how to proceed. Primness was an albatross about her neck. But Mr. Nate Denison, an expert in barter and buying, would certainly know what to do. Instinct propelled her on. Slowly she untied her short cape, then unwrapped it from her shoulders and handed it to him. His brows dived into a frown, as if he couldn't believe his eyes. So when he stood there, unsmiling, and raking her up and down with his eyes, she was nonplussed. But, she told herself, it might take him a minute to adjust.

She clamped her eyes shut. "Let me know what I should do next."

Truth be told, she was still trying to believe what she'd done herself. After all, she should have been shocked at going to a man to trade her reputation for money, especially a man who had publicly humiliated Thaddeus Gordon and all Jennie's family, especially her sister. Instead she was only shocked at the depth of her desire, at the wanton streak she'd never known existed. Why, she was actually looking forward to Nate's teasing response to her. She wanted to feel his hands on her, look into his eyes, have him murmur against her lips. . . . If a woman was going to remain a spinster, she reasoned, she was entitled to one flirtation, one affair of the heart to warm her old age.

One by one she reached for the pins in her hair, and one by one by one slid them out and dropped them. Strand by strand her hair fell about her shoulders. He said nothing, so she reached up to the top button of her shirtwaist.

Suddenly he grabbed her by the arm, propelled her into his library, slammed the door, and leaned against it, arms folded.

With wide-open eyes she stared, openmouthed, at Nate Denison's angry face.

"Is Thaddeus sending the mercantile wares door-to-door now?" he said, voice cold. "What are you selling? Hairpins? Lily-of-the-valley scent? Castile soap? Or does the mercantile have something more intimate to hawk—petticoats perhaps?"

All she could do was stare back, heart thudding, as a dull flush stole across her cheeks. She hadn't mistaken the promise in his words. *Everyone has a price, Jennie, and before that new school is ready, I'll find yours.*

"Answer me." He circled her, looking her up and down as she'd seen ranchers look over their cattle. "Answer me, Jennie!"

With an unexpectedly shaking hand, she reached up to touch his face. "I—I thought this is what you wanted?"

He wrenched her hand away. "Don't do that!"

Looking up at him, she ran a nervous tongue along dry lips.

"Why are you so angry?"

All she received in reply was a glare. His eyes were positively glacial.

"Say something, Nate. What are you thinking?"

Nate was torn. Here was Jennie Beasley, dressed as demurely as ever in dark skirt and high-necked shirtwaist. And yet she had sashayed in here as if she were a bored matron from back east. Where had she learned to do this?

"You're trying to seduce me," he said calmly, displeasure in his tone.

"You mean you can tell?" She sounded pleased, and his body responded; she had the ability to create instant desire in him. The trouble was his head was rebelling, saying no.

"Why did you change your mind?" he asked softly, striving for control. He did desire her, yet with all his willpower he was resisting. "I thought you were different," he muttered as a numbness stole over him. He'd begun to admire that difference. Jennie's unpredictability had become her charm.

And now she was destroying everything about her he'd come to like. "What do you want?" he asked, suspicious. He'd play along just long enough to figure out what had driven her to something this desperate. "You said you had a price. What is it?" Even to his own ears, his voice sounded strained, hollow.

"Eight hundred dollars," she whispered. Her eyes were cast down, so he couldn't read her face. "I need help. Grace needs help. This is a last resort. Can't you tell?"

"Of course I can tell." He was yelling, but it seemed as if he were listening to someone else's voice.

Turning, she tripped. He reached for her and caught the baffled look in her eyes. She turned her head, but not before he saw the tears well.

His anger flared so quickly it surprised himself. He shook her. "Look at me."

She turned. "I—I thought this is what you wanted."

His hand shook as he raised it to her chin and searched her eyes. Had he destroyed the Jennie he'd first come to know? Was that naive sprite gone forever? Slowly he forced her head back and looked down into her eyes and read the truth.

"Couldn't you have just asked me for the money? You asked me to use the mansion." Despite his better intentions, his voice rose. "Why not just ask?"

"Because you've made it clear this is the only way you deal with women . . . with anything."

Her words might as well have been a mirror of all he'd become, and he hated what he heard. Hated himself.

"You naive, foolish woman, Jennie." His voice rose with each word. "I *don't* want you, do you hear?"

After a flinch, she nodded. Her face had drained of color.

Still, he couldn't stop himself. "I was only teasing you, amusing myself in this two-bit town because you were the handiest female and an easy target to overwhelm. Do you understand? I never really wanted you."

He let her go and crossed the room. It was true. He didn't want her. Not in the way he'd taken other women. Not if it meant shattering his last hope. How could she act like just another female? For the first time in his life, he'd thought maybe, just maybe he'd found someone who wouldn't sell their soul for his money. And here she stood, shattering the illusion.

Just for a while he'd begun to think that one woman in this world might be different, better, worth fighting for. He was wrong. Jennie was like all the others.

"You don't want me?" Her voice trembled.

He had to fight from taking her into his arms. Damn all the women of the world. Damn his money. It was a curse, a wall between him and all he really wanted.

Tears coursed down her cheeks. "What did I do wrong? I know I wouldn't know how—"

"That's the whole point!" He watched her flinch, resisted the tug to go and take her in his arms. "Pin up your hair. You look like a two-dollar strumpet, and you're acting as if I'm the king in my countinghouse."

"Please, Nate . . ." Standing, Jennie held her hair up with one hand, and with the other tucked in her shirtwaist. "At least explain. Why is it all right for you to tease me all the time, but when I tease you, you act morally righteous? No wonder women despair of ever getting the vote. You men are all alike. Hypocrites!"

He rounded on her. "I take back the offer. I don't want you selling yourself—to anyone."

"Then you've changed."

"No, you've changed. You're not the same meek woman who came here asking for shelter for fourteen kids, Jennie."

That silenced her. For a minute she stood there, gulping back tears. "My sister's family means more to me than—than anything."

"Is that all?" He strode to his desk and yanked open a drawer. Females. They were all the same, every last one. . . .

The door squeaked open and he spun again, a fistful of bills sticking out of each hand.

All of a sudden money showered down around her. Bills and bills of paper money. "Take that and leave."

She watched it rain down around her, her shoulders slumping.

Jennie stood there, eyes downcast, humiliated that he was rejecting her.

After fumbling with the latch on the front door, she brushed the rest of the money off her skirt and ground her foot in it. "Keep it." She hurried out into the cold, her little cape trailing off one arm, her pulse beating in her throat. She'd gambled and lost. Not only did Nate Denison not want her anymore, but he'd deceived her. She was a total abject failure.

Mariah paused on the road to Yellowstone. She'd been walking forever, it seemed, and now she wasn't sure where Pa's cabin was. It was like the cabin was being contrary tonight, playing hide-and-seek. She thought it was at the boundary of Yellowstone Park, but it had been a whole year since she'd followed her brothers here. She had to find it because the cavalrymen would come checking on it, and they'd help her runt pup. Helping animals was what they did best, after chasing tourists away from hot pools and watching for fires.

She walked some more and some more, till her toes tingled with cold. Inside her coat, the runt pup shivered. "We're not lost, pup. We'll find them, you'll see. It's straight under the moon—that's what Pa always said. His shack was right under the moon."

She looked up at the big silvery moon and gasped in wonder.

Up on the hill, right under the moon, a white plume of steam gushed toward the stars. A geyser! None of the tourists ever said a thing about. Maybe it waited for the tourists to leave and then gushed. She giggled. "C'mon, runt, let's go see it. Pa said the shack was near a geyser hole. That's it!"

Clutching the pup tighter, she turned off the road and ran across the frozen snow, her gaze fastened on the path made by the moon and that big gusher spewing white up into the sky. Like a lantern, it was beckoning her to come this way. This way, Mariah, and you won't get lost.

She could almost feel the spray on her face, was almost at the top of the hill when the earth sucked the geyser back in. Like hide-and-seek.

Then she heard men's voices. "Hey, kid, what're you doing up there? Don't move!"

She looked below the moon and saw a lantern coming toward her, closer and closer. "Don't move," said a male voice. "Don't take another step."

She hugged the runt to her face and then waved at the pair of men. Cavalrymen. Dressed up in funny leggings and California coats and hats with earflaps.

"Hirum? Orvil? It's about time you got here on rounds. Did you see the gusher?"

And then strong male arms scooped her up.

Nate Denison stared for a long time at the door, then turned to the decanter of whiskey on his desktop, unstoppered it, and drank deeply. Finally he sank down into the chair and leaned back, trying to analyze his anger.

Helga's footsteps sounded at the doorway. "I'm back. Do you wish anything?"

"To be alone."

"That is nothing unusual. That is not a request. That is a habit with you."

"If you want to quit, Helga, now would be ideal. I'm going to torch the house."

"Such a waste." She clucked, hands on hips. "Just when I've put up dozens of jars of corn and beans for the winter, and we've hardly begun eating it. If you're going to burn down this place, could you wait till spring? That way we'll have the food eaten . . . and the new school will be ready."

"Bake me a ginger cake then."

"At this hour?"

"Do it, Helga, or quit."

"I'll make lefse, no ginger cakes, and your temper, Mr. Denison, rivals that of the buffalo. It is a wonder the pretty little teacher does not leave town entirely, and consider herself lucky."

Leave town. She'd never do that. An unaccountable panic seized him, and standing, he paced to the window, staring out into the blackness of Castlerock. A few kerosene lamps winked in distant windows. Faint glows. In a while they'd be extinguished and the town would be pitch-black. With a quick toss, he downed the rest of his whiskey and caressed the empty glass, studying how its many facets caught the lamplight.

What had happened to him? Why had he reacted to her so harshly? Humiliated her?

The only plausible answer—that he cared for her—was immediately rejected. Nate Denison would never care for a prim little schoolmarm from Nowhere, Montana. So why then had he turned her away?

She hadn't changed, of course. She'd acted out of desperation. No, it was he who'd changed from the man who preyed on women with a cavalier's casualness. Now he realized that wasn't really him any more than Miss Jennie Beasley was a Fifth Avenue debutante. Nor did he want his old life back.

He wanted, deeply and fervently, to have a woman's love and tender wifely devotion. He wanted a family. Children like Jennie's niece Mariah. To grow old with the same woman.

His chest ached, somewhere in the vicinity of his heart, an ache that had grown steadily worse since she'd run out.

But then, hadn't he practically thrown her out? Fool. A fool in spades, thinking he could judge all women by Daisy. Daisy had been fool's gold, false. But Jennie, ah, Jennie was the real thing. Only a blind man could fail to see she was infatuated with him, that she'd confused his teasing for something else. Certainly she deserved something better from him than anger. She deserved gentle words. And more than that. He needed to talk to her, to take back his anger . . . better, find out why he'd been consumed with an anger that cut deeper than when Daisy had jilted him. Jennie Beasley had completely confounded him, and he'd know why.

The Gordon house resembled the stock market the day of the panic. Only instead of stockbrokers reeling, children sat quietly, faces reflecting the bottom of some awful abyss. Tears streaked Grace Gordon's face, and the golden-haired boys huddled around a cold stove, staring morosely at a potful of lumpy oatmeal. A wailing baby dominated the entire scene, and Nate had the feeling he had just walked on stage during the final act of a melodrama.

"Where's Jennie?" he asked while simultaneously lifting the lid to stoke the fire. Everyone shrugged. He'd had a hint of how hard life was for the average citizen of Castlerock. The schoolchildren had given him that—with their pathetic lard-pail lunches and patched overalls and runny noses. But now reality came crashing in. This was far, far different from the world out of which his bored paramours had come.

He might not be able to fix a wagon axle or play house-keeper, but clearly some direction was called for, and he had gotten used to starting the furnace in his mansion. He did know how to heat a house.

"You boys go get wood," he said, counting on them to have long memories of his woodshed.

Instead of obeying, they stared at him.

Finally Thaddeus Jr. got some words out. "Edgar locked the woodshed because of Pa's tools."

Nate made a note to withdraw what money he'd put in Edgar's chicken coop of a bank; enough by Edgar's standards to hit his bank's assets like a fox cleaning out the henhouse. Edgar, for all his puff and paunch, could not compete with Nate.

"Then go get some from my house," he said now. "The place is unlocked. Just walk in." Hang the furniture, the bric-a-brac, the antique table. They could chop it up and burn it all. Quickly his gaze swept around, taking in the abject poverty, and suddenly he understood what had driven Jennie to come to him with her desperate offer. "Go in and bring some food back here. Whatever you want."

Grace half stood, face proud. "Mr. Denison, we don't want charity."

For the first time he felt humility. "It's a neighborly gesture. Isn't that how it works out here? When one neighbor needs help, another neighbor pitches in? Now, as I see it, unless you let me help, you're saying I can't be a part of this community."

"Mr. Denison, it's Thaddeus—he wouldn't want you to give to us."

Nate took a step toward her, determined to gain her trust. Not buy it. But gain it. It was a new concept, one he'd have to feel his way through.

"Now, I know he thinks I've brought him to ruin, but I don't hold the power over the cavalry he thinks. If I planted any suspicions in their heads, though, I'm sorry."

Grace swept back a limp strand of hair, and her eyes filled with tears. "I know you didn't. He's just a stubborn man, and proud too. But none of this is for you to worry about."

Nate, feeling utterly conspicuous in his fine wool coat and leather gloves, moved close to Grace Gordon and took her work-reddened hand in his. His experience at consoling weeping women was limited, usually because his absence was the cause of their tears. This was, he realized, perhaps the first time he'd seen a woman weep because of what some other man had done.

Then he heard Jennie's voice, talking to the littlest Gordon. "But you *must* have some idea where Mariah went. You *must*."

The Gordon boys—with their matching golden curls—all

looked like raggedy Gainsborough boys, and he'd never quite
sorted out the names, but one replied, his voice scared. "She
was with the pups and everyone was worrying over where Pa
went. We just thought he went hunting, but now Mariah's
gone too."

Grace now paced the floor of the kitchen, baby on her
shoulder, face drawn, a nagging cough adding to her plight.

Mariah. Run away? Whatever needed to be said to Jennie
would have to wait, and for the first time Nate admitted to
himself that a feeling of affection had sprung up unknowingly
between himself and the lonely little girl who loved animals,
who'd insisted on seeing the buffalo calf, and who had named
his buffalo sight unseen. Whether Jennie liked it or not, he was
going to help.

"Jennie," he said, and she stopped dead in her tracks, a myri-
ad of emotions washing over her face. Surprise . . . hurt . . .
humiliation . . . then finally anger.

"What are you doing here?"

"I came to talk to you."

"Your timing is off. I can't talk. Mariah's missing now
on top of all else. Why don't you leave and go check on
your telegrams? Maybe your buffalo are arriving, or some
new tassels for your draperies."

In three quick strides he closed the distance between them.
"Jennie, let me talk to you. Alone." There was raw pleading
in his voice.

"You had me alone."

It felt like a slap.

Couldn't they quit sparring with each other? Even in the
midst of disaster? She backed away from him, but in two
steps he grabbed her by the arms.

"Don't play heroine now," he said, ignoring her watching
family. "Whatever happened earlier doesn't matter."

She tried to wrench away. "Let go!" Then she stared up at

him defiantly. "It doesn't matter anymore."

He half shook her. "I'm going to help, and you can't stop me. Now, what do you mean, Mariah is missing?"

Jennie, who stood there wishing the floor would swallow her up, felt overwhelmed. With one sweep of the broom, she could probably chase Nate Denison out of here. In his eyes, she'd sullied her virtue—practically. Yet that seemed so long ago, insignificant now.

Thaddeus Jr.'s voice continued. "The runt pup's gone too."

"Do you suppose she went after her pa?"

"Who knows?" Grace said. "Thaddeus never told me where *he* went."

Well, this was one fine mess. Men!

Looking up, Jennie found Nate staring directly at her.

Jennie couldn't meet his eyes, couldn't stand the apology, the patronizing look of those beautiful blue eyes. She only wanted him to go away so he couldn't further witness her humiliation. "This is a family matter."

"Not anymore. This is a town matter, and I live here too. Now, where could Mariah have gone?"

For a long minute he held her like that, staring at her, and without warning she sagged against him. "I—I don't know. No one knows. And since it's freezing out there, you'll excuse me while I bundle up."

"You're not going out searching alone."

Swiftly, as he did in business, Nate took charge. Where a naive schoolmarm was concerned, he could win—no, that wasn't the feeling. It wasn't a matter of wanting to show her up. He simply wanted to help her . . . and find the little girl, Mariah, whom he was scared to death for. He needed to help. Needed to find that little girl.

"Would she go to town? The new school? She'll show up sooner or later. And if she doesn't then we'll organize a search party."

Jennie's shoulders sank in despair. "Sooner or later isn't good enough. It's below freezing outside, and she's got a dozen or so hiding places for all her animals. She's not in town. I know that child and I know she's gotten some notion in her head about saving that pup, and that means she's headed out of town. I'm going out to look right now."

"Then I'm going with you."

"You? You can't even fix an axle. How are you going to keep up?"

They stood a mere six inches apart, daring each other to back down.

He could have wrung her pretty little neck. "We can stand here fighting all night about who's going or we can both go and find her. Now, which will it be?"

He was right. Jennie slowly exhaled. Darn, but he was right. Every minute she argued with him was another minute Mariah spent lost out in the cold.

With Mariah's safety at stake, she couldn't say no. Anything else that needed to be said would have to wait.

"Say something." He ground the words out.

"Together." It was a grudging acceptance.

His face relaxed. "And we'll have a plan. First, you pull on all the warm clothes you can find. Borrow some of Thaddeus's long underwear—and the warmest coat in town. The boys here are going to look around town. And as for Grace . . ." He looked at Mariah's mother and quickly designated one Gordon boy to stay with her. "Don't worry. I own all this property now, and I'm not going to evict you."

Jennie whirled at the doorway. "Since when do you own it?"

"As soon as I tell Edgar at the bank that I'm buying it, which will take me all of one minute. I think he'll like my price." And before anyone could shut their mouth on that announcement, he had another novel idea. "On my way back here with the sleigh, I'm going to telegraph down to Fort Yellowstone."

Sleigh? "The cavalry?" she guessed. "You're going to call out the cavalry to find Mariah?" Gratitude, profound and weary gratitude, laced her voice. Just like that, he'd thought of everything.

"Wow," little Caleb Gordon said, "you think the cavalry's going to chase Mariah like they do poachers?"

"That's part of their job—to look for lost people in the park while they're on rounds. Don't worry, we'll find your sister. Mariah's a very bright child, but she can't walk as fast as my sleigh can glide."

"She's dumb to run away." This from Thaddeus Jr. "Isn't she, Jennie?"

Jennie would rather have been watching the Armstrong boys sail spit wads at her new blackboard than face this.

"Nate?" She needed him. However she'd humiliated herself, she needed him now.

His voice was soft, reassuring. "I suspect Mariah thought this through, that she's got a plan. I don't know what it is, but we'll find her." He moved a step closer, looked down into her eyes, ached to reassure her. "Jennie, I promise, we'll find her." His hand reached out to touch her face, then he realized how quiet the room had grown, how everyone was staring. He dropped his hand and headed for the door.

"Twenty minutes," he said.

"All right, then."

When he returned, exactly nineteen minutes later, there was Jennie waiting in the doorway, arms hugging her middle.

She was buttoning a navy-blue caped coat—hastily borrowed from Ingrid Jensen, who, scenting gossip of the first order, had followed the boys back to the house. It was, she proudly reassured Nate, the very warmest coat in town, and Nate decided the widow had an admirable streak after all. He watched, impatient, as Jennie stuffed her hair up inside a knit hat and pulled on heavy mittens. In a heartbeat he could have her in his arms, but instead he offered her a hand up into the sleigh, tucked her under a pile of buffalo robes and blankets, set her feet on a bucket of hot coals Helga had dug out of the furnace.

"Turn to me." He pulled the funny cap further over her ears, wrapped the loose ends of it up over her cheeks.

"Drive, Nate. We've no time to lose."

And they were off. Side by side, they said not a word. Jennie, pride clinging to her like icicles, stared straight ahead, her cheeks already pink from the cold. She sat, prim as could be, mittened hands outside the robes, and he reached over and laid his hand on hers. She pulled it away, staring out at the rocky landscape leading into Yellowstone.

Let it go, he told himself. Find Mariah, and then have it out with Jennie. Staring straight ahead, he clicked the reins and spurred on the pair of bays that pulled the cutter.

They were heading south on the road to Yellowstone, now covered with a slick coating of frozen week-old snow. Jennie's collar was pulled up as prim as could be, but he could feel her, warm and trusting, beside him. It was the first time he'd felt human in weeks.

CHAPTER

~17~

"You're heading for Yellowstone, for the stagecoach road."

Jennie's tone was skeptical, but at least she was talking to him.

"Why?" she said, grabbing his arm urgently. "Not one of your famous predictions or hunches? This, Nate Denison, is not the stock market." Hysteria tinged Jennie's voice.

It was night, but a full moon had risen, lighting the sky. If they didn't find her soon, though, Mariah would be in danger from the arctic cold.

Nate looked down at the way she gripped his arm. "Believe in me." She turned away. "Jennie, I may have done little to earn your trust, but try."

"Why should I?" And she let go, pulled away, and scrunched herself up on the far side of the little sleigh.

No, he didn't suppose she had any reason to trust him, not after the way he'd spurned her. But there'd be time enough to sort through that.

"I put myself in her shoes," he began, "and knowing her and animals, I thought of the cavalrymen—who protect animals."

He stopped.

"You're not making a bit of sense."

"When I called the fort to report her missing, I mentioned her pa's cabin, thinking they might send out extra men on patrol up that way."

"And . . . ?" Something in his expression gave her reason to hope.

"The cavalry wired right back that they'd already picked a little girl up. A pair of cavalrymen decided to use the full moon to do a little poacher searching and instead they came up with a little girl and a pup."

Jennie was staring up at him, tears shimmering in her eyes. "You're sure?"

He nodded.

Her mouth was open, her heart thumping wildly, wanting to believe, afraid he was teasing her. "Truly? Can I trust you?"

"Truly." For the first time he knew the feeling of giving someone joy with a single word. It felt unexpectedly satisfying.

Before he could ponder longer about the power of words, she was pummeling his arm. "Why didn't you tell me? You let me come this far and not know she's been found? How *could* you?"

His gaze lingered on her mouth and then he turned back to steer the reins. "Because I'm selfish. We have to go down into Yellowstone to bring her back, and this way I got you alone. If I'd told you before we left, you wouldn't have come."

Her silence was forbidding, so after a few minutes, he reined in, stopped the sleigh right there on the road to Yellowstone.

"Jennie—"

"Keep going."

"She's fine."

"Not until I see her."

"You won't see her until you talk to me."

"Nate Denison, drive this sleigh on to Yellowstone. Mariah might escape, might do anything."

"Jennie, they've got her in the commander's quarters. Hirum and Orvil identified her, so she's safe, and so's the pup, and she's not going anywhere until we get there."

She stared at him. Silent. Impassive. Until five minutes later when a wagonload of cavalry officers passed by on its way to Gardiner.

"You folks want that little girl, better hurry on or the fort'll have her adopted. You two'll freeze to death, too, if you don't get the sleigh moving. Fair warning."

They looked at each other. Her glare was hard to sustain and evolved into a giddy grin. "You should have told me the moment you knew. What a heartless trick, Nate Denison."

Guilty, he shrugged. "So was the trick you pulled—coming to my house, throwing yourself at me. I never know what you're going to do next. Mariah must take after you." He flicked the reins and they continued on the road to Fort Yellowstone.

Jennie wasn't going to argue. Instead she peered out the side of the sleigh, unsure how to respond. What would *this man* do next?

At length Nate spoke again, just some gentle conversation to break through Jennie's icy facade.

"It just came to me, Jennie, what I'm going to do—with both Mariah's pup and with that little herd of buffalo I bought."

Mariah, Nate realized suddenly, reminded him of himself at the same age. Lost and alone. And very fond of animals. But he'd been forbidden to have any by his fastidious parents and even fussier housekeepers. He could understand Mariah's fervent desire to save a sickly pup. And even though buffalo weren't much in the way of pets, maybe, just maybe, he'd keep them. His wealth would buy something worthwhile, something enduring, and no one could condemn a man for that, could they? He could see Mariah's solemn little face brighten up when he told her that. After he bought that black runt from her.

"Don't you want to know what I'm going to do, Jennie?"

"You're fanciful."

"So are you."

She was silent a minute. "You mean earlier."

"You were pretty desperate."

"To bargain with a man like you? I guess so. You don't know what it's like to love your family that much, do you?"

He whipped around to glance at her. How did she know? "I wish I did."

"Why did you get angry?" Her voice sounded very small, almost swallowed up in the dark and the cold.

"That's why I came to find you. So we could talk."

"There's no need. I'll never do anything so foolish again. It was as silly as Mariah running away. And near as dangerous."

"I want to talk."

"Am I stopping you?"

"Jennie, I got mad when you walked in there acting as if I was worth no more than my money. Which may be my own fault . . . but I've never known a woman like you." He glanced at her. "Truly, Jennie. If you're angry at me for spurning you, don't be. It was a compliment."

"You're a real swell with words, Nate. Save them for Cornelia."

"No . . . I want you, Jennie. Not her. It's true." But he wanted her to want him for himself, not his money.

"Well, I'm going to be a spinster teacher and attend college, so you might as well save your breath." Shrugging, she shaded her eyes from his scrutiny and looked off into the darkness.

A coyote howled, serenading them.

After negotiating another curve, he slowed. The hills were steeper here, the road more dangerous.

"Keep going," she instructed.

He urged the horses forward, and after a few more moments he said, "I've never known a confirmed spinster before. Why?"

She sighed, as if the answer were so obvious. "Do you think I want to marry a man like Grace did, a man who can wander off whenever he pleases with not a word, bully his children, and dominate his wife? I might bow to principle in order to survive, but I'd never choose a dreary predictable marriage like that."

Momentarily stunned, Nate reined in the sleigh and stared for a minute at the horses stamping impatiently. Other than that, the snowy hill was perfectly still, and at last, like a window being cleared of steam, everything came clear. Why, she'd described exactly what he dreaded about marriage. The predictability of his friends' marriages left him cold. And the ruthless predictability with which Daisy had wed. He could, he knew, have kept Daisy, but realized now why he'd not called her duke out for a duel: he didn't want a traditional marriage either, one whose dreary pattern he could predict down through the years.

"Drive on," Jennie ordered when he slowed again. "You're a terrible driver, Nate."

Nate stopped the sleigh completely.

"Jennie, you're talking to me as if I'm your personal groom."

"So?"

"So, can you actually see yourself knuckling under if you and I were wed?" He reined in and turned to her.

"What do you mean?"

"Do you think I'd ever be able to dominate you?"

"Of course not. I don't care how rich you are. You're just like everyone else."

"Good."

"Good?"

"We're quite compatible."

"In what way?"

"You are unpredictable when I least expect it. The things we have in common are the best things—our mutual eccentricities and friendship—I hope—and a similar distaste for conventional marriage patterns. That's more than my parents had in common. No, we'd never have one of those dreary predictable marriages."

She stared at him, nonplussed. "Are you asking me to marry you, Nate Denison?"

There was a long pause, and he half turned to look at her, as if he'd surprised himself. "Am I? Yes."

"You'd do anything to get your way, wouldn't you?"

"I guess I just realized I want you to give yourself, not be bought. I'm asking as nice as I know how."

She looked defiant. "Nate Denison, we're on the road to Fort Yellowstone, and Mariah is waiting."

"I won't ask twice." My God, women back on Fifth Avenue would curtsy for a proposal from him.

She sighed in resignation. "I accept, then." And she looked at him, as if he'd lost his mind. "Are you satisfied? Drive on. We have to get Mariah back before Grace worries to death and before you make any more rash promises and vows."

Smiling, he picked up the reins and urged the sleigh on toward the lights of the fort. "I bet right now Mariah's showing off the runt pup and making friends."

He grabbed her hand, and though she sat primly staring out into the darkness, he thought he saw her blink back tears, and he held her hand all the tighter. Earning her trust would take time. Trust. It had no price. For the first time in his life, Nate knew the helplessness of wanting something whose price was beyond money. His feelings for Mariah and Jennie made him realize he'd never really risked anything of value before tonight.

They rode around the next bend and the next. Five miles separated Castlerock from Fort Yellowstone, and Mariah luckily had been found near the Park entrance. Nate could have given the cavalry a medal.

When Nate arrived at the Fort with Jennie, she was out of the sleigh and would have marched right into the men's barracks unannounced if Nate hadn't rounded her up and taken her to the headquarters. More wooden buildings.

An officer of the U.S. Cavalry met them at the entrance. "Your telegraph came just as our men were bringing her in. A couple of the men here knew her, so she's been plenty content. Lucky little girl, though, to get found in the first place."

"I'm her aunt," Jennie said anxiously. "Please tell her I'm here. Let me see her."

Moments later they were inside the commander's room, judging by its map-covered wall and imposing desk. A potbellied stove crackled away.

Mariah, hand in hand with a little blond girl the same size as herself, appeared in the doorway from another room, looking like the cat that swallowed the canary. The commander of Fort Yellowstone followed them.

"Aunt Jennie," Mariah said. "You're not mad, are you? I made a new friend, and she likes my pup. She's got a real Colombian wheel and a kaleidoscope both."

Jennie knelt to hug Mariah, and her niece's arms came around her, soft and oh, so welcome. "Dear Mariah." She was so happy that she very nearly forgave Nate for frightening her on the ride down here. "I'm not mad. No one's mad. But very worried. That was quite a scare you gave us. You should have left a note, you know." She brushed aside Mariah's bangs and then watched them fall over her forehead, dark and feathery.

"I brought the pup here for safekeeping," Mariah explained.

"Yes, Nate—Mr. Denison figured all that out."

"He's very smart, isn't he? I knew the cavalry would find me, but if they didn't, I figured Mr. Denison would know where to find me, so I was never worried. I only had to find a place for my pup. All the animals are protected in here, and no one can let him die now."

Jennie and Nate exchanged a glance. "Yes, well—he'll be fine," Jennie said.

"Will you give me the pup, Mariah?" Nate knelt down to Mariah's level. He'd been intending to ask if she'd sell it, so the request to give away the pup surprised even him. This was new, learning to ask for a favor.

"You mean let my pup live in your house? Right in Castlerock?" Her expression grew hopeful, then fell. "The cavalry's got rules."

The commander cleared his throat. "We reassured her no animal could be taken from the Park . . . but maybe we can bend the rule on this one." He winked at Nate. "The pup's yours."

Mariah smiled wide. "You'll let me visit him?"

Nate nodded. "I think I'd like that."

"Can I go play with Lucinda now?" Mariah asked, as if nothing very exciting had happened save for playing with the rotating wheel from the Colombian Exposition that she held. The girls ran off, Lucinda having earned the honors of feeding the pup from a doll's baby bottle.

Joy . . . relief . . . Jennie couldn't put a name to the emotions she felt. But it was the most natural thing to wrap her arms about Nate for joy, hug him so tight she couldn't breathe. It was natural for his arms to come up around her, to embrace her back. "I told you they'd take care of her, Jennie," he whispered hoarsely.

"Oh, Nate, thank you." Their words tumbled on top of each other, hurried, anxious, then they fell into a mutual silence. She couldn't seem to let go; if she had her way, she'd go on hugging him forever.

How long they stood embracing Jennie didn't know.

The commander of the fort cleared his throat and then his deep voice pierced her consciousness. "Mr. and Mrs. Gordon?"

Jennie turned. "Oh, no—"

Nate had gone perfectly still.

"We've got most anything you need in our guest cabins. Nothing fancy of course. Army style, but comfortable. We're quite self-sufficient here. Anything else you only need to ask for. Extra blankets. Food . . . hot coffee. That's it. I should have ordered something to warm you two up—"

"No—" Jennie stared at her feet.

"Mrs. Gordon, are you all right?" the commander asked.

"I'm not Mrs. Gordon." Her voice was very small.

"Did I read the message correctly? It said her parents were coming to find her."

"I guess I did put that in the telegraph message," Nate confessed. "We were in a hurry. I thought parents would carry more clout. This is her aunt."

"Ah, aunt and uncle. Mr. and Mrs.?"

"Jennie's her aunt—Jennie Beasley."

The commander coughed discreetly. "Let me get this straight. If you're not her uncle, who are you?"

Nate turned and shook the officer's hand. "Nate Denison. I live up in Castlerock. Friend of the Gordon family. If you meant it about being self-sufficient, would you happen to have a preacher somewhere in this fort?"

Jennie thought she was hearing things and quickly looked

up. Nate was staring down at her, a question in his eyes. Grabbing his hand, she led him off to a corner right beneath a stuffed moose head for a hasty whispered conference.

"I have a price too," Nate told her. "I want you, but on my terms."

"Which are?"

"I want you to say again you want me—here, alone, away from my house, my wealth, the Castlerock gossips."

"Nate, none of that means anything."

"Then marry me with nothing but my hand in yours," Nate said, his voice suddenly rising above a whisper.

"Now?"

"Now?" The commander blinked like an owl, then called for his wife.

"Now." That was Nate's voice, firm and steady and resolute.

"This is rather hasty." Jennie sounded flustered.

Nate untied the frog closures on her borrowed coat. "Exactly. Do you know how many fussed-over high-society weddings I've attended and hated? It's now, Jennie. Impulsive and spur of the moment. I've never done a thing without predicting its outcome and speculating on its advantages and disadvantages. For the first time in my life, I know this is right. Instinct tells me. It's right. Now."

"We'll shock the entire town of Castlerock."

He grinned from ear to ear. "Exactly." He smiled gently. "I told you. I'm the only unorthodox man you'll ever find to match you. Besides, think of what Ingrid Jensen will say if we spend the night out alone, without benefit of a snowstorm, and I don't marry you. I doubt she'll give us the benefit of the doubt two times." Briefly he touched her cheek with the back of his hand. He looked as if he were searching for the right words, then finally said, "I'm not teasing. You won't regret it."

Jennie looked into his eyes and saw, if not passion, then loneliness and honest hope. Nate wasn't offering love, but she doubted he'd ever love a woman. He would, she knew, honor his promise to be good to her, to accept her as she was, and as he said there weren't many men out here who could do that . . . and then, too, she loved him. Loved him more than all her dreams for herself. Dreams were all good and well and could come true later, but Nate was now, and she didn't want to ever be parted from him. Instinct said yes.

Yes, she loved him, and that's finally what decided it.

"You'll have to marry me in my schoolmarm clothes, I'm afraid."

"Just exactly how I think of you." He reached for her funny little knit cap. "Just take this off, and let me see that copper-penny hair. That's all I want changed." He slid her hat off and watched her hair tumble about her shoulders.

Oh, there was some fussing about by the commander's wife, who insisted on helping pin up her hair again, then found a Bible for Jennie to hold, along with some dried Queen Anne's lace. For a ring, they borrowed one from the commander's pinky. And Mariah and her runt pup stood up as witnesses for Jennie. Hirum was summoned to stand as witness for Nate. Of course no one could find a license, but the preacher yawned and said he'd find that in the morning.

"Lots of rules get bent down here. See no reason why we can't bend any rules about marriage certificates," he said.

And with no more to-do, other than waiting for the preacher to pull his suspenders up over his long red underwear, the simple service began, Nate in a borrowed tie, Jennie in her dark skirt and schoolmarm shirtwaist. Neither Jennie nor Nate thought about the details any further. It was done on instinct, and some instincts could be trusted.

"You may kiss the bride," the preacher finished, then yawned and cleared his throat.

It was a sweet lingering kiss. Jennie tasted of rum and spice and her hair was faintly scented with lily of the valley.

Still, the preacher waited, as if he weren't done.

"Two bucks," the commander prompted in a stage whisper. Nate and Jennie looked at each other. Nate turned his pockets inside out. Empty. Jennie dug into the pocket of the coat and, after a bit of fumbling, came up with a few coins Ingrid had sewn into an inner seam.

With another yawn, the preacher snatched the coins. "The balance is on the house for now. Pay me next spring."

They shared an amused smile, then as reality sank in, a bit self-consciously they drew apart. Had they acted in haste?

The small wedding party—the fort commander, Hirum, Nate, and Jennie—shared hot cider, while the commander's wife rounded up some fresh-baked carrot cake for their celebration. They ate and talked of mundane things—the sleigh ride in, the telegraph operator, the poaching problems.

Jennie looked up at her husband. "I'm going to make sure Mariah's tucked in."

Nate tugged her back. "Jennie, she's content with her new friend."

"Just let me be certain. It would be selfish of me to get married and go off without tucking her in."

In truth, she needed just a few minutes alone to gather her thoughts. Oh, what had she done with the owner of Denison's Folly? And who was the foolish one now?

She'd married the man. Oh, mercy, no one would believe it. This was far worse than making papier-mâché birds in his dining room or allowing Mariah to go chasing after a toad in his kitchen. And never had she seen *this* in their imaginary window.

By now, Mariah was half-asleep, tucked up in a pair of woolen blankets, her dark hair unbraided and damp against her cheeks. Beside her on the floor was the toy Colombian wheel and a game of Authors. On the other side of the bed slept her new friend, Lucinda, the captain's eleven-year-old daughter.

Bosom friends already.

Well, Jennie guessed if she could elope with Nate just like that, Mariah could make a friend that fast.

"It'll be all right," the commander's wife reassured her with a knowing smile. "We'll lend Mariah some of Lucinda's clothes for the trip back to Castlerock tomorrow and have hers washed. And you're all invited to eat breakfast with us. Seven o'clock sharp."

Outside, in the office, the commander scraped his fork across his plate and then coughed. "Well," he said, still clearing his throat, "marry in haste, repent at leisure. I shall leave you to repent." He gave his wife a meaningful look. "It's getting late for old married folks like us. Time to retire."

Tactfully his wife collected their plates—clear glass ones— and set them aside, then directed Hirum to show them to their cabin.

"I knew you wanted to flirt with the schoolmarm," Hirum said with a smile. "Got caught too. Wait'll I tell Orvil."

"Hirum," Jennie said quickly, "could you do me a favor and telegraph Grace that Mariah's fast asleep and safe?"

"My pleasure." Hirum wore a look of polite bemusement. Oh, but *this* news wasn't going to stay secret long. Why, from the look on his face, he'd have it telegraphed up to Castlerock before Nate and Jennie could shut the cabin door.

Imagine, she thought, watching him hold open the door for her. Nate Denison had spurned her and then, hours later, married her.

Yes, the man was definitely unpredictable.

And she had little idea what to expect next.

CHAPTER

⮟18⮞

Married and alone with Nate. They stood side by side, looking at the spartan little room. Hardly the place for a man of wealth to spend his wedding night. Log-hewn with a floor of bare wooden planks, it was the epitome of simplicity. Already a fire roared in the potbellied stove, radiating warmth to each side of the room, where a pair of army bunks sat, each covered with a gray blanket. A kerosene lamp near a washstand cast a soft glow. Pegs for clothing lined one wall, and a single window allowed the wintry moonlight to spill across the floor. A room more unlike Nate's bedroom she couldn't imagine. After taking in the furnishings, she cast a nervous glance at Nate, who looked down at her, equally uneasy, it seemed.

The commander's wife had, at the last minute, thrust into Jennie's hands a hastily made-up package. She walked over to the bed on the right and opened it. Out fell a nightgown—a prim confection of lace and ribbons. A hairbrush fell to the floor, as well as a bar of scented soap, something far more elegant than the utilitarian army soap that sat by the washstand. Blushing, Jennie bent to pick up the brush and, glancing back, saw Nate standing there watching her.

Hastily she bundled up the nightgown and, before Nate could comment, stuffed it under the pillow. She wasn't going to change in front of him? Was she?

Then she turned back to face Nate's chiseled face. His coffee-colored hair was wind-tousled, and this time he was grinning at her. Somehow, from that look, she knew she wasn't going to have to worry about how to take off her clothing.

"Well, you got your wish," she said, dusting off her hands. "You've got me apart from the schoolchildren."

"Willingly. Without having to bargain for you."

"You didn't have to go to extremes and marry me, though." It had happened so fast that she needed to be reassured.

He untied the fastenings on her coat and shed his own. "I don't do anything I don't want to, Jennie. A man gets lonely out here. I've gotten lonely when you're not in that house."

"With a houseful of telegrams and velvet settees to keep you company?"

"Telegrams don't warm a man at night."

"Oh." She stood stock-still, staring at him, touched at his confession. Even rich men got lonely. So lonely that they'd settle for the local schoolmarm for a wife? But, she tried to remind herself, he had suggested they'd be compatible.

"Lonelier than you know. No one in town thinks I fit in. I get very lonely, indeed, Jennie. Don't tell me you haven't been lonely too."

Yes, in the midst of that crowded house, she had known loneliness. There could, she decided, be less worthy reasons

for marrying. Her heart pattered a little harder, which was
the only predictable thing about being around towering Nate
Denison. Always, when she looked at him, her heart beat
faster.

Especially now as he hung up their coats on a peg.

She loved him for admitting his loneliness. She loved him,
plain and simple, though that was such a predictable thing
for a bride to say. She'd not spoil the mood with predictable
words. Not tonight, maybe not ever. After all, he'd proposed
because she was unpredictable. He wanted, he claimed, an
unconventional marriage.

"What are you thinking?" he asked, watching her from ten
paces. "You look as if you're about to bolt the fence and go
chasing after that dream of college."

She sighed. How often in her life had her impulsive actions
boxed her in? Now she'd gone and eloped with Nate and had
jeopardized her chances of a university education. Oh, Grace
would laugh. "I'll figure something out."

"Somehow, Mrs. Denison, I have this awful feeling I'll end
up building you a college—"

Her face brightened.

"Not so fast. I'm not sharing you with your dreams tonight."
He came over and took her in his arms. "You're confined here
with me. And for tonight you're going to be only mine."

"Nate Denison, this is supposed to be an unconventional
marriage. We're each free to come and go, as if there were
no fences around us."

"Starting tomorrow."

His arms were too seductive to argue with. She put on her
brightest smile, tried hard to keep her words casual, bantering
about fences so she wouldn't slip up and do the conventional
thing, say the conventional words of love. Words of love, she
expected, would confine Nate as much as her. Like a fence.
A fence that he'd bolt right over too. Why, he was no better

than the pot calling the kettle black.

He tilted her chin up so she was looking right into those compelling blue eyes. "Tell me, what are you thinking?"

She said the first words that came to mind. "That it's December the eighth, and I'm a bride with a borrowed wedding ring." She half smiled. "A borrowed wedding ring, and I was married by a sleepy preacher in red long johns after the cavalry rescued Mariah. Nate, our children will never believe this. *I* scarcely believe it." As soon as the words were out, she realized the implications. Children, of necessity, required the act of conception. She spun out of his arms.

"Well, it's late," she said ever so casually, hoping to avoid the subject. "You haven't picked the bed you want."

Big Nate Denison, richest man in three states, looked uncertain. "What I want, Jennie, is you." He stared steadily at her, the smile deepening to crinkle his wonderful blue eyes. "But since you insist, this one." He pointed to the one that did not have her nightgown hidden under the pillow.

He held out a hand, as if to reach for her. "Come here, Jennie," he said softly. "Come here. . . ."

Next thing she knew her hand was in his, and he'd pulled her over to sit on his lap on the bed he'd chosen. Nearby the potbellied stove still crackled away.

"What are *you* thinking?" she asked.

He brushed a strand of hair off her face. "How much I want you. That at last I get to play teacher to you, and I can't wait another minute."

"I was always a quick study." Her heart was thudding so loudly she could scarcely hear her own words.

He was kissing her then—her hair, her throat, and at last her lips. As her arms went around his neck she and Nate fell back against the bed, clinging . . . kissing . . . melding . . . at last unleashing desire. The only barrier to their yearning was clothing, and it quickly became hopelessly tangled.

Arching back, she moaned. "Nate Denison, your teaching methods are unorthodox. I feel on fire."

"A man and a woman coming together *is* like fire—not the kind that destroys, but the kind that warms. A fire that warms."

"If this is the kindling," she said, "I think I'd better have a bucket of water ready for when you light the match."

Laughter rumbled up from his throat, and he hugged her to him.

"Jennie, I've wanted you ever since you threw that water on me."

"You have?"

"Of course. How many women have had the nerve to toss a bucket of water on me? That was passion then, Jennie. Pure, beautiful passion hiding under your prim skin. Enough to tempt a man to set fires just to have a glimpse of it again."

"And are you going to find it now?"

"Passion can't be hidden forever . . . and it can't be taught," he murmured. "Not if it's good, not if it's real passion. Like fire that explodes without reason, passion ignites between a man and a woman—whether they want it to or not."

"Like between us now?"

"Exactly so," he said huskily, tracing the outline of her figure, wondering how long he could stand it till he stripped her bare of corset and slip. He reached for the buttons on her shirtwaist, hesitated, reminding himself of her innocence. "Kissing is the kindling."

"And what makes it take spark?"

"It builds up step-by-step—just like the fire in the school. It smolders a long time and then suddenly it explodes, the way a spark catches and becomes a blaze."

"You've been lighting the furnace at school," she murmured, "so demonstrate. Show me," she murmured in between kisses. "That's always a more effective way to teach than telling. Show me. . . ."

Sassy schoolmarm. With an easy movement, he rolled onto his back, and before she knew it, she was on top of him. Already he was fumbling with the hooks and eyes at her waistband. She buried her hands in his hair, delighting in tousling it, and leaned down to kiss him herself. He rolled her over onto her back and against the insistent pressure of his mouth, her lips opened, a delicious warmth spread through her, an ache between her thighs.

He backed away, grabbed a shaky breath.

She pulled him back. "Nate, don't stop . . . finish."

There was a glint in his eyes, and it was not caused by the reflection of the flames. He was staring at her, and that deep warm ache inside intensified.

Moonlight spilled over her hair, highlighting the copper streaks. Reaching for her, he began to pull pins from her hair, until it all tumbled down around her shoulders.

"Are you going to kiss me again?" she asked.

And when he was done showing her all the answers to that question, she lay limp in his arms. He finally did what he'd been yearning to do for weeks—unfasten that top button on her prim shirtwaist and then the second and the third. His fingers shook so that it took time to work the tiny pearl buttons through the buttonholes. Moments later he gazed on the lace-edged camisole and petticoat and the creamy skin of her shoulders, her wrists. "Are you all right?" he asked.

"Mmm." Could Jennie tell him how her heart was pattering faster than ever? No. But she didn't want him to stop touching her. "If you stop touching me, would the fire go out?" she asked, reaching for the buttons on his shirt.

"Not as long as you touch me."

"Like this?" She reciprocated and unbuttoned his shirt. One by one by one.

Nate shut his eyes briefly at the gentle feel of her fingers undressing him, then looked at her, at the trusting face. Trusting him to take her gently . . . It would be hard, but there was nothing he wanted to do as well as this.

"Jennie . . ."

As if she'd read his mind, she smiled wistfully. "It's all right. Grace told me about her wedding night." She lay there waiting, steeled for him to take her.

"Jennie, it is not the same between every man and woman." He touched her cheek, tenderly, and when she opened her eyes, he gazed into them, at the trust. "I mean, it is different for every couple. The first time may not be perfect. . . ."

"Well, Nate, teachers don't expect perfection, but always best efforts."

His grin was wry. Nate's "best efforts" had reduced at least half a dozen women back east to groveling for his favors. This would be even better. Instinctively he knew it. Despite her virginity. Or because of it. He didn't know. All he knew was that holding her in his arms was even better than he'd imagined. And different. Different from any other time. He couldn't say why, nor did it really matter now.

But something about this lovemaking was new to him, and so he ceased trying to put a name to it, and simply, gently, tenderly showed her where to touch him, where to kiss him, in return. His Jennie was indeed a quick student.

Now he nudged her lips open and teased her with his tongue. She hesitated, then the tip of her tongue touched his. And while he slowly deepened the intensity of the kiss, his hands slid up her bodice to untie her camisole, slip off her petticoat, and fling both in a heap on the floor. When he broke off the kiss, she leaned back, as if satiated, and he kissed the hollow of her throat while moving his hands down to touch her breasts, slowly igniting a deeper kind of passion.

She stared directly at him, lips slightly parted, breasts heaving. Desire was there, but fear as well.

His mouth again found hers, touched her lips in reassurance, then moved to her breasts. He pressed her back against the rough blanket and slowly ran a hand from her cheek down her belly, lingering until her breathing quickened, till she moaned beneath his touch.

Lily of the valley drifted from the crevice of her breasts. If he did this right—and God knew it had been years since he'd dallied with a virgin—it would be good for her. If he could but see a glimmer of passion in her. That would be his satisfaction.

He pulled back, stared at her. That was an utterly unselfish thought on his part, and truth be told, he was losing reason. Beneath him, she moved, instinctively seeking.

He let his hands rove, generously explored, gently touched, tried to match her in unpredictability . . . until she moaned her pleasure, arched against him in longing, instinctive and sweet.

"Jennie—"

"Please, Nate . . ." Shyly her hands ran up his torso, clung to him.

He didn't know till later when restrained exploring stopped and passion took over, but he could recall pausing once, staring down into her flushed face. "Jennie," he murmured, and again it was she, ever unpredictable, who surprised him.

One flesh. To cherish. To honor.

When it was over, he lay staring at the ceiling. She was nestled in the crook of his arm, and the only sound was the low crackle of the fire. The faint scent of lily of the valley clung to him, and she was limp and warm. Usually, at this point, he always got up and walked out. Done. Finished. This time he wanted to linger, with her nestling close. No wonder he'd been bored with the women back east. They knew too much, took all the wonder out of such a wondrous event as the coming together of man and woman—especially for the first time.

For long afterward, he held her close against his wildly beating heart.

"I liked it," she said softly at length.

"Did you?" He smiled to himself.

What would she say tomorrow and the next day? Would she ever regret tonight?

Propped up on one elbow, Nate looked down at her, this fiery little woman who asked such impertinent questions about lovemaking. In truth such a question called for a declaration of feelings, but he wasn't a man to engage in sweet words. Such talk was cheap among the people he'd come from. Hadn't he given Daisy sweet words . . . and to what end? His vow not to love again was still the best idea. Sweet words fenced a man in, made him vulnerable to humiliation.

He got up to stoke the little fire, came back, and saw that she had dived under the covers. He hesitated. The beds were but cots.

He'd never asked if she'd mind if they shared the same one.

Again, with any other woman, he'd have taken the other bed. He was used to his own bed. His own room. But this time he wasn't feeling noble or selfish. Detached? No. Cynical? No . . .

Perplexed at himself, he raked his fingers through his hair. Unable to pinpoint why he wanted to stay as close to Jennie as he could, he simply gave in to the yearning. Carefully he edged in next to her in the tiny cot and slid her closer against him. She stirred but fell asleep. Blissfully he wrapped his arms about her, his hand just below her breasts, where he could feel her heart beating, and he buried his face in her sweet hair.

In the morning she woke him with a drop of water from her fingertips to his mouth. Quickly she bent to kiss it away.

"Nate."

Instantly awake, he pulled her into his arms and down onto the bed with him. "You're not thinking about starting another fire, are you, lady?"

"Not yet . . ." She kissed his sandpaper cheek. "Get up. We've got to go to breakfast and collect Mariah."

He looked at her. She was fully dressed, the prim schoolmarm. "What'd we do last night?" he asked carefully.

Jennie, blushing, stared down at the floorboards of their spartan cabin. Doubtless he'd regret last night as soon as he remembered the details. To her it was too glorious a night to talk about yet, except for the prosaic happenings. She walked to the door, stared out the tiny window next to it. Everything was white; that much was still constant in the world.

"We need to collect Mariah and head back to Castlerock. Everything's waiting—breakfast, the sleigh . . . we'll need to say our thank-you's to the cavalry for finding her, for putting us up—"

"For marrying us too."

She whirled around, anxious to see his expression. No teasing, just deep yearning, a reflection of everything she felt. That surprised her, but she wasn't going to spoil things and mention it.

Instead she stared, unashamedly, while he fastened his clothing, and then followed him to the basin, watching while he splashed water on his face, lots and lots. "Are we very late?"

She nodded with a rueful look at one water drop that angled its way down his jaw. "Very." Reaching up, she licked it away and backed away, still the unpredictable robin.

"We'll skip breakfast. Mariah shouldn't have to worry . . ." Words trailing off, he stood looking at her. Just his glance started a fiery ache inside her abdomen.

"Shall I go ahead?" she asked softly.

"No." He reached out and pulled her close. Water from his face dripped onto her prim shirtwaist. If they weren't already late to get Mariah . . . Desire flared in his loins, but he fought it back, toweled his face dry, then dropped the towel and gathered her suddenly into his arms. Her arms were so tight about him that her feet came up off the ground and the only barrier to passion was petticoats and trousers and time . . . of which they had none. With a gentle kiss, reluctantly, they parted, and gave each other a wide berth. Their gaze swung constantly back to look at each other, as if for reassurance.

Her funny little hat was lying on the other cot, the unused one. He reached for the hat and came over to her. "Trust me, now," he said softly, and once again tied it about her face, helped her tuck her copper-penny hair up inside it. When he pulled on his own coat, she reached for hers. She'd only gotten her arms in the sleeves when he came over to her and tied the frog fasteners for her. One by one by one, from bottom to top. Once again, they came together, bodies touching at strategic points, smoldering. "Nate, please . . ."

He stepped back, banked the embers. He was used to being in control with women, and by God he'd maintain control today.

The leave-taking was uneventful, and before long they were tucked in the sleigh, Mariah and a squirming pup between them, buffalo robes over them, newly heated bricks under their feet, and a box of sandwiches and tarts and apples tucked in the back with the snowshoes. Someone had handed Jennie a jar of pickled beets along with their marriage certificate. It was one of those glorious days of almost winter—when the sun shone in a wide blue sky and glinted off every dab of snow on the hills and road.

"You're sure you want my pup?" Mariah kept asking. "You'll have to name him Coal."

"That's a fine name," Jennie said. She touched the certificate, still not believing. Nate had shared her bed. She was shamed at her wantonness. And what if he'd married her only because he felt obligated to help her family? Because it was the only way to spend the night together honorably? Because he was lonely? Because he'd made some obscene wager with the cavalry to wed her before the school was finished? Because she'd practically thrown herself at him hours earlier, and he was curious? Because she was a money grubber?

Doubt after doubt assailed her, like so many snowflakes that wouldn't stop. And to hide her sinking spirits, she turned her head away and pretended to stare at the scenery. He was rich enough to buy his way out of anything, even a hasty wedding. Would he, now that he'd *had* her?

Oh, but she'd give anything to know what was going on in Nate's head. What must he think? Certainly that he'd acted hastily. Why, he'd scrawled his name on that license, declaring pieces of paper were like fences, confining people. Oh, Nate, is that what you think? Did he regret his impulsiveness? Is that why he was so quiet, except for the occasional glance at her?

Nate dared not look at Jennie one more time. She refused to meet his glance, refused to talk, and there was so much he needed to talk over with her. Did she regret her impulsive marriage? For once in her life had she overdone it? Maybe this was too impulsive a thing to have done to a woman . . . cheated her out of a fancy wedding, a party, an engagement . . . all those traditional trappings she said she disdained. How could he convince her he meant what he said about wanting a marriage different from the norm? He couldn't build a fence to keep *her* in. Not Jennie.

He longed to touch her hand, the tender nape of her neck, her waist, anything to make her look at him, to see if, after last night, the trust she'd given him was still there in those soft brown eyes . . . but Mariah sat between them, chattering, and so he had to bide his time until the sleigh covered the distance between Yellowstone and Castlerock.

CHAPTER

~19~

As they approached Castlerock's Camas Street Jennie took the squirming puppy from Mariah. "He's to live at Nate's mansion now. Lucky pup."

"Just like you."

Her breath caught. It still didn't seem real. "Just like me." There was a trace of disbelief in her voice.

Mariah, cheeks rosy, looked up at Jennie, and when she spoke, her breath came out all frosty. "I'll be all alone in our lean-to."

The puppy squirmed, but Jennie managed to hold him under one arm while with the other she reached over to cup Mariah's face briefly. "Baby Pearl will share with you soon enough, I imagine."

Mariah looked up at Jennie. "She can't talk—not about imaginary windows."

Nate turned, obviously puzzled. Blushing, Jennie gave her full attention to the pup, hoping if she made no reply, he'd drop the subject.

"What?" he asked, taking his gaze off the road long enough to draw a return glance from Jennie.

"Windows," Jennie said softly.

"I heard that," he said quietly. "It was the imaginary part I didn't understand."

How to explain? Desperate to change the subject, Jennie handed the squirming pup back to her niece, which didn't stop Mariah from doing the explaining. "We have a pretend window in our room and make wishes on it."

"What kind of wishes?" he asked, smiling.

"Jennie usually wishes that she could go to college. I wish for everything . . . but don't worry," Mariah reassured him. "You've got real windows in your bedroom, so Jennie won't talk to them, and pretty soon she'll forget all about me."

Over Mariah's head Jennie exchanged a smile with Nate, whose hair was tossing about in the winter air. The sleigh turned the corner and they were home.

Their welcome into Castlerock was a whirlwind of yipping puppies and cheering children. What a memory this day would be. . . . But of all the memories Jennie would treasure, one stood out: her sister, Grace, smiling again, lifting her little girl out of the sleigh, and then, miracle of miracles, thrusting out her hand to shake Nate's in thanks.

Nate helped Jennie out, and it must have been her imagination that his hands lingered on her waist because a minute later he handed her the jar of pickled beets. Their fingers touched, they looked at each other, and she longed for his kiss, then, as if aware of prying eyes, Nate backed away from her and climbed back into the sleigh. "I'll see you in a little while?"

he asked. "After you've packed?"

She nodded. "It won't take long. The good-byes may take me longer."

Nodding, he climbed into the sleigh, looking somewhat at a loss. "I guess I'll go check on my telegrams and tell Helga to set the table for two tonight . . . if she's there." With uncharacteristic awkwardness, he stared down at his hands. They were bare and red with cold.

"Nate."

He looked up at her so suddenly she thought he was going to say something. Instead he pinned a glance of longing on her so intense it could have melted the snow beneath her feet.

"You forgot your gloves," she said simply, and picking them up from the step of the sleigh where he'd dropped them, she handed them over.

Without taking his gaze off her, he accepted the gloves and put them on. "Take your time with the good-byes. I'll see you in a while."

She nodded, uncertain, doubts assailing her. Had he changed his mind? She watched him take the sleigh back up Camas Street without her and swallowed down a hard lump. Foolish, impulsive Jennie, however are you going to get out of this? This was more permanent than a snowstorm. That marriage certificate up her sleeve wasn't about to melt anytime soon. Alone, in the doorway, she pulled it out and read it, just to be sure she wasn't dreaming.

Nathaniel Denison and Jennie Beasley. Joined in matrimony this eighth day of December, eighteen hundred and ninety-three. Nate's signature was as large and decisive as John Hancock's. With a sigh she folded the paper back up. He probably signed sell-and-buy orders for the stock market the same way.

Ingrid Jensen managed to arrive just as Nate vanished from

sight. The woman's lips were pursed, her spectacles fogged from all her talk.

"We all heard," she sniffed, "how the schoolmarm had to pay for the preacher because the rich groom had no money in his pockets."

Jennie smiled mysteriously. "Actually I believe we owe you some money, Ingrid."

Ingrid's expression turned incredulous as she bent to examine the seams of her coat. "I'd forgotten about those coins."

"I do apologize for not asking permission in advance. We . . . we were in a bind. I'll have Nate pay you back at once."

"Well!" The widow blinked in consternation, and what might have been indignation softened to resignation. "I'm glad that old coat was able to help out in more ways than one. My very best wishes, Jennie."

Jennie wished the woman would leave the family alone, but still, Ingrid persisted in forcing Jennie to think about insignificant details. "Is it true you're going to tear out the wallpaper, Jennie, when you go to live there?"

"Only in the dining room, where I splashed flour paste around," she said, deliberately vague. Most of these humble town families were lucky to have newspapers for wallpaper. "The parlor's too nice to change. Besides, if I changed, how could I invite all of you up for oatmeal cookies?"

Ingrid beamed in satisfaction. "You let me know, now, if you need any advice on how to do things up proper. This town is going to have some refinement yet, and," she whispered confidentially, then gave a pained look at Jennie's hat, which didn't flatter Ingrid's caped coat, "if you need help with more stylish clothing, I can copy the latest Paris gowns from the paper-doll fashions in the newspaper. It'd be awfully good for business if you tried to set the fashion pace, Jennie."

"Thank you, Ingrid. You'll be a fountain of good advice on style, I'm sure."

Oh, but the gossips had been working overtime like knitting needles for a premature baby, and pleading cold, she at last unfastened the coat and, after returning it to Ingrid, escaped inside.

But in the humble little Gordon house, she stood at the kitchen stove, uncertain whether to stay or retreat to her little room to pack. "You must be ecstatic." Grace sighed, draping mittens and scarves and hats to dry from a line over the stove. "Well, aren't you?"

"Yes."

Grace half turned. "You don't sound excited. If you're like me, you're probably numb with joy."

Jennie reached for a mitten that fell onto the stove, picked it up by its thumb, and draped it over the makeshift line. Actually she was terrified. Nate Denison would never want a humble bride like her. True, she'd lain in his arms, given him her virginity, but who was she to become mistress of that place called Denison's Folly? Nate must have been out of his mind with loneliness. Maybe she'd better move her things into the new schoolhouse, because now that he was back in his mansion, he was liable to be having second thoughts.

A wedding with four witnesses held in the middle of the night in remote Yellowstone could easily be annulled. And after all, he'd never told her he loved her. Just over and over how much he wanted her. And Nate Denison was a man who got whatever he wanted, took it any way he had to. And he'd made no bones about setting his sights on her. He'd simply taken what she'd offered, but on his own eccentric terms. If he wanted to change his mind, he had the means to do so.

She'd been woolgathering long enough. Already, Grace had the tin tub filled with hot water and Mariah soaking in it. With no more preliminaries, her sister came up, embraced Jennie around the waist, and distracted her. "You too. Out of those cold clothes and, as soon as Mariah's done, into the hot tub.

The boys are all outside," she added reassuringly.

Jennie glanced at the homely contraption and thought of
Nate's fancy zinc-lined tub, the newfangled kind that drained.
"Yes, all right then, one bath for old times' sake." She was,
she realized, shivering.

"Hurry up, Mariah, dear," Grace said, "because Aunt Jennie
gets it next." Then Grace turned to Jennie with a wistful smile.
"I still can't believe my confirmed spinster sister married."

"News travels fast."

"The cavalry telegraphed it up. As soon as we knew Mariah
was with the cavalry, we knew about you and Nate Denison.
Oh, Jennie, Ingrid Jensen is beside herself with envy, and
Thaddeus would be livid. Another teacher lost to marriage.
But poor Karl lost out."

Dear Grace, still putting on a brave front. "You haven't
heard from Thaddeus?" Jennie asked gently.

Grace shook her head, pressed her lips together, and busied
herself adding wood to the stove. As Mariah splashed in the
hot water she turned stricken eyes to Jennie. "I've had no word
at all. And as for Edgar, he doesn't deserve any of Castlerock's
teachers—ever . . . unless a grouchy cantankerous one comes
along."

Jennie could understand Grace's ire, but didn't know what
to do. "I'll stay with you, Grace."

Her sister gave a rueful smile. "You enjoy your honeymoon.
I'm doing some cleaning for Ingrid. I could do the same for
you, Jennie—if Helga ever quits."

"No, Grace. I'll talk to Nate."

"Don't you dare!"

"Well, if I want to talk to him about bringing in an extra
teacher, I will."

"An extra teacher?" Grace looked up from baby Pearl in
her cradle and then back again. "I could teach, if it wasn't
for Pearl."

"You could bring her—temporarily. I think it's time the school split into two. The town's growing. One half for lower grades. The other for upper grades. That way there'd be two teachers. With our big new school we could do it. Karl can build a partition . . ." She bit her lip. Everyone would think she was getting fancy ideas now that she'd married Nate, and in truth she still wondered if he'd have second thoughts. She guessed she'd know when she saw his face again, heard his voice. "It's an idea . . . we'll figure something out. My own sister and nephews and nieces are not going to starve right under my nose."

"Oh, Jennie, we've had so many offers of help. It'll turn out all right. I know it will. But let's wait a day to talk about it. This is your day, your wedding, and I want to plan a party."

Brave Grace, acting happy for Jennie when Thaddeus was still missing. Jennie stared down at the well-scrubbed wooden floor. The scent of soap and coffee filled the air. The coffee reminded her of Nate. She ached to see him, and maybe the yearning showed in her face.

"I—I guess I'd better not put off packing any longer or baby Pearl will have outgrown her cradle and still be waiting to move in with Mariah."

"But first you get out of these cold clothes." Grace, with a touch to her elbow, steered her sister toward the lean-to bedroom. "How soon is he coming back?"

"I don't know."

Grace said, "I'll help you change, and while you're bathing I'll pack. Out of the tub, Mariah."

The kitchen door opened, and as one the women turned. Nate couldn't be back already. Quickly, Grace moved to drape both a towel and quilt about Mariah, then as it registered who stood there in the doorway, both women froze in place. There, none the worse for wear, conscience apparently unbothered, stood Mariah's father.

"Thaddeus!"

"Pa, you're back." Mariah, who'd scurried to the lean-to, peeked around the curtain into the kitchen, eyes wide.

Grace stood staring at her husband, disheveled, golden beard unkempt, boots wet. "Thaddeus," she said softly. "You came back." For all her gentle words, there was accusation in her eyes. "Where have you been?" Her words voiced the question on everyone's mind.

One by one the boys crept into the house, and Mariah hastily pulled on a dress and stockings and, clutching the quilt about her shoulders, came to stand near the stove. Thaddeus Gordon was hanging up his coat on a peg and removing his wet boots as if nothing were amiss.

Grace sat in the rocker, nursing Pearl, who had started to cry. "Are you going to tell me where you've been?" she repeated at length.

Her husband brushed back his hair. "I went to job-hunt," he said as matter-of-factly as if he'd gone to collect kindling. When no one replied, he looked around at their accusing stares. "What's the matter with everyone? I thought you'd be glad."

While Grace rocked the baby Jennie helped hang up the boys' jackets.

"I found mine work in Butte," Thaddeus said. "We can move anytime." Looking quite pleased with himself, he reached for the coffeepot.

Silence, except for the slosh of coffee into a mug.

"What's going on here?" he asked, turning, looking at his wife. "Grace?"

Everything was happening at once. Suddenly exhausted from all the events of the last day, Jennie sank down into the nearest chair. It's a good thing Nate had said to take as long as she liked for the good-byes. There was, it seemed, much more than good-byes to talk about.

"Grace, what happened while I was gone?" Thaddeus was a stubborn man.

Finally Grace looked up and met Thaddeus's gaze with a steely look Jennie had rarely seen. "While you were gone, Edgar foreclosed on our store . . . and house both."

Thaddeus didn't say a word for a long minute, then moved from the stove to Grace. "You didn't let him bully you, did you? All he did was fly off the handle like the coward he is. He'd crawl under the table if his steak mooed. If he was a real man, he'd have had the guts to wait until I was here."

"Well, he didn't." Grace's voice trembled. Baby Pearl whimpered, and when Jennie made a move to take her, Grace held up a restraining hand. She rocked the baby on her shoulder. "He foreclosed on us, Thaddeus. Me and six children."

"I just thought you'd assume I'd gone hunting—you know, for meat to feed us."

"You left your rifle," Grace said icily. The boys shuffled their feet uncomfortably.

Jennie stared in embarrassment, sadness. This was exactly why she'd never wanted to marry. Would Nate ever walk out on her and make plans without consulting her?

Thaddeus was doing his best to pacify Grace. "Well, who cares what Edgar does? I told you, I've got mine work in Butte. Aren't you going to say you're glad?"

"No," Grace said. "We're not moving. You can, but I'm not. Butte is a rough town, I hear. Full of soiled doves and painted ladies and John Barleycorn, same as Gardiner. Besides, I always believed once a man and wife had children, they should look to the children and stop roaming. We're staying here. We'll work through the tough times, and after the scare you gave me, that's my final word on the subject. This is our home."

"Now, Grace, don't be unreasonable. We have to feed and clothe the children. I have no money."

"We know," Grace said with a meaningful glance at Jennie.

Thaddeus turned then to Jennie. "I'm sorry, Jennie." He stared at the floor and then up, abashed. "I had to buy a train ticket. I know I should have asked, but I didn't want Grace worrying like now."

The silence told of everyone's lack of enthusiasm for his answer.

Guiltily Thaddeus stood at the head of the table and looked around the accusing faces of his family. "I used the money for train fare, nothing else, Jennie. You can't know what a man will do when he's desperate for his family . . . I'll pay it back, with interest."

"I appreciate that, Thaddeus." Jennie was going to chalk this up to desperate need and never look back or mention it ever again.

Thaddeus knelt beside his wife. "I'm sorry," he said softly.

Suddenly Grace's eyes filled with tears. "You should be, you stubborn Scotsman. And taking Jennie's savings was unforgivable."

Mariah moved up to kneel by her mother. "It's all right, Ma." Then she looked up at her pa. "It's all right, Pa. Jennie's going to live in the big house. She's not too mad about the money."

Thaddeus looked back at Jennie, who felt the blood drain from her face. Hastily she stood and, smoothing her skirt, started to back toward the lean-to room. "I'd better pack."

"What do you mean, she's living in the big house?"

"Jennie got married, Pa." The news came from Mariah, in bright tones.

"Married . . . ?" Thaddeus stroked his beard, frowned as if trying to see the world from a new angle. "Who to? Karl?"

"No, Pa," Mariah said in exasperation. "To Nate Denison."

"Nate? The rich dude? What for?"

Jennie felt herself blush to the roots of her hair and was grateful for her sister's quick reply.

"Don't ask ridiculous questions in front of the children, Thaddeus. She and Nate eloped to Yellowstone. That's all."

"But why Yellowstone?" Clearly Nate was having trouble piecing together all that had transpired since he'd taken off.

"Because," his wife said, in obvious impatience, "because, on top of all else, your daughter . . . Mariah . . . ran away last night."

Thaddeus whipped around to stare at his wife and then searched out Mariah. "She did what? Would you put all this in chronological order?"

Jennie stood immobile by the stove while Grace sighed and rocked back and forth. "Your daughter ran away, and everyone—even Nate Denison—has been searching for her." Her voice caught and she wiped away a tear. "Anyway, Nate Denison's a better man than you've painted him, judging him out of hand, implying because he's got money, he's heartless. Why, he's as nice as any of us regular folks."

At once, an image of Ingrid and Edgar flitted through Jennie's mind.

"Nicer than some," Jennie put in, and Grace smiled her agreement.

"It was, you'll be interested to know," Grace went on, "Nate who organized the entire cavalry, and it was the cavalry who found Mariah and took her to the fort for safekeeping. And then Nate and Jennie drove in by sleigh through all the snow and cold and wild animals to retrieve your daughter." Briefly she sketched in the details about telegraph messages and the town's concern. "And when they returned, not less than an hour before you this morning, they were already married. And since you've come home, you can bathe and shave and get ready for the wedding party tonight."

Thaddeus spared a brief look of surprise for Jennie, just long enough to see if marrying a rich man had changed her any. Then, apparently satisfied she was still the same old Jennie, he turned to his daughter, who stood, head bowed, hugging the quilt to her like an Indian robe.

Without a word Thaddeus moved to Mariah and knelt beside her. "Why'd you run away?" he asked.

Jennie looked on in sympathy. Did a child ever know precisely why she did something as impulsive as run away? But with all her heart, Jennie wished Mariah could tell her pa.

When Thaddeus put his hands on her shoulders, Mariah, damp hair unbraided, only buried her head on his shoulder.

"Why, runt?" her father persisted.

That did it. Jennie had been a silent onlooker until now, but couldn't keep quiet any longer. She took a step toward them. "I'll tell you why, Thaddeus. Because you persist in calling the child a runt, and she takes it to heart. You say you want to let a runt pup die, and you expect a child with the nickname runt to expect different treatment?"

As she spoke Thaddeus slowly turned to stare at his sister-in-law. Now he turned back. "That so?" he asked Mariah.

"Of course it's so," Jennie said. Oh, but men could be so thickheaded, and once again, she wondered what she'd gotten herself into last night with Nate.

Then Thaddeus pulled Mariah into his embrace. "That's different, child. I thought I explained that."

"No." Mariah managed a whisper. "You won't spank me? Or throw me in the river?"

"Spank you? Throw you in the river in this weather?"

"I only wanted to save the runt pup."

His face softened. "Heck, child, we don't have to sell the runt. You can keep it." He gave Mariah's head an awkward pat. "You can keep it. We'll figure out a way to feed it too."

Mariah's face fell in misery. "But now Nate's adopted it."

As that information sank in, Thaddeus broke into a grin. "That pup's loose in Denison's Folly with all the fancy furniture and carpets?" His smile deepened. "I bet if you go ask him real nice, he'd let you have it back."

Mariah looked up at Jennie. "Would he, do you think?"

Somehow, as Jennie remembered Nate's uncommon concern with his furnishings, the thought of him readily returning the puppy was indeed quite easy to imagine. Dear Nate.

"Would he?" Mariah asked.

Jennie nodded. "I think he would."

"Would you care?"

"Only if he *didn't* give it to you."

"Now?"

"After a bit . . . the family still has things to talk over." Grace turned to Thaddeus. "Now, about this job in Butte."

"I don't want to move," Mariah said.

"Me neither," moaned Thaddeus Jr.

"Well, what do you expect us to do?" Thaddeus, relaxing into his old role as patriarch, poured himself more coffee.

"Stay here with Jennie."

Thaddeus glanced from his sister-in-law to his daughter. Then, after he cast a lingering look at the little girl, his glance came at last to rest on the face of his wife. Grace. Brave Grace.

"Yeah, well, it's a hard blow to lose a business. I admit I didn't manage things as well as I could. I never had my father's talent with accounts. If it wasn't for him buying that little store before he died, we might never have that mercantile. But I still might have made it until the panic. Lots of folks are hurting this year, except for the likes of Nate Denison. Anyway, I wanted to line up a job before I told everyone the bad news."

Grace stood and walked baby Pearl back and forth. "I've got it all figured out. I can teach. Jennie says the school can use a second teacher . . . and you can make do with sweeping or doing handyman work." She drew in a breath and shuddered, then continued. "For Ingrid or whoever can pay you."

Thaddeus leaned against the table and sipped his coffee while Jennie moved toward her room to pack. It was past time to give Grace and Thaddeus some privacy to sort out their lives. Her brother-in-law stared at her as she moved away and suddenly grinned as if he'd invented toothpicks.

"Jennie . . . moving into Denison's Folly, eh? Come to think of it, now that I've suddenly acquired a rich brother-in-law, maybe I can ask him for a loan to tide us over—"

"Thaddeus Gordon, don't you dare ruin Jennie's marriage!" Grace got good and mad. For the first time ever.

Grace stalked over to Thaddeus while Jennie stood trying to think of the diplomatic answer. Oh dear, if she had to ask Nate to help her relatives within one day of marrying him, he'd think for certain she'd only married him for his money. No wonder he'd not given her any tender words of affection. And probably never would.

CHAPTER
～20～

Jennie took Mariah by the hand and led her off to the bedroom to help her pack while her sister and Thaddeus finished solving their problems. But if she thought she'd escape thoughts of Nate, she was mistaken. She and Mariah sat on the edge of the bed. Grace's voice carried through the gingham-curtain door, and this time she had most certainly lost her temper.

"You mean you're going to put on airs about being too proud to use a rich relative?" Thaddeus's voice filtered through next.

Jennie and Mariah stared at the imaginary window. If Jennie wished hard enough, Nate would come and take her away, and Thaddeus would miraculously be able to provide for his family. But this was not a year when miracles happened. As

Grace was now aptly pointing out. In loud enough words to be heard down at the fort.

"Thaddeus, if you want to arrange a job with Nate Denison, that's one thing, but not because of Jennie. You can ask Nate for help only if you can prove you can keep the mercantile profitable so he'll not lose money on his investment—and that's *if* he did indeed decide to do business with Edgar and the bank and purchase the mercantile. He's no fool with his money, or he'd not be rich, I daresay."

"What makes you so smart?" Why, if Jennie wasn't mistaken, there was actually a trace of awe in Thaddeus's voice.

"I pay attention to more than just recipes and dress patterns. And even if Jennie had married a simple carpenter, that wouldn't give you the right to free nails. You have to make it a business arrangement, pure and simple. First you must convince him to hire you, and then you have to stop acting like the lord of the manor and strutting about town as if you were more important than everyone else. Your father may have been a successful keeper of a castle's accounts, but this is no castle, and this is not Scotland. Just a humble little town in Montana. But with hard work you can prove yourself in the mercantile, and to Nate Denison, Thaddeus. I know you can."

Then there was silence. Mariah ran back out and Jennie heard her voice through the curtained doorway. "Pa . . . I'm glad you're back." The words were sort of muffled and then there was more silence.

"Heck, runt, I never meant for you to run off."

Alone in the bedroom, Jennie began to feel self-conscious, if not downright ashamed for eavesdropping. She pulled her single trunk out from the foot of the bed and began to fill it with her few possessions.

"Jennie . . ." It was Grace's voice. Jennie looked up to find her standing in the doorway, gingham curtain pushed aside, and looking very tired.

"I came to help you. Forgive me . . . and Thaddeus. He's gone to talk to Edgar. Pearl's asleep. I can't let you move out with this kind of mood in the house."

"It's all right," Jennie said. She should have remained a spinster. All her instincts had said to.

"It won't be like that with Nate, Jennie. I just know it."

"But you *are* glad Thaddeus is back, aren't you?"

"Yes." With another sigh Grace dropped onto the bed and helped Jennie fold her petticoats. "I'm glad, but I'm also worn-out. Anyway, everything's worked out for the best, and now you can settle into being a new bride." She paused. "About what I told Thaddeus . . . It doesn't matter if Nate doesn't want to invest in Thaddeus, or the mercantile. He's not beholden on account of you."

Jennie folded her nightgown and laid it in the trunk next to her hairbrush. "Grace, I heard every last word you and Thaddeus exchanged, and even though I agree with everything you told him, I'm going to ask Nate on the sly . . . to say yes about investing in the mercantile—"

"Jennie, you didn't listen. I don't want to be beholden."

"You're not. Nate will *want* to say yes . . . after I talk to him." She laid her camisoles into the trunk, then glanced at Grace, who was grinning widely.

"Oh, Jennie, where did you get so wise?"

"From you."

Grace stared down at her folded hands. "Just promise—please promise, you won't ever tell Thaddeus. I want him to think he arranged a loan all by himself. He needs to think that."

"I know," Jennie said easily. "And Nate, whether he knows it or not, needs to be allowed to help . . . even temporarily. It'll make him feel he's accepted here at last."

Jennie returned Grace's smile, then reached over and hugged her sister. They hugged like they hadn't hugged since they were little girls waiting for Christmas. As they finally drew apart Jennie prepared to say her farewells.

"There now," Grace said all proper like. "Everything's worked out, even your marriage." She bustled out to call two of the boys to carry Jennie's trunk.

Alone, Jennie sighed. Even her marriage? Then why did she feel so uncertain about Nate's reasons for marrying her? Was his commitment as strong as that of Thaddeus? Because for all his faults, Thaddeus at least kept money matters in perspective. He might be impractical and stubborn, but he'd come back for Grace. Grace was loved, and that had no price.

Swallowing hard, Jennie marched out. "Well, I'm going."

"There's to be no bridal journey?"

"I think last night was enough of a journey."

"Indeed! The both of you acted so impulsively. I still can't get over it."

"Well . . . now he needs to stay at home . . . to wait for the buffalo."

"Ah, yes, a stay-at-home period to receive visitors and good wishes, except you *have* to come out to your party tonight, else the town will never forgive you. Wear your dark blue church dress."

"We'll come. I'll change up there." Jennie's glance fell on the tub of now-cold bath water that had warmed Mariah. "I guess I never had my bath."

Thaddeus Jr. was dragging her trunk out the door, but now he paused. "You gonna use that bathtub in the mansion? I've heard tales that it sucks people right down the drain."

"Thaddeus Jr., that is an inappropriate question to ask a lady."

"Well, if she'd doesn't get sucked down, her big toes might get caught."

His brothers giggled, and Grace handed off baby Pearl to Mariah.

"Thaddeus Jr., go out and chop some wood so we can heat water for our humble kitchen tub for your bath. The only drain it's got is your arm power." This from his mother, who, to Jennie's delight, was sounding much stronger. Much.

Now it was Jennie who was full of fears. Her hands went clammy at their stares; inside, at the memory of Nate's love-making, she began to melt like snow in July. "I guess it'll take some getting used to living there," she admitted, "but I'll try to make it homey. The first thing I intend to do is get rid of those stuffy gold drapery cords. And add some Christmas greens. Put away the silver. And put the stereoscope in the center of the dining table so my nieces and nephews can view it anytime they want." Oh, yes, just by rearranging things a bit, even a house like that could be made homey. Between Helga and her, it wouldn't be hard at all.

Thaddeus Jr. scoffed. "Heck, Aunt Jennie, Nate Denison ain't gonna let you fool with his house any more than he let us fool with his dining room."

His mother swatted his bottom with a broom. "Get." Then she turned to her sister. "Well, before you do anything to his house, Mr. Nate Denison can carry you over the threshold all proper like."

"Actually," Jennie said on a shaky voice, "I'm not going straight to the mansion. I—I need to collect some belongings at the new school. If he comes, just show him my trunk there on the stoop and tell him I'm at the school."

"My, so calm for a new bride," Grace commented, and gave her sister a last hug for good luck.

Alone, Jennie walked up Moose Street and into her new school and sank into one of the new little desks with the inkwells and pencil grooves before she allowed her knees to really shake. Calm? No, not at all. So terrified she put her head down on the little desk and shut her eyes, praying Nate would not let her down. Praying all the doubts would vanish.

Oh, Grace, I can't believe I'm a bride either, she thought with panic. It was a whirl in her mind, and she looked at her bare hand. She'd just wed the richest man in three states and didn't have even a plain gold band as proof, never mind riches and jewels. All she had were fleeting images.

The cavalryman and his wife who served as witnesses. The brief words by the preacher. A hasty license procured from a dusty drawer. The night in the guest cabin, sharing a single bed, the army-issue towels, the army-issue blanket. A spartan setting compared with Nate's mansion. But luxurious in their passion . . . all night in each other's arms, finally yielding to the longings they'd been fighting all these weeks.

And then . . . and then the sleigh ride home this morning with Mariah and pup bundled up with them as they rode out past the Mammoth Springs Hotel, past a pair of elk grazing in patchy snow, past a pair of beautiful trumpeter swans taking wing off the river, past the market wagon on its way to Gardiner, past the wool-clad cavalry out on snowshoes, waving from their morning patrol.

A wedding night in wonderland. Everything she felt was a wonder. Too good to be true. "I never thought I'd fall in love with any man," she whispered to herself, "and now I have, and I'm scared to death that I don't love him enough, that I don't love him as his own kind of woman would." And Nate—now that he'd had her, would he still want her? Ever love her? Or would she end up back where she'd started? Teaching in this little schoolhouse?

Oh, why had romance ever come into her life? Especially with such a complicated man? Life as a spinster teacher would have been ever so much easier. Her thoughts had come full circle and gone nowhere. And then a new fear raised its head.

Grace, thankfully, was calm now that she had Thaddeus back, and that's what scared Jennie so. The fear that she needed Nate as much as Grace did Thaddeus. That her need for Nate would swallow her up. Her and all her dreams. Despite what promises Nate had made last night, she didn't want to be just a piece of property to him.

Oh, yes, if Nate still wanted her, he'd have to come and reassure her that their wedding was more than an impulsive piece of fun, a bargain won. She couldn't risk a second rebuff.

Mariah sat on the floor watching her parents embrace. They were still arguing, but now it sounded more like teasing. She liked this kind of arguing better.

"It all started when Jennie went to teach in that dude man's house and the youngsters picked up ideas," Pa said.

Ma reached up and touched Pa's face. "It all started when the cavalry accused you falsely."

"That they did. Undisciplined louts, trying to impress their commanding officer by accusing anybody."

Pa was going to be mad at the cavalry forever.

"They apologized for their error. They're only doing their job, trying to find a poacher, nothing more. Why, if it weren't for them, we might have lost Mariah—" Grace's voice caught. "As I see it, things are even."

"I guess so," Pa agreed.

"Then we can stay here?" Mariah, looking up at her parents, ventured a question. She wanted very badly to go visit the black pup at Nate's house, but Ma had said absolutely not. Now she came to the table and stood peering down at baby Pearl, at her crown of dark hair. "If we don't stay, baby Pearl will never remember this place . . . or hardly know her aunt Jennie."

Pa looked around at his children's eager faces and nodded.

A chorus of cheers went up from the boys. "Then we'll be here to see the buffalo arrive."

"When?" Mariah asked. It wasn't fair. Thaddeus Jr. always knew the fun stuff first.

"No one knows," her brother said with self-importance, "but they're coming, and we're all going to watch."

"You most certainly are not going up close to them," their mother said, moving away from Pa and tying on a clean apron. "A calf is one thing. Full-grown bison another. Besides, you've lots to do to help your father. And you can start now. You four boys, get going."

"What about the runt?" Thaddeus Jr. stared resentfully at Mariah, who sat rubbing Paddy's ears. Puppies, not yet old enough to sell, waddled around underfoot. "She never has to work like us boys do."

Mariah looked up, surprised. "That's not so. You boys get to do all the fun work." How could her big brothers possibly think she was the pampered one. Her? The runt? Impossible.

"Mariah," her mother said clearly, "is going to have a talk with her father. Alone. Now get. You can start by going door-to-door and thanking the townspeople for their help with prayers for Mariah and reassuring them she's safe."

"Heck, Ma, everyone knows that already."

"Then go see if Edgar will take the padlock off the mercantile now so you can empty the mousetraps and dust the merchandise. Let him know you'll care for the place till . . . till he works out the sale . . . and the hiring of a new manager. And if he says yes, get a good fire going. I have a feeling Ingrid Jensen and Mrs. Vane are going to be coming by to sit a spell and plan a wedding supper. Those gossipy women aren't going to let Edgar leave the place closed too long."

"A wedding supper? When?"

"Didn't I tell everybody? Tonight. So there's no time to waste."

"But Nate and Jennie already had their wedding."

"Better late than never, Mariah. Remember that saying. It will serve you well. Anyway, if that handsome bridegroom and my unconventional sister think just because they did an impulsive thing like get married in the middle of the night down at Fort Yellowstone—with absolute strangers among the witnesses—that they can avoid a celebration, all proper and organized, they're wrong. It won't be as fancy as what Mr. Denison's used to, but it's time he got used to our ways now. I bet I make a nicer coconut cake than any of those Fifth Avenue belles do anyway." She reached for a mixing bowl and wooden spoon and pulled a cigar box of her own out from behind the kettles—a box full of precious coconut, saved for only the most special occasions. "I've got a cake to start. Mariah, you set here with your pa and hear what he's got to say."

No spanking. Mariah sat there beaming, grateful. Still, she wondered what Pa could possibly say that would top the lectures from first the cavalry and then from Jennie, Nate, and her mother and brothers.

Pa pulled up plain wooden chairs by the stove, just as if they were over in the mercantile for another gossipy chat with the townsfolk. Only he looked older, more tired, and when he asked Ma for coffee, this time he said, "Please."

"Thaddeus," Ma said softly. "I've told you for years—grief unspoken only festers and hurts others. Now, after what happened yesterday, you've got to tell her."

Tell her what? Pa pulled out his watch, opened the case, and Mariah grew curious. There was an old picture in that case of a dark-haired girl. It wasn't Mariah, and it wasn't Ma, and the one time Mariah had asked Pa who it was, he'd snatched away the watch. "You don't touch it and don't ask so many questions, you hear?" he had said.

Now Pa cleared his throat and cast a nervous look at Ma. Mariah liked the way Ma spoke up to Pa with a bit more feistiness. Maybe Pa would quit making speeches.

Pa picked up a stick from the woodpile and, drawing out his pocketknife, began to whittle at it.

Paddy came and plopped down at Mariah's feet, and the little girl stroked her ears with her foot. "I'm gonna bring your runt home," she whispered to the dog. Oh, hurry, Pa. Give her the lecture and get it over with.

"Thaddeus," said his wife, "put down that stick and talk."

Pa glanced over at Mariah, uneasy. "Guess I should have seen how you'd misunderstand about me calling you runt so much, but it's not the same for children as it is for animals."

"Why not?"

Pa was silent, then swallowed hard. "I guess I called you runt, out of affection, only I never told you."

"Why don't you call me Mariah?"

"Because you weren't the first Mariah in the family," he said, dangling his watch in his hand.

Mariah looked at it, recalled the dark-haired girl, and waited while Pa told the story of the first Mariah.

She listened solemnly, then at last, when he wound down, she repeated in wonder, "I had an aunt named Mariah. Was she your big sister or little sister?"

Pa tucked the watch in his pocket, then resumed whittling. "Baby sister. In fact, no one thought we were related. Just like you and your brothers. I had this golden curly hair I hated, and my little sister was dark like you."

"Did she like animals?"

Pa nodded. "Just like you. You're her all over again."

"But you still haven't told me what happened to her."

"Mariah?" Thaddeus stopped whittling and stared at the stick. "We were pretty young. I was younger than Thaddeus Jr., and we were left in a wagon out on the plains while my own pa went after a gopher. Shot it. But buffalo were grazing just over a nearby ridge. I doubt Pa even saw them."

"What happened?"

"Oh, well, you know what buffalo are like. Got shaken by the gunshots and took off at a dead run, just like a train coming at that wagon. I should have gotten my sister out of there, but I sort of froze, and then there was only time to raise my rifle, but it was unloaded, and the next thing we knew a pair of those buffalo butted that wagon over. I thought they'd run around it—they do that you know, divide at a wagon—but these two didn't. Didn't behave like I predicted."

"And—"

"And my little sister lived a few days, but she never came awake again. We had no doctors out there, and in any case the horses had run off, but some Indians were near, and they helped us . . . loaned their horses so we could carry Mariah— my little sister, Mariah—back to our shack."

She knew Mariah's fate. "What did the Indians do?"

"After they helped us get home . . . Oh, they hung about outside, at a distance, waiting, in case we needed help. Ma was afraid of their kind of medicine. But before they left, they gave me an arrowhead. I saved it. My sister liked the Indians . . . and the buffalo too. It was a tragic accident . . . and Ma never got over it. Ma died of a fever the next winter. If it hadn't been for me, my pa might have gone back to Scotland, back to Gillycairn, but we stuck it out here in America, him and me. That's when he came here and started a trading post, he called it. Indians used to stop by . . . before the tourists came. Later, when the town got named Castlerock, I started calling it a mercantile."

Silent, Mariah stared at a smudge of dirt on her hand, which, no matter how many times she rubbed it, kept blurring.

Pa cleared his throat. "Maybe that's why I never used the name Mariah for you. I wanted you named after her, then didn't have the heart to say the name."

"Say it now, Pa." Her voice was a whisper.

Pa cleared his throat. "Mariah . . ." The name drifted out into the silent room, then he said it again, more firmly this time. "Mariah, I'm glad you found your way to that cabin last night and didn't get lost."

With a smile Mariah looked up. "No, Pa, it was dark and I couldn't remember where the cutoff from the road was to the cabin, and then this big geyser gushed up, and I followed it right up the hill, and the next thing I knew the cavalrymen found me and took me to Mammoth, to the fort."

"The cavalry said you were standing by a dead geyser hole—real close to my old shack."

"No, it was a live geyser."

"You know there's no geysers by the cabin. We've been there in summer, and there's never been one. It was a low-hanging cloud."

"There weren't any clouds last night, Pa. Just millions and trillions of stars and a big round moon . . . and the new geyser."

Pa smiled indulgently. "Well, there're a few places where geysers used to blow—maybe one near that cabin—but they're dead. And once a geyser is dead, it's just a hole in the earth. None of them ever come back."

"This one did." Mariah's voice was decisive. "Last night. I saw it, and it's just like the stories. A big white plume with wings."

"All right, geysers never were predictable, so we'll suppose, just suppose maybe it had one more gush left—just for you."

Just for her. Mariah liked the sound of that.

"Well," Pa said, turning practical again, "all this jawing about ancestors and family that's gone before doesn't put meat on the table, does it?" He rose to go. "Guess I better get changed before Jennie's dude comes to visit."

"You won't call me a runt," Mariah said. "Will you?"

Pa hugged her. "No more runt. Baby Pearl inherits that name."

"Pa!"

And as soon as Pa was gone to the bedroom, she turned to her ma. "I get to sprinkle the coconut on over the icing, don't I? I get to do the coconut for the cake because I was at the wedding!"

Ma smiled, and she looked content, pleased. "I think that would be lovely, and so would a thank-you—especially to Nate Denison."

"You mean now?"

Ma hesitated, as if wanting to take back her words. Mariah knew what was worrying her. Jennie had just married Nate. Grown-ups acted as if kids knew nothing. Absolutely nothing. "I'll only stay five minutes . . . please?"

Ma nodded. "Not a second more."

Mariah grabbed her coat and mittens and was already half out the door, on the run.

CHAPTER
~21~

For long moments Nate stood, head bowed over the carved walnut sideboard, waiting. She'd come to him. All women did, especially this one. He'd married her. Paid the ultimate price. She'd come.

But what was taking her so long? Time dragged by, an hour and still another hour, alone in his vast cavern of a house. He felt hollow and couldn't wait for the prim woman with copper-penny hair and banked passion to come warm the room, warm his arms again.

How many possessions did a schoolmarm need to collect? A vial of lily-of-the-valley scent and that funny hat. Her teacher's satchel. He'd told her he'd buy her whatever she needed. And he was going to have this sideboard hauled away. It reminded him of Daisy, who was ruled by artificial things like possessions, while Jennie . . . Jennie had wed him in an impromptu ceremony at a fort, shared a wedding night in an army shack.

At a knock on the front door, he rushed out to open it himself. There stood Mariah.

"Hi ya, Mr. Denison." The child looked none the worse for her trek into wonderland. If anything, she was more confident, especially with the black runt, Coal, bouncing around her feet, yapping and wagging its tail.

"Hello there." He looked behind her for signs of Jennie.

"She's not with me, but it's all right because I need to say thank you. I guess you're mad at me, huh?"

Mad? For leading him to a preacher and willingly bunking with a captain's daughter so Nate could finally have Jennie. . . .

"No, I'm not mad."

"Then how come you look so glum?"

He was a bridegroom without a bride. But perhaps, if he played along with Mariah's talk, the child would shed some light on his bride's whereabouts.

"Don't be sad. Your buffalo will come, and they'll be safe too. Last night when you were looking for me, the cavalry caught Vernon in Yellowstone with poaching gear. It was Vernon sneaking in and out of Pa's shack."

"Ah, Vernon, of the burned-down school. Still haunting us with bad deeds. Last night was a busy night at the fort. A wedding and a poacher and a runaway. The cavalry must be done in and sending for fresh recruits, I expect."

"Ma sent me to apologize," Mariah said. "I didn't mean for people to think I ran away. But I had to save the runt pup. I had to because no one else cared." She fussed with a piece of lint on her coat, then looked up. "I'm sorry I troubled you."

"It turned out all right, I'd say," Nate said, picking up the pup before it ran out the door. Mariah followed him into the parlor.

"Do you want to hear some special news before Ingrid Jensen does?"

"A rare honor, I'm sure, Mariah."

Nate was sitting on a footstool, rubbing the puppy's stomach. It lay on its back, all four feet up in the air, batting at Nate's hand. Oh, dear, Mariah thought, maybe he would want to keep the pup. He looked up, expression noncommittal. "What's the news?"

Mariah gulped then plunged ahead. "Pa's back—"

"When?" Nate stood, the pup suddenly forgotten.

Mariah knelt down and stroked Coal between the ears. "Just after you left the house."

"Where was he?"

Mariah looked up, then back down. "It's all right. He only went off job hunting, but Ma won't move, so we're staying no matter what." Out of air, she paused and looked up to see Nate Denison, the ogre of Denison's Folly, smiling down at her. With fondness.

"After I told Pa why I took the pup down to Yellowstone, he said I could ask you something. He says maybe you'd be tired of puppy puddles and—"

"You want the pup back?" Nate guessed.

Mariah nodded and, looking up shyly, pushed a braid over her shoulder. "If he's a nuisance." She gave a meaningful look at the pup, which was now busily chewing the tassle on one of Nate's parlor cushions.

Without another word Nate knelt and scooped up the pup, pried the soggy tassle from its mouth, and handed him over to Mariah's waiting arms. "All yours."

"Thanks . . . oh, thanks, Mr. Denison." She gave him her biggest smile, then bent to nuzzle the pup's face. "You're sure?" She was so worried he'd change his mind.

Nate chuckled. "If I get to missing him, I'll come visit. Jennie and I will come visit."

"Of course. Anytime you miss him, you can come. You're family now." She looked around at the doorway into his parlor. "Where *is* Jennie?"

Nate shrugged. "Still packing, I guess. Don't *you* know?"

"Oh, no, she's done. She doesn't own near as much as you do, you know."

"I'd assumed that," he said in dry tones. "Do you want to know a secret?" he asked.

Nodding, she sat Indian style and, punching an indentation in her coat-clad lap, created a little nest for the pup. "What? Tell me."

"I miss Jennie right now."

"Miss her?"

"Like you miss the runt pup—Coal, rather." Except a thousand times worse. His heart clenched, and he looked at Jennie's niece, hungry for any scrap of information. "Do you suppose, Mariah, that you could tell me if you've seen her? She hasn't come home."

"Home? Oh, you mean here now. Well, she was packing at my house and Pa says he bets you get cold feet and change your mind, and Ma told Pa he couldn't have any apple dumpling if he didn't quit joshing about you. Gosh, Mr. Denison, didn't you know you're supposed to go get her and carry her over the threshold?"

"Carry her?"

"She doesn't weigh much."

"Of course not . . ."

Poor Mr. Denison. Hadn't anyone ever taught him how things were done? "You have given the bride some sweet words?"

"Sweet words." He sounded puzzled.

"You know. Cooing. That's what lovebirds do. Lots of animals say sweet things to their mates. In their own way, of course, but the boy always sweet-talks the girl. Even buffalo do it. I thought everyone knew that."

"Buffalo say sweet words?"

"Well, not exactly, but they let the girl buffalo know they like her. . . . You mean you've been married almost a day and you haven't said a single sweet word to Jennie?"

"It was a busy night." Mariah was too young to know the half of it.

Mariah didn't miss a beat. "Well, that was last night. Gosh, for a rich man, you sure are dumb. Not even a wedding ring and no sweet words. You have to *take* her to your house. Ma says you'll carry her over the threshold, so that means you have to go get her. Why didn't you figure all this out before you married her?"

"I acted on impulse, I guess, and nothing else. I'm glad you set me straight. Does your pa sell wedding rings in that fancy case at the mercantile?"

"What'd you do with that scent bottle and that vanity set? You could give Jennie those."

Nate smiled. "Those have been mailed off to my aunt for Christmas."

"You've got an aunt? An aunt like Jennie?"

Now that he thought on it, yes, his aunt Ethel, a staunch bluestocking who spent her share of the family fortune to finance her feminist principles, was a lot like Jennie. "Aunt Ethel and Jennie would get along famously, I think. But meanwhile, Mariah, I need a wedding ring for Jennie."

"I don't think Pa's got any. You'll have to order one. But he's got a few other pretty things, and I know exactly which one Jennie would like."

"Well, I guess you've set me straight about how to treat my bride."

He was already grabbing his coat off the hall rack and was shrugging it on. By the time it was on, he was heading down the street with Mariah and her pup.

Suddenly he couldn't wait to tell Jennie what he'd learned from a child. He wished Mariah were as knowledgeable about words as she were about fancy ornaments for women. He'd never done this before. Chased after a woman. His own wife, no less.

Mariah pushed open the door. "We're here, Ma . . . Pa. Nate's come for Jennie. And Coal's back."

Thaddeus appeared from the bedroom door, baby in his arms. "Nate," he said warmly. "Thank you for helping."

"Jennie?"

"She's gone to the new school."

The deuce. Probably having second thoughts about trading in her beloved school for life with him. He turned on his heel. Ignoring all the rest, Nate zeroed in on two words. The new school. From here he could almost see it, all newly painted white with green shutters, a bell up in its belfry, hooks waiting in the cloakroom for school to resume. He strode to the mercantile for a brief but special purchase and in no time was on his way to Jennie.

"Don't forget," Mariah called after him.

Moments later he entered the school that Karl had built. The place still smelled of fresh paint and lumber chips and brand-new blackboard. Four rows of wooden desks, seats folded up, sat empty, waiting for the Castlerock youngsters. A fire burned in the new stove, and instinctively he looked in that direction.

There, curled up by the stove, by a half-unpacked box of books, lay Mrs. Nathaniel Denison of New York and Castlerock, Montana. She used her homely little cape for a pillow and appeared just to have laid down in midtask. Sleep last night had been hard to come by as he'd played tutor in the ways of the flesh. Now he needed Jennie to teach him about sweet words.

He stood looking down at his wife. In the past whenever he'd been with a woman and wanted to sleep, he'd walked out. It was new to him to have one leave him and fall asleep.

It should have been a blow to his ego, but instead he stood there like a schoolboy wondering what to do. What did one do with a sleeping wife?

Except for the steady rise and fall of the lace and buttons at her bodice, she never stirred, and he knelt, counting the lashes against her cheekbones.

Kissing her awake occurred to him, but he liked watching over her, liked the trust implied. A sleeping waif she was, whom he had just last night promised to cherish . . . What else was there to say?

Words? They were not the coin in which he dealt. Trinkets and money. That was his coin. In his pocket lay the pin-on gold watch he'd purchased from the mercantile—a sentimental memento of when they met . . . when she lost her other gold watch in the fire. But he would give it to her later, when the moment was right. Now the coin in which he had to deal was words, and he'd never felt on shakier ground.

His wife. My wife. His wife. Wife. Darling. Darling wife. He tried it like a schoolboy fretting over his grammar. "My wife. My wife. My wife."

He belonged to Jennie now. Somehow, last night, they'd bonded, in more than just a physical way. He didn't belong to the high-society set anymore. This was his wife, Jennie. Mrs. Denison. And he'd do anything to protect her, even if it meant never returning to New York. Any number of debutantes on Fifth Avenue would gladly stab her in the back, with as much ruthlessness as predatory hunters, with no more conscience than poachers. When he wasn't looking they'd attack her clothes, her hair, her . . . Her. But he'd keep her away from it all. This place, Castlerock, is where he'd spend the rest of his life, protecting Jennie.

"Jennie," he whispered, against her cheek. "Jennie, don't give up on me yet. I need you to teach me what I left out last night."

What, dammit? He knew the words to buy and sell on the stock exchange. The words to flatter Fifth Avenue hostesses. The words in which to ask "how much?" in Spanish and German. The entire Morse-code alphabet. He'd even managed not to falter on a single one of the marriage vows.

Of course he'd had to repeat them. Love, honor, and cherish was all he recalled now. Strange that the one word with which he was most familiar—"passion"—was not spoken by the minister. Alarmed, he gently shook her. "Jennie . . ."

Stirring against him, she moaned and then blinked. Her eyes flickered open, and when she saw him, she sat up, as if horrified.

"Nate!" She blinked. "I didn't fall asleep here. Oh, no, I put youngsters in the cloakroom for sleeping in class."

"School's out."

"What are you doing here?"

"Don't you remember?" As if he'd asked for a dance.

Her eyes grew large.

"Jennie?" It was as if the question had been bled out of him. "I married you."

"It's true, isn't it?" she said with a tremulous smile. "I didn't dream it?"

Relieved, he smiled. "No, it wasn't a dream."

"It was terribly impulsive of us," she suggested, her face going serious. Shoving aside his coat, she got to her knees and brushed wrinkles from her shirtwaist. There was a lovely red crease on her left cheek where she'd lain against the coat.

He looked at her the way he'd once stared at a rare statue at a New York auction. Of all the items on which his father had bid, nothing interested him, except the statue, and it was the one thing not for sale, and neither he nor his father had any idea who owned it. Given the means, he'd have stolen it, whisked it away to some private corner of the cavernous house in which he lived.

"I've always wished I could be impulsive."

Flustered, she blushed. "I came here alone. I mean, in case you've come to your senses and have changed your mind."

"I *have* come to my senses," he said, and as she flinched as if waiting for a blow, he added quickly, "I'm not a man who changes his mind easily. I've run my life by hunches and predictions, but once I make those predictions, I stick by them."

"Have you ever made a wrong prediction?"

"Very few." Raking his hand through his hair, he felt haggard, at a loss. "Teach me, Jennie."

"Teach you what?" There was surprise in her face.

"About marriage."

She flushed. "There's nothing I can add to what you showed me last night."

"Yes, there is."

"What?"

"Dammit, if I knew, I wouldn't be asking you!"

In one fell swoop, he had her in his arms and was striding out the door with her.

"Where are we going?"

"Home. Mariah suggested I carry you over the threshold and that I give you a wedding ring or trinket."

"She did!" Giggling, Jennie said, "But you can wait till we get to the door to pick me up."

But he carried her all the way. Whatever a ten-year-old child suggested, Nate figured must need done ten times as good. At Denison's Folly, all was bright and warm. Helga, back from her son's, was scurrying down the hall, tying on an apron, and stopped midway, staring at her employer. Mariah and the pup gaped from the dining room doorway.

"So it's true. *Ja,* you really did marry the schoolmarm."

Nate set his bride down and helped her off with her cape while he sparred with Helga. "Did you doubt it?"

"No. But it was sudden. I leave for one day, and you buy buffalo. I quit for another day and you have an entire school set up in the dining room. Another day gone, and you've got rich folks for dinner. Another day and you've gotten married. What, I ask myself, would you do if I quit again?"

"I suggest, Helga, that you stick around more often, because never knowing what I'll do next is what is going to keep life so interesting around here." And with that, he once again swept Jennie off her feet and up the stairs.

He put her down outside the bedroom. "This, Jennie, is where you live from now on. Go in and tell me what you like about it and what you want changed, and then tell me what else you know about marriage that I don't."

Jennie, after an uneasy glance at his dark elegance—even with the shadow of a beard and rumpled clothing—walked in. It was just as she remembered it, just as she'd often thought of it since. At once her gaze flew to the bed with its high dark bedstead and snowy-white pillows. How often had she daydreamed about this bed? About herself lying on it? How often had she pulled away from the dream for fear of being disappointed?

"I let the girls sleep here the night of the storm," she said shyly.

"Yes?" he asked as if she might have a major revelation.

"I always wondered what it would feel like." And she sat down and bounced on it, pulled him down beside her, and gave in to her joy.

"I can't believe it. Mariah did this and I envied her so. And now you and I will sleep together here!"

Her face was lit up like a brilliant candle. He leaned over to kiss her, and together they fell back against the bed. The quilt was soft; he was hard—all muscle and sinew against her soft contours. When he kissed her eyelids, her eyebrows, her cheeks, her nose, his whiskers tickled.

He lifted up and looked down into her shining brown eyes; her hand came up to rub his jaw.

"What have I left out, Jennie?"

Her arms came around his neck. "Shaving, that's it," she said on a teasing note. She pulled out of his arms and rushed to pour water in the basin. "The groom shall shave every day. I never want a bushy-faced groom." Like a robin in spring, she darted here and there, exploring. Opening the armoire, she pulled out the maroon robe. "Throw out this ridiculous robe and let me see you in long johns."

"I don't have any."

"You were going to live through an arctic winter here without long johns? We'll have to pay a visit to the mercantile— be among its first customers now that it's reopened. Oh, and you'll have to learn to eat oatmeal . . . porridge. You know." She darted to the vent that led from his fancy coal furnace, the only one in all of Castlerock. She stood right over it, and the warm air blew up her long skirt.

"Stay there."

With a tug at the impossible hooks and eyes, he made short work of the skirt and stood watching the heat rustle her petticoat. "You constantly surprise me, Jennie," he said huskily.

"Oh, Nate, don't you see, there aren't any rules about all this."

"What about sweet words?"

"Oh, absolutely. Far better than sour words, or bitter words." And then she thought how handsome Nate was with that baffled look on his face.

"I don't know any sweet words."

"Oh, Nate," she teased, "they're just instinctive. Don't worry. You'll spoil the mood."

And she flitted to the washstand to tidy up. It was an action calculated to get Nate off the subject of sweet words. She could say the words "I love you," but why? Like rich demanding mistresses, they were, naming their price, asking for matching words in return.

Perhaps in time, he'd feel an affection for her, and she'd not worry about disappointing him. For now, that was enough. Still, like a stream about to overflow, the words were on the tip of her tongue, yearning to be said.

"What about the vows we made? Will they make you feel confined?" he asked.

"Oh, Nate," she said. "You've been worrying too much about your buffalo fence. There are different kinds of fences."

"How so?"

Smiling impishly, she twirled back to the bed and bounced on it. "Since you're so smart, you'll have to figure that out for yourself." With nimble fingers, she was parting buttons from the buttonholes on his shirt. Down . . . down her hand slid . . .with surprising boldness for a bride of one day. On the brink of daring territory, she suddenly reversed course. Up his chest came her fingers, all the way up to his lips. He captured her fingertips and kissed each one, then made short work of her shirtwaist.

"Have you ever slept on your carpet?"

He stopped, surprised, with his hands on her corset laces. Few of his many society ladies had suggested anything other than the bed. The predictable women would expect the bed. But not Jennie.

"I slept on the rug," Jennie said. "But I had one of the frilly-cased white pillows." She slipped away and threw them to him.

In a second, white pillows on the Aubusson carpet cushioned their heads as the heat from the coal furnace vent tickled their feet. Neither could wait on preliminaries. As they became one the words just slipped from her. "Oh, Nate, I love you."

Loving? Did he? Was that why he felt this way toward her? Could that be it?

"I'd give up all I know or have to keep you by my side, Jennie, darling Jennie." His kiss plundered her mouth, his heart beat wildly, as sweet words just spilled out, unbidden. "I don't know whether you'll run away tomorrow, darling Jennie, chasing after dreams. I love you, dammit." When the words came out, he didn't plan them. It was instinctive, as Jennie had told him.

"I don't know what to do beyond build a fence around you to keep you. How, Jennie?" he moaned, his head against her breasts. "How, how? I don't know how a man guarantees love. Love in return."

She half pulled away. "Say that again."

"All of it?"

"No."

He knew then what to give Jennie. His trust. His heart. Into her care. "I love you, Jennie." He knew it as surely as he knew he breathed and that blood pulsed through his heart, and that snow was cold and sun was hot. He loved her. "I love you . . . Jennie, I love you."

And then as husband and wife, they both said it over and over again in the oldest language of all. I love you. At some point the words overflowed and washed over them both.

Freely given.

CHAPTER

❧ 22 ❧

Later that day, while the women of town scurried about decorating the new schoolhouse with pine boughs and silver bells for a belated wedding dinner, Nate finally tackled the stack of congratulatory telegrams. Sitting cross-legged on the bed, he and Jennie wore matching long johns from the mercantile and read silently, companionably, the crisp paper rattling, the wind outside mingling with the faraway whistle of the incoming train.

"We have two hours till the party," he said with a significant look at her. The long johns, though droopy, could not conceal her breasts, the swell of hips.

"Then we'll read the telegrams." Her own gaze dropped to his chest, where the buttons were undone, exposing his chest.

"What if we run out of telegrams to read?" he asked with a sly smile.

She looked down at the small mountain of paper that had poured into the train station that afternoon as news of their wedding had spread to the most far-flung places. It would take a while to read all these.

"We'll think of something spontaneous and impulsive and unpredictable, won't we?"

He folded the next telegram into a paper bird and aimed it at her. It flew right at the valley between her breasts.

"Cornelia Van Altman!" Jennie ripped it up.

"Naughty teacher." He handed her another.

"Teddy Roosevelt?"

"Don't you dare rip that one up." And snatching it back, he handed her another.

"The commander of Fort Yellowstone," Jennie said, marveling at the man's polite good wishes on their marriage and his expressing his great honor at having been present for the "solemn" occasion. She giggled. "It was hardly solemn. He must have told the entire country."

"He's being polite. Here . . ." Their smiles caught and held, and then slowly he passed another telegram over to her.

Jennie unfolded it.

"President Cleveland! Nate!" She was stunned, so stunned she sat there staring at him, ready to sweep the entire pile off the bed and fall into his arms. He was bent over another telegram, his coffee-colored hair temptingly rumpled.

As she watched, Nate's expression changed. He looked up at her, mirth in his deep blue eyes.

"Who's that from? The Prince of Wales inquiring after the dining table?"

"The buffalo!" He was on his feet, tugging on trousers.

"Nate! Where are you going?"

"They're on the way." Outside, the train whistle again pierced the white landscape, but it stopped outside of town. He rushed to the window and peered out. "Damn. After all these delays, the contrary beasts pick today to arrive."

Reaching up to smooth his tousled brown hair, she nestled close to him. "You like the unpredictable, Nate," she reminded him. "Or have you forgotten? I think it's entirely fitting that they arrive today."

He kissed the crown of her head. "I can see you'll be correcting me for the rest of my life."

Then he pushed up the window sash and called down like Scrooge on Christmas morning to a young boy passing by. "You there. Jennie's nephew? Go run to the train station and find out what's coming in on this train. Hurry up, and it's worth a Morgan dollar."

The train whistle was silent now, and strangely the train had never appeared at the depot. Jennie joined Nate at the window, then pulled him to the floor beside her. Wrapped in his arms, she nuzzled at his lips until her nephew returned and shouted up.

Nate stuck his head out the window, and after a moment of listening, he sat back on his haunches, defeated and exultant both. "We're all to stay in our houses till the wranglers get the buffalo unloaded off the train and moved up to the rangelands. Confined to my own bedroom with nothing but my bride to keep me company. I'll have to resort to field glasses," he teased, "if I'm not going to miss anything."

In the end it was Jennie who got to watch through the field glasses while perched at the window on Nate's lap.

In the distance the sharp commands of wranglers guided shaggy, travel-weary buffalo from the train into a holding pen. Then the gate to the holding pen was opened and on cloven hooves the dozen buffalo took off at a dead run. From the window Jennie stared awestruck as in the distance cowboys zigzagged on horses, expertly herding the great beasts toward the outbuildings on the Denison property.

"Tell me, Jennie, how do they look? Worth keeping?"

"Of course we'll keep them. If they'll stay. They're big and shaggy with humpbacks. They're fast on their feet, and look dreadfully glad to get out of the train. Do you want to see?"

He shook his head, face buried in her hair. "There's plenty of time to see them." Hopefully, years.

Occasional gunshots shattered the wintry air—blanks, Nate reassured Jennie—meant to guide any straying buffalo back in line so they'd all end up in the same place. And sure enough, one by one, they ran right into the opening in the great wall of a fence that Nate had built. "Look," Jennie said. "Look at them going into your fence."

"A fence not to keep them in, but to keep the poachers out. That's all."

"The best reason possible."

Nate thought that over a second.

Some fences had reasons. Like marriage. A boundary, not to keep Jennie in, but to keep others out.

To protect, and to cherish.

To keep her his. And as she watched through the field glasses his arms came around her waist.

On the buffalo ran, spreading out into the hundreds of acres he'd fenced and made ready. Until finally there was nothing confining them, nothing crowding them, and they slowed, began to nuzzle at the hard ground, rooting here and there for wild grass beneath the snow. A mere dozen scarcely made a difference in the empty landscape. They were close to extinct, close to vanishing from the earth. He couldn't imagine a world without Jennie, and his arms tightened about her; he nuzzled her neck, breathed in the lily of the valley of her skin. "I'm going to keep them," he said softly. "Protect them. Does that sound impossible?"

"For a man who won the hand of the local spinster school-marm? Kiss me, buffalo man," she teased, and molded herself against him.

They were still kissing when Mariah rushed up to the house.

"Nate! Nate!" the little girl called up to the window. "I've got the list of names."

"Names?" Giddy with desire, he tried to follow the thread of Mariah's logic.

"For the buffalo. There are a dozen, and they're all named."

He leaned out. "For presidents?"

"No, for Indians. It's fitting. There'll be Sitting Bull, and Red Cloud, and White Feather and . . ."

Now Jennie leaned out the window. "Mariah, you go back inside until they're all in the pasture," Jennie ordered.

"They're charging up the hills now—like kids let out of school. Come see. Hurry." She stood out in the snow, jumping up and down for joy, dark braids bouncing.

"I used to think she was such a quiet little child. What happened?" he grumbled.

Jennie, laughing, stood and bent to kiss his deliciously tousled hair. "She changed, Nate. It happens to people."

The bell on the new Castlerock School had been pealing across the wintry landscape for some time when later, much later, Nate and Jennie headed arm in arm up Camas Street, snow dusting their hair like powdered sugar. On and on the bell continued to ring, both giving an all-clear signal for the arrival of the buffalo and an invitation to a wedding party in Castlerock's brand-new school.

Briefly the newlyweds stopped to gaze in wonder at the small herd of buffalo roaming the hills above their home. Except for one that was rolling in the snow, the rest slowly roamed their snowy pastureland, heads down, nuzzling for grass, great mantles of brown fur distinguishing them. Majestic. The royalty of the old old West. Jennie's heart swelled in awe, and she looked up at Nate, at his expression of pride.

"Hurry up," Mariah called from the schoolhouse door, where she stood ringing the bell. "The buffalo made everything late."

"Better late than never," Jennie called out, and as she glanced up at Nate again, they exchanged a secret smile. Embracing her shoulders, he pulled her close while she in turn slid her arm about his waist and hurried on, matching his long strides.

The school bell was still ringing, tolling her joy.

FROM A SCRAPBOOK OF
CASTLEROCK NEWS STORIES

May 7, 1894: President Cleveland signed into law a congressional act making the wanton destruction of buffalo punishable by a fine and jail term. Extremely rare, bison number only 50 to 100 in all of North America, some in Yellowstone Park, others in the possession of private owners. Local resident Nathaniel Denison recently acquired a dozen along with an orphan calf, and hopes to see his herd prosper. The sight of the shaggy beasts on rangelands outside Castlerock brings to mind many tales from old-timers when the noble beasts roamed freely in the millions.

May 23, 1899: Mrs. Nathaniel Denison was graduated from Castlerock College in southern Montana, its first woman graduate. Because Mrs. Denison was unexpectedly blessed with a second son two days earlier, she was unable to attend the ceremony. Her husband, a founder of the college, filled in for her, a task he says he's had the honor of performing in the past. Mr. Denison is owner of a buffalo herd, now over two hundred in number. Local residents will recall the arrival of his first small herd the same day he and Jennie Denison, a former schoolteacher, wed unexpectedly at Yellowstone. The unions have prospered.

ACKNOWLEDGMENTS

Exactly one hundred years ago this winter, America came close to losing a national treasure—the bison, commonly referred to as our buffalo. In writing *Winter Song,* I owe thanks to many people in Montana who shared historical and animal expertise—personnel at the Grant-Kohrs Ranch, the National Bison Range, and the State Historical Society. Thanks also to the historian of Yellowstone National Park, Wyoming, as well as to wildlife expert and fellow writer Bob Sherwood, and to Wayne C. Lee, author of an invaluable reference book, *Scotty Philip, The Man Who Saved the Buffalo,* which provided both inspiration and much helpful information. I did my best to keep the facts correct within the framework of fiction. Any errors belong to me; the buffalo, thanks to men like Nate Denison, belong to all of us.